WASHOE COUNTY LIBRARY

3 1235 034

P9-DVY-383

Praise for Mark Henry and *Happy Hour of the Damned*!

DATE DUE

ILL
2000 95938
JAN 0 2 2020

Demco, Inc. 38-293

wear... shui... drink...

who... story... fresh... and... caus...

with...

dari...

gros...

book... be s... as th... dead... look...

Please turn the page for more praise for Mark Henry!

"Hilariously wicked, *Road Trip of the Living Dead*'s Amanda Feral's antics had me rolling on the floor with laughter. Between the snarky footnotes and the quirky, sassy voice, this book rocked my world."

Tate Hallaway, *New York Times* bestselling author of
Romancing the Dead

"A spew-licious snark fest straight from Winnebago hell—Mark Henry drives this adventure with masterful wit."

Dakota Cassidy, author of *The Accidental Human*

"I didn't see how Mark Henry would be able to top Amanda Feral's first adventure, but *Road Trip of the Living Dead* is even more raucous, lewd, and hilarious. How could I have doubted his genius? His *savoir faire*? His ability to create scenarios so horrifyingly *and* guilt-inducingly funny? Amanda Feral rules the urban fantasy landscape. To miss out on this novel would be *très gauche*!"

Michele Bardsley, nationally bestselling author of
Wait Till Your Vampire Gets Home

HAPPY HOUR
OF THE DAMNED

MARK HENRY

KENSINGTON BOOKS
http://www.kensingtonbooks.com

KENSINGTON BOOKS are published by

Kensington Publishing Corp.
119 West 40th Street
New York, NY 10018

Copyright © 2008 by Mark Henry

All rights reserved. No part of this book may be reproduced in any form or by any means without the prior written consent of the Publisher, excepting brief quotes used in reviews.

If you purchased this book without a cover you should be aware that this book is stolen property. It was reported as "unsold and destroyed" to the Publisher and neither the Author nor the Publisher has received any payment for this "stripped book."

All Kensington titles, imprints, and distributed lines are available at special quantity discounts for bulk purchases for sales promotion, premiums, fund-raising, educational, or institutional use.

Special book excerpts or customized printings can also be created to fit specific needs. For details, write or phone the office of the Kensington Special Sales Manager: Attn.: Special Sales Department. Kensington Publishing Corp., 119 West 40th Street, New York, NY 10018. Phone: 1-800-221-2647.

Kensington and the K logo Reg. U.S. Pat. & TM Off.

ISBN-13: 978-0-7582-2523-8
ISBN-10: 0-7582-2523-7

First Kensington Books Trade Paperback Printing: March 2008
First Kensington Books Mass-Market Paperback Printing: February 2010

10 9 8 7 6 5 4 3 2 1

Printed in the United States of America

To Caroline, my wife.
She couldn't be any more supportive and wonderful.
It's just not possible.

Acknowledgments

This book is a miracle to me. Really. A cocktail-swigging, flesh-eating zombie miracle, sure, but a miracle, nonetheless. I'm deeply indebted to a number of people who either got the ball rolling, supported that ball on its roll, or lubed it up and pushed that ball through the tight orifices of the publishing world.

A million and one thank-yous go out to . . .

My mother, Edna Henry, the most avid reader I know. She taught me to read and always told me I could do anything I put my mind to.

My father, Wayne Henry, who's the kind of guy that does *everything* he puts his mind to. Plus, he tells a hell of a story. Ask anyone.

The South Sound Algonquins—originals Monica Britt and Sherylle Stapleton; and the newbies Megan Pottorf, Manek Mistry, and Tom Wright—put up with my foul-mouthed readings so graciously, and never held back in critique. You guys weren't holding back, right?

Gina Craig, my first copy editor, gave my first few chapters as much polish as she could.

The talented Joe Schreiber gave me the push I needed to get an awesome agent. He's also a top-notch author pimp.

The Friday night dinner crew: Kevin Macias, Jo Rash, Dana Krapfl and later, Mike Green, Ann Bowen, Shannon Hills, and Yolanda Macias, for listening to my rambling publishing stories. Your excitement has been the greatest cheerleading.

Supercool editor, Liz Scheier, took a pitch and a chance

on an idea. Not even a completed manuscript, mind you, just an idea. People: that just doesn't happen. Her enthusiasm got this book written.

My agent, the delightfully sarcastic Jim McCarthy of Dystel & Goderich Literary Management, rocked me a deal lickety split (I love that phrase). If I have my way, we'll be selling many more.

Kristine Mills-Noble brought Amanda to life on the fabulous cover.

My copy editor, William Mehlman, caught stuff I'd have never seen, even with my bad high school French.

My editor, John Scognamiglio, believed in my crazy little story enough to buy the fucker. I'm still amazed. Every day. Plus, he dishes on the reality TV like a pro, and that's my number one criterion for awesome.

Finally, to the readers, there are only two kinds of people in the world.

Chapter 1

It's Saturday; It's the Well of Souls.

A few hints: the damned of Seattle congregate at the Orphanage on Tuesday nights for half-price nibbles and cocktail specials, Convent on Thursdays, for Burlesque of the Living Dead, and Pharmacy on Fridays, which is brand new, and I have never been (don't let that stop you, I hear it's mind-blowing) . . .
—Otherworld Weekly

Saturday night is all about the Well of Souls—see and *be* seen is the rule—there is no excuse for an absence, least of all a bad hair day. Shit, even if it looks like broom straw or the waxy coils plunged from drains, just throw on a hat, a wig, or whatever you have to do; the worst that could happen is public embarrassment and mockery. Nobody's died from those. Fortunately, Wendy and I didn't have to worry about that; we were looking hot as Hell, and ready to burn it down.

She wore her trademark mix of lush patterns in silk and wool, which she's been cultivating for a decade like a rose hybrid. On this particular night, she was working it short-short-short in a devilish Galliano skull and crossbones print dress. She wrapped the frock in a constricting bouclé sweater that cupped under her breasts and showed them off like a slutty European peasant girl. Her blond hair hung in perfect esses, framing her fair skin in a glow of spun sugar.

I must stop there. If Wendy had her way, the subject would never veer from her.

So let's move on . . .

I sported my "Variations on Black" vintage Azzedine Alaia[1]. I pulled it out on occasion to air like a favorite strand of pearls. It molded to my curves like a second skin—the very fibers followed each shift and undulation. My kicks were black, strapped, and towered on a heel that could impale the most amorous vamp. My hair is brown to the point of black with caramel notes—think of the first crema rising through the black of a properly made espresso—and up in a loose twist to show off these big retro hoop earrings I was rocking, like it was the '70s all over again.

Sexy? That's certain, but enough about fashion; let's move on to the *oh-so-important* seating arrangements . . .

Our reserved black-velvet-draped banquette was centrally located between the restrooms, the dance floor, and the ice bar, perfect for witnessing both fashion atrocities and supernatural scandals. Ricardo, the Well's owner and bartender, was so good to us, always assuring our favorite spot, and providing eye candy to boot. I spotted him across the room shaking a metal shaker with a flourish. Which brought to mind the question: *where's my fucking Flirtini*?

Normally at the Well, I have no complaints, but, on this night, Ricardo was breaking in a new waitress. That's right, I refuse to call them cocktail servers or waitstaff, and if anyone commented as to the political correctness of my terminology, I'd have their head and everything else. Her name

---

[1] *Azzedine Alaia:* Tunisian designer, famous for banding a woman's body into its proper form, regardless of her actual shape, a God at turning cows into shapely visions of sublime modernity.

was Isobel, and she was exactly what you'd expect—slow, boring, obnoxious, and—wouldn't you know—pretty. To describe her as a doe-eyed starlet-type would be fairly accurate, but would neglect an account of her childlike intelligence and subpar vocabulary.

I was scanning the crowd for our regular waitress, Jezebel, when my eye caught on a table pressed against the farthest crescent of the club. Those booths, set deep within swags of thick jewel-toned curtains, were normally occupied by the evil bloodsuckers of Karkaroff, Snell and Associates, and some of them were even in attendance, but Dona Elizabeth Karkaroff was the only one worth noting, believe me, and don't ever look her in the eye, everyone knows that, never in the eye—I cannot stress this enough. The legal firm was a nasty crew, dealing in divorces and disillusionments, of the mysterious sort.

Mannish creatures flitted around her like butterflies, their thorny heads covered in fedoras, berets and caps, in shapes and sizes that must have put their milliners through Hell. They leaned in, whispered to her, roamed the area, covered their mouths. The lady herself slouched elegantly, legs crossed and protruding from the shadows into that space between tables, like a track hurdle for the waitresses. Maybe Isobel tried to get through that way and didn't make it back. Karkaroff's cigarette glow lit her angular face. Her dark probing eyes searched the cavernous space.

I averted my gaze.

On that night, a darker than normal presence spread a dense layer of gloom through the already murky yet sophisticated atmosphere.

"Is that Cameron Hansen[2]?" I asked.

Wendy tracked my nod to a deep copse of tables, and her

[2]A word of caution: This name has been changed to protect you from the evil that is this particular celebrity and he is certainly not Bruce Willis, Ben Affleck or Brad Pitt (although he may have worked with one or all of them in the course of his career).

eyes widened as they lit on the shadowed celebrity. "It is. Jesus, what's he doing here?" Her face fixed in a grimace, as though she were about to vomit across the table or had turned a corner and was surprised by the glaring eye of an asshole, crowning a thick brown mass. "I can't stand that shrimp."

"I certainly didn't get the memo." I lit a two-tone, pink-on-green cigarette that I'd had personally rolled and drew a mouthful of the pungent apricot-flavored smoke. I glared in the actor's direction, and blew without inhaling—obviously, the lungs don't exactly work anymore. I quit years ago, but after my death, I decided, what the hell?

Cameron Hansen appeared benign enough, sitting with a blonde pile of vacant silicone on one side and a shiny Asian boy on the other, but so many of his kind do, not that I'm remotely aware of his actual species. On the outside, he was awkwardly handsome, albeit far beneath most people's height requirements; inside Cameron was one hundred percent monster, or so I'm told. On several occasions, Ricardo shared, under his breath, tales of having to clean up the actor's sloppy kills, following previous visits to the Well.

We might have left, just then, simply to avoid the actor's bad energy, if we hadn't been waiting for Liesl and Gil to arrive for our weekly snarkfest. Nothing was more enjoyable than the four of us volleying hilarious barbs, at the expense of the moronic undead and neverliveds. Liesl was on her way, and Gil was perpetually late to the point of actually being punctual, but he never missed the chance to rail on his peers or drink blood from sparkling martini glasses. We loved him, and when I say we, it's not the royal plural; I'm including you. So we just sat, spat gossip, and grew increasingly irritable about our cocktailless hands.

The Well of Souls is certainly in no Seattle guidebook, and no one will direct you to its doors. It is a nightclub that does not exist in your world. Well, that's not altogether true and frankly, you should know, I can slip into a bit of drama.

The truth is, the Well of Souls is our bar, just as are Convent, Pharmacy, Malevolence, Orphanage and the aptly named Les Toilettes. Our places are right out in the open, just like yours, but you can't see them, and it's too bad, because they are amazing feats of sinister architecture and engineering.

"There they are!" Our drinks bobbed on a tray, afloat on the sea of pouty-lipped club goers, Isobel's hand invisible in the murk. My pink Flirtini and Wendy's Melon Ball nodded right past Cheryl Rand, the famous water sprite and owner of Discreet Dry Cleaners, and Cash Zinsser, a vampire and social essayist, who had just written a scathing review of the all-demon-owned Malevolence. In it he reported the drinks were overpriced, the appetizers, inedible, and the victims, flavorless. The two were wrapped in a furtive embrace, groping, clawing. He grazed from her neck like a cow chewing cud. It made me feel icky[3].

As the drinks swung past the dance floor, a forest of arms rose to obscure them. They bounced to the rhythm, some glowed fluorescently with rows of Band-Aids lined up like dominos, because, this season, it's all about cloud, and cloud is the new crank. The faces attached to the flailing limbs were giddy, mostly fanged-out and with eyes like saucers. The cloud was having its known effect, euphoria. Across the room, the bathroom seemed to be home to the "paster," a male wearing a retro Kangol hat and massive gold chains. He supplied the drug from a repurposed Crest tube and slapped on the bandages to keep it in place for maximum absorption.

Isobel drifted past the ballet-dancing werewolf, Lina Peritzkova, who hunkered over her drink, one of Ricardo's secret recipe Black Devils, thick as syrup. Lina still nursed the hurt of failure; she couldn't seem to test out of the chorus, despite an impressive arabesque. Wendy and I used to joke that one day we would take water pistols filled with Liquid

---

[3]That's what Mommy calls bad touch.

Moonglow™ and blast her from the orchestra seats during Swan Lake[4]. But, seeing her in this downtrodden state stripped the humor from that idea.

A single margarita rode alongside the two martinis; I watched it, longed for its sweet warmth, and salty aftertaste. Because this is not a perfect afterworld, the margarita's owner was served first. A long-fingered hand coiled around the offered cocktail as Isobel wrinkled a cloying smile. The hand belonged to Shane King. Isn't a margarita an odd drink for someone so masculine? I wouldn't mind mangling him. He looked to be about twenty-eight, a shade younger than I, but was probably over a hundred. He wore a square jaw, kind eyes and the tousled blond hair of a surfer. The golden boy vampire—I'm not ashamed to admit—was the subject of at least two early morning pillow hump fantasies. I tried to erase his drink choice information from my mind and focus on the image of his butt; I sometimes called upon it. Whatever it takes, right girls?

"Look over there." I pointed in Shane's direction.

"Mmm, yummy. Dibs." Wendy shoved out of the banquette before I could protest, slipped through the crowd like a professional[5], touched shoulders and winked, and stopped to grind hips with a familiar face, or three. And then she was with *him*, sliding in close. Was he alone?

I turned away with an *ech*, to find Gil bumping and pushing his way to the table. Gil looked very much the part: his hair, jet black, and skin, a golden-blushed olive stretched over a lean muscular frame, a vampire, obviously, but so sadly, stereotypically gay[6]. But still, I could look.

"What up, bitch?" he said as he plopped down into the

[4]Poor swans.
[5]Hooker.
[6]A certain horror author has made it their concern to develop a blatantly homosexual shtick for their vampires. This has bled into both human and supernatural consciousness. I couldn't have spun it better myself.

banquette, slouching, one leg splayed into the passing lane. I thought of Karkaroff. Was it becoming a trend to block walkways, or a cry for attention?

"You're working that fashion editorial vibe a little hard, don't ya think?"

"Gotta glitter." He motioned to his black and grey pin-striped jacket, presenting it like a game show hostess playing up the crap prizes. "It's Armani."

The drinks arrived, and Gil ordered a vodka martini with two olives, an extra glass, and a pint of warm red. He explained that the vodka was a sheer sensory pleasure, sniffed and rolled over the tongue. Isobel would have to bring a spittoon if she expected a tip. I tried to avoid eye contact with the incompetent waitress, lest she cause me to become irritable. Regardless, the Flirtini was perfect (see inset); it glowed hot pink under the disco's black light. Ricardo was on point. The frost clung to my cold dead fingers, like sugared fruit on a holiday centerpiece.

> ### *Flirtini*
>
> *1 part X-RATED®*
> *Fusion Liqueur*
> *1 part vodka*
> *Splash of Cointreau*
> *Splash of cranberry juice*
> *Squeeze of fresh lime*

"Is that Armani with an 'e'?" I asked. Although, in truth, the whole outfit hung on that jacket, and it was a beautiful cut.

"Funny. Where are the others?"

I directed his eyes to the other side of the room. Shane nuzzled against Wendy's neck. His lips were parting and beginning to bare canines. It startled me a bit. I wondered if Wendy was aware of the possibility of being scarred by her encounter with the pretty boy[7].

---

[7]Dead flesh doesn't heal and spackle is only cheap in bulk.

"*Ew*, whore," Gil said, stretching the accusation into two distinct syllables.

"No doubt. Could you?"

"Absolutely." Gil shook the look of faux-disgust from his face. He bit the inside of his cheek and blew a vibrating blood-fueled whisper across the room. It unfurled and coiled and stretched as though a snake of pink mist escaped from his mouth. It stained the air until it found its target ear, and then slid inside, snapping from view. No one in the club seemed at all interested.

He's going to bite, bitch.

Wendy pushed back from Shane and took his upper lip in her fingers; she examined his slowly retracting teeth and then let his lip go. He gave her a sickening smile, she returned a playful slap, and then darted from his side, galloping back to our table, leaving him looking around, embarrassment spreading across his cheeks like fresh blood-kill.

"Gilly!" she yelled. "Love you."

"And you." He leaned toward her and gave her a Euro double kiss.

"Thanks for the heads-up on the biter. I swear to God if he'd left a mark I would've torn him apart. Is Liesl here yet?"

"No," I said. "Haven't seen her. Let me text her." I fumbled for my BlackBerry and danced the familiar patterns to create the message:

Bitch, where r u? The crowd is grossly overrated, Cameron's here! Ick!

"I told her that Cameron's here."

"What?" Gil's neck craned to gain a view. Wendy pointed out the actor's location. "Holy shit! Do you know who that is with him? It's that skank weathergirl from Channel 8."

"No way," Wendy said. "*Ew.* She's got legs like uncooked spaghetti."

"What's her name?"

"Rochelle somebody, I think."

"He brought a pseudo-celebrity victim to the Well?"

"Looks like it." Gil walked off toward the bar, and slid between a severely butch demonette with short blonde hair and curly goat horns, and a cute young gent of USO[8]. He lingered on a well-rehearsed stare into the man's eyes, then leaned across the bar and spoke to Ricardo.

Ricardo Amandine was a burly abovegrounder and tall. He had a cherubic face with cheeks like peaches; in other words, a zombie hottie like Wendy and me. He was a master entrepreneur—an undead Trump—and had turned the crumbling warehouse into the hottest club in the nation. He existed in death, as he had in life, with rich aplomb. Self-confidence dripped from him like marketable sweat; the musk hung around him tucked with dollar signs. I needed a bottle and an ad campaign.

Gil grabbed something paper from the bar, and scribbled a note on it; he handed it to the man next to him as if the paper were magical, and pulled from thin air, or from his ass. He winked and strutted back to the table, actually strutted. Desperate.

"How do you make strutting look natural?" I asked.

Gil slid in close to me and whispered, "Practice."

"So what are we talking about?" Wendy asked.

"How about the freaky-ass weather?"

Normally far too banal for cocktail banter, the Seattle weather had gone full-on biblical. Raining or drizzling, at least, every day for the past two months. There had even been a tornado in some rural town that doesn't bear repeating, a farm destroyed, or something. It hardly seemed worth mentioning. Once you're dead there's no need for agriculture.

"I've been wondering why it's been raining so—"

"It is total ass. My hair is—"

"Next!" I shouted; the topic was tiresome regardless of its timeliness. I was sorry to have brought it up. "Zombie plague, anyone?"

[8]USO: Unknown Supernatural Origin.

"That's just a rumor," Wendy said. She stirred her drink with her pinky and scanned the dance floor, eyes as dull as if she were trying to stay awake in first-year botany.

"I heard . . ." Gil said, leaning in with that in-the-know conspirator, gotta-listen thing, ". . . there was another outbreak just last week. Are you bitches out on a taste test, or something? Because someone is doing a bite and run. Anyway, it happened at some coffee shop in Renton. Six caffeine-pumped zombies just chewing through customers and baristas alike. The reapers cleaned it up before the media got there. Although they might have let it go public. Renton could use the exposure."

"Totally."

"What a dump."

Three sips around the table and a new topic popped.

"So, how's your afterlife going?" Gil asked.

I sighed. "Are you serious? That topic is as fresh as Wendy's poon[9]." Wendy punched my leg. I blew a kiss. "Let's talk about your conversation with Ricardo."

"Yeah," Wendy said, chiming in, almost singing the words; we love her. "Let's."

"I just wanted to be sure that he was keeping an eye on Cam. There's no way he can kill the weather-ho and go unnoticed."

"Well yeah, the reapers would be on him in like a minute," I said, "right after the media, in her case. Channel 8 probably has her lo-jacked."

"Ricardo said he had it under control," Gil ended the topic. All three looked over at the celeb's table. "And it seems Cam is looking for something other than a kill tonight."

In the shadows of the booth, the three were making out feverishly. The actor was in the middle, trading off his mouth first to the weathergirl then the Asian adolescent. Thick ropes

[9]The answer: Exactly as it was before death, BORING.

of spittle stretched between puffy lips and hands groped and stroked under the table.

"You know, I knew that weathergirl was nasty," Wendy said.

Just then my BlackBerry vibrated, alerting me to a text message, I hoped from Liesl. I pulled it into sight and checked.

Help.

That's all it said.

Help.

"Look at this shit, right here." I leaned over to display the message for Gil and Wendy.

"Help?" Gil asked. "That *must* be a wrong number." Then, an aside to Wendy, "Do we *do* help?"

"It's from Liesl."

"Oh shit." Wendy was already grabbing for her purse.

Christ, I thought, *how are we going to help? Not a caring nurturer in the bunch.*

Chapter 2

The Narcissistic Search Party of the Year

Do bring an umbrella. The locals may be okay with scraggly overhumidified hair, but we all know it won't cut it on the red carpet.

—Ghastly Miss

Getting out of the Well of Souls proved to be a hassle. By 2:00 on Saturdays, it's a given that the club breaches the fire code, and that night was no exception. We snaked our way through the crowd, slithering between the hot backs and cold fronts of horny and horned devils, cloud-doped bloodsuckers, musty shifts[10] and a wealth of zombies in various states of decay. The wall of water that signaled the club's exit seemed farther away the deeper we delved into the crowd. We passed Claire Bandon by a video wall that featured a loop of the Well from that Japanese movie about that dirty-haired dead girl. Claire was a shapeshifter with the most extraordinary control of her ability. She changed seamlessly between human and

[10]Werewolves, wereleopards and, to a lesser degree, werebears, who prefer the more masculine milieu of Les Toilettes, if you know what I mean.

any animal in the zoological spectrum. Needless to say, she made a killing in her consulting business, appropriately named Globalshift, Inc. She winked and waved me over. Her face mashed to make room for an overzealous smile.

"Hey, Claire. We'll do drinks next week. 'Kay?" I yelled, and slid through a hole in the throng to palm her my card. "I've got some great ideas for promoting Globalshift. Call me." She nodded and her smile faded as she realized our interaction would end there. I didn't have time to make nice.

As we neared the wall of cascading water, the deluge parted like a curtain and did so throughout its width, creating a small tunnel. The effect was fun, fabulous really. I have never gotten so much as a drop on me, in the many times I've passed. Coming out the other side, we spilled into a wet alley, where rain fell in fat drops, spotting the bands of fabric in my Alaia like ink. Destroying it.

"Goddamn it!" I yelled. *Why don't I ever carry an umbrella?* Wendy flashed a thin grin of sympathy. Gil grimaced at the fashion disaster. Even Seattle's most well-known cultural event, Bumbershoot, is named after an umbrella. Because news flash: it rains here. *So stupid.*

Just then, a racket of metal clanging accosted us from above.

"You ingrates! Be quiet down there!" said a curt voice.

We looked up to find a loathsome Hitotsume-kozou yelling from a third story window, two pots dangling limply from its hands. He was the size of a ten-year-old boy, with a huge glaring single eye distinguishing his bald head.

"Shut up freak!" Wendy yelled. "If you don't like the noise, get a real estate agent, and move your annoying ass."

The kozou's face stretched into a glower. The pans he white-knuckled dropped to the street with a clatter, and he exploded into an obscene stream of Japanese, that was undoubtedly curse-ridden[11].

---

[11] The fucking potty mouth.

"Ooh," I said. "Those are supposed to be really bad luck." Notoriously unlucky, if you're familiar with the lore. Not that I'm an expert or anything, but it doesn't take too many verbal assaults from cyclopic foreigners, before you do the research.

"That's just superstitious crap," Gil said. "I just wish I had a stick. I'd whack him."

"You're gonna whack him?" I laughed, so did Wendy. "Who are you, Joe Pesci?"

"I wish *I* had a stick," Wendy said, looking off at an amorous couple pressed into a doorway, poorly sheltered by a shallow brick overhang. They were locked in a pleasant molestation.

Gil drove an old Jaguar Vanden Plas, in British racing green. He said the queen had one, which was appropriate, considering. So, the drive to Liesl's place was smooth. Wendy played with the mahogany "picnic tables" that collapsed from the seat backs like in an airplane. Gil shamed her for it on multiple occasions. I spent most of the ride smoking and making extended eye contact with food at stoplights. Sometimes they would notice and I would fake a smile. It was hard to pull off enthusiastic responses when your Saturday was ruined and you didn't know why. We propelled through the city streets of the real world, past the cars and homes of humans, and some of our own, too. We are not completely without a presence. The percentage is actually quite high, ten percent. That's the highest in the country and growing. We're so proud.

Liesl's apartment took up the entire first floor of an updated Victorian on Capitol Hill. Gil piloted the Jag into the driveway. The lights blazed from inside and the front door swung open on creaking hinges in the slow night breeze. The upstairs unit was dark. I was the first one out and running. On the sidewalk, which had not fared well in the last earthquake, I tripped on a jut of concrete. I scrambled for a sure footing, horrified that I'd tumble and scar myself beyond my artistic makeup abilities. But, Wendy was behind me, pulling up on my waist, stabilizing me.

"Jesus. Thanks."

We continued up the front stairs and slowed to a stop at the door. Wendy and Gil seemed to lock up, frozen. I noticed I wasn't moving either. There wasn't any supernatural event that prevented their entry. It was a tiny object lying a mere foot inside her door, small, shiny, and silver: Liesl's cell phone.

"Liesl? Sweetie?" I called. The door was all the way open now, and the hall beyond stretched deep into the dark, seemingly further than the architecture allowed. "Are you in there?"

There was no response. I knew there wouldn't be. No one leaves his or her cell phone on the floor with the door open. It screams take it, make free calls, drive out of town and use my roam at ten times the rate. Liesl wouldn't be caught undead without it although, come to think of it, Liesl was the opposite, quite alive, in fact. Or at least I hoped that was still the case.

"So what do we do now?" Gil peeked through the front window.

"Go in," I said.

"Who?" Gil pressed his palm to his quiet heart.

"She's talkin' to you, bitch," Wendy said in a thick Latina burr, mimicking a line from her favorite movie, *Freeway*. She says Reese Witherspoon hasn't been as endearing since, and if I had to hear that one more time. . . .

"Me, why me?"

"Well let's see. You can heal," I said, shrugging. "You know; if something gets you."

"If something gets me? Gets me what?"

Wendy pulled her thumb across her throat, for the internationally known symbol for a Colombian choker.

"Oh hell no!" Gil pulled a pack of cigarettes from his inside jacket pocket and lit up; started puffing, then pacing.

So did I. My mind drifted to the text message again.

Help.

I leaned over the open doorway and picked up Liesl's phone, flipped it open and checked caller ID for recent calls and messages: mine, one from Sanguine Industrial Bio Products, likely a telemarketer, and two missed calls, both restricted. I checked the outgoing calls and found that the help request had been the second-to-the-last call.

2065559056 was dialed at 1:48 A.M. Local. I looked at my watch. 2:38 A.M. Almost an hour ago. I pocketed the cell.

Cars crossed the intersection two houses away, bad '80s butt rock blared in the distance, and the oak in the yard lost its leaves like anvils dropping from the sky. But any sound worth hearing, someone lurking inside, escaping out the back, jumping the fence, was washed out by Gil's paranoid stomping. The boards were cracking with his insanity. It must have been viral; I started pacing myself, partly from fear, partly out of a familiar hunger that was building gradually. It started in the car, progressed to my head, and then sat, squatted really, polluting my stomach[12]. I needed to complete the search to take my mind off the growing inevitability of coming unglued in a maniacal George Romero way, like a mindless bitten mistake, a flesh-junkie.

Liesl's car, a metallic cinnamon-colored Mustang, clogged the driveway; close in to a single-car garage, the door to which was the kind that swung out instead of retracting into the ceiling. The bumper blocked that entry. I called inside, but there was only a faint scrabbling in response, too weak to be human, and certainly not humanish, rats probably. Ivy cleaved to the building's side like an abused child; wood rot proved neglect. There was no other way in.

Back on the porch, the view from the window into the living room revealed no movement, just an eclectic eye for

---

[12]The opposite of a living person's hunger pang, which goes: stomach, head, car, McDonald's.

décor—retro davenport and Eames chairs, a Lucite coffee table stacked neatly with architecture and home magazines, some framed photos hung from a picture rail, no fireplace—and no evidence of either a struggle or a rushed departure.

Beyond the living room, the kitchen was shrouded in shadow: appropriate, since it had likely never been used. Liesl only consumed restaurant food and souls. The window to the right of the front door was blocked from view by thickly drawn curtains.

Gil stepped off the porch and stamped out his cigarette on the walk; he turned, puffed up his chest, and walked back up the two steps, passing Wendy and me, into the apartment. He stopped just past the threshold, and clicked his tongue.

"Well . . . are you bitches coming, or what?"

I followed. Wendy crept inside behind. Gil tossed a look back at us shaking his head as if to say, *You three will be the death of me*—only there were just two now. A six-panel door to the right was closed, two other doors farther down the hall stood open, and an arch led from the thin hall into the living room. The vampire's back visibly tensed as he stood to the side of the first door. We all listened for a moment and then Gil twisted the knob and pushed in; peeked around the corner.

"No one here." His shoulders relaxed to a slouch.

We walked down the slim hall as a single mass, clutching each other like drowning victims. The next doorway was open, her office. The room had the musty attic smell of the elderly. A heavy oaken desk and leather office chair, situated near a small window, were coated with a layer of dust. Liesl wasn't big on work any more than cooking, or correspondence, either.

"No one."

The bathroom ahead was clearly empty; the shower curtain was left open. The tiles sparkled with anal retention. Unless they were flattened in the tub, the place was vacant. Gil pressed into the bathroom doorway and seemed about to speak, lips parted. Who were *they*, exactly, I wondered.

"Well—" Gil started.

"—Alright, big man, obviously there's no one here," I said, cutting him off and pushing away from the pack. "Let's start trying to figure out what the fuck happened." My hunger was spreading out from my organs to my muscles. They were twitching. I looked over to Wendy who was standing facing the wall, bracing her forehead against her arm like a school-girl in corner punishment. She was hungry, too. "And we have to hurry; us zombie girls are breaking down."

Gil studied our faces, our stance, and understood; his hunger was similar, only we eat our solids. *Big Baby.*

"Got it," he said. "Me too, though. I could totally go for a bite."

We ignored the lame pun and spread out inside the apartment; I took the bedroom. The door opened into a disorient-ing pool of red. A heavy scarlet duvet patterned with sharp *fleurs-de-lis* weighed down dark crimson sheets; the walls were slathered in red, too, three in flat and the other, a glossy shimmer behind the bed. This degree of monochrome may seem strange and would be for anyone but a succubus[13]. Not that there's a connection between her breed and the color choice. A matte black shadow box created a focal point against the shine of the wall, over the bed. Inside the box, a clean spot provided the image of a shape, defined by a thin layer of dust. The shape was of an amulet of some sort. An antique dresser was canvas for a still life in silver and gold. An embossed hand mirror angled across a black lacquer tray, a powder puff rested in a round bowl of glass in silver filigree. The look was way too Grandma's house. No amulet.

"Hey, guys!" I yelled. "C'mere."

---

[13]*Succubus:* A demon that can take the form of a female, in order to drain the life essence from its male victims. Often these demons work in tandem with an incubus, a male version of the demon, who will use the collected semen of the succubus's victims to impregnate women. Sound sexy? Not so much.

Wendy and Gil scuttled into the bedroom and flanked me.

"Do you remember what was in this shadow box?"

"Nope. But it looks like it could be a sand dollar, maybe," Gil said.

"Or a monocle?" Wendy approached the bed, leaned across it to examine the box. "Could have been a monocle. Aren't they about that size and shape?"

"A monocle? Who do you think she is, the guy from Monopoly?" Gil was pleased with his jab, and giggled to himself from the doorframe.

"Whatever."

"Did anyone ever see her wear a necklace with a pendant that looked about this size?" I asked. "It's familiar to me."

"I don't think so," Gil said.

"No, Liesl's taste was too clean to disrupt a line with jewelry that overpowering."

"Oh well. Did you two find anything . . . at all?" I wondered if they'd even looked. Their painfully bored expressions gave away no hints. But, I suspected they'd been flipping through fashion magazines in the bathroom. Wendy drummed her fingers against the carved rosewood headboard. Hungry.

They shook their heads like a couple of vacant teenage girls. Gil lit another cigarette. I tsked.

He shrugged. "Listen, there's nothing more we can do tonight. Let's go. You two feed; I'll go suck on Mario and we'll talk tomorrow. Whaddya think?"

"Your booty call slash blood bank is such a whore, Gil. It's kind of gross. Aren't you worried about catching a fungus?"

"Sh, Wendy." He pressed a finger to her lips, smearing the line of her lipstick in the process. "Don't make me bring up your nasty habits."

"Shut up."

Sounded like a plan. We had little to go on anyway: the

phone number and the absence of an object that none of us recalled seeing. Not exactly promising leads. It was probably best to quell the hunger before making a serious effort toward investigating, a prospect none of us had ever attempted.

Back in the car, the windshield was dotted with sap. On cue, Gil started bitching. I ignored him as best I could and stared at the empty apartment windows, aglow from within. I thought about turning the lights off. The stitch in my stomach tugged.

Where the hell was Liesl?

Help, the text read. I understood the feeling. Damn right. But it would have to wait. Someone needed to *help me* get some food.

Chapter 3

On Bingeing: Fun Food Facts

Seattle's in-crowd relishes a smorgasbord of gastronomical delights. The town caters to supernaturals with the broadest spectrum of tastes; those in the mood for casual fare might consider the plethora of choices found in the misty waterfront hunting grounds; more scrupulous palates venture into the lush and diverse tent cities; they are vast, woefully insecure, simply a must for visitors . . .

—The Abovegrounder '97

"It is *not* normal to have this much difficulty finding food, Amanda," Wendy said.

"Sh, please, I'm concentrating."

"Whatever. We're both starving. It's been like a week since we've eaten[14]."

"Jesus Wendy, would you quit whining and let me drive?"

---

[14]An exaggeration. Saturday, after the Liesl situation, Wendy and I binged on two guys coming out of a salsa club, yummy Latin boys with just enough spice. Couldn't dance for shit, though.

As it was, I had enough difficulty focusing on driving when I was hungry, let alone while listening to the pretty blonde zombie moan on and on incessantly from the passenger seat. Emaciated, irritated, and stuck in traffic, I was absolutely wooly. Wendy had a right to gripe; it was true, neither of us had eaten since Saturday, the night Liesl dropped off the face of the earth. Which if it had been Sunday evening would have been bad enough, but it was Tuesday and my hunger was festering like a gangrenous wound, bubbling over. Even children were looking tasty, and normally they were on my off-limits list[15].

I was frazzled for another reason, of course; Liesl had still not turned up, and the phone number I'd found in her cell was out of service. Question: what kind of person doesn't use their contacts list? There wasn't a single stored number. It might as well have been a rotary. Liesl was a complete techtard.

I started to do some Internet research on succubi but hit a dead end after the basics, which appeared to be sex, sex, and sex. Humans are notoriously unreliable historians, so the information was suspect. It was interesting to think that Liesl may have had a male counterpart, or incubus, that she was aligned with. This seemed to be a universally known fact about the succubus—to everyone but, of course, me. Liesl never mentioned it. In fact, as far as I knew, she could have been a human; we only talked about other people, never much of her own issues or history.

"I'm taking the next exit."

Not only did driving Interstate 5 leave us few food options, I had driven too far south, outside of my comfort zone. This would make safe hunting impossible without a flip map (I can see it now on the bookcase in my office); as a rule, I must know my exits. One wrong move and you've driven

---

[15]Along with animals (so cute), the elderly (too chewy) and people with cold sores, because honestly—ew!

down a rural road, pulled over, and munched out on some tweaker, behind a shed covered in blue tarp, reeking of kitty pee. Quick note: meth-heads are horrible for the skin, and the aftertaste is icky. Why not just munch on a camera battery?

As I scuttled into the far right lane, a hideous lump of blue metal on wheels tore past and cut me off. My vision was clouded by a plume of noxious exhaust.

"I swear to God, Wendy," I said, pointing at the sky blue and primer grey Datsun B210 slowing in front of us now. "Can you believe this shit?"

"I know; I totally hate that."

"Fucker!" My voice shook, and I noticed my jaw tensed to match the pressure of my alternately clenched and grinding teeth.

I wasn't disturbed so much by the near-collision—I'd learned to tolerate that kind of rudeness[16]. No, I was referring to the dingy-socked foot resting on the driver's side dash. That early '80s piece of shit was the driver's couch; the dash was his ottoman. There was no way possible for that car to be comfortable enough to warrant kicking back. It was a rolling wreck. The driver was likely enjoying a loose spring up his ass.

The sock fabric was grayed and spotted with clumps of hair, dust bunnies and food stains, like a used Swiffer pad. The collected filth told the whole unsanitary story at the end of a single wiggling foot. It conjured images of rusty trailer courts, dusty dollar store knickknacks, and fleas nesting in green shag carpet.

"It just has to be dingy, too. Like he's never picked up a bottle of bleach in his life."

"Are we supposed to be impressed at his dexterity?" Wendy grated her nails with an emery board, fashioning them into points. Functional, as well as elegant. She looked past her lethal extensions, eyeing the other car. It was unusual to

---

[16]This is America, after all.

see the driver of a car perpetrating this particular social offense. Usually, it was the narcoleptic passenger, fresh from a feeding at the Old Country Buffet troughs.

"I'm sure we're to notice the general size of it and make an association to his penis."

"We're gonna eat this asshole, right?" Wendy was locked on target, and assholes were totally on the list. In fact, let this be a warning: there are those among you who view exposed vehicular feet as an invitation to dine. Don't let a need to be lax while driving be your death sentence. Actually, that goes for passenger feet, too.

"Well, *you* can have the asshole, but, yeah—" I stopped in mid-thought, remembering the dirty feet, then quickly added, "Heads."

"Fuck you! You got heads last time. Besides I know what you're thinking and those feet were nasty."

"Okay, okay, split down the middle then and I'll get our next one on my own." She sighed at this and seemed to relax into the seat. Wendy appreciated nothing more than an easy kill, particularly if I was the one doing all the work.

"Fine."

Without another word passed between us, I accelerated to match our boy's pace and pulled around on his left to line him up parallel to Wendy. He was twenty-two or twenty-three at the oldest, scruffy around the collar but tan (or was that dirt?). In tandem, we began the stare[17] and he sensed it immediately and sold us on the most adorable of expressions, boyish fear piggybacking on horny excitement, a deadly combo for him. The boy looked over and, obviously interested[18], agreed to pull off in response to Wendy motioning to the exit.

---

[17]The stare is our signature move; our victims, in that brief calm time before the realization, describe it in the sexiest way as, get this, "a vibrating recollection."

[18]As if this needs clarification; I mean, who wouldn't be?

I nudged the car in behind his, and we proceeded onto a street with a large three-digit number, 320th or 270th; anyway, something with a zero on the end. All the good streets are in the double digits, so I knew we were firmly in the slobburbs. At the first parking lot, we made our introductions.

"I'm Amanda. Amanda Feral," I said. "Not Amanda Amanda Feral, just Amanda Feral. I use the doubling up sometimes, for memory reasons. In advertising, which I am, we find that the more times a product name is used, the more it connects in consumer consciousness." Mid-speech, I was surprised to find that I was nervous and blathering on and on, needlessly. I had to turn it over to my partner. "This is Wendy." I gestured to Wendy, who was playing the slut for an Academy Award. "She's a pole dancer."

The boy's eyes popped. He was mortified and shaking. So was I, with hunger and something else. It must have been the nasty traffic. Or . . .

Help. I could almost see the text, floating in the air. It was Liesl. She was ruining my meal.

"She's a lying whore." Wendy brushed the backs of her fingers across his cheek. I worried that those nails would slice him right there in the parking lot. "What's your name, pretty?"

He paused, eyes moving too rapidly; here it comes . . .

"Joel," he said. A lie, of course. The predictable is unacceptable.

"Joel, do you have any friends that might want to party?" I asked. My mind was hunting for stomach memories. I was going to need a lot of food.

"Uh." His thin lips hung wide open. I could have slid three fingers in, and toyed with the idea of doing just that.

"The only reason I ask is that Wendy here . . ." I pointed to Wendy, who was brandishing a crystal and silver Hello Kitty flask, took a mouthful and winked. "Wendy would just love to pull a train tonight." Wendy blasted a spray of Grey Goose vodka onto the concrete.

Joel grabbed his cell phone and thumbed in a number with the feverishness of adolescent masturbation. Two calls and very little effort on his part assured a cornucopia of food.

That's all it took—really—in less than fifteen minutes the three of us were holed up in the Pine Lodge Motor-on-Inn— swear to God; how could I make *that* up? The motel sign touted its numerous luxury amenities. They were slightly exaggerated. A pair of double beds with threadbare coverlets offered "Exotic" massage action, a Magnavox TV with rabbit ear antennas that magically accessed a "wide array of adult movies," a carpet stickier than peep show booths, yet not as tastefully patterned, low, low hourly rates, and best of all, two totally sexy undead glamour killers.

We were on Joel before the door even closed. Wendy ripped into his throat, and I tore off his cheek, exposing a quivering jawbone. He would have screamed if my girl hadn't clamped down on his vocal cords with her first bite. He was tasty enough, but starving as we were, we made quick work of him and waited for his friends, "Steve" and "Lou," to show up for the "gang bang" we promised.

"Gang bang? I can't believe you said that." Wendy wiped tears from her eyes, still giggling.

I tossed a wicked smile and blew a kiss to my friend, who was sitting on the now-activated bed, jiggling and licking the blood from a tibia, or was it a femur—no—it was a tibia[19]. From the corner of the room I retrieved a Nordstrom shopping bag, removed its contents, and lined them up across the cheap dresser top: a box of wet naps, cans of Formula 409, Pledge wipes, and a bottle of Mountain Spring Clorox. I gathered the few remaining bones and fabric scraps and put them in the bottom of the bag—for midnight snacks—as I

[19]The tricky bitch had snapped off the fibula; it looked just like a femur though, huh.

wiped the corners of my mouth with the dainty delicacy of a true deadutante.

Laugh as she may, I had hardly exaggerated Wendy's sexual appetite. Her taste for male victims is well known in our circle and she often incorporates elaborate sexual fantasies into her kills. Sometimes we call her black widow, but, only to her face, because we're good people.

"You know what would go perfect with this meal?" she asked.

"Hmm?"

"Salsa."

"Oh yeah, chunky."

"Or that kind with mangos in it."

"Nah, too sweet."

"I guess you're right." She picked a finger from the nightstand, popped it in her mouth, and wiped down the surface with a fresh Pledge wipe.

Wendy and I became so proficient in our dining that we rarely left a drop of blood behind. So the evidence was not piling up. The bodies were simply gone. Mostly, we only took those who wouldn't be missed. Usually. Though it's not our style, any youth, between sixteen and twenty-two, is a fairly good target. They tend to be flighty and could take off for Hollywood at any second. Unless their parents enjoy pornography, they are rarely seen again. The leftovers are an easy fix, thanks to the cleaning aisle at Target.

The knock on the door was light, almost inaudible.

"Who is it?" I said, countering their hesitance with a conspiratorial whisper.

"Is this where we go for the—um—gang bang?"

Wendy nearly shook apart with laughter. "Shut up." I threw open the door and took in the view of the most pathetic creatures to cross my path in months. "Steve" and "Lou" looked far more suited to the type of role-playing that was done over a game board with their wizard friends than the handcuffs and butt plugs shit they'd been promised, a real couple of blue-ballers. These boys had definitely reached the crescendo of their lives. It was never going to get any better than the idea of this moment, and isn't it comforting to know that?

"Absolutely, this is the gang bang," I whispered into one's ear, an unfamiliar thickness of breath crawling out past my lips. "Oops." If I crossed my eyes, I could see the change in temperature floating briefly between us; a pale white wisp of smoke curled and hung for a moment. My mind drifted to another time, a small, enclosed space.

I was not alone.

The boy's eyes ballooned. He gasped, slurping my solid breath from the air like a hit of linguine.

"That shouldn't have happened," I said.

"Huh?" The boy's teeth filled up half his face in an overly eager grin. His eyes bounced from my face to my chest, to Wendy's chest, to the sad bulge in his jeans. "No, no. It's okay. You can blow in my ear."

"What's up?" asked Wendy, disregarding the boys' presence. The fun had left. Her face was slack with concern.

"The breath," I told her.

Wendy puzzled a look from me to "Lou" or "Steve" or whoever he was, back to me, and then to him she said, "You're fucked." To me her eyes bulged, they beseeched, and seemed to say "eat quick, bitch!"

He turned to his friend, a question dangling. In the time it took to move his head, Wendy pulled the other one into the room, slammed the door, and unhinged her jaw like a living Pez dispenser. Her mouth opened with a slew of ratcheting clicks. She shook and twitched with each transformative widening. The boy's face registered terror, for only the second before that shark mouth clamped down. Wendy caught a stray spurt of blood ejecting from a large hole at the base of his neck, and moaned. My boy's head jerked back to look at me, and I took off half of his face, while pinching his windpipe closed. He struggled for a moment and then went still. I binged, for the second time that evening[20].

In the denouement, my thoughts returned to the breath. The breath was wrong, all wrong. I had never made it before, neither had Wendy, nor do we know how. The dead do not breathe, except to reproduce, and not every zombie could do it. It's a rare gift. I guessed I was the lucky recipient. Somehow, I didn't feel like I'd won the lottery. The breath, of course, brought up *the* memory . . .

[20]I know, I know, I'll have to exercise twice as long tomorrow.

Chapter 4

Of Donuts, Hair Plugs and Rude Wingtips

It only takes a breath to start that undead wheel a rollin'...
   —"The Ballad of the Zombie's Apprentice"
     by Chuck W. Hickock, Jr.
     (from *Supernatural Country Hits*:
     Volume 1)

Five months earlier . . .

On my way in to Pendleton, Avery and Feral, a familiar stitch crept into my stomach. I noticed a quickening of breath. Goddamn stress. The campaign pitch was in two hours, and I intended to kill. Coming down Pine, I noticed the monolithic zinc and glass frontage of Elite donuts looming over an empty parking space. I followed my first instinct; an empty parking space at that time of morning was a sign from the Goddess Bulimia. My Volvo SUV gas sucker filled the space like hand to glove; the tires screeched a bit against the curb—I'm no expert at parallel, but I was on a mission. I was in front of the counter before I realized I'd left the car running and unlocked on a city street. I ordered as quick as I could and ran back to the car with the square pink box tied in chocolate brown grosgrain ribbon, an early morning take on Tiffany's signature.

By the time I folded into the front seat, I was bouncing like a little girl at a surprise party. I positioned my precious cargo gently on the grey leather of the passenger seat and flipped on the seat warmer. All I could think of was the box and its dreamy contents. My mind wandered, daydreaming ads[21].

A binge is a sincerely personal thing; no two are alike, at least that's what my therapist says, and he should know, eating disorders are his specialty, not that he's particularly good

---

[21] *Triple Chocolate Cake:* a crunchy exterior reveals a cascade of moist devil's food (aptly named) and chocolate chips, topped with a ganache worthy of a truffle. When warm, like on my seat next to me, it's like one of those molten chocolate cakes from Cocoa on Market.

Chai Tea Cake: This is really more of a palate cleanser as it really only has a hint of tea flavor, but is spicy nonetheless. This spiciness combined with the creamy glaze is brilliant. I would brave India and fight off the throngs of street beggars, if these lovelies were sitting in baskets on the table next to the naan.

Oregon Marionberry Fritter: The first of a trio of raised donuts, a holy trinity, if you will, and I think you will, because I'm going to. Think apple fritter, with marionberries instead of apples, spotted evenly through a lump of fried yeast dough (mmm, fried dough) then drenched with Elite's glaze from heaven. It truly is like the skies opened and God handed these to his favorite creation: me.

Mandarin Orange Glazed: Now this one is the same dough as the fritter, but is all about the glaze. You can almost feel the burst of flavor, like biting into a fresh orange. Sometimes I cut this one into wedges and pretend my mouth is full of juices. Oh wait, that's saliva.

Peppermint Crème Filled: That's right. You read it correctly, peppermint crème. What you don't know is that the dough is the flavor and shade of hot chocolate. A perfect holiday memory, only Elite has it year-round, and for that we should all pray that the donut bakers should receive only the finest head available.

A Second Triple Chocolate Cake: See above. This flavor needs to be the last thing you taste. It coats your mouth like silk and, miraculously, is maintained for a good hour after. I cannot stress enough the importance of ending with this lump of lusciousness.

at treating them. That is not why I saw him, anyway; well, it was initially. Okay, I'll admit, I was fucking him.

His name is Martin Allende, and he's the hotness. But wait . . . enough about him; I'm not ready to entertain a lengthy discussion of my sex life. We'll dissect his character later, among other things.

Anyway . . .

It took hours to get from Elite donuts to the parking garage by the office, or, at least, five minutes. Everyone I passed, either in their own cars, rushing to work on the tree-lined sidewalks or lounging about on cardboard beds with comfy newspaper blankets, seemed to be in the thralls of donut consumption. I even found myself jealous of the bum, whose dirty face had a fresh smudge of raspberry jelly and powdered sugar. Of course, when I saw him, he was washing it down with some Boone's.

The garage was nearly empty, only a few cars spotted the early morning spaces. So I felt a bit better about the screeching the tires made up the spiral ramp. When I got to my reserved space, the frenzy began. It was 7:36 A.M.

By 7:40, it was all over.

I tossed the box on the ground for building maintenance, as if it were the '70s, and the box was a full bag of McDonald's trash flying out the window and landing on the side of the freeway at the foot of a tearful Indian stereotype; I headed in to my office, searching for coffee.

Did I say "office"? A brief interlude, if you will, because my office is the shit. Let's make that "The Shit." Take notes, I'm going to go pretty fast here. The bones:

Corner office.

Floor-to-ceiling windows.

Ebony-stained hardwood plank floor, hand-distressed.

View of Lake Union.

Private bathroom, with shower.

Furnished in glass, plastic, steel and leather.

Can you say mid-century modern?

In a word? Superb.

My work afforded me other perks, naturally: an 1,800 square foot, 18th floor condo, for one, with a patio garden and unobstructed views of the Puget Sound and in the distance, the snowcapped peaks of the Olympics (even from the tub). From my deck, I could see the Space Needle. And on some summer evenings, my ears stole the music drifting from the concerts at the pier, while I lounged on linen-cushioned teak.

"For all intents and purposes, the faux-hawk is swiftly becoming the metrosexual comb-over and we all know it." I began the pitch with my legs crossed and ankle popping, just like Momma, my hips balanced on the mahogany buffet of the conference room. "Your father had that slick soft serve swirl piled up there, but with your faux-hawk you've got at least a semblance of style, or do you?"

Gardner shifted his ass in the chair, from left cheek to right, his face said, "I'm not sold." But his ass, sunk deep into plush comfy leather, said, "This bitch is making me uncomfortable." I half expected him to reach up and flatten the peak in his own hair. Chang stared and focused on me. I glanced at my partner, Pendleton, his shrewd face softened into a smile as he nodded. I reached for the remote and clicked. The room lights dimmed and the plasma opposite Gardner and Chang filled with light and color.

A montage of images: men in beautiful Italian or bespoke suits and shined shoes descended stone steps from between stone columns, the financial sector—cut to—the same men at the vanity struggling with hiding their hair deficiencies—cut to—a man at dinner with a less than attractive woman, her makeup poorly executed and hair unkempt, longingly watching a nearby banquette—close-up on—the aging male model with the full head of hair making out with the young pouty-

lipped blonde we hired from the pages of FHM—cut back to—
a pained expression, despair.

"It's a cover-up, gentlemen, a lie." I paused the ad, stood,
and bent toward them for punctuation. "It's not about style,
or a last grab at a youth they never knew." How many of
these faux-hawked men were ever punk, honestly? Certainly
not Gardner; he looked like an accountant, hair grey at the
temple, beady eyes shielded by cheap wire-framed glasses
and worst of all a short-sleeved dress shirt, the definitive
oxymoron. In fact, Gardner himself was an oxymoron, a rich
plastic surgeon masquerading in blue collar drag[22]. I went
on, "What it is . . . do you want to know?" I held them both
in the cold warmth of my eyes; they nodded, mesmerized. "It
is truly about pain, or rather, pushing it down, covering it up.
Your product, your service, is miraculous for these men, a
blessing." I pointed to the screen, but did not avert my gaze;
I was locked on target, Gardner and Chang in my sights.
"They've bought into societal expectations. They've had to
because women certainly have. They have to look a certain
way to be loved; a full head of hair is essential to wholeness.
Because the media demands it, it is so; women have been the
targets for as long as modern advertising has existed and
have fallen right in line. Despair. This, gentlemen, is how we
sell Renewal Clinic to the balding masses. Dismay."

A punch of the play button sent the screen into rapid-fire
punctuation of my point. Face after face, sunken, sorrowful,
hopeless, all with sparse heads of thinning hair, just like
Daddy used to make. And then, the screen snaps black; rays
of sunlight break the darkness rising from the Clinic's
logo—a piece of crap rendering of a phoenix, I'd have to sell
them a new one—violin and cello drift from the speakers, rising, powerful. Blah, blah, blah.

My pitch to the partners of the Renewal Clinic was on
fire. Doctors Chang and Gardner had approached the firm

---

[22] Were those Dickies? Jesus.

for an ad campaign, a hair transplant program, and I was giving it to them, hard, and they were giving me soft grunts of approval. Pendleton and Avery beamed; I gave them a wink as the commercial went on. "The technique is innovative; it's ground-breaking; a legion of men will now be spared from maddeningly brushing their thinning hair to a messy point, in the vain hope of disguising their pattern baldness." At least that's what we'll say in the commercial. I have no idea whether it's true, but it sounded good, not my best but good enough; I've never been much for fact checking; I'm the creative type. Regardless, they bought it, every word, every image—and applauded, even.

"Thank you, gentlemen," I said, standing and extending my hand to firm shakes, Chang then Gardner. "I take it we have a campaign?"

Agreement. Smiles. More handshakes and ass kissing.

I pushed the parking button in elevator two and the door, closing, was interrupted by a rude wingtip. The shoe's owner, a black man of about 6'2", had something wrong with his skin. I noticed that right away; obviously, I am, after all, me. But, honestly, you couldn't help but notice. Small sores were weeping noxious yellow ooze and there was a general sag to it. He pulled a handkerchief from his inner suit pocket and dabbed like a Southern gentleman on a sultry day; at least he was attempting to freshen.

"Could you push the P2?" he asked. His voice crackled like a tire crossing rough gravel, in slow, popping tones.

I stepped forward and pushed the button until the light blinked on. Behind me, there was movement and from the periphery, shoe soles shuffling. I noticed that the man was now on my heels. What was he doing? I glanced at the floor display. The elevator just passed the lobby, or I would have slammed my finger into the L button and gotten out early. I felt a breath on my neck, cold and forced, as if filtered through the air conditioning. Shivers quaked from the epicenter of my neck as goose bumps spread across my skin like breath becomes frost on a winter window. I stood rigid, expecting to be assaulted at any moment, or, worse, molested; my finger hovered rigid next to the open door button.

The breath was cold and yet somehow thick, as though textured. The shock of the proximity of the elevator's other passenger forced a gasp that drew in the man's dense breath.

Wouldn't you know something cliché would have to happen to me? That's right, time stood still.

Only a second before, I had realized I wasn't breathing and drew in that quick gulp of air, but my fear converted this into a soothing food thought, and I swallowed the breath. It tasted of sour milk, dust and a vinegary tartness that instantly started my gag reflex. The air didn't actually travel the full distance to my stomach before it was on its way back out, in the form of a burp. Because, what is more appropriate when you are about to be killed, than belching? So ladylike.

Burp. I thought I heard a snicker. And that was all it took to launch a full-blown belch attack.

Burp. I turned to see the man hiding his face behind his hankie.

Burp. His shoulders were unmistakably shrugging with silent laughter.

Burp. He exploded then, laughing aloud. There was something in the laugh that I interpreted as sinister[23].

Thankfully, the door retracted; my parking level appeared, and I sprinted out of the elevator and through the lot. A quick glance over my shoulder, and the man was still in the elevator, hunched over now in a full-blown guffaw, clutching his stomach; the door closed, and I hoped he pissed himself. By the time I neared my car, and for no real reason other than that I'm a freak, I was in a full-on run. That's when it

[23] Hmm, maybe it was the deadish breath?

happened. I tripped. My left leg flung straight out in front of me, followed by the right, followed by the inevitable death crunch as my head slammed into the oil-spotted concrete. Time really does slow down when you're about to die. So, instead of a single thought to encapsulate my feelings on my impending demise, I had five[24].

---

[24] "That bitch's breath stunk."

"No more cocktails (I'm going to miss kamikazes and ooh, zombies)."

"Who will they get to dress my corpse?"

"I hope they have carbohydrates in heaven." And, finally,

"Goddamn donut box."

Chapter 5

Into the Lion's Den

Convent teeters on the edge of the ridiculous. Its Goth-by-Disney vibe makes this club a <u>must visit</u> on our tour of hot spots. Throw in the human element— yes, Convent is one of the few supernatural lounges that lures human victims into the space for our enjoyment—and you've got one hot evening . . .

—Supernatural Seattle

I'm not sure how long I was splayed out like a dead hooker under a Vegas box spring. Both Pendleton's Hummer and Avery's Mercedes were missing from their assigned spots— numbers 13 and 14. Mine was 15 and farthest from the elevator, but near enough that they would have noticed my prone figure, if they weren't so goddamn self-absorbed. Those bitches just drove their inferiority complexes right on by. On any given day, they left around six o'clock, so, it had to be after that.

I must have cracked my head harder than I thought; there was a small puddle of blood that smacked and sucked at my head as I pulled my scalp out of it. Shaky hands followed the curve of my skull, prodding gently for damage. I was relieved by the absence of anything scarier than a sore pucker, no openings. My biggest problem was another puddle, a yellow one. I could smell the musty tartness before I felt or saw. I was sitting in it. I must have been really out of it, to relieve myself in silk Versace. At the very least, I was thankful that I'd already voided the donut binge—four cups of coffee helped—and other than my pride, nothing else seemed to be broken, not even a heel. *It could have been worse.*

But the atrocity done to my fashions wouldn't do. I had to get to Convent, to meet Martin, therapist slash lover. I touched on him briefly before, you may recall. Here's the scoop: gorgeous Mediterranean with brown eyes like Ex-Lax, hair the color and consistency of Spanish hot chocolate, and a body that could cause a woman to take a lenient stance on kink[25]. In fact, the first time we met, at his office for a session, I grabbed his *churro*, if you'll forgive the food reference. *Gracias.*

The sex wasn't what I'd consider dirty either, no matter what you're thinking; it was great because it was mildly dangerous. The receptionist was in the next room, and being considerate individuals, we came with our hands over each other's mouths. Ethics? I'm neither here nor there on the subject, but I will tell you that he didn't charge me. So it's all glitter, baby.

Thus my need to get cleaned up and moving.

The Volvo's bumper was grimy and greasy but gave me enough slippery leverage to pull myself from the urine, so I couldn't complain. My legs were fine, no bruises or stocking runs, thank God. I dashed back to the office and took a quick steamy shower in my *en suite* bath. I couldn't very well show up to a date with a bloody scalp and a pissy cooch[26]. I was careful to not reopen the tender spot on my head, but was relieved to find that it didn't hurt.

---

[25] I'm talkin' anal, bitches. Don't be coy.
[26] That's pissy cooch, not Prissy Koch, she's from Accounting, and a real cunt. Honestly, who keeps receipts?

While I was blow-drying, the fog began to loosen from the mirror and my face came into focus. I gasped. The image revealed a hideous pallor to my skin; a pale white, and if I looked close enough, the veins were lightly visible. Jesus! It was time for concealer, foundation, blush and shimmer powder, the full line of cosmetics; I depleted my inventory in one application, and that never happens. I was in shock from the fall. Had to be. I convinced myself that a smart cocktail would snap me out of my depression. I threw on my backup impromptu party outfit, a little black dress—I affectionately call her Audrey—and fled the office for the creature comforts of electronica and hard alcohol.

I spotted him immediately from across the room. He waved, from under a large painting of Carmelite nuns, three of them, each face dustier and more somber than the last, habits black as obsidian. I pressed a quick kiss onto Martin's cheek, anything more intimate and I wouldn't be able to stop. We were in public, after all.

Convent was stellar atmosphere, dark, draped in rich fabric, religiously affected, and crowded as hell. Instead of the Benedictine vows of "Chastity, Poverty and Obedience" painted over the gothic carved bar, it read "Debauchery, Wealth and Recalcitrance." The ceiling tented in bloody crimson velvet and glowed moody from rotund black iron hanging lanterns, inset with stained glass crosses. They jumped on chains in time to the techno beats, and glowed Christless—the only martyrs here were the aimless temps on the bar stools looking for husbands and finding only serial victimizers. But props to them; they were on the hunt, not sitting on their fat asses waiting for Mr. Right to step out of that Lifetime movie.

"This place is fucking fantastic," I said.

"Are you feeling alright?" Martin reached for my forehead. "You look a little pale."

I pulled away. "I'm fine, really, fully functional." The

waitress sauntered up for our drink order. "What's the house cocktail?" I hoped to change the subject and the waitress was a lifesaver.

"The Penitent Abbess."

I winked at Martin. The server, awash in a black habit cut far above the knee to reveal garters and those adorable retro stockings with the seam up the back, continued her description, "It's a muddle of Absolut Vanilla and fresh fire-roasted pear sorbet with a float of crème de menthe."

"Mmm, I'll take one now and one in twenty minutes, sister." I scooted in close to my man candy. He wrapped his arm around me, pulled me in tighter. "So get this," I said, starting in. Martin was a great listener; the benefit of our dual relationship was the ability to work out my issues for free. "I slipped and fell in the parking garage and must have passed out."

"Oh my God, are you okay? I knew you looked funny."

I let that comment pass and continued. "Anyway. When I woke up I noticed that both Avery and Pendleton had left for the day. Can you believe those scumbags?"

Martin shifted to face me sliding his right knee up onto the seat. "Fucks, both. How did you fall?"

That part was still hazy. I let my left hand fall to rest on his thigh. "I was running . . . for some reason." I struggled for the details, but they wouldn't come. I only recalled the running. "Hmm. I don't really remember from what, or why, but then I slipped on a box[27]."

He reached to touch my head and as his hand rose past my face, I caught a smell off him that made me want to eat him alive. I ran my hand up his thigh and let my pinky rest against the bulge at his groin. He patted the back of my head.

"There's a little bump, but if you could drive I think it's

---

[27] He didn't need to know about the donuts any more than the incontinence, so get off me.

probably okay." He brushed my cheek with the back of his hand, tilted his head abruptly and then palmed my forehead. "You're pretty cold though. Here." He took his jacket from the hook at the end of the banquette and rapped it around my shoulders.

"Thanks doc," I said. Sister Chlamydia brought the drinks, and we slurped and snuggled, watching the animals do their mating rituals[28]. And, they were animals; in fact, a few were getting a little rough on the dance floor.

Later that evening, in a more literal interpretation of the phrase mating ritual, Martin and I went back to his apartment and after a nightcap of nondescript but chilled champagne he had on hand, I stripped out of Audrey and wriggled between the Egyptian cotton sheets.

Our sex had become familiar by this date and regular to boot, so he was used to the idea that kissing was enough to get me going. His hands moved down my body toward my thighs and then stopped. His face registered confusion.

"Why are you so cold?"

"I don't know, keep going." *I* felt warm. Maybe he was feverish.

He spread my legs and scrambled between to find his leverage, kissing my neck, breasts. I could feel his hard cock slide across my thigh and press against me. I shifted my hips, curling my pelvis against him. My hunger grew from the moment I smelled his scent, the morbid sweetness of overripe peaches. It clung to him like cologne, an essence, liquor. Peach Schnapps, perhaps. He pressed his lips into mine; our tongues circled, and again, I resisted the urge to bite. He positioned himself to thrust and then . . .

---

[28] If only the lies of human dating could be replaced by a simple ass sniff. Think of the wasted tears that could be avoided. *Sniff.* Yep. That's an asshole.

"Jesus!" I yelled.

He was prodding my vagina, poking, attempting to insert his finger, now.

"I don't think you're letting me in."

Martin was right. I was cold, too tight and dry as Death Valley. For the first time in our relationship, I was feeling a little disconnected from my privates.

He slid down the length of my body and pressed his mouth to my vagina, started to lap and then stopped. He seemed to question whether he should speak. "No" would be the correct answer. I was totally out of the mood, by then.

"You can keep knocking on that door, all you'd like. But, it's not looking good for tonight." He looked like I'd taken away his favorite toy. So, I finished him off[29], pulled on my clothes, left him with a kiss and made off into the night.

Outside, there was an eerie silence, no cars passing, a breeze too gentle to crinkle leaves. The only atmosphere was a soft drizzle. I pretended to lock the door to the apartment building, stalling. I had the uncanny sense of being followed by a pair of eyes, a cold breeze up a wet spine. I took tentative steps, stopped to listen for unfamiliar sounds, before continuing. At the gap between Martin's building and the next, I scanned the street for signs of human activity; I saw none. But then, a resonance came, from the direction of the darkened alley, a swishing breezy sound accompanied by fast footfalls. I scurried for my car, scrambling in my purse for keys, stupidly dropped back in, instead of fanned between my fingers like a deadly set of brass knuckles—as seen on Oprah's self-defense show. Just three car-lengths away, I felt a brash hand circle my wrist, and lock on. My feet flew out in front of me. I was drawn backward into the darkness; a Jimmy Choo fell off, and was left teetering on the curb above a particularly mucky brown puddle. A thick, gloved

---

[29] Use your imagination. Jesus! Do I have to tell you everything? I blew him. Don't make that face. You've done it, too.

hand muffled my screams; I could smell the quality calfskin. And then as quickly as my abduction had begun, it stopped.

"*Ew* . . . I'm sorry," my attacker said.

He released his grip and I ran, or a close enough facsimile to running—more of a hobble, really, but graceful, I can assure you, as refined as a woman can be while fleeing a possible rape in a single stiletto. I clutched the Balenciaga purse to my chest, a $1,250 security blanket, and that was on sale.

"I said, I'm sorry," the man repeated, in a surprisingly meek tone. *Did you smell that?* I thought. *Weakness.* My cue.

"You're goddamn right you're sorry," I said, spinning to confront him. Odd, since he'd closed the gap with nary a sound. Quick fucker. "What the hell was that?"

"I didn't realize. I mean, you seem so . . ." His arms spread out redemptively.

"Seem so . . . what? Realize . . . what?"

"Look, why don't we go get some coffee and I'll make it up to you."

"Excuse me, but what the fuck? You attack me out of the blue and think we're going to start a fucking coffee klatch? Unbelievable." I turned to walk away and remembered I was on one shoe, so I stopped and stepped out of it.

"Listen," he said, probably in his sincerest voice. He emerged from the shadows, revealing himself. He was beautiful. He had shiny blemish-free amber skin and dark hair; his eyes were these amazing black pools. He seemed to look through me, but not in a Helen Keller way—Latino, Cuban maybe. "I was simply hungry, I didn't realize you were an abovegrounder, or I would have never, I swear. Scout's honor." He held up the three middle fingers of his right hand and grinned, revealing two-inch canines that retracted into black slits in his gum line as he shrugged.

"Jesus Christ!" I screamed and put my hands up in front of me forcing a makeshift cross out of my index fingers. "Back to Hell, you unclean spirit."

"That's for demons. I'm a vampire." His smile faded. "And I've never been to Hell, so." He looked off in the distance and muttered, "Although, I do have the frequent flyer miles."

"Whatever." I turned and dashed for my car, cursing myself for still not having my keys out. I was still struggling for them, when I reached the driver's side door. I found them at the bottom of the purse, of course, under my Coach signature wallet, make-up bag, and a large tube of shea butter hand cream. In the end, what made it most difficult to find them, were the handfuls of loose change that populate all my bags. I promised myself to gather the change and go to the bank; I probably had enough change for a car payment. I clicked the unlock button, and looked into the window to the passenger side. The Mexivamp was sitting there, holding my Jimmy Choo. He smiled sans fangs, a little smug for my taste.

"I thought you might appreciate that I rescued this one here, just prior to a heinous plunge into a wet gutter full of used condoms and hypodermic needles." He held the shoe like a *Price Is Right* blonde.

I laughed, tried to stop myself and laughed again.

"I'm Gil," he said. "And you . . . sweetheart, are my new friend."

Chapter 6

The Last Venti® Triple Decaf, Not Too Hot, Sugar-Free Vanilla Breve Latte

If it is your first time in the lovely "Suicide Capital of the World," let your first foray into the social under-ground be the Well of Souls, an architectural marvel of charmed water, both flowing and solid. Welcoming, despite a tricky entrance, our clip-out instructions are simple and easy to follow . . .

—Way Off the Grid (Summer Issue)

I drove. Gil rode shotgun, forcing friendship down my throat like an emergency room doc with a handful of charcoal—not that I've ever had my stomach pumped. Suicide is so self-indulgent.

"Vampire, then?"

"Yep." Gil nodded, twisting on the radio knob. A horrible whining issued from the speakers: Dave Matthews. Gil nodded along with the squelch, shifting his hips in the seat, snapping his fingers. Now, what kind of straight man would rock the seated dance of the uninhibited, after only minutes of knowing me? I'll tell you what kind. The gay kind. Now, the vampire was even less threatening. I hit scan on the radio. The Pussycat Dolls were whoring themselves two digits over, while four away found some country bumpkin mooning over beer or lost poonani.

"What, you don't like Dave Matthews?"

"Uh . . . no. Of course not, he's the musical equivalent of backwash."

Gil crossed his arms and huffed. The radio settled on the '80s hits station, *I'm in Love with a German Film Star* by The Passions. I couldn't recall ever hearing the song (or the band for that matter), and I distinctly remembered the '80s. It was kind of a jam, though.

"Now *this* is shit."

I brushed over the sour grapes and went for the subject change. "So then what am I, that you can't take a bite, you picky bastard?"

"Why, a debutante, of course, and we're off to your cotillion."

"Quit fucking with me."

"You're a zombie," he said.

"Am not." *Wait . . . did he say zombie*? Mindless shuffling corpses, arms outstretched, chewing on hot intestines, bumping into shit—that sure wasn't me. "Besides, there's no such thing as zombies."

He nodded, either in agreement or along with the song— so fickle. "Vampires either." He pointed to his mouth and curled back his lips, revealing dark slits in his gums, above his canines. His jaw twitched. Thin daggers of bone slid from the black gashes, about an inch and a half long. He winked; they retracted with a slurp. "Trust me: you're a zombie."

"No way, it's not possible. I just have a cold."

"Okay, you're a ghoul, then. But, the politically correct term is abovegrounder."

I decided to play along. I wasn't going to change his mind, and he was clearly insane. I mean really, Dave Matthews? I was a little chilly, though. I rubbed my arms, trying to produce warmth, but only achieved the chilling of my hands. "Well, I won't be adding that to my everyday vernacular. Political correctness rubs me the wrong way."

"Oh yeah? Call it what you like, debutante."

I caught his eyes rolling and an unpleasant smirk, so I didn't respond. The rest of the ride was silent and stuck in slow motion, like the goddamned projectionist went on break, right when the projector hit the skids. Gil played commando with the radio again, landing on some middle-aged soundtrack that kept rolling out the painful "hits."

Me: scowling and judgmental.

Him: glib and nonchalant.

Us: stuck like that on a hanging swirl of flypaper.

Rain trickled in streams down beaded windows, at each stoplight. The air was damp, humid. It should have been cold, but wasn't. Outside, pedestrians seemed more alive, sparkling as they passed, shimmery, almost haloed. Inside, I felt dull. Dead. *An astute observation, no*[30]*?*

I drove us from outside Martin's apartment on Queen Anne, down the hill toward the center, and through the soppy streets of Seattle, following the vampire's one-word directions—left, right, right, straight, left, straight—until I could take it no more. Where the hell were we going? If it was for coffee, as I suggested, we passed the Starbucks on Denny, the SBC on Fifth, the Tully's on Western, not to mention Café Lladro, City Perk, B&O, Grounds for Coffee, The Bean Tree, Jitterz, and a host of Photomat-sized percolator drive-thrus.

"You realize, we've *easily* passed twenty coffee shops."

---

[30]Zombie or retard? You be the judge.

"Yeah?" The flat look on his face screamed boredom, his eyes nearly glazing over to punctuate.

"*Yeah!* This *is* Seattle, you know."

"Hmm, right, and who said we were going to a coffee shop? Turn right here and find a space." Gil checked his face in the vanity mirror and ran long fingers through his dense crop of hair.

I turned off Western, driving out of range of a pack of tipsy modern furniture purveyors; at this time of night, the employees of those stores littered the streets, like bums under wet newspaper, although it's doubtful they'd been swigging grape Mad Dog, although, I could be wrong about that. I bowed into an alley, just past a particularly bland Danish furniture store, its front window awash in white on white.

"So where are we headed?" I slid the shifter into park and shut off the ignition.

"Just a little place, to meet a guy, and get you some coffee."

"Would I have heard of it?"

"Unlikely," he said and then sniggered.

Talking to him was like pulling grey hairs instead of going in for a CitySpa tint—cheap—and a complete waste of my lovely vocal timbre.

"Listen, *Gil*." I lingered on his name like a freeway accident fatality. "I have specific places where I find coffee palatable. If you give me the name, maybe I can generate some enthusiasm."

"You know, Amanda, these are treacherous times for coffee snobs. The Starbucks Gestapo will be knocking on your door."

"Very funny, asshole."

But he continued, "They'll take you *auf* to *ze* camps."

He laughed and snorted; I sneered and pretended to ignore.

Now, don't get me wrong, I bought the whole vampire thing. There was some residual fear, although with every one of his crap-ass jokes, it dwindled. Anyone in close proximity to those fangs and his cold grip would have no difficulty with belief. What I didn't buy was my own undeadness. When, exactly, did that happen? The fall was an obvious choice—a single lousy head-bump. No way, it wasn't bad enough. How was that possible?

"So where were you leaving, when I ran into you? A boyfriend?" he asked.

"Yeah. Sort of."

His gazed drifted off seeming to be lost in the black and grey swirl of cumulus. "I'd settle for a 'sort of.' I haven't had a boyfriend since the '80s. Not one that has lasted longer than a month."

"What are you doing? Bleeding them dry?"

"No!" he snapped, then relaxed. "I don't know. Yes, maybe, figuratively. I'm just lonely."

Forlorn and lovesick, a pathetic vampire, he could be fun. Project!

Instead of heading off down the sidewalk, Gil led me deeper into the alley, where the stink promised piss puddles and trannylicious crack whores with butterfly knives. About halfway into the alley, amongst drifts of broken bottles, rat smear and unmarked warehouse doors, Gil turned to face an ordinary brick wall.

"Here we are, princess."

"Suck it[31]." I looked around, asked, "Where is here?"

"The Well of Souls." He gargled the words like a '30s horror voice-over.

"Is that your *best* spooky?" I asked. "I believe what you're going for is scared shitless, not bored to tears."

He smirked, pressed both hands flat against the wall, backed off and then traced the mortar between the bricks. His fingers found a gap there, a deeper space. He dug in. It

---

[31] Without a scathing comeback, I revert to a haughty adolescence. I'm not proud. It's shameful. Lazy.

gave a bit, releasing puffs of dust into the night. Columns of light revealed a door shape in the brickwork. The rectangle of bricks opened into a glow of fog. The incandescence spilled out, squeezing around Gil's silhouette.

"Impressive," I said and followed him in.

The interior was straight out of *Frankenstein*—the black and white one, pre-HDTV—including the centerpiece of the room, a stone well, that could have done double duty in that pseudo-Japanese horror remake a few years back. The walls were, on one side, veneered in grey stone, where a fire code travesty of sconces sputtered with gaslight. On the other a realistic forest grew from the walls. Columns of bark and roots spread out under a canopy of leafy green. The ceiling was a high dome painted to resemble the night sky. Rows of banquettes sat on levels like a stadium, which spoke to the massive size of the place, made all the more spacious by a lack of patrons. A shiny dance floor surrounded the Well; it could easily sustain two hundred grinding whores and their drunken penis-afflicted partners. To the right of the trees, a waterfall dropped into a frozen constriction of spray. The bar was carved from the block; behind it stood the tender. He was a tall man with a stare as icy as his surroundings.

Gil walked right up to the man and started talking. I straggled, taking in the atmosphere. The tall man glanced at me a few times, head tilted in interest, I thought.

I caught the tail end of their conversation.

"She's brand spankin' new," Gil said.

"Well bring her over, I suppose we've got some talking to do." He polished glasses from a row of highballs. He finished up and forced the blue and white striped towel through a belt loop.

"Amanda Feral," Gil said, gesturing to me with an open palm. "Meet Ricardo Amandine, proprietor of The Well, statesman, and all-around great ghoul."

Ricardo winced, but then softened. "Hello, Amanda, it's a pleasure."

"Nice to meet you." I offered my hand.

He took it, squeezed, and lingered long enough for me to become uncomfortable.

"What are you doing?"

"Do you sense anything?" His voice was deep and soothing like a steaming mug of dark Sumatran spotted with half-and-half, sugary. "Anything between us?"

I looked around. Gil watched from nearby. The bar was between us. It seemed an inappropriate time for a pass.

"No, no," he said, and squeezed my hand, again. Then, again, tighter. "Here. *Between* us."

There was nothing, his hand was rough, and mine was, obviously, perfectly moisturized and smooth. He wore no rings, whereas, my index finger was garnished with Mother's emerald. *Silly, she thought the maid took it.* What the hell was he talking about?

"Nothing, as far as I can tell," I said. This man piqued my curiosity. He was good.

"We're the same temperature." He squeezed my hand once more and released. "Sixty-eight degrees, Amanda. Room temperature. That's the first lesson."

> ### *Seattle's Holy Communion*
>
> *or*
>
> *Venti® Triple Shot Decaf NTH Sugar-Free Vanilla Breve Latte*
>
> *Steam 15 oz. half-and-half. Press three shots. In the mug, add 1–2 shots of sugar-free vanilla syrup.*
>
> *Add cream.*
>
> *Pour shots in a row, leaving three dots of stain in the froth.*

Gil smiled. "The lady was hoping for a coffee, Ricardo."

"A triple decaf, not too hot, sugar-free vanilla breve latte, if you can manage it?"

"Comin' right up, sweetheart." And then turning to Gil, he said, "It'll be lesson number two."

At that, they both broke into a disgustingly proud brand of maniacal laughter. Apparently, death has no effect on testosterone-fueled idiocy.

I came out of the bathroom cursing under my breath.

"Goddamn motherfucking dead people."

"What's wrong, princess? Can't hold your coffee?" Gil asked, grinning, Cheshire-like.

"Cut that smile, man. You look like a retard."

I had spent twenty minutes rocking and heaving brownish fluid from my ass; it burned as though I'd been raped with the serious end of a red-hot poker. When there was nothing left to pass, I dabbed, yelping at each thunderbolt of pressure. I stood at the mirror a good five minutes, clutching the vanity, then ventured out to be humiliated.

"Lesson number two," Ricardo said, sliding a vodka martini across the ice in front of me. "There are only two things you can consume and coffee's not one of them."

"No doubt. It's a good thing alcoholism runs in the family."

"That's the spirit!" He either ignored my joke, or took it as sincere. "Alcohol and human flesh, blood, muscle, sweetbreads, and bone marrow is particularly tasty, but primarily for the epicure. Pig will do in a pinch but plays havoc with the bowels."

"Are you trying to gross me out?" I asked. But I found I was not in the slightest queasy or disgusted, just kind of sad. His words meant no more pizza, garlic fries, coconut cream pie, and greasy *churros* dipped in hot chocolate. I would need to beef up the black in my wardrobe for the mourning period.

"Nope. Until they come out with Zombie Chow, those are your options."

I thought back to my temptation to bite into Martin. It explained so much. The pangs in my stomach, prickling like a bag of thumbtacks; my inability to self-lubricate[32]; the ghostly pallor of my skin, not to mention the bluing of my veins, now visible through my foundation; and the chill coming off me, like an ice storm. It sunk in then, the death. Or I sunk into it. Either way, I was dead.

"Hungry?" Ricardo asked.

My head snapped in his direction. I was unsure how to respond.

"I guess the real question is: hungry enough, right?" As in: hungry enough to eat a person, Amanda? Hungry enough to kill? Hungry enough to go balls-to-the-wall *Night of the Living Dead*-savage on a human being?

Ricardo resumed polishing cocktail glasses; he studied me over his work. A sly grin danced across his mouth.

"I don't think so," I responded. "Not yet."

"You will be. Soon. But, it's not a problem. Luckily, for you, you live in a city—a state, really—that houses a significant underclass. The best thing for us, as hunters, is a welfare state. And, you live in a prime example of that concept. The tri-county area spreads out like stockyards of human cast-offs."

"So—let me get this straight—we feed on welfare recipients?"

Gross, right? Where do you procure one, the Dollar Store? Jesus!

"Welfare recipients, criminals, runaways, the homeless, those who, once gone, go unnoticed. If there's one thing you can count on in this town, it's people not noticing. There's a

---

[32] Which has never, I assure you, been a problem.

plague of self-absorption, self-help books, yoga studios, on-call psychotherapy and twenty-four-hour massage. For Christ's sake, we'll never go hungry." Ricardo was laughing, hard. A hearty bellowing laugh, the beef stew of laughs. Gil hunched over in silent glee, seizing in fits.

He took a break to say, "Tell her about the *fun runs*."

Ricardo spit his drink across the table in a fine spray, his eyes tight with laughter. A bit may have come out his nose. "Once a month, we rent a van—and by we, I mean some-body, whoever—we load up and drive down to the welfare office. Someone, usually a werecreature of some sort, in human form, waits outside with a clipboard and screens *applicants* for computer training, day labor. The goal is to get them to agree to get in the van. When they do . . . it's a feast, and we laugh and laugh. We keep going like that until we're full or security notices, which is *so* rare."

"That's really nice," I said. "Way to go with the empathy."

Ricardo and Gil busted up; there was God's-honest knee slapping.

It was viral.

I started to laugh, too. Then flinched, from a delay in processing the conversation, "Did I hear that we eat *sweet-breads*?" Ricardo nodded. I gagged. He giggled, and mo-tioned for me to take my glass. We settled into a cushy banquette. Gil hung from the end and lit a very thin ciga-rette—did it have to be an Eve?

"These are exciting times," Gil said. "Parents are so freaked out about their children and so worried about fuck-ing them up, they've become hypervigilant. That used to be a symptom of mental illness, you know. Now it's a value. Kids growing up today expect to be protected. They're weaker than ever." A shudder rolled through him, as though someone passed a box of Girl Scout cookies under his nose, or in Gil's case, a crate of actual Girl Scouts would be more evocative. "By the time this generation are adults, they'll just line up for dinner."

"One can dream." Ricardo swallowed the remaining vodka from his glass.

"Well probably not to that degree, but it's gotten easier every year. You've got to give me that."

"True. So how did you die, princess?" Ricardo asked, swirling an olive around his martini, but not tasting it, just flavoring the vodka. Lesson two, well learned: food is a no-no. Got it.

"First off, you two." I pointed at both with either index finger. "You two *must* shove the pet names up your asses. Second, it's Amanda Feral, and if that's too difficult for you, then don't refer to me at all." I enlightened them about the fall in the garage and then waking up dead and fabulous.

"Nope," Gil said. "That's not it."

"Something before that, maybe you're forgetting."

It had only been a few hours. I tried to remember. I fell because I was running. But from whom? It didn't seem likely that Avery or Pendleton could create enough speed to break a sweat, let alone have reason to chase me. An image of a floating box drifted into my head[33]. *Not* the donut box. Was there something about an elevator?

"The memory just isn't coming."

"It will," Ricardo said. "In time."

"In time," Gil mocked. But, his was a direct quote from the possessed girl, Regan, in *The Exorcist*, complete with demonic accent.

I rolled my eyes and swallowed the rest of my martini. It warmed all the way down.

"Well you're clearly not a mistake." Ricardo lit a cigarette. He shook another out of the pack and offered me one. I waved it off.

"Thanks, no. I quit years ago. So, was I murdered, then?"

"No, no, nothing like that. You see, there are two types of zombies, those who have received the breath, like you and I.

---

[33] Mmm, donuts.

We are *made* zombies, we sometimes call ourselves ghouls or abovegrounders, but the term is inconsequential. The other kind of zombies are total mistakes, either the victims of a bite or a scratch from another zombie. You or I could go out right this minute and create one. They're highly danger-ous to both humans and the rest of the supernatural world, as they are not at all discreet and can easily expose us to the liv-ing."

Gil piped up, "They're sloppy and don't give a damn about appearances. Most of them have visible injuries that make it obvious that they are dead. You see, despite a large population of supernatural beings, we have been able to go unnoticed. We work *very* hard at blending into our land-scape, creating an atmosphere of trust with certain humans. It ensures that as a group, we'll go overlooked. That's what en-ables us to inhabit dwellings next door to our human cousins, and have places like this." He gestured around the club. "The mistakes fuck with that balance."

"And, you'll have to watch out for them, as well," Ricardo said. "They are incredibly violent and have a tendency to claw. As long as you consume human flesh, your own de-composition process will be stalled, but you can't afford any damage or accidents on your person. Nothing that happens to you from now on is reversible. You will not heal. Do you see where a confrontation with a mistake can become a seri-ous issue?"

"Absolutely." I skimmed my fingers across the pale skin on my arm. "So, is anything being done about the *mis-takes*?"

"Oh, there's a group that takes care of them," Gil said, flippantly, discarding the topic, as if to say, *we don't discuss the help*.

I looked to Ricardo for elaboration, but none followed.

Gil palmed a business card into mine that simply read Gilbert on one side and his phone number on the other, an old-fashioned calling card. How old was he? Ancient was my guess. He excused himself and sauntered up through the amphitheater of booths.

Ricardo and I discussed some basic principles of the living dead[34], while prowling the nearby waterfront. It was quiet, despite the cars rumbling on the viaduct above. An anorexic drizzle flitted through the air like the mist at the bottom of a falls.

We settled into stride, one hundred feet behind two street kids that Ricardo suggested were likely runaways or hustlers. He listed several identifying characteristics, for which I found immediate rebuttals.

"Jeans shredded at the ankle and knee," he said, gesturing.

"You can't use that. That's totally in fashion, right now."

"Dirty, unevenly shorn hair?" he suggested. Throwing it out there to see if it would stick.

"Well, they *are* boys, Ricardo."

"Alright, point taken." He tilted his head in the air, breathing in a familiar scent, indicating for me to do the same. "How do you explain the pungent aroma of patchouli oil, and underneath that, unwashed filth, old sweat, and dried semen?"

"Whatever. There is no way you can smell—" I stopped talking. There *was* a smell in the air. I closed my eyes to focus. A combination of odors—the sharpness of dirty, crusty human creases; the slight chemical smell of ejaculate—it wafted from the boys like a rest-stop washroom; and the topper aroma—that '80s pot smoke cover-up—patchouli. "Jesus. How can we smell all this?"

"Some very well-known sommeliers are part of the family," he said.

---

[34] In a nutshell: Eat people and drink cocktails, wear expensive foundation that really covers (as if I needed to be told that) and moisturize (duh). Carry a small box of moist towelettes and breath mints, wherever you go. Oh. And don't allow yourself to be maimed, or disfigured, because forever is a long fucking time.

"Seriously."

"You are a hunter, now. It is very important for you to sniff out appropriate victims, to determine both accessibility, and the potential for violent struggle."

"Uh—No," I said, pointing at the boys. "Filth plus sweat plus semen equals an unscathed survivor. The only way *those* boys are going into *this* mouth is after a thorough scrubbing. I'm talking rubber gloves, bleach, and steel wool."

"That can be arranged." He wiped what could have been drool from the corners of his mouth. "But I think, if you'll just smell again. Inhale, deeper this time."

We gained on the boys, who ducked into a covered bus shelter. We stopped in the shadows of a boarded-up chowder house, still a good twenty yards away from our proposed quarry. I closed my eyes and sniffed the misty air, this time with more detail. First was the fallen rain, but beyond its freshness, patchouli, thick, seemingly impenetrable, faintly moldy, like the icky proximity of a rock concert queue. The scent hid the sweaty perfume of unwashed armpit and ass, and another, what Ricardo must have picked up as distinctly hustler—semen. These two boys, neither older than sixteen, survived the streets by way of their mouths. *How does it come to this?* I thought, but I knew—intolerance, alcohol, rage, neglect, the kid becomes fed up, tired, and runs. Everyone knows. Disney and Simba don't tell you, but moments like these are points on the circle of life; on your knees, taking some old man's cock-spit on your cheek and dirty clothes.

Secondary smells came, deeper than those first, obvious fragrances: mustard crusted at the corner of a mouth, the ashy stink of smoke on a breath, the yellow of bile in a stomach. My head swam in the combination of scents; a drunken feeling passed through me; I was spinning, floating. I was no longer connected to my body.

Swirling. Swirling. I thought of tidal pools and eddies and swirling.

It seemed like minutes passed, not real time, but the cloudy minutes of a dream. It could have been as long as an hour, or a few seconds, or days.

Then, as soon as the spell came on, it dissipated. The aroma of freshly butchered meat filled my nose. It was the only scent. I noticed my teeth grinding, a fullness in my stomach. Calm.

I was sated.

I opened my eyes to a scene of horror. At my feet lay a pile of shredded fabric, bloody bones and assorted body parts[35]. The glass of the bus shelter was sprayed with blood. It dripped around me. Ricardo was chewing on an ear, like a potato chip, and winking.

"Full?" he asked.

"What?" I was groggy, like I had a hangover.

"Are you full, no longer hungry?"

"What happened?" I nudged the heap of remains with a gore-stained high heel; a jawbone slid out and skittered a few inches. It registered. The boys' scent had drawn me. I hadn't even noticed my own body's movement. I was in a trance. At some point, I was on them, biting in, tearing at flesh and muscle, slurping at sinew and entrails.

"You fed." He brushed some loose hairs from his wool coat. "You caught the scent and you let it take you. It's how it works. It's lesson three."

"But, I didn't have any control over it," I said, pacing back and forth in the confines of the shelter. "I always have control. Always."

"Calm down. It's a totally normal part of the process. You become more sentient as you grow into the new life. On some kills, you will be completely aware of your actions."

---

[35] Lips and assholes, the makings of hot dogs.

"That's comforting," I said, absently massaging my jaw. It was tired and sore, like I had given it a serious workout. Which, of course, I had. I continued to rub, until a sharp pain bit into my cheek. Reaching in, I withdrew a minute shiny metal chunk: a filling.

"Jesus Christ!" I yelled, swooning, dropping the small piece of metal.

Ricardo bent over and picked up the shiny ball from the concrete. "That's not a problem, fillings are replaceable. Even for us. I know a very discreet dentist."

"That's not it," I said, looking back to the pile.

"What is it, then?"

"All *my* fillings are porcelain."

Lesson four was something I would have to deal with on my own. As it turns out, it wouldn't pose a problem. You see, Ricardo told me that I would need to break ties with my friends and family, and likely, in time, my job. He told me this on the way back to the Well, after a quick spray of Scrubbing Bubbles, and a brisk wipe of the bus shelter. He even stopped mid-stride to comfort me, should the moment necessitate. It didn't.

Oh, where to begin?

Right here . . .

Ethel Ellen Frazier was a mother—mine—in the loosest, most perfunctory sense of that word. I was the product of her first marriage to my father, John Shutter, a carpet salesman who worked the hours of a long-haul trucker, with the same truck stop cravings (greasy prostitutes). He worked so often, I became Ethel's confidante—as so many only children do— leaving the growing-up part to the other kids, orphaned to rec room cocktail mixology, doilied social etiquette, the proper delivery of humorous anecdotes, and the moderately interesting discussion of current events. These were Ethel's primary pursuits and she accomplished them with a style—she called it panache—often mimicked by her acquaintances, but rarely up-to-par.

I refer to the people that hung around our house as "glommers." They seemed to have no other purpose than to reinforce my mother's ridiculous ideas or negate her stream of brutal self-critique (the brunt of which transferred to me, with more frequency than I'd like to admit). One particular glommer, Mary-Beth Winters, had it in for me. A jealous bitch and cold—I often mourned the shriveling of Mr. Winters' dick, as surely the weather called for snow flurries with each creaky spreading of Mary-Beth's thighs—she'd often whisper to me, "You certainly like your food, don't you Mandy?" or "Scared away your daddy, didn't you?"

Ethel dumped my father in a whirlwind of china shards and chilly barbs about scabrous floozies and infantile earnings. I braced myself in a doorjamb and waited for the earthquake of foot stomping. My mother wore a crisp housedress patterned with black roses, the perfect choice. It said so much, her demeanor, her thorns, and that heady perfume she wore: Evil by Satan.

Mr. Shutter was replaced. Ethel took up with a horse-faced financier named Asher Fable, who lived up to his name on both counts. Ash, as Ethel renamed him, turned out to be a low-level con man with ties to the old Vegas mob. So the money, too, was a fairy tale. The ashy part was too, too true. I found this out after a cocktail party, which left Ethel passed out on the davenport, her arm draped unapologetically over the squared-off pillows. An extinguished cigarette held its burnt cargo for the full two and half inches, ready to drop and gray the shag, but had stamina. At least that wasn't true of Ash. He crawled into my bed that night and fondled me with hands that had never seen moisturizer.

I was twelve.

The therapists that my mother gathered to deal with the situation were the first positive men in my life. It's probably why I'm drawn to them, now. If anything the whole experience made me resilient, and, only a smidge bitter. I didn't need to be around people.

I became a loner. I carried this into my adult years. Don't get me wrong; I was social, when it suited me. I accumulated very few friends, but plenty of glommers. So cutting people out of my life would be a quick process.

Martin.

He would be the only real loss. My family was better left in the dark about my present condition. I hadn't spoken to Ethel since high school graduation, anyway. That exchange had gone like this (I'm paraphrasing):

"Why couldn't you wear the pearls I left out for you?" Ethel's lips pursed in perpetual disappointment.

"Why couldn't you use your big-girl words and ask?"

"Look." Mother pointed across the courtyard to Stickgirl, the only anorexic in our class that had managed to avoid inpatient treatment. "Your friend Andrea looks so nice in that silk dress."

"Yeah. Like a praying mantis. What are you trying to say?"

"Oh, nothing." Ethel turned to snatch a glass of champagne off a passing tray.

"C'mon. Spill it," I demanded.

"Just that you could look nice, if you tried."

I clenched my jaw, and fists.

Right about then she grabbed me, spun me around and embraced me for a photo op. Rocky Kornblatt, her latest bunkbuddy had a thing for 35mm cameras—collected them, or something. The result: an expression on my face somewhere between startled from sleep and saying "alfalfa" rather than "cheese". My mother looked adorable, straight from a Disney movie—only this Mary Poppins came with shark teeth, standard.

This was totally representative of our interaction. Her: flippant and denigrating. Me: angry and defensive. I couldn't take it anymore; I was packed and gone before Ethel made it home from one of my own friend's graduation parties.

As you can see, severing ties with Mother wasn't going to be a problem. We didn't have a relationship, anyway. Certainly, nothing any normal person would call loving. Dad was outtie, who knew where he'd settled. Ash was long gone, which was too bad, really. I'd like to think I could sort him out, in my present condition.

Which brings me back to Martin.

What to do with Martin?

I walked alone through the city streets, taking notice of the dark places and individuals and creatures that were never visible before the change. A romantic couple in the sloppy throes of passion became a vampire sucking his struggling victim dry. A stray dog reared up on its hind legs, stretched to the height of a burly lumberjack, and howled at a moon hidden by heavy clouds. A zombie roamed the streets, with sluggish tired feet, but sexy-ass heels.

I needed to get home.

Chapter 7

The Great Cosmetics Heist

Most clubs have no formal dress code; however, the Seattle scene is haute-haute-haute. You know what that means girls, glamour hair and face, designer clothes and pricey stilettos. Without? Don't even bother to come . . .

—Undead Times

A half an hour later, I was in the shower, exfoliating like a rape victim. The steaming water hit from three angles, a sunflower blossom in the ceiling of the marble stall provided a typhoon of warm rain, while two sheets of water emerged from thin slits on either side of the wall. I leached comfort from the undulating warmth.

I twisted the faucets closed.

What's the difference really? I thought. *Warm, cold, comfortable, miserable, I'd never be clean again, anyway.*

The face, in the mirror, was unacceptable; blue veins netted across it, liberally, like the shaft of an engorged penis. Even with the most high-octane concealer and foundation, the spider webs pierced through, mocked me. Then, there was the issue of the bags under my eyes—sweet Jesus, don't let me get started on the bags—thick and dark, like my tear ducts had turned to inkwells.

And, my eyes—Oh my God—they'd turned on me.

My eyes used to be my best facial feature, stormy ocean blue and cat-like. Now, I could hardly look into them. They had turned a light grey, only one or two shades darker than the whites, and despite the welcome sympathy I might glean from a Helen Keller shtick, I had no intention of faking blindness. Besides, a white cane with a red tip is not "*in*" this year, or any year.

What hadn't been affected by death? I tried to make an inventory. My hair, for one; it fell from my head to just below my shoulders, in deep brown waves. Who would have thought? Death is all about great hair. And, under the web of veiny white skin, my body rocked; muscles tighter than ever, they felt powerful, energized, like after an electroshock treatment.

But, you've had enough of the self-love, back to the trauma.

I turned the vanity into a graveyard of empty makeup containers; yet, I still looked like my dead Aunt Margene. This was clearly going to be an issue. Where could I go looking like this? To work? Unlikely. Although, the partners were self-absorbed enough not to notice, there were plenty of judgers who'd notice right away. The gossip would be flying through the office like horseflies, and the biggest buzz would come from Prissy Koch in Accounting. I imagined her sneaking up and snapping a pic with her cell, and then posting it on the agency intranet, with some heading like: *The New Face of Alcoholism*, or *Those French and Their Veils*. I wasn't about to let that happen. I'd sooner die.

Oh, wait . . . heh, heh, too late.

When I was eight, I dragged my mother kicking and screaming to Aunt Margene's funeral. Ethel hated Margene. Ever since she named her second daughter Cassandra, after

Mother told her that was to be my name—I ended up with a complex anyway.

"I love my name," I'd said to Mom.

Her response, "Ech, it's so pedestrian, so . . . last minute." Then, under her breath, "Fuck that bitch." A model parent.

I wanted to go so bad; I expected the chapel to be draped in black tulle and cobwebs like a Billy Idol video. Instead, we were greeted with thin blue-grey carpet and dusty pews from the bargain bin. The last time I saw Margene, she was shoved inside a white-satin-lined mahogany casket; my mother and I took turns flinching at her whore-like visage; her face was uniform beige with pinched red cheeks and lids heavy with blue powder. We made bets on the depth of the pancake make-up smeared on her face. I won—eighth of an inch—by going in with my pinky nail. I barely left a mark, a little half moon. No one else would notice; the rest of the family was too busy faking tears and rolling in drama like a puppy on birdshit.

Then it came to me. The answer to my skin care dilemma: the morgue. Their makeup is heavy-duty shit, thick and seemed to cover everything. Despite Aunt Margene looking like a used-up hooker, I couldn't recall a single blue vein.

"Field Trip!" I shouted and giggled to myself, before I realized that doing so meant I was completely insane.

I scampered to the phone book, and flipped through the yellows until I found the listings for funeral homes. A quick scan led to one, on Capitol Hill, that I was fairly certain I could find. I called the number, a message responded. I was in luck: closed for another four hours.

I drove like Gina Lollobrigida, through a blue screen Italian cityscape, looking over my shoulder, repetitively, hair trapped behind a floral scarf, and eyes guarded by oversized Gucci shades. Of course, Gina would have been driving a sporty convertible around the "s" curves of the Amalfi coast, while I coaxed a dirty SUV up slick Seattle hills.

The Prader-Willy Funeral Home was a black hole on an otherwise lively avenue of shops, restaurants and dance clubs. The two-story building was dark, except for its sign and a few tall thujas in the landscape beds, lit from below. I drove around back and parked in the alley.

While the front of the building was classic Georgian, with a low-slung roof and four unlit dormers, the backside of the building was designed strictly for utility. To the left, a truck bay dug deep, flanked by a Dumpster on one side and a ramp on the other. At the top of the ramp, a paneled door with a small window was shut and presumably locked. Dark windows pocked the right side of the building; a few were at ground level, but those were covered with bars.

I waited for a thinning of traffic and then darted from the Volvo into the truck bay. Halfway across the alley, my foot slid ankle deep into a flooded pothole. This could only happen to me. I limped in beside the Dumpster; from there, I was out of the sight of passing motorists. I poured the water from my shoe and cursed the heavens, with a closed fist. *What could it hurt, right?* I figured I didn't have a shot at meeting the old man anytime soon, since I just ate some people and all.

The truck bay ended in a bumper-high wall, padded with a row of three tires. On the right, metal rungs were embedded in the concrete. I climbed them like an epilepsy patient, slipping and trying to find balance with each step. I promised myself, the next time I burgled, I would wear flats[36]. I should have remembered the first time, I'd risked an arrest for beauty.

My obsession with skin care began before college, but oddly enough, after the melodrama of high school; that single hurdle of a summer transformed meek honor student,

[36] Cute ones. I'm thinking Retro '80s.

Amanda, into a chaotic raving lunatic. Pimples weren't the issue for me, and if one did rear its ugly white head, it was in fierce competition with a trifecta of mental afflictions. My skin care routine developed out of my obsessive-compulsive nature, itself growing out of some perfectly age-appropriate generalized anxiety, which of course blossomed from the standard low self-esteem and distorted body image-induced bulimia[37].

During that summer, I had the misfortune of seeing a vampire film, *The Hunger,* on cable. While not particularly scary, and seemingly erotic to some, David Bowie's character went through a rapid aging. It seriously freaked me out. I couldn't sleep; I got out of bed every hour to stare at the skin around my eyes and mouth. The next morning, I arrived at the mall early and stood at the entrance nearest to the only department store with cosmetics kiosks, waiting for them to open.

I didn't have a penny on me, so this was a full-on scam mission. As everyone knows, those skanks at the cosmetics counters are required to offer free makeovers to sell their shit. With my mother's Louis Vuitton purse slung over my forearm, as a distraction, I was intent on taking full advantage. I barreled through that door as soon as the haughty saleswoman turned the key, speed-walked through the racks of clothes and then changed to a leisurely pace as I approached the Chanel counter. I perused the rows of lipstick

---

[37] The following self-diagnoses are a result of years of introspection and research, plus I stole a book called the *Diagnostic and Statistical Manual of Mental Disorders* from my therapist's bookshelf:

1. *Obsessive Compulsive Disorder (OCD)*: I'm not imagining this one. You're reading a list, aren't you? Is it really necessary? I'll answer right after I wash all the doorknobs again, excuse me.

2. *Generalized Anxiety Disorder (GAD)*: My understanding is that this is a disorder where everything makes you anxious. I'm not sure whether I actually have it or if I just like to think I do.

3. *Bulimia Nervosa*: Before you get any ideas, I do not puke, I exercise, like a demon.

samples and plucked a fuck-me red from the rack. The clerk watched from within reach.

"Can I help you with something?" she asked, all puffy cheeks and squinty eyes.

"I don't know," I said, my hand lingering above the eye shadows.

"Some eye shadow, perhaps?"

"I'm not sure I'd know what to do with it. I've never really worn make-up."

"Well, I'd be happy to teach you some tricks. If you've got some time."

"Uh, I guess so." I was giving her a thoughtful Kansas farmgirl, complete with wide-eyed blank stares and heaving exaggerated shrugs.

"Have a seat and I'll just grab some things from back here." The clerk ducked below the counter and I made my move, pocketing a compact of blush. Within the hour, I garnered a twofer, a face of expensive make-up applied by a chic woman trained in Paris (I was pretty sure), and a lovely black compact with mirror image C's emblazoned in gold. The next weekend, I hit Dior.

The funeral home heist was considerably more complicated; first off, how would I get in? The exterior windows were either too high to reach or firmly imprisoned by iron bars. Through the wired glass in the locked rear door, I looked in on a dark hallway. Without risking going around to the front, the only thing left to check was the rolling shutter of the truck bay.

The door was about seven feet tall, and at least that wide. Its corrugated metal was cold to the touch, yet surprisingly flimsy, a tinny flick revealed. At the base of the door a strap of thick fabric lay dusty on the concrete. It was locked.

So, I was either going around the street side of the building, or breaking in through a prime example of shoddy American craftsmanship. Neither Prader nor Willy must have been tremendously concerned about break-ins, or they would have upgraded to an actual door. I trotted to the car for a crowbar.

With very little effort, I wrenched the door up a foot, so I dropped back into the bay and grabbed a tire block for a wedge. After another shaky trip up the ladder, I put the block in place, lay on my back, and slid underneath, into linoleum-lined darkness.

The room was full of oblong crates, stacked nearly to the ceiling. On the far wall stood a machine that looked like a crane, with wide bands hanging. The floor was thick with dust; by the time I hauled my ass up, my hands were coated in gray must. A heavy odor permeated the room and likely the entire basement, a thick syrupy smell. Rot. Under that lived the wet stench of mildew, common to all basements, and a slight wisp of bleach. The silence of the space was impenetrable.

The room funneled into the murky black corridor. I approached the square of light projected from the outside door, and squinted down the hall, trying to distinguish shadow creatures from the very real monsters. Small alcoves were unevenly spaced and caught the light like snags, only to distort it into malevolent figures. I caught myself trembling, and, then, realized I had nothing to fear. *I* was the shadow creature.

I was the monster in the dark. People would be afraid. Not that they'd know right away, I was no *mistake*, lumbering around like some idiot, in a damaged body, constantly attacking, clawing, chewing, and killing. No. This creature was sleek and attractive. I might even get some volunteers.

The muscles in my back loosened their grip, with that bit of revelation.

I started down the hall. My heels clacked and echoed like a fucking Clydesdale. From somewhere in the bowels of the charnel house came a noise—*choop-choop-choop*—what could only be described as a mad shuffling and then silence. I froze, listened for more.

Nothing.

Nothing but dark hall and death stink. I was imagining things.

Why was I here? Oh yeah—makeup. Okay, it's not such a bad smell after all. I can live with it. Sure.

I slipped into the first door; a white rectangular box sat flat on a metal gurney, dead center of the empty room. It was spotlit by a dim sliver of firelight projected from a hole in the opposite wall; beside the door hung oversized ice scrapers on broomsticks, like pizza paddles. *But is it art, Eddie?* I thought and my mind's voice hit all the right Patsy Stone quirks. "No. It's the crematorium," I muttered, in response. I closed the door as I left.

The next doors were a supply closet, a moldy restroom, a small desked office, and a stairwell leading up out of the darkness and into the mourning. The last door on the left[38] revealed a large space with a wall of metal drawers and cabinets and counters, just like your dad's workshop, if he were a crazed serial killer.

I switched on the light.

In the middle of the room were three stainless steel tables. I glanced over the first table and saw gutters around the edges that led to a drain hole; a metal pail sat below. The embalming room. There were machines nearby, like pumps with coils of tubing and . . .

Choop.

The sound came from the far table, from a lump covered by a slip of fabric. It was body-shaped. *Had it been there all along? How could it not be the first thing I'd notice?* I stood stony like one of those Vegas mimes that does nothing—no walking against wind, no trapped in box—nothing but pretending to be a Venetian statue, solid and unresponsive[39]. The

---

[38] And, just typing that gave me Wes Craven–style creeps.
[39] Except by a tip, of course. That'll get 'em moving. This is America.

lump followed suit, no movement. My slender hand lingered on the doorframe, petting.

If I hadn't heard the shuffling from the hall, I might've chalked this latest sound up to morgue rats; the presence of a corpse rotting away on a table, instead of tucked away on a cozy refrigerated metal tray in the wall, the result of good old American incompetence, plain and simple. But I had heard, and it was the sound of fabric sliding too quickly against other fabric, or flesh.

My focus turned visual: the lump was a human shape, maybe, another zombie, a *mistake*, obviously, or a ghost, a phantom, some wicked specter readying itself to take me to Hell. My first instinct was to run. Just turn and clack off down the hall, and out the door; just jump in the car and drive away, just like not every single character did in a horror movie. But instead I opened my big mouth.

"Did you just move?" I asked the lump.

The sheet moved at its head. The mistake was sniffing the air for meat. Maybe I wasn't dead long enough. Maybe I smelled like prey. *Jesus! It's going to eat me.*

The corpse sat up with a start, the sheet dropping to its waist. *Oh my God!* I grasped the wall to hold myself up; I couldn't decide what to scream about first, the corpse's sudden movement, or the fact it wore a garish clown mask; its exaggeration of a blood-red smile, painted on like a flank steak, took me back to childhood dread. Three puffs of scarlet fuzz aged the clown at about forty-two. A horrible thought crossed my mind. It was no mask at all, just a loose slippage of skin on a real dead clown, killed in some terrible balloon animal accident. Ricardo had described zombie mistakes. This might be one of them[40].

---

[40] Point of fact: The presence of a dead clown(s) is rarely cause for concern. Normally, their corpses signal that someone has simply been considerate enough to dispose of the rotten creatures, before you have to.

No.

It was one of them. I screamed. The note echoed across acres of stainless steel, seemingly the only décor theme.

The clown on the table waved its open hands as if to stop me.

"No, no, no, no, no," a female voice said, staccato, the words muffled behind what was now clearly a mask. The clown reached up and pulled it off, revealing a pale blonde waif of a woman, washed out, completely, with eyes the same color as her surrounding skin. I relaxed. The clown was a zombie, and not a mistake, either, but like me, made.

"I'm Wendy." She slid off the table and clacked as her feet hit the floor. She offered her hand, and we shook. I gave her the up-and-down[41].

"I'm Amanda. Nice shoes," I said. "Blahnik's?"

She winced, shook her head. "Christian Louboutins."

"Pretty, and not at all clownish. I was expecting larger feet."

"You really scared me," she said. "I thought you might be the fun director or a ghost—they fuckin' creep me out. I was just rustling through the makeup kits for foundation." She went back to her heist and pulled out a large tub, stuck her finger in and extracted a glob that looked like beige spackle. She rolled it between her fingers. "Found it."

"You beat me to it, then. Is there more?" I asked. "I have no intention of walking around looking like the underside of a hard-on."

"No way!" Wendy screamed, turning from the boxes and shoving my shoulder.

I jumped back, my eyes wide. "Jesus, what?"

"I can't believe you call them that," she said, turning back toward me, a second tub of foundation clutched to her chest, like an Emmy. "I call them scrotal veins."

---

[41] The Assessment: Shorter by a couple of inches, pretty face, thin, smallish tits, vintage shirtdress tied with a gold chain, cute shoes.

"Get the fuck out of here. You're my new best friend."

We broke into teary-eyed guffaws. Those settled into broad comfortable smiles. Wendy handed me the jar of concealer.

"Is this pretty good?" I asked.

"You know, I think it's a halfway decent base coat. Creates a really even canvas." She stopped, put her hand to her hip. "What *are* you, new?"

"Not even twenty-four hours dead."

"Holy shit! You are going to be a handful. Not even a day into your undeath and already worrying about skin care."

"I intend to make this body last."

"Then here's a tip: while your skin still has some flexibility do a final shave. Our hair still grows, but much slower."

"Let me get you my number," I said, scrambling through the cabinet drawers for a pen and some scratch. "Why don't you and I meet for drinks? I could introduce you to a vampire friend." I found a stub of pencil and scratched my number onto the corner of a file folder lying on the counter, tore off a piece.

"Sounds good."

Wendy and I scheduled to meet for drinks the following night, and as we left the building, without discussing it beforehand, both of us serpentined into the alley like a couple of special ops commandos in six-inch heels. I had found a soul mate.

Chapter 8

Bernard Krups's Satyricon

A wicked fun time, to be sure, but there's so much more . . . all this—and hundreds of dollars' worth of valuable coupons, accepted at nearly all undead establishments . . .

—The Bacchus Guide

You know, I could just sit here and ramble on about the nightmare of being dead, eating helpless people, breaking and entering, not having circadian rhythms. I could tell you that I was horrified with the direction my life had taken. I'm on a downward spiral into a vision of Hell not glimpsed since a Nine Inch Nails video. Blah, blah, blah. Who wants to hear it? It's not true, anyway. The truth is this: I wasn't enjoying life when I was alive. Now that I'm dead, it's gonna be another story.

I plan to enjoy the hell out of it. *Am I bad[42]?*

For instance, I can't tell you how many pathetic holidays I spent in the office covering for Pendleton and Avery, this when I was but a lowly copywriter. It took two years for those assholes to notice; two years of throwing myself on the

[42] A rhetorical question, obviously. I don't give a shit what you think.

holiday pyre, as well as writing the best ads in the firm—
hello, just wait until you see the list of accomplishments
(coming soon to a chapter near you). When they did catch
on, it was drinks after work, spiteful eye daggers from my—
ahem—peers, and the inevitable partnership offer. Satisfying, yes, but still not really living.

I'd be delusional!—I know I'm eccentric, but not psychotic—if I believed it was only ambition that chained me to
that desk; sometimes I was simply killing time, so I wouldn't
have to go home to an empty apartment (this was long before my digs improved).

Listen to me.

Boo-hoo.

Jesus, can I whine?

My place wasn't *always* empty. I've had a few boyfriends,
from time to time. I'm not a fucking nun[*]. But those relationships were so tragically short-lived[**]. I'd get bored with
them. Take Elden Ford, seemingly interesting mortgage bro-
ker with a full head of Patrick Dempsey waves. His hobbies:
hiking, travel, and talking about himself incessantly. Or
how about Reece McCallister? He was cute enough, with
his sandy blond locks, chiseled jaw, and sad puppy dog
eyes—eyes that were set a tad *too* far apart for my taste.
Reece enjoyed a certain sexual proclivity that I allowed on
a single occasion. An act I don't care to elaborate on
here—I just don't like the idea of it being documented.
Let's just say, it involved an egg of Leggs pantyhose (his
choice), knots, and an orifice designed for output rather
than intake[***].

Shall I go on?

Let's see. There was Gregoire. Just Gregoire. He wouldn't
tell me his last name, and spoke in no detectable accent to

[*] Not that there'd be any question of that.
[**] Thanks, Mom!
[***] His!

warrant a moniker so patently French. What drew me to him, I'll never know. He was hideous, puffy, and rouged up by alcoholism, to the point of looking like a character from *Chitty Chitty Bang Bang*. I nearly always left our dates singing, "Toot Sweet." For that reason alone, he had to go. Well that and the whole one word name thing.

See? Anyone want to trade places?

Now that my situation is . . . uh . . . different, I plan to enjoy the hell out of it. *Is that so wrong?*

Let me prove my point in a more intellectual, didactic way, chock full of hands-on examples.

Take a look at your definition of zombie. Go ahead, humor me, I'll wait . . .

See?

Now take a look, wherever you are (assuming you like to read in coffee shops, parks, squares, or somewhere equally public).

Do you see them? They are all around you, shuffling between work and home, home and daycare, school and soccer practice. Repeating the same motions over and over. Trying to find meaning—or escape—through monotonous cycles. Birth, life, death. It's all so last season.

Sure, they look okay on the outside, but on the inside they're dead.

Take vampires, for that matter. They're definitely all around you. Ever have the feeling that someone was sucking the life out of you with incessant droning or a static condition of high drama? Vampires. They're not just blood drinkers anymore. They've evolved. Now they feed on emotions. There's one two cubes over from you. Isn't your sister a little needy? See what I mean?

That being said, let me get down off this high horse, I think I can just reach the soapbox . . .

The sun rose, promptly at 6:47 A.M., as unwelcome as your aunt with the hacking cough, the one that shows up early for Thanksgiving; you remember, the one with the male pattern baldness. I knew the exact second; the clock in my condo lobby all but shouted it as I returned home. The foyer was a bit bright for my taste, too cheery. Not that I was tired—no sleep, tons of energy, oh, the opportunities.

I needed to figure out how to deal with Pendleton, Avery and the drones at the agency. I couldn't very well just quit. I owned a third. Ricardo and his lesson four could kiss my ass. I'd sooner eat glass than walk away from that kind of money. I had an hour and thirteen minutes to plan.

If you'll remember, I love my work and I'm damn good at it. I know you don't hear that a lot. Most people just go through the motions. That's not me. I was not about to allow a touch of undeadness, and the fear of discovery, to creep in and ruin my confidence.

I took my shower and sorted out the grey skin issue. Despite the seemingly cheap product the foundation went on smooth and not at all greasy. The coverage was excellent and my cheeks were smooth as a baby's ass. I slipped from the bathroom, dropping my towel on the maple planks. The vertical blinds colluded with the dawn; the sun's fingers tinkled a tune on the hardwood floor like piano keys. I was glad I'd opted against the wall-sized mirror in the bedroom. Despite my zombie power epiphany, I was still self-critical and avoiding direct examination of my body.

My closet was arranged by color and then in subsets by activity (work, play, exercise, etc.). The day's look was power bitch—starched white shirt, pointy collar, French cuffs, high-waisted jet wool pencil skirt, and opaque human skin tone stockings. The black stilettos were standard, as were the Dolce and Gabbana shades. Do you get the picture? I think you do.

I chignoned my hair to the ceiling, like a doomed Hitchcock heroine, tight on the sides, coiled like a nautilus shell in the back. I snatched up my favorite black purse, the Balenciaga, and stormed off to work, feet crushing the floor like a paparazzi-lit runway. Hot, unstoppable. *You can bank on that, bitches*.

The drive to work was unremarkable. I suppose I could describe it once, and then you'd be able to picture every rain-flooded pothole of Seattle's roads. The Volvo spat me out into the garage, the scene of the crime. I half-expected a fabulous chalk outline in one of those fashion editorial poses. But, all that remained to mark my death was a dark grey spot of wet, on the parking garage concrete, and a heavily trod donut box, edges gone to pulp. I snatched up the culprit of my slip and crammed it into the garbage by the elevator.

The elevator.

There was something I forgot about it, about yesterday. My memory was hazy. Had there been a man? I pressed the up arrow and watched the numbers descend, struggling for the memory.

The 14th floor lit and I dwelled on donut boxes and urine stains.

12th floor: athletic equipment, running shoes.

11th floor: uncomfortable silences.

10th floor: boundary breakers.

9th through 6th floors: overstock of fear.

(Is this list too Macy's? Bear with me; I'm going somewhere.)

5th floor: skin care for ethnic tones, men's suits.

4th through 2nd floors: heavy breathers.

Lobby: death rattles and rotten eggs.

P1 and P2: zombie-making machines.

I remembered, that fucker was dead—undead, but he breathed. *Don't you just love shopping?*

The metal doors slid back into the wall, revealing a group of pay-per-day parking garage goons, checking watches, tapping their briefcases, sneering. *Jealousy is so ugly*. They made room for me, and I stepped in with a series of clicks, my personal space bubble projecting needles.

"Nineteen?" I asked, to no one in particular, more to the

nonchalance of air, and rude or no, a random finger stretched out and tapped the round key. The "19" lit up like a ring of power. Lemmings.

"Thank you."

I needed to talk to Ricardo. *This* was the memory. Zombie in the elevator. The thing that both Ricardo and Gil had expected to hear. He'd be able to explain why it was important. I dredged my purse and flipped open my cell. 411.

"City and state." The voice was mechanical, by way of accent-free middle America, the regional twang sucked out by multiple viewings of the five o'clock news.

"Seattle, Washington."

"Listing?"

"The Well of Souls," I said, but in a whisper, covering my mouth, which instantly seemed conspicuous and idiotic. A woman on my left glared at me, her lip curled up, as if to showcase the cigarette divot in her lipstick.

I mouthed, wide-eyed and nodding with each overaccentuated and soundless word, *piss—off—okay—great*, as though the woman were a naughty kindergartener.

"I'm not finding a number for that listing, ma'am."

I don't know why that surprised me; how could it be listed, and where? Above Zombies-R-Us? Right after Undead DVD and Video? In the same list as Phantasm's Emporium of Eccentricities? Where?

"Okay, how about a number for Ricardo . . ." I blanked on his last name. "Ricardo . . ." The bitch was looking again; I started the stare down, eyes blazing white. "Forget it." I flipped the cell phone shut and dropped it into my bag. She turned her head away and I smiled. What would they all do if I just opened my mouth and bit her? Was I even hungry? Did that matter when I was alive? I thought about donuts.

Nineteen was a long way off, but the elevator emptied out by 12.

The doors opened directly into the sprawling modern space of Pendleton, Avery and Feral. Walls of both clear and frosted glass, depending on the need for privacy, vied for time with shiny stainless steel reflecting ghost forms with each passing shape.

Marithé, our receptionist, was making that art school nostalgia thing happen, but a closer look revealed a tongue split at the end; she could strike venom with the best of them—I should know, I hired her. Her hair was bobbed, cruel and black. She wore cat-eye glasses, librarian low, and a Zac Posen frock. The effect: Sadistic Prude, Chic.

"Good morning, Ms. Feral," she purred.

"Good morning, Marithé," I responded. "Anything for me?" I watched her harsh eyes scan me in trademarked *jugement de Marithé*, her lips pursed, like a Pomeranian's asshole. If anyone would pick up the difference in me, it was this woman. And, if she knew something, she was not letting on.

She handed over a large white envelope.

"The website CV, for your final edit." She plucked up the stack and straightened, patting the edges with her fingertips to achieve some level of perfection of which only she was aware. "Messages arranged in order of importance." She passed the pink slips across the desk. "And, a woman named Wendy called to confirm your attendance at a seminar. It's at 1:00 P.M. She said she'd sent you the brochure as requested. I didn't see it on your calendar." Marithé fingered through a stack of papers and withdrew a black envelope printed in white, addressed to me. "This is it. Couriered this morning."

Wendy, what are you up to?

There was no telling what the "seminar" was about, if there was one. I suspected inside the envelope, I would find a note about going on a "manhunt," or a "fun run." Thank God, Marithé hadn't opened it, although her take on "manhunt" would be much more benign, *or would it*? I headed down the glass halls toward my office, slapping the stack of papers into my hand like a riding crop.

"Amanda, Amanda!" A familiar voice called from behind

me. *No*. I turned to find Prissy Koch scuttling up the hall like a roach.

An assessment, from the ground up: white nurse clogs, wool socks, knee-length pleated skirt, argyle sweater set, fake pearls. Jesus Christ, like a fashion magazine had never been printed. Prissy Koch must enter a store[43] and suffer immediate hysterical blindness. Her face was a shade lighter than her arms, and accented with a pink blush that could only have been created by smudging an Easter Peep across those giant apple cheeks. Her bangs stood at attention over a short forehead, like a shellacked line of defense, protecting the damaged ranks behind.

My hand settled on my hip, the loose papers whacking in time with my irritability. "Yes, Prissy?"

"I need your credit card receipts for end-of-month," she said, just like that, like end of the month were one word. And, that single word spilled out of her ugly mouth like slosh from a urinal. The woman made me sick.

Can you tell we have history?

Six months prior, Prissy Koch marched into Jeremy Pendleton's office like a Salem witch hunter and announced that I was embezzling funds. She slapped down a file of her "research," and marched back out. Jeremy and I went over Prissy's printed paranoia and found that her sticking point was my clothing allowance. Statement after statement, yellow highlighter pointed to various store purchases (Nordstrom, Barney's, Betsey Johnson). My mother would call her an ignoramus or a buttinsky, but I prefer the classics; Prissy Koch was a c-u-n-t, cunt. Jeremy wrote her up, the following day, for insubordination. That gave me some time to spread the word, through the back door.

To Claire in the mailroom: "I'm worried that Jeremy's gunning for Prissy." With that, my work was done. The gossip

---

[43] Wal-Mart, would be my best guess, or somewhere equally *haute*.

spread like influenza at a daycare center. The rest of that day Prissy hid in her office like Anne Frank.

"I'll get you those receipts before lunch, Prissy. Thank you for bringing them to my attention."

"Thank you, Amanda." Her words were terse, pecked one by one from the air. Prissy turned and clopped off the way she'd come.

"Oh . . . and Prissy?" I asked.

"Yes?"

"Cute shoes!"

Her reply—get this—"Humph[44]!" *Couldn't you just die?*

I set the stack of papers on my desk, sprawled out on the love seat and watched the lake like a movie. I tore open the envelope and retrieved a brochure that appeared to be hand-made. It did, in fact, advertise a seminar, entitled: *Getting the Most from Your Afterlife, A Field Guide for Supernaturals.* I decided to just go and call it an adventure. It would also allow me to stall on what to do about the business.

I worked through messages and returned calls: Renewal clinic—check, Rigel shoes—check.

Check, check, check, check, check.

I turned my attention to the biography sample for the website.

AMANDA R. FERAL, Vice President

Graduate of UC Berkeley, where she earned a Ph.D. in Organizational Psychology, in addition to an MA in Sociology and an MBA with emphasis in Advertising and Marketing, both from Stanford.

The winner of three AdYear awards and a Copywriter of the Year for 2005, Ms. Feral's past campaigns include:

• Rigel Athletic, *Cloudrunner* (2005)
• The 2005 Bridge the Gap Games
• Peach, iMind (2006)

---

[44] An actual "humph." So rare, these days. I hadn't heard one since Roz in a repeat of *Nine to Five.*

- Arhea Home, *A New Bed for Sally and Jane* (1999)
- Platinum Hotel, *Lux* (2002)
- BellyBurger, *Swallow* (2004)

Doesn't all that sound so super impressive? It should, I wrote it myself and some of it was even true. The education was exaggerated, a bit. I have been to Berkeley, where I spent many a hazy stoned summer evening searching for torn panties after frat keggers. I've also been to Stanford, where Ben Moretti, of steel-belted-radial fame and a proud Kappa Beta Pi, took me, and my drunken virginity (at least that's what I told him). Lest you think that my only experience with education has been of the drinking and fucking nature, I did complete a degree at Seattle Community College and some work towards a BA at UW, in advertising of course. It was enough to get me started. My brazen nature (and to a lesser degree my good looks) took me the rest of the way. As for organizational psychology, I am a good judge of character[45] and a highly organized person (please note my fondness for lists). Sociology? I'm a social butterfly and I think that counts (I'm going to the Well of Souls for drinks after work—or the seminar depending on how long that took—and not just anyone can get in, now can they?). The impressive array of ad campaigns were all me. Those idiots Pendleton and Avery couldn't come up with a decent slogan if their lives depended on it; they were along for the ride.

I sketched a smiley on a Post-It and underneath wrote: *Run with it.* I slapped it on the form and put it in the out box. Marithé cleaned it out hourly.

My thinking: I'll just keep working, fake it until I come up with a plan.

Thinking about drinks reminded me that I needed to talk with Ricardo about the black zombie breathing on me. What

---

[45] Except for the time with Ben Moretti, oh and Joel Watts and that time with Rachel somebody, after that stupid Wicca meeting, but that was a long time ago, a long time.

was Ricardo's last name? I was sure he mentioned it, or Gil did. Why did I want to say peanut? It was a nut! His last name was a nut. Ricardo Macadami-no. Ricardo Brazi-no. Almond? Ricardo Almandine? Almost, Amandine, that sounded right. I reached for the phone.

411. Got me a ring.

"You've reached Ricardo, I'm either sleeping with the dead or too busy to pick up. Leave me a message." Beep.

"Ricardo, this is Amanda." I paused, waited, as though my name would be enough to make the tall dead guy pick up. I assure you in most circumstances, it's plenty. I rethought, added, "Princess, whatever. Listen. I remembered something about my death. Give me a call."

The Oak Alley Business Park abandoned its namesake plantation roots at its ramshackle sign; a low-budget enamel-on-plywood affair, strapped across a shattered Plexiglas column. It stood unlit, shadowed, and ineffective under the dark gloom of rain clouds. It was a wonder I'd found the place. There were no oaks, as the name implied, nor any trees, at all. The site was the opposite of an oasis, a patch of bland in an otherwise evergreen landscape. The little foliage to be seen, a variegated ivy, furred the low brick structures; windows pocked their surface like mange.

6106 Suite B squatted amidst the willy-nilly cluster of buildings, like an imposter. Cars dotted the parking spaces of the other buildings, but my destination was marked by only two: a gray VW Vanagon suitable for serial killing, and a far-too-yellow Xterra, that seemed puffy, Fisher-Price, except for the heavily tented windows. Wendy's Audi was conspicuously absent. I wheeled into the handicapped spot outside the smoked glass doors, and snatched my purse.

The lobby was humdrum; flat white paint, industrial grey carpet and dropped ceiling; boring. It could have been a prison common room. A copper-topped zombie head examining nails that wanted a French manicure, bad, stopped and glared up at me. Gerilyn would be my greeter and warden for the day's event, and happy to be so. Though her teeth were in desperate need of veneers, she showed them off with the pride of a psychotic pageant mother, albeit a white-eyed and dead one. She sat prim-postured at a cheap plywood table skirted for the Fourth of July, in pleats of red, white and blue plastic. A handwritten table tent read:

REGISTRATION
A–Z

She extended her hand with the stiff-jointed squareness of a robot. I took it.

"Welcome to *Getting the Most from Your Afterlife with Bernard Krups.*" The words flowed out from monotonous practice. I could, almost, hear the italics. "I'm Gerilyn. Did you get a field guide?"

I broke off from her jerky handshake. "Just this brochure." I extracted it from my purse and held it in front of me like a used Kleenex. It was a poorly produced tri-fold of the kind I could have manufactured at age seven. "I'm Amanda Feral. I'm supposed to meet my friend Wendy. Has she checked in?" I knew the answer, but one could hope.

Gerilyn scanned the names on a brief list and returned a pert, "Nope, not yet." She handed over a stapled stack of lightweight bond printed with the title of the seminar in slipshod blurriness. Under Bernard Krups's name, I saw that the workshop was subtitled, *A Field Guide to the Supernatu*real. I hadn't caught that the first time. The sloppy creators loved their plays on words. Me? Not wowed.

The woman wrote out my name on a "Hello my name is . . ." sticker and passed it to me, along with a pen that pronounced, "You're a winner." Duh[46]!

---

[46] Weird, right? It was like they knew me.

Gerilyn pointed to double doors to my right. "The seminar is through there. There are snacks if you'd like, depending on . . . well, you know." I didn't pick up on her meaning until I saw the buffet.

I slapped the Balenciaga and paperwork down at a table near the back of the room, the kind you don't cross your legs under for fear of becoming attached to it by a wad of moldy gum.

There were two others in the room, one held a bottle of red liquid and slurped at it, occasionally gnawing on the spiral threading the top, with a fine-pointed canine. She was a woman, vampire, clearly, and bored. Her head rested in her palm. She stared at the wall, window and then the other person in the room, a man wearing a short-sleeved dress shirt, a beige polka-dot oxymoron. Gag! My eyes followed hers, from the man's laptop, to its connected projector. Oh shit, I thought. The woman turned her gaze to me and mouthed, "PowerPoint." Her head rolled back on her shoulders as though she was near death and she shoved a pretend stake through her heart.

The man was average height and weight—you'd never pick him out of a crowd, except for one oddity. Grey hairs sprouted from above his ears like wings on either side of his bald head. Was this Bernie Krups? If it was, we were in trouble, in real danger of being bored to death. Or else, we had been dropped in the middle of a pyramid scheme. I feared I would be forced into selling knives or participating in a Ponzi.

Where the hell was Wendy and how did I let myself get roped into this?

The food *was* interesting; I'll have to admit. Eight bottles of a red liquid, surely blood, in plastic bottles, were kept warm in a chafing dish of water. A tray of appetizers displayed cracker-sized spinal cord segments, each dotted with a spherical glob of jaundiced fat; if we were at a French restaurant, it would be called an *amuse bouche*. Severed fingers protruded from a crystal bowl of ice—the fingernails had been removed[47]. The blood and body parts shared space with humdrum turkey subs and bags of Doritos[48]. I snapped up one of the vertebrae and cracked through the bone like a carrot.

I scanned the room for reading materials, a *Vogue* or an *Entertainment Weekly*, some bit of glossy gossip—you know, news. Nothing but laminate covered in the greasy finger-prints of past attendees. I popped another nibble down my craw, this time a tasty finger—and not bad, probably Geri-lyn's specialty. I took my seat.

As I was fumbling for my phone to text Wendy, a pair of regular flesh-toned humans strode in chatting about the weather, traffic and other sundry blah, blah. Their name tags—which reminded me that mine was mixed in with the papers on the table—read Tim Torgerson and Shanna Tate. They looked exactly how you'd expect them to, blond-haired, blue-eyed, Ken and Barbie fresh from Malibu. Suh-nore. They sat at the table in front of me, but didn't offer a greeting. So, screw 'em.

I thumbed a quick message out to Wendy:
Where the fuck r u bitch?

The doors behind me banged open, slamming against ei-ther side of their frame. A squatty shirtless creature appeared, with the streaky bronzed skin of a last-minute invite. Despite its hairy-pitted maleness and smirking Buddha head, the beast wore C-cups like a pinup, and the muscled legs of a goat. The pink hot pants were the clincher. He was fabulous.

"Welcome!" he bellowed, spreading short arms as wide as possible. "Oh . . . so few attendees. That is too bad. I'm Bernard Krups the Third. I guess you could say I'm a benev-olent gift to the malevolent. A real helper."

Gerilyn trailed behind him, her lips spread in a giddy

---

[47] Classy.
[48] Moment of silence.

smile. She clapped her hands with the enthusiasm of a game show contestant. Bernard marched to the front of the room and shooed the tech geek away, with two quick flicks of a wrist. He hopped onto the table there and spread across it like a centerfold, dragging a stubby finger up his side, circling the thick aura of skin around his nipple. I could imagine him crowned with grape leaves and carrying a diamond crusted pimp cup, but his origins escaped me. I was thinking Roman, but it could have been Greek. God of parties, or something.

"Bacchus?" the little thing offered, plucking the question from inside my head. *Was he reading me like a goddamned book? Am I that transparent?* "But that was so very long ago, what makes you go there? Miss? Miss?" he asked, searching for my name.

I looked around to see if he were talking to someone else but his bloodshot eyes were trained on me. "Amanda, Amanda Feral."

"Mmm, feral, makes me want to come over there and tangle with you, you feisty little pussycat." Bernard was on his hands and knees and reached out with a curling movement and clawed at the air. It would have been sexy if he was remotely pleasant to look at, or I was completely drunk.

"That can be remedied," he said, growling.

The woman in the front of the room was heaving. Tim and Shanna's mouths hung open, wide enough to attract flies.

I didn't respond. Bacchus started his song and dance.

"Getting the most from our afterlife. Isn't that why we're all here?" He spread his fingers and fluffed an imaginary pillow in front of him. "This afterlife can be so boring, really. Eating people, sucking blood . . ." He gestured to Tim and Shanna. "Seemingly pointless attacks under the full moon, or . . . whenever. Isn't there more?"

Of course, there is, I thought.

"Exactly, Amanda."

"I—"

Tim, Shanna, and the bored vampire looked back at me with questioning eyes. I had a question. *How the hell did a vampire get to a daylight seminar?* I wondered about the dark tinting on the car outside. Was it dark enough?

"There is more to this life than pretense. An entire world is available to you, if you'll just open your eyes."

"Duh," Shanna said. "Preach to the choir much?"

He waved off her comment, with a shudder that rolled through him like that first bite of lemon.

My cell began to vibrate on the table. I snatched it up and quieted it, maintaining eye contact with Bacchus in the process.

The little troll pressed a key on the laptop; the screen lit up with a slide show of undead hot spots: The Well of Souls, Convent, and other clubs, but also retail stores, dry cleaners and restaurants that catered to our kind, all open twenty-four hours per day. Shiny-skinned zombies with white eyes danced together, silly vampires laughed at tables with friends. Same old crap.

"And none of this we share with our living cousins. They cannot see them, as you are probably aware. How many of you have been to a supernatural bar since you were turned?"

We all raised our hands, like some pathetic AA meeting. We all know those people are quitters.

"Good, a wicked fun time to be sure, but there is so much more." He flicked another key, and a book flashed onto the screen. A thick hardback with the title: *The Bacchus Guide to the Supernatural World*.

Here it comes, I thought. He caught my thought and winked. Was I the only one thinking—they all looked pretty vacant—or could he only read zombie thoughts?

"'Here it comes,' is right, ladies and gentlemen. The Bacchus Guide is the premiere . . ." His voice trailed off along with my interest. Wendy had sent me to a sales pitch.

I glared at the message on my phone.

Ha ha ha luv wend c u.

I responded with,

U bitch the well 7

I reached for my purse. The last words I heard from the sales pitch were, ". . . and hundreds of dollars' value in coupons, all for $79.99. You can't beat it . . ."

Sad. The patron saint of fraternity row was reduced to direct marketing sales and from the look of things, tanking. I swished to the front of the room and handed Bacchus a business card, "We could work on a new marketing plan."

Bernard Krups's mouth hung open. He flipped the card over twice and then shook his head yes.

I let the doors slam on my way out.

Outside a raggedy woman trudged across the parking lot pushing a grocery store cart loaded with cans and bottles.

I took one whiff, winced, and went deeper, past the stench of homelessness, to the meat of the matter. I didn't drift as much this time. It still held the feeling of a dream sequence, like I was eating the woman in a big bowl of marshmallow fluff. I crunched on bones, and slurped up loose tendons. Despite the actions, it was a surprisingly comfortable experience.

The cart went rolling into the side of a red Tempo, leaving a dent the size of a cake plate. I threw the pile of leftover shredded clothes behind a holly bush and got in the Volvo.

I had become an expert at directing gore and splatter away from my expensive designer clothes; who would've guessed? I also used to eat butter-slathered corn on the cob without a single slobbery drip. But there's always some smoosh in the corners of your mouth. After a quick wet nap and a cosmetic pick-me-up, I hightailed it out of the business park. I was ready to hit the town and Wendy.

Chapter 9

Way Too Much Information

The history of the supernatural settlement is intriguing, to say the least. Back in 1902, Jeremiah Barrelman was the first creature to happen upon Seattle, and instantly took a liking to it . . .
—The Secret Lives of Dead People

Two blondes stuck to the ice bar like wet tongues, their hip-bones jutting as if in an attempt to escape their skin. They ground their respective pelvises against a pair of horny ghouls, one of whom being only slightly more hideous than the other. The girls were human and under some kind of trance, drunk, or just not at all particular.

"Thank God for necrophilia," I said. "Those rotting corpses wouldn't stand a chance of getting laid without it."

Gil nodded, adding, "Here's to celebrity blood donors." He raised his glass for the toast and took a deep slug of warm blood from the Riedel Syrah glass in his hand. "This, for instance." Another swallow. ". . . is a lovely *Square Pegs*–era Jami Gertz. It's Jami-licious."

"Sounds yummy." Come to think of it, it probably was a

good year. *Square Pegs* was fabulous and Ms. Gertz's Muffy Tepperman was a spot-on caricature of the preppy bitch. Brings back memories.

Wendy arrived with flourish[49], tossing her purse into the booth and flopping down with a bounce. "Cheers to mortuaries with fully-stocked cosmetics inventory." She spoke with the ease of indifference, as is apparently common among the dead. She slathered crimson stained lips with a fresh coat of gloss. Snapped a gold compact shut with a click like a castanet.

"Hear, hear!" I yelled. "Oh, and by the way, thanks a lot for the fucking infomercial."

"No prob." She shielded a laugh like a Japanese schoolgirl.

"Such a cooze. This is Gil."

He stretched his arm across the table and pumped Wendy's hand, lightly. "I think we've met before."

"Yeah, totally! Armani trunk show."

"That's right."

I motioned for Ricardo; he trotted from the bar, a white towel bouncing against—what were those—oh my God, *black* jeans. Only Ricardo could pull off black jeans without leather chaps, and to think, so far downhill of the gay ghetto.

"How are the beautiful people tonight?" he asked, scooting in next to Wendy, who had moved on to jiggling and blinking like anime.

"Perfect," I said, nudging Wendy and raising my vodkatini ('cause anything else is just garnish). "This flirt right here, is Wendy, I met her at a cosmetics convention. On your way to the line dance?" I pointed at his jeans. "Could you hook the bitch up with something strong yet pretty?"

"You were probably much more cute when you were still alive," he said. His face had gone all smirky-flirty.

"Mmm. But oddly enough not so sweet."

[49] Is there any other way?

"It's wonderful to meet you," Ricardo said, leaning in to Wendy. He may have sniffed her hair.

"Isn't it just?" Wendy said.

I got the impression they'd met before. Sliding in close to Wendy, I put my face in his line of sight. "Hey Ricardo, did you get my message?"

"Yeah, yeah. I meant to call you and just got bogged down. You remembered something?"

"There was a guy in the elevator before the garage. He got up way too close to me. I could smell the flesh coming off of him."

"That's right, we knew you'd received the breath, otherwise you'd be stumbling around mumbling about brains."

"Brains!" Gil yelled, his arms stretching out toward Wendy.

"Shut up," she said, but giggled.

"They really say 'brains' like on the movies?"

"No." Ricardo pursed his lips and rolled his eyes. "Not at all. What'd the guy look like?"

"Black guy, gray hair . . . he'd seen better days."

"I think I know him, comes in here every once in a while, I'll speak with him when he shows up. Arrange an introduction." Ricardo patted Wendy's shoulder. "I'll get that drink right now."

With a disturbingly broad smile for Wendy's benefit, Ricardo bounded off for the bar. Wendy wore a similar grin. I wondered what was up between them.

"So have you sated your curiosity?" Gil asked, interrupting my Nancy Drewness.

"For now. But how about you?"

"How about me what?"

"How did you become such a sexy vamp?"

Gil sipped at his Gertz, the blood shot straight into his cheeks. "I'd rather not say."

"Oh, come on," Wendy begged.

"It's really embarrassing."

"You're among friends." I winked at Wendy. She chased a plastic monkey around the rim of an empty glass, grinning.

"Alright."

I expected a paragraph, not a hijacking.

Hanging Out at the Flat

Inconsiderate Interlude of the Bitter & Pathetic
Part One: Gil

"Let me paint you a picture." Gil wrapped his arm over the back of the seat, shifted his ass into a comfortable spot, and set off on his self-indulgence.

"It was the seventies and Tacoma. Grey skies filled with pulp steam and the distinct stench of dirty diapers from the stacked mills in the tide flats. A scent that—I think, you'll agree—lingers today. The grey stubs of buildings that composed the city's skyline appeared to have risen from an ashtray. Completely utilitarian.

"But that's too much history lesson.

"Okay.

"So, needless to say, I looked hot—'cause, well just look at me—and not all Castro mustachioed with short-short Levis cutoffs. I'm talking Sergio Valente hotness, and that needs to be clarified when we're talking about the age of polyester. I was twenty-six and trolling for the unspeakable: love. I know, I know, it's hard enough nowadays with all the six-packed gym sluts, but back then, forget it. No one was looking for long-term relationships. They were considered the plague; that is before the real one showed up.

"My best friend's name was Howard, and we'd known each other since grade school. His girlfriend was Bethany

Brindle—I just loved her name, it reminded me of jodhpurs and shooting parties, still does. They had an unnatural interest in my romantic life, prodding for information, showering me with empathy, and oftentimes setting me up on blind dates.

"In those days Tacoma gays only frequented bars with sailor themes, or the back room at Lucky Wang's; I met my blind date at The Rusty Bucket. The place reeked of poorly wiped butt, a heady blend of musky sweat and Old Spice cologne, like a mediocre Cabernet gone to vinegar under Grandma Pearl's sink. The bar seemed repurposed from a defunct bordello, its ceiling, once covered in a carved crimson velvet, hung loose like the felt roof lining of a shaggy Saab hardtop. Despite the grunge, The Rusty Bucket was a much more desirable locale than the Poop Deck, which a week prior had seen Dayton's first gay riot, Deckwall—Poopwall seemed too irreverent considering that nasty business in New York.

"Chase was his name. Chase Hollingsworth. Three hundred pounds and a fake British accent that went in and out like pirate cable. Chase snorted Vicks from those old dispensers that looked like little dildos. He kept reaching across the table for me with these greasy sausage fingers. I cringed and flattened myself on my side of the booth. There was only one thing to do. Drink.

"Over several pitchers, Chase regaled me with his love of all things British, particularly fish and chips with lots of malt vinegar in the newspaper cone and never on a plate, from the stands and not a restaurant, although, he let on, he'd never been to England. I was trapped in Hell. I poured another beer.

"I noticed a man ordering something from the bar, a tall sexy thing with sandy blond hair, a strong square jaw, and most importantly, not three hundred pounds and wrapped in the Union Jack. His drink was coffee, and lucky me, he carried it to the table next to ours, so I could ogle him easily while pretending to listen to Chase. He met my gaze a couple of times, seemed to be interested and then resumed his preferred activity: smelling his coffee.

"It was about the time when Chase started in on the importance of Benny Hill, that my memory started to fuzz. I calculated my beer consumption at or about a pitcher and a half, maybe three quarters. I kind of remember being helped into a cab and landing on a foreign sofa, before passing out entirely.

"When I woke up I was in someone else's apartment. The coffee table in front of me was draped in crocheted doilies and stacks of dog-eared and bookmarked *Hello* magazines, the top one splashed with Prince Andrew's youthful face and a headline that read: Andrew Snogs Porn Strumpet. There was a picture of Queen Elizabeth on the wall, but I didn't need that clue to realize I was at Chase's house. Chills coursed through me, and over me like permanent goose bumps.

"Particularly, around my nether regions.

"I glanced down at my crotch to find my dick hanging out of my open jeans—I'd taken to going commando, so it was all the more garishly displayed. I hugged myself and rocked, imagining Chase's melon head bobbing up and down on me as I slept, the hot-dog pack of his neck rising and falling. I gagged. The beer was coming up. I got up and frantically scoured the room for a trash can, my jeans sliding down to my ankles in the process. My spew ended up flooding an adorable bluebell and vines china teapot, each of its six surrounding cups and saucers, and a bit on the TV tray where they were all displayed.

"I vowed never to drink again.

"I was a mess. I picked myself up, pulled up my pants and went in search of a bathroom. I thought I heard Chase snoring from deep in the house. Past the doilied parlor, a short hall led to the front door in one direction and three closed doors. The first was an empty space with a sewing machine in the corner and bolts of fabric strewn about. A shade was drawn over the window. The next room was the bathroom. I rinsed the spatter from my face, snatched a towel and wandered back into the hall.

"A slurping sound issued from behind the final door, as though a dog were going at a bone. I knocked softly. 'Chase?' The lapping ceased. 'Chase, I'm going to head home.' No response.

"I turned to dart out the front, and as I did the door behind me opened.

" 'Do you have to go so soon?' a throaty voice asked, decidedly free of British inflection.

"It was the coffee-snorting guy from the bar, and he wasn't wearing a shirt. He was smirking, lean and tan—like I like them. My thighs shook. I thought my legs would give out. I managed, 'Well I guess I could—'

"And, then he was on me pressing his lips to mine, parting them with his tongue. A smell of Jovan Musk drifted from his throat, musk and something else I couldn't put my finger on. Something like rust, iron, pungent. But he was too good a kisser to allow myself to drift into critique. His mouth moved to my throat, sucking at the skin there, scraping his teeth against the taut flesh.

"That's when I saw Chase. The man had left the bedroom door open. Inside, Chase lay on the bed, his head bent back over the foot of it, upside down, eyes wide but vacant, a huge smile on his pudgy dead face. He did look thinner, though.

"At some point, the man's interest in my neck had become less sexual and more epicurean. The lapping sound returned and I blacked out for the second time, and when I woke up, I was a vampire."

"That's it? How did you turn?" Wendy asked, for my benefit.

"I didn't know then, the specifics of it. But it's kind of

simple. Just drain out the old blood and blow in the new. Like this." Gil bit his cheek and blew a bit of spray into the air, where it kept traveling across the room, finally coming to rest in a scatter of spots on some guy's cream linen jacket. Frankly, it improved the look. Really, linen?

"Well?"

Wendy and I just looked at each other, then back at him.

"Well what?" I shrugged.

"Don't you have anything to say, a comment, anything?" His face reddened, no small feat for a bloodless creature, but the Gertz was creeping in, and he did seem to be channeling some of the snotty prep of Ms. Muffy. I wondered if that was a real side effect. If so, the practical joke possibilities would be endless.

"You probably should have kept that to yourself, chubby chaser." I almost couldn't get the words out. They were followed by a rolling explosion of laughter that quickly enveloped Wendy, who pointed at Gil, convulsing in fits of hilarity.

"He didn't blow me!"

"Then how was your dick out? Do you have a habit of airing it?" I asked.

"Shut up!"

"Oooh, defensive." Wendy blew him a kiss.

"I guess we'll never know, unless . . . was there any clotted cream around?" I asked in my best British accent.

"Yeah! Did you check around your bangers and beans?" Wendy had to one-up me with a spot-on cockney.

"Jesus! I'm not telling you guys anything, anymore."

From then on it was chatty barb slinging.

Wendy to me: "Do you always talk like a drag queen?"

Me to Gil: "You really should take Ricardo out to gay boot camp for a refresher. He's working it *so* last year."

Gil to Wendy: "Don't mind the Princess. She's just jealous. Ricardo is straight as a coffin nail."

Wendy to me: "Good to know."

We sat in silence after the exchange and drained our drinks. At the banquette directly across from ours, a woman sulked, nursing what looked like a strawberry margarita. Her face was doll smooth and ebony; large brown eyes wandered the crowd like runaways. I envied her sugar intake, but wondered what it meant. A zombie would be shitting their bowels out; vampires only drink blood—Gil says the response to other stuff is total projectile vomit; and I didn't make her for a shapeshifter. So what did that make her? I nudged Gil.

"What's up with Strawberry Margarita, over there?"

Gil followed my gaze to the pixie-haired black woman, a crazy straw dangling from her pouty lips. "Hard to say, from here. Could be a hemoglobin smoothie."

Wendy executed a weak spit take that dribbled down her chin like baby formula. I handed her my napkin.

"You can't be serious."

"You're right, I made it up. Maybe she's a witch, or a switch," he said.

"Could be some kind of demon," Wendy proposed.

I just wouldn't be satisfied with speculation. I scooted out of the booth; behind me Wendy yelled, "Fifty says demon!" She dug in her purse for the bet.

I ferried my glass and joined the mystery woman, passing several gyrating bodies far too early to be on the dance floor. A geeky-looking zombie in broken glasses taped at the bridge flicked his tongue at me like he had a shot. She spotted me and seemed to study my progress toward her. I stuck out my hand.

"Amanda Feral," I said, grasping and pumping her outstretched hand. Her shake was firm and she gave excellent eye contact.

"Liesl Lescalla. I'm pleased to meet you." Her smile was genuine and filled the lower half of her face. She had large almond-shaped eyes, dark brown, nearly black. There was little definition between pupil and iris.

"Ooh pretty name. Like the opera house, or that sweet girl from *The Sound of Music*."

She laughed, catching the play, nodded and volleyed. "And you? Feral like a barn cat?"

"Mmm, yes, and twice as promiscuous."

We both laughed, so I supposed we were cool.

"So, Liesl, I'm at a disadvantage. I'll let you know, I am differently animated—no, that doesn't work—I'm a zombie, my friend on the left over there . . ." I pointed across the club, to where Gil and Wendy were pointing and laughing at some less-thans canoodling a couple of banquettes away. "She is too. Our gay is a vamp. We saw you drinking the margarita and questions came up, a bet actually. So what is it, witch, werewolf, demon?"

"It's a secret. Promise not to tell?" she asked. Her eyes were still on the other booth; Wendy had risen from her seat and was waving at an attractive blond man, shaking her tits at him. Lovely.

"I swear to God."

Liesl sneered at the mention, but went on, leaning in to play to my confidence. "I'm human. I just like to slum it in the underworld."

"A dangerous hobby. A girl could get a little roughed up in this kind of club, or worse, particularly by those hambones. And, well, me of course."

"You seriously want to know?" She seemed surprised that I'd expressed interest at all.

"Yeah."

She looked me up and down, assessing, and must have decided I was worthy of the truth.

"I'm a succubus." Her lips curled into a coy smile.

Demon it was. What did I bet on again?

"So is that like an incubus?" I asked. "'Cause I saw that movie in the '80s and didn't that guy fuck people to death?"

"Um . . ." Liesl's eyes dropped into a squint. She was mulling the question over. That was probably smart. I could easily have been making fun—and would, over and over throughout our friendship. It's a defining tool. Plus it wears down all that nasty political correctness. Over time you just slough off anything, like hosing yourself down with RainX. It's a blessing, trust me.

"Yeah. That's right," she answered.

"Great! You'll fit right in. We love to talk dirty."

We crossed the dance floor and Liesl tripped the geek, who spasmed in midair, trying to keep his footing, before crashing to the floor and curling into a ball of embarrassment. Poor thing. I kicked him in the head on the way by and spat an obscenity his way; fucker, I think. We joined Wendy and Gil midconversation.

"They *are* our most precious resource, Gil," Wendy said.

"Scooch over." I slid in next to Wendy. Liesl saddled up next to me. "Allow me to introduce the very sexy and dangerous, Liesl." They glared at me, then her, so I continued. "She's good people, besides, we need a fourth."

They welcomed her then glowered at me like parents would a naughty child. I bounced back a glib shrug. I wasn't sure where the urge to congregate had come from. It was not in my nature to gather people around me. I collected acquaintances, not friends.

"So, you were talking about children, or some shit."

"Kids? What?" Wendy looked at me like I was nuts.

"You said something about 'protecting our most precious resource'. . ."

"Oh, that's rich." Wendy giggled. "No, sweetie. *We* were talking about diamonds. The kids can fend for themselves."

There was something in Wendy's look that held a question. What was I doing? She wouldn't ask, but she seemed to, *what do we need a fourth for, exactly*? A reenactment, perhaps? Bridge? She scowled at Liesl.

I thumbed through memories like a card catalog, looking for similarities in situation. The closest match was this:

In high school—nasty old Barnaby Ridge—I had been a

lonely girl[50], so disconnected from people my own age. I was used to entertaining the glommers, after all. I would sit in the cafeteria, alone, leafing through a salad and stabbing my fork into a dog-eared *Catcher in the Rye*, trying to look brainy, but managing only to send out that freakish vibe.

Carly Bookman ruled Barnaby with the iron fist of a third world drug lord. She was eternally flanked by a harem of her own glommers, namely, Sue Preacher, a.k.a. the Barnaby Ridge Blow Job Queen, whose specialty, the "corkscrew," garnered rave reviews from half the senior boys, Glennis Groin, who earned her name after a poor fashion choice in the sixth grade—overalls that bulged at the crotch, like she was packing some serious transgendered heat—and Tigra Pierce, a downright malfeasance of a girl, whose heinous mouth spewed obscenities like a merchant marine.

The four had these things in common: beauty, popularity, and my complete adoration.

I remembered daydreaming about becoming the fifth in their elite group, stalking the halls like jungle cats, trailing fear and jealousy. It was never to be, of course. Four years together and never closer than twenty feet. I used to wonder what they did outside of school. What amazing adventures were entitled to the most popular? I thought they could probably do anything they wanted. I fantasized that they each held a license to torture, maim, kill, or at least, mock, shame, and denigrate.

Could I be reliving this fantasy? Was that the real reason for gathering this particular group of killers, albeit far more glamorous than Carly and her bitches could dream of? Where did such a desperate longing for companionship come from? Had it been there all along?

---

[50] If this comes as a surprise, then you've overlooked the fact that I'm a total bitch. Totally unacceptable, considering, I've given you plenty of hints. It should have you reconsidering that YouTube bitch.

Chapter 10

I Am Not Cleaning This Up

Wander down the quaint side streets; you never know what kind of interesting characters you might meet. This is Seattle, after all. You're bound to run into an anomaly, if you look hard enough.

—Supernatural Seattle

An hour later, we left the Well a bit tipsy—the first few do the warming, while the next four knock you on your ass—but no worse for the wear, certainly not staggering. A thin mist laced the air, hung there like attic dust motes. Liesl suggested a coffee. The idea hit and that ingrained habitual craving kicked in; I could smell the dense aroma and . . . wait, hold up. I should have thought about banking a blast of diarrhea off the back of a public toilet seat. There was no way we were going to have coffee. Over my dead bowels.

Wendy said, "Sure, Liesl, I could go for some coffee."

"But, but, but, it's not alcohol." I nudged Wendy in the side, repeatedly.

"So?"

"It'll pass right through!" I imagined the toilet after my "lesson"; it looked like an autopsy.

Wendy leaned in close to my ear and whispered, "That's

what Depends are for, silly." She winked and pursed her lips like an extra from *Pink Flamingos*. Obviously, that shut me up. Did I have a lot to learn? Or was my new friend June Allyson[51]?

She must have sensed my total mental collapse; she looped her arm through mine. We slowed our pace, and fell back a few yards behind the others. Ahead, Gil and Liesl were doubled over laughing; no doubt a sexually charged slur at someone's expense. Probably mine.

"I, for one, am not giving up coffee. I won't." She shrugged. "I, simply, found a solution. It's a bit messy, but I'm a quick changer." I remained stunned. "Do you really think you're going to go on—business as usual—in this town, and avoid coffee?"

Could I? Was that a reasonable expectation? In Seattle, a hand not holding a heat-sleeved paper cup may as well be lopped off; even tea drinkers are looked upon as lepers. And, though, most people in the country joke about the predominance of espresso in Seattle, those people have no real idea the degree to which it has taken hold. It's like our gas. If there were a coffee shortage, lines would wrap around city blocks, industry would grind to a crashing halt. The revolution would start here.

"Do you have an extra?" I asked. We stopped walking as she dug through her purse for a small plastic wrapped package.

"You know, it takes some getting used to but if you're game later, we could sneak back to my place, sit on some buckets and gorge on a chocolate cake."

"You're kidding, right?"

"Yeah, that time."

Gil and Liesl had stopped, too, and loitered a half block ahead of us. Their presence blurred like film noir conspirators as a weighty fog bank blew through from the waterfront.

---

[51] She was dead, after all, and blonde.

The Starbucks was just ahead, on the corner—shocker—its big round logo lunged from the building's face.

Wendy placed the pad into my palm. "Remember to keep the plastic baggy, after you shit your . . ."

Her voice trailed off as screams cut through the air like piano wire. Ahead at the coffee shop, the windows exploded into the street, the shards tinkled like, well, broken glass[52]. More screams, and a three-foot-long sausage, bent in the middle, followed this; it jettisoned from inside and thudded against the wall on the opposite side of the street. A second look showed that the sausage was a human arm. Either way, it looked très yummy. A woman climbing from the broken window was grabbed from inside and tossed sideways into a sharp triangle of glass still stuck in the frame. It sliced her clean in two; both parts dropped to the ground with a sickening—but oddly yummy—*thunk*. Her torso crawled another few feet toward the road, trailing intestine and gore, before it slumped still. A dull moan echoed from inside, Corinne Bailey Rae, I thought, or Fiona Apple.

Wendy and I caught up and huddled with Gil and Liesl.

"What the fuck?"

"Ssh!" Gil said, the words turning to red mist and circling us like butterflies. "Mistakes." He spread his arms in front of us, a mother putting on the brakes, and backed us to the wall.

The lament grew in volume and the gaping window and door gave birth to six well-dressed, but completely uncoordinated zombies, two men and four women. Three carried Starbucks cups in their shaky hands, one dragged a barista's battered and bitten body, its jaw floppy and disjointed. Her hand gripped an espresso tamper; it clinked and scraped against the concrete. These were, clearly, furniture salespeople who stopped off for a caffeine jolt and got something else

---

[52] It's my memoir, and I like lazy similes.

instead. Their ability to earn that commission would be dampened by their new appearance, I was sure. The last in the bunch was the other undead barista. This one seemed more alert, almost cognizant.

Their faces were twisted and dripping with the blood of the innocents—joking, obviously, I don't believe for a second there's any innocence left. They were, however, dripping with a lot of blood. I almost yelled "plug it up." But thought better of it. Best not to attract any attention.

"Ew," I whispered to Wendy. "This is horrible PR, for us."

"No shit, and they're relatives, too."

"Just wait." Liesl's face took on a wicked grin, her eyes glinting with specks of fire. "The best part's coming up."

When she spoke, a female of the herd jerked her head in our direction with a sixth grade schoolyard pop. A pathetic moan escaped her yawning mouth. She ambled in our direction.

"Goddamn it." I looked around for a two-by-four or a broken bottle of Boone's, although, anything to keep her from scraping or scratching or biting me, would suffice. I decided Gil would do, and pushed him toward the ghoul. He stumbled and spun his arms in a madcap lawn ornament sendup.

"Whoa! What are you doing?"

"Hello . . . you're the vampire. Fast healer. Super strength. Go on. Work your magic. Keep that bitch away from your fragile friends."

"Hey, I don't even know you that well."

A hissing sound began during our exchange, like air escaping a fine hole. The whistle turned into a low hum, almost mechanical. As we were backing away from the approaching mistake, a light seemed to go on in the middle of the street, as if a bulb was hanging in the air a yard above the pavement. The undead secretary, shopgirl, or whatever she was, turned to gawk, head tilting and tongue out like a dopey little Yorkie. Her suit fit her well, pinstriped, though it was; the pants had a nice length and width[53]. The hum stopped dead and a black line split the light in two, opening into a dark ellipse[54]. The light, still emanating from around the hole, made it difficult to see inside.

A figure appeared, merely a dark silhouette. The light dimmed and the shape became a golden haired darling of a girl. Her cheeks had that chunky plumpness that made you want to pinch, but you didn't dare without coming off like Grandma Fern. She seemed at home there, filling the frame of the floating snatch, a fully formed Shirley Temple fetus, replete with Heidi uniform. She was probably nine years old.

The girl started to move, alternating sniffing her arm, and mock biting it. "Mmm," she said, beaming and shaking her head up and down; her tone spoke of birthday party pony rides and jelly beans. "Yummy. Come on."

The zombies shuffled forward toward the slit in space, releasing various body parts, the coffee girl's body, and even their beloved paper cups. The girl dropped to the bottom, crossed her legs Indian style and rested her head in her hands like it was story time.

"That's right, come on li'l mistakes. Wouldn't I just taste so good? Like a big ole piece of chicken, and I'm super scared, too. I promise I am."

As the first zombie approached, the little girl stood and walked backward into the now fully darkened space, becoming no more than a blonde smudge. The dead walked up to the hole, one after another, crowded there for a moment, before rushing in like mad bargain shoppers. Our interested "lady" friend was the last to step into the hole. When she did, the hum came back with a roar, and jagged, rotten, "meth mouth" teeth sprouted from the sides of the ellipse[55]. Reveal-

---

[53] You knew I'd notice.

[54] Is it wrong that I thought it looked like a floating poon? I don't think so.

[55] Making my initial reference all the more disturbing, no?

ing what it had been all along, a mouth. The teeth came down on the final zombie with a crunch and her right leg dropped to the ground twitching. With the mouth closed, the ghoul's moans ceased. But as it opened again, their groaning returned, more urgently. A black tongue protruded, slithering across the concrete. It coiled around the amputated leg like a python. And, with a snap, it sucked the leg into its throat. If it was a throat—more like another dimension, or something. The mouth closed into a line and someone turned off the light. The hum became a whisper. In the distance, I heard someone running away, feet beating the pavement. I wondered if the other barista might have been one of us.

"Reapers." Wendy's eyes had a dry look, as though she'd stopped blinking.

"So coffee's out, then?" I said.

Chapter 11

Mama's Little Helper

It's almost a given that supernatural singles won't be disappointed—or leave empty handed. The Well is a hotbed of sexual tension, particularly on weeknights. From its eroti-lectronica dance grooves to the "speed séance socials" lorded over by the club's owner, Ricardo, you'll be sure to find your match . . .
—Supernatural Seattle 2.0

When I got home, Martin was sitting on my sofa, and he had that look in his eyes[56]. He'd taken advantage of my key maneuver; I'd given a set to him a week ago, under the ruse of hanging on to my extras, in case I lost mine. There he was, and despite being exhausted, I wanted him bad, like a kid wants an all-day jawbreaker. But something caused me to tense.

"Late evening, huh?" He walked over to meet me at the table by the door.

I mumbled a quiet yes, and set down my keys in a molded steel bowl. His arms snaked around my waist from behind, and squeezed, molding me to his frame. Our eyes met in the

[56] Yeah. That one.

foyer mirror, lingered there. He rubbed his cheek against mine, a slightness of stubble scraped, breaking the fantasy. His eyes were heavy-lidded, sleepy. He smelled of soap and woods and leather and . . . meat.

"I couldn't wait to see you."

"Oh yeah? So I'm safe; you already jacked off, then?" I wiggled free from his embrace. "I don't see any wadded-up tissues."

"Very funny, Mandy. But you know me better than that, I'd just let it fly."

"Gross. Remind me to go with leather when I redecorate, will ya?"

This was exactly what I needed, right? An amorous boy-friend standing in my apartment, ready for some dirty loving, whom I would, in turn, have to struggle against devouring. And, this, after the last twenty-eight hours of my undeath, my defenses worn down to a stub. Let's recap shall we:

1. Tripped and died in a parking garage (a total piss/shit nightmare).
2. Attacked by a vampire (gay, but purse awareness is a plus).
3. Found out I'm a zombie (but made, like Ray Liota in *Goodfellas*, only dead).
4. Lost a battle with my exploding bowels (gag).
5. Ate some street hustlers (porcelain is the way to go for fillings).
6. Broke into a funeral home to steal cosmetics (high point).
7. Barely escaped a low-budget zombie outbreak (*ew!*).

Suffice it to say, I was not feeling particularly horny. Not to mention, the issue of feminine lubrication and my makeup ending at my cleavage. Below that line was a hot body clad in a grey catsuit with blue veins painted on. Do you think I could convince him?

When I spun back to turn Martin down, he had already stripped off his shirt to reveal a black ribbed wifebeater. Oh, I thought, trailer park sex. Musty, sweaty, groping, white trash sex. I had to think quick. *What to do? What to do?*

"Give me a sec," I said, rushing off to the bathroom. I made a quick side trip to the nightstand for my bottle of lube.

The bathroom was a mess, an avalanche of compacts, bottles and makeup sponges. I would have to clean before the maid even showed up for her weekly visit. I tore through the drawers, hunting for that special something that might take the edge off. And, since alcohol brought some warmth to my surface skin, I yelled out for Martin. "Honey, could you make me a brandy?"

"Comin' right up."

In the last drawer checked, a blue glass jar with white lettering drew my attention, it read: Heet. I opened it, and fingered out a glob. I dumped the rings from a small dish on the vanity and knocked the glob off into it. Like a biochemist working for a cancer cure I mixed the thick paste with the lube. I brought the dish to my nose. Smelled okay, dense with vapors, sort of like childhood sick days, only this stuff wasn't for rubbing on congested chests. If it worked, I'd find a way to market it to the sexually arid undead.

"What a mess!" Martin was standing in the doorway with a snifter. His pants were gone. He wore accountant boxers in white, and I wanted them, they'd look so cute on me. He turned, exposing the boxer standard baggy butt and carried my drink into the bedroom.

"Yeah, yeah."

He was right. The bathroom was disgusting. When I bought the condo it was out of a deep resounding love for the bathroom. The scale and warmth of the fixtures. This love was second only to that of my skin—need I bring up the summer after high school? Steam, exfoliate, rinse, tone, rinse, again, and moisturize. Sweet Jesus, if you take anything from our relationship, let it be to moisturize your ass off. My skin-care regime was so easy even the most brain dead among you could follow it[57]. God help those who don't heed my dermal warnings and their ruddy, dry (or oily, we are all uniquely afflicted), unappealing and inextricably flawed skin. I'm talking about blemishes, people, I know it's not something we like to talk about, but by bringing it to the surface, maybe we can put an end to senseless dating tragedies and vomit-worthy family photography[58].

"Where are you going with that drink?" I asked. I set the dish on my nightstand. Martin handed me the brandy and I sipped it gone, feeling the warmth spread to my extremities. Better make this quick, I thought. The alcohol had a tendency to burn off, and he'd made such a fuss of my tempera-

---

[57] Please stock up on the following items:
   1. *Spasteam 2000*: There are other steamers on the market, but this one seems to be able to extract a blackhead without stripping ten layers of skin. If we wanted that, I'd have suggested a belt sander.
   2. *Otani Alcohol-Free Exfoliating Gel*: Alcohol-free is a must, particularly for dry skin. An alcohol-based exfoliate will render your skin a desiccated wasteland, and no one wants to see that.
   3. *Egyptian cotton extra soft washcloths, natural:* If you're going to spend $42 on an eight-ounce bottle of Otani, do you really want to scrub with that Target shit?
   4. *Fiji or Voss water for rinsing:* Okay, I'm being elitist here but I don't know where you live, your tap water could smell like raw sewage. Some do, you know.
   5. *Clarity Spa's Fluff Toner:* Most toners will be effective, but if I can create an excuse for a quarterly visit to the spa, then, it's on.
   6. *Hypoallergenic Softdiscs:* Please disregard the need for these applicators, only if you reside in a singlewide trailer and call metal flashing a foundation.
   7. *Matsuma Conditional Moisturizer:* Creamy, bordering on edible, even the name of the company suggests food. Your skin will look so fresh, bystanders will have to resist the urge to lick.
   8. *Brookhaven Valley Pinot Noir:* To drink, silly. Essential. The more you think of this as an experience, as pampering, the more likely you are to spend the time required to look fabulous.

[58] Steam. Exfoliate. Rinse. Tone. Rinse, again. Moisturize. Please commit it to memory.

ture last time—and we all know how that ended. I had him turn off the lights before I joined him in nakedness, under the guise of a lapse into teenage self-consciousness. I, certainly, couldn't just bare deadened blue skin, my human-looking head stacked on top, like a mask, now could I? Until I could figure out all over coverage—like a spray tan—the dark would have to do.

So we did it, made love, screwed, fucked, all of the above, whatever. The hopped-up lube worked like a jalapeno-spiked tab of Rohypnol. Martin even commented that it felt like he was inside a hot watermelon. Which caused a bit of concern—pervert? But who was I to judge?

We lay in each other's arms, talking about his work (clients were still crazy and that's good for business) and planning a weekend getaway. With the first lull of conversation, Martin's breathing deepened with an inkling of sleep. I pulled away. I was sure my skin had begun its cooldown; any colder and Martin might take notice.

It's amazing, really, that Martin didn't suspect, or if he did, he didn't show it. He was wonderful, gentle and warm; so *very* warm. Don't judge me; there was a battle going on in my head. It played out like this:

I wouldn't hurt him. I won't. I couldn't. I love him. I love Martin. And my love is the kind that says no matter how much I want to, I will never pass into that dreamworld and eat him. He doesn't have to worry. I'll never nod off and bite into that delicious olive skin—I bet it snaps like an apple, though, ooh and sourly sweet. No, I will never, when nibbling his ear, drunkenly take the lobe off and swallow. I promise. My love is pure and true and isn't that what life is all about or death, in my case?

With those pleasantries playing like a frenetic symphony of notes in my head, I drifted into Martin's sweet musk and underneath that into the tantalizing aroma of flesh.

Chapter 12

Old Acquaintances and New Questions

Burlesque of the Living Dead—Convent (Thursdays @ 10:30 P.M.; shows every two hours). Those nasty little abortions, the Mylings, have cooked up another hot draw for Convent. Burlesque is a balls-to-the-wall grossout and Delia Daylong is one hot nightmare . . .
—The Undead Science Monitor

Okay.

I know what you're thinking: enough with the flashback, already. What about Liesl's disappearance, weird breathing, and cocktails?

I couldn't agree more. I just like to give you all the facts, and not go running slapdash into a mystery. That wouldn't be at all original, or frankly my style.

Let's recap.

It was the evening after Wendy and I pulled a *midnight meat train*[59] on the geeky youth of America, and Convent was a happening, wall-to-wall professionals. Absolute glit-

[59] Shout out to Clive Barker!

ter. I grabbed my cell and dialed; got voice mail, said, "Wendy, you have got to get your dead ass down to Convent, it's all-you-can-eat down here." I flipped the phone shut.

The last time I'd been to Convent was the night of my death. We didn't know it at the time, but Martin was in serious danger, sitting alone, waiting for me. Beneath the gothica and mood lighting, supernaturals scoped out invited victims, and mimicked the morbid machinations of humans, to ensnare them. It was a mixed club, the undead, never-liveds and "down" humans dancing to the beat of the same drum and bass loop. Martin had been possibly seconds away from an untoward advance of the most visceral kind. When I showed up, my peers must have acquiesced to my ownership of Martin, leaving him for my dining pleasure.

Of course, on this night, I would not be dining; I was there for the client meeting with the shapeshifter Claire, soon to be famous for her mastery of the shift, if I had anything to do with it. She had secured the very same banquette that Martin had, under the heavy-handed portrait of the pensive Carmelites. Her hair was severe and blunt, make-up minimal and poorly executed. The bitch needed a makeover for that man face, bad. If only she were pretty on the inside, but sadly . . . not so much. Claire slid a full drink to the empty spot at the table.

"Hey Claire." I nestled into the banquette. "Great to see you, and this." I picked up the drink and took a sip. "Nice."

"You too." Claire leaned forward, shielded her thin lips from the crowds and said, "Fine dining, here tonight." She pointed to a woman in her mid-twenties dancing atop a tall speaker column. The woman had long black hair with a skunk spot of grey that might have actually been natural; she whipped it around her head like a cyclone, writhing with the music. While it would have been fine for Wendy, Gil or Liesl to make lewd suggestions, someone from outside the group only identified themselves as crude by doing so.

"Heh, heh." I feigned. Claire always had difficulty remaining strictly professional and I wasn't comfortable with her same-sex-oriented innuendo or blatant passes. In the past, I'd been the object of her unmanicured groping—you'd be proud, I only threw up a little bit.

"I heard about your friend," she said. My head spun at her like a top; I must have looked stunned. "Oh. I'm sorry, Amanda. I didn't mean to bring up such a tough subject."

"It's alright. I just . . . well, I'm very concerned."

"Absolutely," Claire continued. "As you should be. A wereleopard client of mine disappeared two weeks ago."

"Is that right? I think I heard about that," I lied. My interest was piqued, there might just be a connection; it never hurt to dig a bit and I hadn't been focused on finding Liesl with any sincerity. I'm embarrassed to admit, I was still a bit irritated that she had taken the entire focus away from me.

"Oliver Calver."

"Excuse me?"

"Oliver Calver, the missing wereleopard guy."

"Mm. What happened?" I asked. "Do they know?"

"His girlfriend told the police that he left for work at the normal time, but then the receptionist at his office said that he never arrived. I've heard nothing else. He just vanished off the face of the earth."

"How did you come by the information?"

"Well, I had an evening meeting scheduled with Oliver and stopped by their apartment. His girlfriend told me what had happened."

"Do you think she'd mind a visit?"

"What do you mean?" Claire's eyes narrowed to slits— not a good look for her. "He's coming back, you know. The girl does not immediately become food."

"Oh no. That's not what I meant at all. I mean, do you think she would mind talking to me about it? I mean . . . me." I gestured to my face, while quite beautiful, striking, really, it may give away my identity, particularly my once-blue eyes, which have become lighter and lighter to the point of ice. Can you say Meg Foster?

"Oh stop it, Amanda. You totally pass for human. And even if you didn't, this girl is familiar with supernaturals. Oliver told her everything." She reached into her purse, a sedate Dooney & Bourke—a surprise, I expected a fanny pack—and withdrew a business card. On the back she wrote in swirling loops the girl's name and phone number. She handed me the card, which I dropped to the table without review.

"Thanks." I said.

"Not a problem. Good luck in your search for Liesl, but you know . . ." She leaned forward again, unblinking. "The succubi are a secretive bunch, they may be off somewhere doing 'things'." She winked on the final word. But then must have seen the look of confusion spreading across my face. "You know. Making little succubi and incubi with turkey-basters, or whatever the hell they do."

Gross, I thought. The idea was disturbing. I hadn't really thought about the possibility of a job-related absence. It would explain Liesl's disappearance, but not her negligence in clueing her friends in and certainly not her last text message. Unless . . . she wasn't in agreement with the process and was forced to comply through some demonic contract. Can you tell? I'm grasping for straws and I don't even understand that figure of speech.

Our concentration was broken by the sudden absence of techno beats and a bass boom of a voice blaring through the room. "Ladies and gentlemen, your attention, please."

On the far wall, an enormous intricately carved altar—various saints and angels pointing at grimacing demons—began a slow spotlit turn and slipped into the wall like a revolving door. The opposite side revealed a red velvet draped stage. It came to a stop, the emcee's voice echoed through the space, "Burlesque of the Living Dead!"

The crowd broke into voracious howls, screams of de-

light and applause. A group of men—well . . . they used to
be men—clung to spots at the footlights of the stage, stomping. Off to the right, another curtained area lit up, and
opened to reveal a three-piece band, plucking out a traditional "bump and grind."

Gold cords rose from either side of the main stage drawing the plush velvet back, revealing a voluptuous redhead, a
silver-satin-covered ruby, arms shrouded in startlingly white
opera gloves; her face grey with death and hips gyrating to
the beat. She was *so* the glitter. The crowd went insane. They
hooted and clapped, some of the men were visibly drooling
and I don't think this could be described as glee, possibly appetite, not glee. To my right, rapid thumps to the underside
of a nearby table signaled public masturbation. I turned to
check out the offender, and wished I hadn't. A burly man
with a basketball head was furiously pumping at himself, his
mouth hung open and a tearstain trailed down his chubby
cheek.

Claire scooted over next to my side and yelled directly in
my ear, "Have you seen this one before?"

"No."

"Fantastic. Wait until you see the finale. It'll make you
spit up your drink."

"Special."

The woman peeled off her clothes slowly and tossed them
spinning through the air into the audience. The gloves were
the first and she used them as a tether for a man's head down
front; she ground her pelvis into his face and then let him
slip to the floor in a mock faint. The dress, she tore away in a
single motion, revealing a '40s era bra, seemingly connected
to the panty by a shiny metal accoutrement ending at her
garter belt and attached to silk stockings, the kind with a
seam up the back. The dancer thrust her pelvis back and
forth as she made her way from one gentleman to another,
each more eager than the next. A greasy-headed business
ghoul unhooked her garters with trembling blue hands. She

used his shoulders to prop her legs on while slipping the stockings off. The bra was next. She reached behind her, unhooked, shook the bra loose with a series of wild twirls and grinding. Beneath it, her nipples were covered in shimmering tasseled pasties, in silver to match the dress, natch.

Claire elbowed my ribs. "Are you ready for it?" She made a quick gesture to imply that people may vomit and to prepare myself.

"Huh?"

Now I'm no prude, you may have gathered, and, yes, I eat human flesh and have seen terrible vile things since my transformation. But what came next was just, well . . . wrong.

Wait for it . . .

The woman turned to the audience and ran her hands up and down the sides of what could only be described as a zipper. It was embedded in her skin from her sternum, to somewhere inside her panties. The music slowed to a pattern of thump and cymbal with no accompaniment; the crowd hushed, some covered their eyes with loose fingers, ready to close them and shut out the vision. The dancer began to do an ad-hoc belly roll and twirled the pasties at the same time; she reached up and slid the zipper down while rolling her stomach, seductively. The tab was drawn to the band of her panties. She tore the underwear off and drew the zipper to its final destination, just north of her vagina. She rubbed the sides of her belly and the motion caused her abdomen to open like a shaggy grin. Intestines spilled out of the cavity onto the floor. The dancer continued to bump and thrust, twirling her guts around her shoulders like a feather boa. I noticed that her innards were either embedded with gemstones, or bound with strands of pearls, emeralds and sapphires. There may have been rubies but those could not be distinguished from the swollen redness of the bowel, itself. A murky slosh burped from her abdomen, onto the stage boards, like chum from a trawler. The woman's face contorted in a stroke of orgasmic acting, as the curtains descended. I drained

my cocktail, a Black
Magic (see inset);
I needed a little
magic, just then, to
soothe my stom-
ach; it was flopping
like a dying fish.

> ### *Black Magic*
>
> *1 ½ oz. vodka*
> *¾ oz. Kahlua*
> *1 dash lemon juice*
> *Serve in a Collins glass with ice.*
> *Garnish with a lemon twist.*

The crowd was
of two minds: im-
pressed and disgusted; hands covered mouths while others
clapped wildly over smiling faces. Screams and laughter
blended together into a roar of astonished bewilderment[60].

Claire nudged me and pointed across the room, where a
woman was, at that moment, rising from a crouch over a
now-filthy spew-covered trash can. When she finished wiping her face, I realized it was Wendy. We ordered another
round and tried to stop laughing.

I'd taken to doing supernatural marketing projects on the
side, just until I got up the nerve to sell my share at Pendleton, Avery, and Feral. We mulled over a marketing campaign
for her consulting firm, but my mind wandered to Liesl,
again. I planned to call the wereleopard's girlfriend the next
day, generate some movement in the search. I glanced down
at the card still faceup on the table; I hadn't taken a good
look before.

Rochelle Ali—555-9063

My mouth dropped open.

"I'm going to get going, Claire." I scooted from the
booth. "It was great meeting with you. I'll have Marithé,
my assistant, contact you when we've prepared a workable
strategy." I excused myself and stepped out into the mist to
clear my head.

---

[60] Or, a cacophony of maniacal incomprehension, your choice.

Outside of Convent, a storm was brewing. Both figurative and literal flashes of lightning pierced the night sky, as well as that sustained darkness that is my mind. I was flabbergasted, flummoxed, one or the other, both. The name was instantly identifiable. I had just seen the bitch, oddly enough, on the same night that Liesl blew town. At the Well, she was on the arm of the diminutive Cameron Hansen. That's right, folks; Rochelle Ali was that princess of the elements, the plastic-surgery-riddled Channel 8 weathergirl. Whore. I struggled to draw air into my dead lungs. A spark was catching fire in me, and I needed Wendy. Where was she?

I headed back inside.

Chapter 13

All the Chocolatey Goodness

You know you want to. Go ahead. Gorge . . .
—Zombie Times

Convent empties its crowd into a hall resembling the Paris catacombs, its walls embedded with dusty vacant skulls and stacks of femurs, tibias and assorted ribs, each set cramped into wall crypts like a Japanese capsule hotel. There was a low rattle in the bones, their reaction to the reverberation of darkwave music shouting from the speakers. A macabre chandelier of antlers blazed overhead in faux candlelight, dried heads hung from it, horns pierced through eye sockets, mouths. A cossacked concierge was embroiled in a conversation with a burly man whose neck shared its collar with hair tufts resembling a cravat. A step closer and I could hear the topic—werebear hunting grounds.

"You should try Les Toilettes," the grim attendant said. He stood on a raised pulpit, surrounded by an intricately carved Victorian gothic rail. He was referring to the club, not the john, but the advice was helpful either way.

I found Wendy in the bathroom, behind the vibrating

stainless steel stall walls, shaking with the pulsing bass. She was shitting her bowels out, into a rarely used club toilet. I didn't envy her position, but imagined it well, hunched over and rocking. You know the drill.

"Wendy? Is that you?"

"Oh God, I wish it wasn't." Inside the stall, the toilet paper roll spun, a lot.

"Do you need another roll, or should I find a towel?"

"There's the Amanda I know, funny as usual." Wendy's voice was a humorless monotone. She groaned, and a stream of wet splattered into the water. "I just couldn't resist."

"What happened, sweetie?"

"I've got a real impulse control problem. I feel like one of those damned mistakes." A low belch echoed from Wendy's rotting bowels, filling the room with a pungent sulfur scent mixed with earthy death, a zombie meat fart.

"I'm sure you're being too hard on yourself. Tell me." I laid out my lip accoutrements on the counter, a stick of matte dusty rose, liner and gloss. I reapplied, dabbing the lipstick on with the precision of a brain surgeon. Perfection.

"I was at my desk, finishing up a column, for my editor, a real dick," she said. Wendy wrote a column for *The Undead Science Monitor* on supernatural innovations[61]. Her prose was sharp and witty, just like our repartee. "I had just hit save when that retard rolled by with his orange-flagged snack cart—I swear to God, my work is all about getting fat—and what did he do? Slowed down, that's what. A pencil cup filled with Twix, hovered a foot from my face. I was doomed. I bought three and devoured them like an off-camera Jenny Craig. It was pathetic. Then, I remembered about meeting you, after your meeting and forgot about the binge. I hadn't planned for eating, so I didn't have my safety panties. God, it's so embarrassing."

---

[61] Some of which are excerpted for this book.

I approached the door, put my fingertips against it. "It's fine. Are you empty yet?"

"I think so." The words were followed by useless grunts, shallow attempts at expelling phantom shit.

"I'll get you some wet paper towels."

While Wendy cleaned up, I called the number for the weathergirl, got her voice mail and left a brief message for her to call me. She came out of the stall and started to touch up the makeup on her tearstained cheeks. I was feeling my most empathetic; so, I gave her a quick hug, and finished the job, adding a shimmery gold dusting to her apples.

Convent

Pathetic '80s Desperately
Goth Afterparty Set List

▨

Skinny Puppy • *Smothered Hope*
Sisters of Mercy • *Black Planet*
Bauhaus • *Lagartija Nick*
Siouxsie & The Banshees •
Cities in Dust
Cocteau Twins • *In the
Gold Dust Rush*
The Cure • *The Hanging Garden*
Mission UK • *Serpent's Kiss*
Echo & the Bunnymen •
The Killing Moon
Shreikback • *Nemesis*
Dead Can Dance • *Cantara*
Xmal Deutchland • *Incubus/Succubus*

II

"You look super hot," I said. She smiled dimly, her face puffed with exertion. "Let's get one for the road, and then it's out of here."

"Where to?"

"To talk to Rochelle Ali, if she calls me back." I took the lead through the restroom's swinging door.

"The weathergirl, what the hell for?"

"It seems when not busy pointing out imaginary clouds on blue screens or whoring around with

Cam Hansen, our Rochelle keeps company with a wereleopard, or kept, is a more apt description."

"So?" A wave of indifference washed over Wendy's already sick and battered face.

"The wereleopard's gone missing."

We walked back into the main club, past the horny partiers, grown rowdier. The afterparty for Burlesque of the Living Dead was raging; the dancers joined the crowd each dressed in a different colored gown and smoking cigarettes like diner waitresses. I scanned for the booth I shared with Claire. She was gone. I didn't see her anywhere.

In that short time, between the end of the strip show and coming out of the bathroom, the atmosphere had changed—scary, but not in a frightening way. Scary lame. The owners were force-feeding the crowd an '80s Goth vibe, which, of course, some pathetic vampires were eating up. You know the scene, Bauhaus or the Sisters of Mercy blaring their dark notes and bass growls (see inset). The antique velvet davenports that lingered on the periphery of the dance floor were draped with maudlin ghouls in little girl's Sunday dresses; you know the type, of course yours are living, if you can call it that.

Needless to say, Wendy and I do not fit in. A fashion refresher: I'm in black Calvin Klein and Jimmy Choos; Wendy's wearing a snappy Stella McCartney and the cutest pair of high cork wedges you've ever seen. We head straight for the bar. The keep was a pale gent, thin and tall, stretched, almost. "What'll it be?" he asked. His skin jiggled loose with each word.

"What's the house cocktail?" I offered my standard reply.

"It depends on your condition, light-aversive, ethereal or abovegrounder." He leaned against the counter for support, as though his next word could be his last.

"You guess." Wendy leaned into the bar, thrusting her chest toward him. She had absolutely no standards. *What was she doing?* He was completely inedible.

"Zombies," he said, just like that, like it was obvious, and it is so not. He grabbed two glasses and filled them with a clear fluid from an apothecary jar and slid them in front of us, then turned his attention to the next customer, a brooding vamp wearing what looked like a homemade dress of shredded black rags. Sad! Her bathtub was probably stained from all the dye it took to create that fashion disaster[62].

"How can he possibly know that?" Wendy asked. "We could easily be two innocent living women, who wandered in here, unaware of the danger all around us."

But what I heard was, "Blah, blah, blah."

Because, across the room, in my banquette, still warm from my ass, lounged the man from the elevator. That's right, RUDE WINGTIP GUY. And he knew I was there, too. How could he not? Honestly, I looked totally hot. I made my way to the table, past the gyrations of the urban evil dead and terminally unfashionable.

"Hi," I said. "Do you remember me from the elevator?"

He was barely able to drag his eyes from the table. When he did, I wished he hadn't; there was less of him to look at than when last we met. His face had slid across his skull; his cheeks settled into a fleshy pouch under his chin; he was missing an eye, the left one; and his nose was exposed skull. He had deteriorated and what's worse, he went out in public like that.

"No," he hissed, as though someone slit a tire. The small word stretched out across the room and lingered like a fart.

"In the Treasury building elevator, about three weeks ago, you breathed on my neck."

"I . . . did . . . nothing . . . of . . . the . . . sort . . . girl." His voice was rough as sandpaper and slower than I remembered.

I wasn't sure how to continue. If I even should. Maybe I

---

[62] It was kind of cute how she thought she looked good.

had offended him. "It's just that, well, I remember you; I was wondering why you did it?" I gestured to my body, which looked pretty good and resisted the urge to do a spin. I was trying to be serious.

"Of . . . course . . . the . . . proximity . . . shared . . . air. Did . . . you . . . have . . . an . . . accident? After?" It took like five minutes for him to get these words out and I was getting impatient, looking at my watch. I'd have to be brain-dead to not know I was a zombie. Some new information would have been nice.

"Yes . . . uh, I *meant* why me?" I dreaded the question as soon as I asked it. He would decompose faster than he could answer.

"W-h-y . . ."

I tapped my right foot, watched some shifts make out and ignored the obligatory cravings.

". . . not," he finished and looked away, brought a shaky lowball to his lips, and slurped like the French hit a soup-spoon.

No, he did not just say that. *Why not?* Like he'd simply had to take a piss.

"So it was like, I think I'll turn someone into a zombie, today, and buy a new sweater, perhaps. Is that it?"

"Sure," he said, just like that, dismissive.

I flashed back to my mother's words, *So last minute.* That was me. *So last minute*—an aside, if you will. I could hear the bitch's voice. *Oh, why bother thinking about Amanda? She's just an afterthought, an unconscious whim. She's a Twix bar binge, double bucket chocolate cake party, a spattered toilet aftermath. Do get the glommers their cocktails, Amanda; they're so much more interesting lubricated.*

"Fuck you," I said.

"Let . . . me . . ." He was going on, but I was done, I didn't have time for another five-word/ten minute sentence, particularly of the rude variety. I stomped across the crowded dance floor to Wendy's side, shoving the night crawlers with my elbows. As I approached, she dismissed some short thing that was hounding her for a date.

"Off you go, little one," she said. The vampire dwarf sneered, revealing impressively large canines[63]. "Oh, don't be mad." He flipped us off with a stubby finger, and skulked away.

Nice, I mouthed, and took a sip from the drink in front of me, what must have been pure rubbing alcohol. "Jesus, it's awful, where is this distilled, Wisconsin? Did they bother to clear out the cheddar curd?" The bartender sneered and pivoted on shaky ankles toward the back of the bar.

"Warms you right up, though." Wendy slurred, head lolling. "Who was that?"

"Hmm?" I dunked a finger in the swill and stirred, an aurora borealis oil slick swirled on the surface.

"You were talking to that guy over there."

"Well, I guess you'd call him my creator, but this is only the second time I've seen him. He's the one that set this sexy dead thing in motion." I shook my hair, but didn't really sell it.

"That's weird." Wendy looked confused.

"What?"

"Well, usually, the one that gives you 'the breath,' chooses you very carefully, because it is extremely difficult to conjure that kind of power. Most of us have been groomed to become zombie."

"So you know your maker?"

"Absolutely." Her eyes trained on me like I was the dumb ass. "So do you."

I gave her my best clueless-irritability look: cocked head, squinty eye, and raised eyebrow. Cute.

"It's Ricardo, darling."

"But you acted like you didn't know him at all . . ." I

---

[63] You know what they say about large canines. Big . . . ego.

stopped myself. The memory of their introduction rolled through my head like film. They *had* been flirting like horny high school kids. At the time, I wouldn't have been surprised for them to rub their butts across the carpet, like a couple of dogs in heat.

Wendy sighed. "I'm starving. Let's eat."

Okay, we've shared a hundred pages; you don't have to be coy. Go ahead. You are dying to ask me what you taste like, right? You're thinking, maybe chicken, because that's what everything is supposed to taste like. Rattlesnake? Tastes like chicken. Rabbit? Tastes like chicken. Cute Safeway produce guy? Tastes like chicken—nope, not so much—that underage kid that you keep looking at like a pervert? He tastes like what I think deer must taste like, gamey, like there is a film across the meat, a sheen of sweat, fear maybe mixed with a metallic, rusty iron thickness. I've come to relish the blood, it's like the gravy, really; it's like Sunday dinner comes five nights out of seven[64].

The first bite is difficult in a challenging way; the flavor is unique and yet varies from person to person and across race and nationality. Despite all the claims that humans are all the same on the inside, it turns out not to be the case, at least in regards to flavor.

Wendy and I have gone through some heated arguments over the past few months as to which race tastes better. I lean toward the Latino; I am partial to the olive-skinned European men, which by now you are aware. Wendy prefers the fresh snap of an Asian boy. She says they have an almost organic flavor, like most all vegetarians. I think they are a bit bland, but will do in a pinch. The additional appeal is that they are moderately easy to snare; their slight physical nature does make them easier targets. I'm, of course, gener-

[64] And, who wouldn't want that?

alizing. There are obvious variations in flavor and texture, but that's all age, diet, and exercise.

The night's repast was pedestrian, literally. When we left the club, we got hold of a teen runaway right outside, like he'd been left there by room service. He thought he'd gotten extremely lucky, and in a way he did. After all, we were definitely the hottest things coming out of Convent.

I looked up from spinning a leg on my teeth like a lathe, and saw a van make a slow pass. It was blue under the streetlamp, and despite large panels of darkened windows, a spark of red light was visible inside. I stood up and took a few steps toward the vehicle. A spray of water came from the van's tires, as it tore off into the night. *Shit*, I thought. *Have we been made?*

Chapter 14

Who Invited the Pothead to the Tea Party?

Our shapeshifting and demonic readers might be surprised and interested to find that several excellent tea shops operate in the Seattle area. Hiroki is a fine example and is located a mere stone's throw from the Green Lake hunting grounds . . .

—Supernatural Dining Guide (Seattle Edition)

My phone sputtered a muffled ring from the bottom of my purse. I took a hand from the wheel and dug around the interior junkyard for the tiny vibrating chunk of plastic. It was raining again. The wipers thwacked on the windshield, like a handball game. I checked the time when I flipped it open.

12:20 A.M.

Five minutes previous and I'd dropped Wendy off at her apartment.

"Hello?"

"This is Rochelle? I'm returning your call?" Her voice was a flashback to the '80s San Fernando Valley, accent on the last syllable. An up-talker. The last of her kind would be wishful thinking.

"Hi, Rochelle, this is Amanda Feral. I got your number from Claire Bandon. She thought you might be willing to talk to me about your boyfriend's disappearance." And, about your taste in men, I thought, thinking of Cameron's slimy presence, the other night.

"Mmm hmm? And, who are you, exactly?"

"I'm not the cops, or anything. My friend is missing as well. I thought there might be something. A connection. Something."

"Mmm hmm?" Her voice was slurred. It gave off the impression that she was slobbering on a lollipop, drunk, or doing her best dumb blonde act for some smarmy casting director[65].

"So could we meet and discuss it?"

"Yeah, I guess? When?"

"How about tomorrow morning?"

"Uh, no? How about tonight? I'm feeling like some tea?" Pushy little bitch, eh? And, tea? This woman was not from around here. It was hard to say exactly from where she might have blown in. I'm going to venture a guess on the land that education forgot.

"Sure. Just tell me where and when and I'll be there?"

"Tearra on Lake Union? One o'clock?"

"Fine," I responded and clicked off.

Tea.

Now, I'd have to stop off at a twenty-four-hour drugstore for the unenviable task of picking up the ever-fashionable incontinence briefs, lucky me.

Tearra, on Lake Union, was a petite converted house on a residential street. Originally a diminutive Craftsman Bungalow, its present incarnation was a hodgepodge of hippie col-

---

[65] Only it wouldn't matter. Her delivery was so awful and standard; she'd still have to blow him.

ors being devoured by a thick copse of bamboo. The only indication that it was a business, at all, was the glow of a neon open sign in the front window.

I parked the Volvo behind a squatty grey Civic Hybrid—it reminded me of a matchbox car. I checked the time.

12:55.

A little early. Just enough time to slip into my . . . into my . . . mutsuki? I was thinking that word was more stylish than diaper. I found it on an Internet translation dictionary. It connotes a certain Japanese Zen sensibility, and isn't that better than burning an image of someone as fabulous as me luxuriating on a pad soaked in tea shit? If there is such a thing as tea shit. My bowels were flushing out fairly clean, by this point.

The porch creaked as it took my weight. Each and every board seemed to be warped with age and the damp of Seattle's climate. Inside a sitar twanged a foreign melody. I twisted the knob and the opening door expelled the aroma of spices, dried leaves and sugared pastries. It had been a fair amount of time since I'd been exposed to human food smells. I found myself drifting and shook my head to counteract a rampage. It was funny. The line between mistake and made was as thin as a paper cut.

It would have been a quick massacre, though. The house seemed to contain only one inhabitant, an emaciated wraith of a woman tumbled from behind a doorway at the back of the entry hall. The passage was obscured, not so much by a drape, but by a series of Indonesian sarongs knotted to a taught hemp twine.

"Welcome to Tearra," the woman said in a forced Indian accent. She was as pale as winter skin, and blonde. A feather was braided into her greasy hair. I expected that this was the kind of person that drove an old VW van with a dreamcatcher hung off the rearview mirror by a roach clip. In fact, the more I considered, the more I could smell the pot wafting off this doobie sister, like the patchouli deodorant hung from her pit hair, and under that mothballs. I'd have to be starving.

"Hello. I'm meeting a friend here?"

"Oh yes, very good. She's already here, I think."

I listened to the sounds of the house; the music was the only distraction. No side conversations, no clinking teaspoons. Wouldn't she know? I wondered. It was pretty empty.

"Could you point me to the ladies' room?" I felt inside my purse for the pad.

"Follow me."

We paraded through the main serving area and past Rochelle Ali, who faced the opposite direction and didn't venture a glance in ours. She gazed out onto the lake and beyond, to the shimmering lights and their matches in the water. Tables were scattered like mingling guests and no two chairs matched, except that they were all wood, ladder-backs integrated with '70s oak numbers. Candles flickered in makeshift tin can hurricanes.

The restroom was directly off the room. I gave a quick order for chai and slipped away from the stoned hostess, and into the john to apply my . . . prophylactic? No. Sounds too much like a rubber. I'm going back to mutsuki.

When I joined the weathergirl, tears clung to her cheeks like beads of dried Elmer's glue. I was not impressed. It's not like she was blubbering, that would have caught my attention, and garnered rave reviews. So I was forced to fake it.

"Oh sweetie, what's wrong? Thinking about your boyfriend?" I spread my hands out palm up on the table, like I'd actually hug her.

"Yes?" she asked—I guess she asked herself, I certainly couldn't answer for her—her up-talking was taking some getting used to.

"Maybe we can find him," I offered, stretching my hand across to touch hers lightly. She withdrew with a jerk.

"Ew, cold. You're a zombie," she charged, turning her nose.

"And you're a weathergirl."

"I'm sorry, I just wasn't prepared." She turned her head to the side and coughed into her hand. If she'd gagged I would have jumped the table at her.

"Claire gave me the impression that you have a great deal of experience with our kind. Supernaturals[66], I mean."

"Absolutely. I apologize, it's just late and I worked the evening news tonight." Rochelle looked off onto the lake, the reflection of headlights from the other side stretched and slid across the surface like grunion.

I needed to gain this woman's confidence if I were going to sluice any information from her. I rummaged through my bag of tricks for a comment that would beholden myself.

"I watch you, sometimes." I said, lying. A surge coursed through me, as though I was feeding on the very act of deception. Of course I didn't watch this woman. Only the excessively boring, or those unfortunate enough to be strapped down by needy children, were home at 11:00 P.M., even on work nights.

"You do?" She looked hopeful. "Thanks."

"So, Rochelle, when did your boyfriend—I'm sorry, what is his name?"

"Oliver."

"That's right, Oliver." I thought about him for a moment, previously, he'd simply been a means to an end, a wereleopard, like in *Cat People*. Natasha Kinski[67] was totally hot in that. I'm not even a lesbian and I'd do her, but I'd have to beat off Claire with a stick to get to her[68]. But this woman

---

[66] That's the word! I'm a supernatural. After all, isn't that what I try to achieve with my makeup? I'll even say it like this: I'm super natural. Très Minnesota.

[67] We used to call her Naughty Kinky. Don't you wish your name could be so deliciously mangled?

[68] If you don't stop thinking those dirty thoughts, you're going to have to seriously consider joining a twelve-step for sex addicts. Now, how would your girlfriend/boyfriend react to that? It's just not fair to them. So embarrassing.

seemed to genuinely care for him. "When did he go missing?"

"It's been like two weeks . . ." her voice trailed off into sobs. "Do you want to see a picture?" She didn't wait for an answer, but rummaged under the table, presumably searching through her purse. She brought out a small bundle of photographs secured by a pink hair scrunchie. She searched the set, and finding one that appealed to her, slid it across the table. Her gaze drifted back to the window. "He used to take me here sometimes."

Oliver was handsome in that rugged Pacific Northwest fashion, like he was never an hour away from a full beard. Didn't seem like a tea drinker. He was smiling but his eyes had the squint of sadness. The backdrop was unfamiliar wallpaper, thin stripes like mattress ticking, probably their apartment.

"He's very good looking."

Rochelle picked up the picture and smiled wanly.

"What happened?" I asked.

The woman straightened in her chair, took a sip from her mug and started in, "It's like I told the police." Her voice lost its Southern California inflection, and every ounce of sadness. "We got up at about six that morning, I sometimes have to get up at four, because I do morning fill-in, you probably know that. But, I was off that day. Oliver has to work on weekends so I was following him around the apartment, while he got ready. He didn't say or do anything outside of his normal routine. He left for work at about 7:30 and just never showed up."

Not *just*, I thought. Didn't her speech seem a bit too rehearsed? Where did the tears go? I realize it's the same story she told the cops, and probably everyone else that asked, but seriously, punch it up for interest sake. She was a weather-girl, an on-air personality; you'd think she could play it up for the entertainment value. Or, was that the ad game rearing its ugly head? Nah. By the way, did I put on my mutsuki for nothing? Where was that damn pothead with my tea?

"When did you find out he was gone?"

"The receptionist at his work called, to ask for him. I was immediately concerned. Oliver is nothing if not prompt. He even transforms right on time with the moon shift. I used to joke that he was like the tide."

"That's sweet," I said, and then yelled. "Waitress!"

The loadie stumbled in from the entry hall carrying a handmade mug with an oddly concave lip, and set it down in front of me. *This is why I do coffee.* There was something most definitely wrong with these tea freaks. Wasn't there a correlation between tea and alcoholism, or a phrase about tea—teetotallers or something[69]? Whatever. I took a swig. It was sweet and spicy, thick, enjoyable. I liked it. I resumed the questions.

"Was there anything odd about Oliver's behavior, prior to his disappearance?"

"Nothing," she said, staring out the window, or maybe at my reflection there.

The table had begun to jiggle. I pulled back feigning a yawn, looked underneath and watched her leg do a steady hop.

"Are you trying to act suspicious, because honestly." I gestured to her leg as if to say, *and you were doing so well*.

"Oh, that. I'm just thinking about work, that's all. There have been some weather anomalies."

"What do you mean?" I leaned in rubbing my chin lightly, as though interested.

"Well, I'm not sure if you are aware, but it's been raining for like two months." Her voice broke into a shocking sarcasm. "A light mist on some days, but the humidity has been

---

[69] You look it up. I'm not big on accuracy. I'm in advertising, for Christ's sake.

constant. It's just not normal. We even had a waterspout a week ago."

"What's that?"

"It's kind of like a weak tornado that happens over water, it sometimes reaches land and it did on this occasion. No one was hurt though."

"Hmm." I guessed it had been wetter than normal. I was a little preoccupied with being dead, and all. Weather was obviously not my topic—now, a flash flood of zombie mistakes from a coffeehouse? That, I could riff on. The questions and answers seemed to be dragging. I needed something to go on, something Rochelle hadn't told anyone. Something the police wouldn't know to ask. I decided to pull out my big gun.

"I thought, perhaps, your involvement with Cameron Hansen had you spooked." My comment sparked in the air like flint, or glitter.

"What? What are you talking about?" The up-talking disappeared; these were real questions, and pointed, like one of those medieval spiked balls on a stick. *What do you call them? A mace? No. Isn't that a spice?*

"I saw you with the pretty boy, at the Well, Rochelle." I didn't mean it to rhyme.

Her eyes went wide and her cheeks blazed.

"Care to tell me how you know him? I could ask the sacrificial Asian lamb you two were with—oh wait, he's probably dead, right?" I was making shit up as I went. I didn't know where on the supernatural continuum Cameron Hansen fell, exactly. But, I was fairly certain that he wasn't a benevolent creature, like me[70].

Rochelle pulled her wallet out of a—and I swear to God, this is true—black Frauda bag. I could see the shoddy replica label, when she opened it. To her credit, the wallet

---

[70] Shut up. I can be nice. Fuck off!

was a real Coach. Her expression was real enough, pursed mouth hiding grinding teeth, eyes shifty.

"You may think you know what's going on here, Ariana—"

"It's A-man-da," I corrected. I tried to be softer in my next comment. "Look, I'm just trying to find my friend. Maybe you've heard of her, Liesl Lescalla."

There seemed to be a glimmer of recognition in Rochelle's eyes or maybe that was just my own stunning reflection. She nodded.

"Listen. Cameron Hansen doesn't have anything to do with your friend's disappearance. You have no clue. This conversation's over." She dropped a five on the table and began to stomp away.

"Oh please, I'm sorry if I offended you," I lied, but I said it naturally, like it was true. And, then, on pure hunch asked, "Could you just tell me where Oliver worked? Anything?"

I figured maybe, the celebutante could send me in a decent direction. She made it to the door and was squeezing the handle, as I caught up with her. I reached for her arm and she spun at me.

"You need to back off, dead girl," she said. "You don't know who you're playing with."

Her aggression surprised me. Did she know whom she was dealing with? The problem was she did. She knew exactly and was somehow not afraid. It gave me pause. I softened. "Please?"

"Fine. He worked for Karkaroff. That's all you're getting from me." Rochelle powered open the door and marched off through the bamboo.

"*Elizabeth* Karkaroff?" I yelled after her. "Wait, Rochelle? Elizabeth Karkaroff?" But she was already winding up the rubber bands on the little hybrid and sputtering off down the street. The drizzle she'd spoken of blurred the other houses and shimmered in the streetlights like television fuzz.

I stood on the porch with my arms dangling like sock puppets.

Holy Shit[71]!

Just my luck, Elizabeth . . . fucking . . . Karkaroff. It couldn't have been someone easy like Bob the waiter or Mary the candy striper. No. Me, the undead Nancy Drew had to get stuck tracking down and talking to the beast with a thousand names. In the human world she was known for being a mega-bitch corporate attorney. Our firm consulted with her when we were young and foolish with our meager earnings. It was a single consultation, and free. She was scary, then. Tough. We left after she listed her fee schedule. No one can afford four hundred dollars an hour, or shouldn't, at least.

I couldn't remember if it was Gil who'd been the one to tell me Karkaroff was the Devil. It seems like it was him. Over the months we'd been talking a lot, between his sporadic boyfriends—emphasis on the sporadic.

He had begun, as most of his stories did, with, "I was going out with this guy, Robert, I think, although it could have been Roger. We were moving into that next phase of our relationship." He gave me a wink, hinting that I knew what he was talking about. But, with Gil, he could have meant anything. I gave him a quizzical look, and he continued, "You know, hunting together. Roger/Robert told me that he had seen Karkaroff whisper into a man's ear—the guy was a witness for something or other—so, the guy gets up and walks over to the balcony rail—they were in the opera house, you know how tall the balconies are—and just leans over, splatters against the floor."

"So what are you telling me?"

"That she's the Devil. No regular demon has that kind of power of suggestion."

The Devil.

---

[71] Or unholy, as the case may be, the unholiest.

Now, before my death, I would have defined that as a real mean bitch, or sneaky but in a cute fun way[72]. Here in my afterlife, I thought Gil meant devil like demon. But no. He meant The Devil. That's what I'm telling you. The Devil lives in Seattle and her name is Elizabeth Karkaroff.

I was fucked.

I jumped in the car, pulled out, and called Wendy. I wasn't about to be the only one in danger[73]. I drove up to Aurora and took the dingy highway back into town.

"Hello?" Her voice sounded ragged. Like she'd figured out a way for zombies to get some sleep and I'd jogged her out of it. I decided she'd drunk one too many cheddartinis on a way too empty stomach.

"Wendy, I just met with Cameron Hansen's skank."

"*Ew*. Did she know anything about Liesl?"

"It seemed like she knew her, but she wouldn't say. Listen, I got a lead on her boyfriend though, the missing one. He works for Karkaroff."

"*Elizabeth* Karkaroff?" A chill gathered in my ass and pulsed up the center of my back, as though someone had traced up my spine with a frozen feather.

"That's exactly what I said."

There was a pause and a tapping that could only be the drumming of sharpened nails against Wendy's phone.

"You're fucked," she said.

"Thanks."

At that point in the conversation, I was driving through an empty intersection on my way back to the condo. The traffic light was solid green. There was not a car visible in any direction.

From my right, a flash of headlights, then an explosion of glass and air bags—everywhere, air bags. My body bounced

---

[72] i.e.: Did I catch you looking at dirty pictures again? You little devil.
[73] Well no more danger than driving while talking on a cell phone, in the rain, whilst in the middle of a total fucking freakout.

between the inflated plastic bladders. After a few moments, I settled into a slump of shock. I'd been hit. As they began to empty, I looked at my arms and found a two-inch tear of skin at my inner elbow. The edges of the cut looked slightly wet, but no blood flowed. There was a foul odor in the car and at first, I thought it was from the gash and then I realized the tea had made its way through my body. I smelled the cut, too—I smell everything. It reeked of alcohol, pure, like my body turned into a distillery.

T-boned, I thought. My poor car.

I heard a voice yelling my name, but from a distance, like from the end of a long tunnel. I thought, at first, it was the driver of the other car. But, how would they know my name? My cell flashed at my feet.

"Amanda!"

I reached between my knees. "Uh, I'm here. I just got in a car accident. I'll call you back."

The Volvo held up inside, just like it was supposed to, a complete tank; the other car did not fare as well. Despite being a Honda and fairly decently safety-equipped, the grey Civic was caved in at the hood. The front windshield was shattered and awash in blood[74].

I leaned to look in the driver's side. The body was pitched over the steering wheel. All of the air bags had deployed except the driver's. Unlucky. The seat belt hadn't seemed to help either. But that wasn't what I noticed first. The body's head—and I could refer to it as a body, because she was most definitely dead—was stretched awkwardly on its neck and facing me. The driver's identity was unmistakable.

I dialed Wendy.

"Are you okay?" she answered.

"I'm fine. You are never going to believe who hit me."

"Who?"

"Rochelle Ali."

---

[74] Is it wrong that my tummy growled? I'd hate to seem insensitive.

"You're right, I don't believe you."

"It's true. She's right in front of me and dead as a fuckin' doornail."

Rochelle's eyes were open and seemed to be staring straight at me. Creepy bitch, I thought, but, much more sinister dead. Smells good, though, just like a porterhouse.

My attention bounced from the gory scene toward the sound of tires squealing from the top of the hill. The blue van was pulling away.

Chapter 15

Dropping in on the Devil

There is no question that the population of super-natural beings in Seattle has reached an all-time high—some estimate the ratio to be as high as one out of every ten individuals. Our dramatic increase is likely due to the number of supernatural businesses and "friendly" employers around. If you can't be comfortable unliving your afterlife here, then where . . .

—The Undead Science Monitor

I was a tad scared. Who am I kidding? I was horrified.

The paranoia crept in somewhere between Rochelle bringing up Karkaroff and the destruction of my Volvo. That fear was driven deep into my shriveled black heart by the second sighting of the blue van.

What the hell? I wondered. *Were they filming me? I hadn't seen a contract.*

The stack of—I hate to admit this—"chick lit" on my nightstand became a pile of bent pastel covers. I had nothing better to do at home than read—the undead satellite company wouldn't commit to a specific appointment, preferring the ultra-vague "between 12 and 6" time frame. That didn't work for me. So, cute cartoons, of women in prettier shoes than you, now circled tents of torn pages, like an old-time wagon train, awash in monotonous pink. I'd never been much of an anxiety shredder, but it seemed as constructive an activity as actually reading Weisberger, Bushnell or Kinsella[75].

I kicked aside the debris with a bare foot and shuffled into the bathroom. I looked at myself in the mirror. Aging, but cute. It was the face of the woman who was going to march straight into hell—the skyscraper version—for what, to find a woman that might just as easily talk me into a high dive as answer a question?

By 10:30 A.M., Marithé had an appointment for me to consult with an attorney at Karkaroff, Snell and Associates, and a fresh Volvo warming in my garage space. The girl was a marvel: cute, snotty and efficient, we love that[76]. Because Wendy demanded that I stay with her, for safety reasons, or to share in the drama, either or both, my luggage was already in the trunk of the rental, again thanks to Marithé.

If only I could work with such speed and accuracy. The tear in my arm was now an amateurish Frankenstein zigzag of pale white thread, skin dotted yellow at the needle holes. Wendy promised to take care of it, after work, but she'd probably scream when she saw the mess I'd made. In the meantime, fashion was reduced to a dull pink cashmere sweater set, over a pink/crème wool herringbone skirt. I wasn't up to developing an ensemble around an injury.

Speaking of fashion, on my way out of the office I was greeted by the grating voice of burgeoning fashionista Rowena Brown. Pendleton calls her "Lollipop" because the color of her hair extensions always matches her tank tops. At

---

[75] Jen Lancaster's memoir is well-read and dog-eared. The bitch is bitter and I love her.
[76] That's the royal "we."

least, I think that's the reason. I hope it's not because he wants to lick her.

Since having a gastric bypass, she melted down at least ten sizes, but her skin hadn't. It collected around her ankles, like sagging brown skin boots. In day-glo miniskirts, tight halter tops and six-inch heels, Lollipop appears less an aging streetwalker than shriveled ghoul. She shuffles down the halls, head balancing Harijuku girl pigtails, and teetering precariously.

Once, she even fell in front of me. The landing scored a 9.5. She settled with her head perched in an odd angle against the copier. A single blinking eye glared up from Lollipop's twisted face; ultimately she was uninjured. Not that I would have eaten her to put her out of her misery. Absolutely not, she looked to me like one big piece of gristle.

But enough Lollipop, more me:

I pulled up to the, oh so chi-chi, Columbia Tower's valet stand, and snatched the ticket from the Latino carboy with a winky smirk. I figured, why not flirt? It's the first step in self-esteem recovery. I was embarrassed with my out of control behavior, allowing panic to shear my self-confidence like ratty old sheep wool, not to mention my reading material. I planned to strut right into that office and do the job up right. *What did I have to worry about?* I was already dead. Plus, I already had my first battle wound.

The building was tall enough to require a second lobby halfway up and an elevator change. Karkaroff was on the 68th floor. My ears popped. This is not normally a notable event, but it did signify that, at the very least, my body remained airtight, or at least my brain. I wished I'd had a stick of gum—sugarless, of course.

The doors opened onto a long thin hall, lined with white leather Barcelona chairs, separated by short white Lucite barrels. The passage ended at a molded plastic desk—you guessed it, also white. The walls were an icy blue and hung from a ceiling of circulating water. The effect was pure Moloko Milk Bar[77]. A pair of receptionists manned the entry, one female, one male, neither pleasant. They could have been twins.

"Are you here for an appointment?" the dark-haired man asked, with the pursed lips of a pageant mother.

"Or just lost?" added the vacant blonde. She didn't look up from admiring her nails: French manicure. I accepted their brazen disregard, although I would require a royalty check— brazen disregard was my move, patented.

"I'm here to see Arthur Snell, we have an 11:30."

"Arthur Snell, 11:30," the blonde whispered into her Bluetooth: the new fembot accessory. She sneered at me. Looked me up and down. Her gaze lingered on my injured arm. "Have a seat. Mr. Snell will be out shortly."

You didn't actually think I was going to confront Kar-karoff? Please, give me some credit for being a little more passive-aggressive.

The bastard kept me waiting fifteen minutes.

Snell was a squatty man in a good suit. He wore a pleas-ant smile, but his eyes squinted behind tortoiseshell glasses, low slung on the bridge of his pointy nose. His hand stretched across the chasm between us.

"Ms. Feral, a pleasure to meet you. I'm Arthur Snell." He spoke in a light French accent.

I made a point of firmly shaking his hand, but with only slightly less pressure than he supplied. Let the manipulation begin.

"Thank you for taking my appointment, Mr. Snell."

"*Pas de problème,*" he said, his hands moving in lyrical gestures. He was comfortable with this method of communi-cating, as though it were sign language. "Feral is an interest-

---

[77] Who doesn't love a Kubrick reference?

ing name. It reminds me that you probably claw your way from the corner."

I resisted the urge to return with: and Snell, only two vowels away from snail but just as slow. Instead I smiled.

I followed him through a short hall. A door to the right was closed and labeled "Private." The hall filtered into a conference room that loomed over a port view like a lofty aerie. The table was a rich mahogany, and in keeping with the mid-century modern feel of the furnishings, was surrounded by slick Eames chairs.

"Have a seat, Ms. Feral. Why don't you tell me why you are here?"

"Well, yes. Of, of course," I stuttered, taking a seat facing the window, a spot closest to the door. Snell sat at the head of the table, reclined a bit, and crossed his legs. His trousers hung in the polite perpendicular of London bespoke tailoring. "I have questions about an employee of yours. An Oliver Calver?"

Snell's pleasant smile decomposed into a glower. He stood up and wandered to the window. "We've told the police everything we know, Ms. Feral." The words came out as an accusation, a question directed to my honesty.

"To be honest, Mr. Snell. I'm not particularly interested in Calver. I'm afraid my interests are more selfish. My own friend, a Ms. Lescalla, has been missing for several days now. I thought their disappearances might be related."

He sat back down. "And, why don't you go to the police?" he asked, the smile returning. "Surely, they'd be better able to assist you, than I."

"I'm not sure that's possible. You see my friend isn't actually a . . . citizen, if you catch my meaning."

Snell stared directly into me. His vision held weight, and I felt pushed back into the chair like gravity had shifted. "Are you sure you wouldn't rather take this meeting with Elizabeth?"

"Uh . . . Ms. Karkaroff? No, no. That won't be necessary." I noticed the pitch of my voice was higher than it should be.

"She's not in. But I could arrange for it. Unless, *you* are certain. Are *you* certain, Ms. Feral?"

"Certainly, certain. I was quite hoping that *you* could help me, sir."

The exchange had turned away from my favor. I'd exposed myself as, at minimum, someone aware of the supernatural, and he'd returned the favor. But, he'd proved his in a manner bigger than mine, controlling the weight of the air. I could probably take him at a brain-eating contest. Brains[78]! The conference room was now a principal's office. I felt scolded. My mouth was dry and I'd started wheezing.

"Allow me to get you some water, I'll be right back."

Snell turned for the door at the same time the female receptionist peeked in.

"Cartouche? Do you have something for me?"

"Yes sir, I have Ms. Karkaroff on line one."

"This may be a few minutes, Ms. Feral. Please relax. Enjoy the view." His arm swept the room in a semicircle, a flippant gesture. The implication stuck in my stomach, like a shank. To suggest that I'd rarely seen the view from such high-rent quarters was ludicrous. But, I smiled and nodded. I'm no idiot. If Karkaroff was the Devil, then her second-in-command was no angel, no matter how pleasantly he presented.

The door was left open at their exit. Cartouche—I couldn't get over that name—flipped her hair and sauntered away, rail-thin and joints popping, emaciated. She needed an IV and a hug. Snell trailed off to the far opposite end of the hall. He slammed the door behind him.

Footsteps quieted in the distance. The only sounds were the purring of air conditioning and the fetid comments of the reception bitches. The topic: some pop princess caught blow-

---

[78] Sorry, couldn't resist.

ing her chauffeur. The closed door with the "Private" sign called to me like the VIP opening of an art gallery. Who am I kidding? I don't give a shit about art. But if there were free drinks, that'd be another story. Were there free drinks?

The knob was cold in my grip, but turned. Unlocked.

The door opened into a massive sparsely furnished space. Sparse was an understatement. The room was the size of a ballroom, and the only accoutrements, a large glass table, a black leather chair and a telescope. It was disorienting, due to an expanse of mirrors across the two inner walls; they echoed the view, creating a sense of floating in mid-air. The white carpet was stained in a scrolling maze of henna. The overall scheme of the design was a cross, although it was crosshatched so many times it began to blur the longer I looked at it. Haitian, voodoo, perhaps.

I crossed the room to Karkaroff's desk. It was made of glass; nothing pocked its surface, no smudged fingerprints, no coffee rings, not even a phone. Who doesn't have a phone? Hmm. Why that would be the Devil. She just knows. She knows when you are sleeping or awake, bad or good. Wait. That's Santa.

I couldn't resist peeking through the telescope. It was pointed into an office window across Seattle, beyond the new Seahawks' stadium and Safeco. The sill was aging brickwork. Inside sat a paper-strewn desk and a man behind it; he rubbed his face with open palms, and then looked directly at me. His eyebrows rose, following the corners of his mouth, turning his expression into a fake happiness that comes from politeness, but barely covered the fear. That same pretty face, last seen looming dangerously over Wendy's neck at the Well. I pulled back from the scope to get a general idea of the building.

"What are you doing in there?"

I had no intention of touching the viewer or moving anything. There was a large-scale building in the distance. At its peak, a familiar green logo hovered above a square clock face set into a brick tower.

Starbucks Corporate.

I was reminded of the last time I'd been to a Starbucks, the zombie outbreak, and the reaper's gaping mouth and gnashing teeth. I shivered and shook it off, that image could not be allowed to linger. It was a far-too-disturbing reminder of this new world I inhabited.

In the distance, a pinkish hue streaked through the air from the direction of the coffee warlord. I hunched over the telescope again and saw the blonde, standing at the window, his mouth wide and spewing red veins like cursive. These streaked and stained the air, unraveling intricate scrollwork that wrapped around buildings and reached toward where I stood. The blood call invaded the office like a sharp, fili-greed épée, its message clear.

"Amanda," it called. The vampire must have had extraordinary vision.

I backed away as the words dissipated, snuck back to the conference room and stood by the window. The Starbucks Headquarters sat in the distance, away from the bustle of downtown, amidst the warehouses and production companies of the Sodo area. I saw no further pinking of the air.

"I'm sorry, Ms. Feral." Mr. Snell breezed back into the room.

"As I was saying, Mr. Snell. I'm only interested in finding my friend. Calver might help me to achieve that goal."

He sniffed and seemed to give in. "Alright, Ms. Feral, a few questions. But do make it quick. I have a lunch meeting with my partner."

I didn't need to be told twice. I sat back down and lunged into the questioning.

"What did Oliver do here at the firm?"

"Oliver was our go-to guy, our runner. Part courier, part bounty hunter. You must understand that we do a different business in the evenings, than during the day. Oliver came in handy for the more, how shall we say, dark work."

There was a question that was begging to be asked, but it felt like a trap. I simply nodded, implying that I was aware of the firm's "dark work" but had no intention of intruding on it, for fear of losing my ever-loving soul. Oh wait, did I even own one, now? "When did you last see Mr. Calver?"

"That would have been about three weeks ago now. He told me he had joined a bowling league, near his home in Ballard, and was excited about a tournament scheduled for that night. When he didn't show up the next morning for work, we figured he was hung-over, too many beers, that sort of thing. But when he didn't call or turn up, our receptionist, Bernard, contacted that girl."

"Rochelle Ali?"

"Excuse me?"

"That girl, Rochelle Ali was her name."

"Yes, he lived with her, a friend or something." Mr. Snell examined his squared-off nails. They shined from a thorough buff.

"Girlfriend," I corrected.

"Oh no, I'm afraid that's not the case. I think Oliver *was* seeing someone, but not that weathergirl." He sucked air through his mouth creating a thin whistle and shook his head vigorously, the most human action of our interface.

"That's odd. Ms. Ali refers to Oliver as her 'boyfriend'."

"That is odd." Snell grinned, as though we shared a secret. I caught on. He knew. Word certainly travels fast through the underworld. I couldn't help but feel that Snell was involved in the accident that killed the poor girl. *Was it even an accident?*

"Do you know the name of the woman he was seeing?" I remembered the picture of Oliver then; his wan smile and sad eyes were captivating. He looked like the type that never needs to sleep alone.

"I'm sure I have no idea." He was finished and swiveled to the doorway. "Are we just about done here, Ms. Feral?"

"Just one more thing."

"Yes?"

"Did you know that Rochelle Ali died last night?"

He lost his smile and his piercing eyes bored holes into my head. "Of course," he said. "What are you implying?" I had no response. Arthur Snell cocked his head and strode off down the corridor, barking, "Cartouche! Bernard! See our guest to the elevator."

"That won't be necessary," I said, passing him.

I had time to consider the exchange in the elevator. Had Snell intimated his or Karkaroff's involvement in the accident? Surely he wouldn't be so stupid. But even if he did, what could I do about it? I certainly couldn't go to the police. What of Karkaroff's office, Starbucks, and the vampire standing in broad daylight?

At least I had a lead on my next step: I'd check into bowling leagues. How many alleys could there be in Ballard? I guessed not likely more than one, and can I just say . . . *ew.* Bowling alleys grossed me out. Do you know studies have found feces in the bowling ball finger holes[79]?

The elevator lurched, with what I thought was a coming stop at an early floor. But, the lights went out, and the darkness was infinite. There must have been a power outage. Except that a steady hum was audible from every direction, the hum of work in the building, voices, machines, the other elevators traveling up and down. The solid sound was interrupted by a thud and then a tinny sound from above, as though a child might be walking across the top of the box. The image caused my shoulders to shrug protectively. My

---

[79] Would you like feces with those bowling alley fries?

mind wandered to the last set of tiny feet I'd heard—the reapers, those creepy little girls. My paranoia was projected into the darkness. I waited for the little Shirley Temples to drop on me with their shark teeth.

Creak.

The sound, again, from above. I looked up into the black, and saw a lighter square in the dark. It accentuated the gloom, hung there, like an obscenity. Two round orbs of white floated there. Eyes. *Oh shit! Were they eyes?* I pushed into the corner of the car, and slid to the ground, my hands clutching my ankles. I needed to make myself small.

The elevator lurched, again. It hopped in a brief descent, no farther than a foot.

Followed by the rapid sound of passing air.

Whoosh!

Before I could get a bearing on my situation, I was stuck to the ceiling of the car, plummeting, screaming . . .

. . . and screaming . . .

. . . and screaming, like a little girl. But not those little girls, they don't scream. They make you scream. My head turned toward the hatch. I thought the dim light caught a glint of smiling teeth. I closed my eyes.

Then the elevator slowed, making friends with gravity. I drifted to the floor and regained uncertain footing. The lights returned and the door opened to the main lobby. I scrambled out on my hands and knees. Certain individuals caught my eye, each stuck on me with the same leering mouth.

Do you think I pissed someone off?

Chapter 16

Mainlining Vodka at Pharmacy

Pharmacy is the new Convent (at least until Mortuary opens). Its medical theme drama is fetish-tastic and the waitstaff is absolutely edible.
— The Undead Science Monitor

Wendy's turn-of-the-century apartment on Queen Anne Hill cost a fortune. The drafty rooms, single-pane windows, and shoddy plumbing were free of charge. In her defense, it was a straight shot from there to downtown boutiques, our hunting grounds and Pharmacy, where we were set to meet Gil. From there, naturally after a few quick drinks consumed, we'd be off to check out Lutefisk Bowl in Ballard[80]. I intended to drag the whole crew along, possibly kicking and screaming—you couldn't possibly think I'd investigate a lead by myself, not after the past twenty-four hours. My death was becoming a very dangerous proposition, and we still had the issue of vanity to put to bed. I unrolled an Ace bandage from my arm.

---

[80] Enticing, no?

"Is this going to hurt?" I asked.

"Nope." Wendy's tongue protruded from her mouth with determination.

Wendy made sweeping popsicle stick circles in white and blue liquid leather, on a sheet of wax paper. Achieving the closest approximation to dead skin color, she rolled the paper into a perfect Martha Stewart cone and snipped the tip off.

"Here we go."

"Are you sure this is going to work?" I looked from the paste to her face. Wendy stared back, sucking her teeth in irritation, as if to say, *duh*.

My skin hung open like a careless gouge in a leather sofa. The string from my shitty sewing job was already removed and lying coiled on a floral plate, its length dotted with yellow goo. Wendy promised the *As Seen On TV* liquid leather repair would do the trick. I had my doubts, but held the rough edges of the tear together, anyway, praying for beauty leniency. Wendy drew a thin bead of paste across the seam, then pressed a patch of flexible fabric across the top for me to press and hold, like a tourniquet, she said. She wrapped it with gauze and tied a flouncy bow.

"There you go. Good as new."

I held out the haphazard wrapping, like I'd been garnished with bird crap. "How long 'til it sets?"

"A few hours, Amanda. You'll be good as new, and you won't even be able to see the cut."

"Do you work for the company, or something?"

Wendy disappeared into her bedroom, and like the undead equivalent of Wonder Woman, returned changed and accessorized. She must have spun into the black lycra exercise jacket with hood, leggings in the same color and material, and black track shoes. Wendy had no intention of exercising; the tear in the illusion was draped about her neck, ears and wrists. She refused to go anywhere without her "babies," her own terminology for bracelets, earrings and necklaces, mainly pendants. Bling would have been more accurate, as she was workin' it tough, like a gangsta rap ho.

"Pretty," I said.

"You don't think it's too much? Nightclub to bowling alley is quite the fashion conundrum."

She had a point, and I came around, losing the sarcasm. "It's perfect."

She sat on the sofa and watched me pull together my outfit.

"Did you ever tell me about how you became a zombie?" I asked her, holding up a dark floral Betsey Johnson dress.

"You want to know about Ricardo?" Suddenly, things were serious[81].

"Yeah." I threw the dress aside and joined her on the couch.

It's my own fault really. I asked the question. I guess it didn't matter that I expected a single sentence response. Without stopping to take a breath, Wendy launched right into her story, hogging attention like an evening news eye-witness.

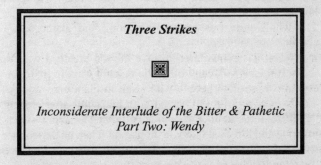

Three Strikes

Inconsiderate Interlude of the Bitter & Pathetic
Part Two: Wendy

"Do you remember that wind storm back in November? The one where we lost power for like a month? Well, I was

---

[81] They'd have to be to employ that overused adjective.

sitting around my apartment, freezing my fucking ass off and feeling sorry for myself. I had every intention of sticking it out, and being the tough bitch. But I'm not that girl.

"I checked into the Inn at the Market, and went looking for a decent bar. I stumbled into the Well of Souls by chance, just followed a random guy in through that back entrance in the brick wall. The place was pretty empty. It was late afternoon, and still light, so that had a lot to do with it. Ricardo was at the bar, of course, and when I saw that man, I beelined.

"He mixed me a Long Island Iced Tea, which I took to be a come-on. I mean there's only one reason to drink Long Island Iced Teas, right? To get drunk and make out in the bed of his truck, right? At least that's the rule in Lynwood, where I'm from. Of course, I didn't always follow the rules, even back then. Like you know how I don't force my bangs into a vertical wall? I was a rebel like that.

"Anyway, Ricardo was just really super nice, totally interested in me, and so sophisticated, you know? We started to hang out. It's like he saw something in me. I see how you're looking at me and yes. Yes, I knew he was dead, it's not like he hides it and people at the Well are not exactly discreet. The whole vibe was just so intriguing and glamorous. I couldn't get enough.

"When Ricardo offered to give me the breath, I was all for it. It means you can't die; who doesn't want to live? Except for those goth people who seem to glamorize suicide. That's so crazy, right? I stayed with him until after closing and he took me to his loft, which is fucking amazing, supermassive and hip. Just like you'd imagine. Then he kissed me; it was the first and last time. He said it wasn't a romance thing, and, I guess I was okay with that.

"When I got home, I couldn't stop thinking about it. I began to obsess on how my actual life would end and my new one would begin. I was certain that however it happened I would be in control of it and there'd be no scars of any sort.

There seemed to be plenty of options, drowning in the tub, suffocation, pills.

"For my first attempt, I decided on pills, I figured a handful of Nytol would do the trick. I loaded a platter with a bowl full of pills and a glass of wine, and set them by the bed. I fluffed a ton of pillows, lit what seemed a hundred candles, turned on the classical station, and put on a satin slip dress. I lay down and fanned the fabric and my hair out like I was readying for a photo spread in *Elle*. It was a perfect environment to start my undeath; soothing, romantic, pretty.

"The first few pills went down fine, so I took more, washing them down with mouthfuls of merlot. My last handful was a mistake, a few too many clogged my throat, and I started to choke. Let me tell you, that shit hurts. I bolted from the bed to the bathroom and Heimliched myself into the toilet. Did that sound dirty?

"I was totally embarrassed, but clear of mind: Pharmaceuticals were out.

"My next attempt was drowning. It seemed so tragic and desperate, so I rented a period costume from Harry's on Greenlake, a real Jane Austen drama queen nightmare. I even did my hair like Emma Thompson's in *Sense and Sensibility* and went light on the make-up. I filled the tub with warm water and got in, pushing the dress and undergarments beneath the water so they'd float around placidly. I was going for a look, more than practicality. Plus, I didn't check the calendar. My brother used his key and brought some skank into the apartment. I wasn't supposed to be there—every third Wednesday is pretend bachelor day. What can I say, he's a pig, but I love him.

"I guess it's true what they say: third time's a charm—It's also true about keeping plastic bags away from toddlers, those things are dangerous. There was only minor bluing but I was lucky to have gone without all the fanfare, because of . . . you know."

"Because of what?"

"The bladder and bowel issue."

"Mmm. I try to forget." I didn't really have a response to Wendy's story. I was kind of jealous that she'd played a role in the decision-making of what we'd become. I wondered if I'd have made the same choice. But then, I wouldn't have been caught dead using an alley entrance, so I'd have never found the Well on my own.

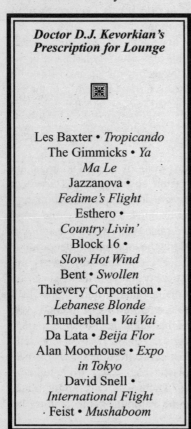

Doctor D.J. Kevorkian's Prescription for Lounge

Les Baxter • *Tropicando*
The Gimmicks • *Ya Ma Le*
Jazzanova • *Fedime's Flight*
Esthero • *Country Livin'*
Block 16 • *Slow Hot Wind*
Bent • *Swollen*
Thievery Corporation • *Lebanese Blonde*
Thunderball • *Vai Vai*
Da Lata • *Beija Flor*
Alan Moorhouse • *Expo in Tokyo*
David Snell • *International Flight*
Feist • *Mushaboom*

We headed off for our premiere at Pharmacy. Gil was supposed to have gone ahead and secured both a scenic banquette (if they had them) and our name on the VIP list. We weren't disappointed—you had to give it up for Gil, he had the social pull of a Hilton or the celeb du jour.

We marched past the line of glowering fashion victims, Wendy in ghetto fabulous and me in my most thoughtful '80s semi-casual chic—hair slicked back torturously into a ponytail, big gold hoops, two black smudges on my eyes like skull holes, big-necked cashmere sweater exposing shoulder, and far-too-trendy leggings (they're having a rebirth, which will soon be followed by a re-death, probably by the time you read this, or by the time I've finished writing this sentence)—we made our entrance.

Pharmacy sparkled like big shiny Tylenols. Towering Lucite columns filled with pharmaceuticals held up the white tile ceiling. The music was Brazilian techno-lounge, so flutes swirled like dust devils between dreamy beats. The waitresses wore naughty nurse outfits and pumped shots directly into patron's mouths with oversized syringes. There were no booths, but we found Gil lounging on a sparkly chrome hospital bed, sucking blood through a straw from a glass test tube.

"*Puta madre,*" he said, in his best Antonio, replete with sleazy air kisses and tongue flitter.

"Listen bitch, you may talk to your momma like that. But it's not gonna fly with me unless you're willing to back it up with some action." I slithered my hands up to cup my own breasts and pretending to lick a nipple.

Gil mock-gagged and reached around himself, pulling an imaginary knife from his back. He motioned for Wendy to squeeze onto the bed, for emotional support. "Wendy?" He drew her close. "Will you protect me from the awful hetero-dead girl?"

"I certainly will, baby. But then you'll have some payback. That's okay, right, Gil? You're up to it." Wendy was nuzzling Gil's ear.

"You're both pigs," he said, pulling away sharply, slurping from his drink. "So what's the plan?"

"I figure I should bring you two up to date," I said, collapsing onto the other side of the bed, like a Southern vapors victim[82]. "While you two secretaries have been busy widening your lazy asses, I've been quite the sleuth—of course,

---

[82] Trauma is the New Recovery. Caution: that tidbit is all mine, folks. When you use it—and you will—pepper it through your speech like veins of blue mold through Roquefort.

the Devil may have me marked for death—but otherwise, it's been a productive couple of days."

"You had a run-in with Elizabeth Karkaroff?" Gil asked, shuddering.

"Not quite, but I did talk to Snell." I held out my hand like a crossing guard. "Anyway, that's *way* getting ahead of myself. I was meeting with Claire Bandon at Burlesque of the Damned, you know, trying to pump her for information about Liesl. She had some unflattering things to say about succubi, but I . . ."

"Like what?" Wendy interjected, doing a little digging in the dirt, herself.

"Well, mainly insinuating that Liesl might be away with her so-called business partner, or incubus, whatever, sucking the life juice out of men and impregnating women with demon seed. That sort of thing."

Gil looked back and forth between Wendy and me, a mirror of disgusted expression, before saying, "But . . . that could be true, no?"

"Absolutely not." I shook the thought from my head.

"Besides," said Wendy. "How could you possibly explain Liesl's text message?"

The glowing green "help" flickered in my memory. I assumed she'd been abducted right after texting, dropping the phone in her entry. What other explanation could there be? Gil said, "I forgot about that. I guess you're right."

"Yeah, because why would she be secretive about work stuff, even if it is semen harvesting and murder." I paused. "Why would we care? We're no strangers to that."

As if on cue, all three of us broke into a laughter that seemed to inform the waitress that vodka injections were in order. She came at us skipping. This one was a cutesy candy striper.

"Open wide," she said and pulled a frosty cold syringe from a block of dry ice on a tray. The liquid went down like an eager prom date, only smooth (see inset). Wendy sucked the

> **Pharmacy**
> *Martini Injection*
>
> *1 oz. chilled high-end vodka*
>
> *Serve in Rx syringes.*
> *From a bed of ice, set to fog by a*
> *splash of dry vermouth.*

last drop from hers and dug out a twenty for the girl.

She glanced at Gil and motioned for reinforcements. An adorable male nurse who could easily have been a porn star before someone turned him zombie, rolled over an old-fashioned IV cart and strung up two bottles of clear—gin, presumably, from the juniper smell—and another filled with AB negative, clearly demarcated. He handed us each a rubber tube with a shut-off switch attached to control the flow. Gil was drooling, Wendy grabbed the zombie's ass; it struggled for release behind the white uniform. He wagged his finger at her and strutted away.

"Anyway," I continued, dabbing the corners of my mouth with my fingers. "While Wendy was exploding all over the toilet at Convent . . ."

Gil patted Wendy's leg and looked sad.

"Shut up," she barked and glared at me for revealing a "girl secret."

I filled them in on everything I'd found out about Oliver, that his girlfriend was the weathergirl, and that after our talk over tea, how the bitch rammed me and wasted herself. Also, that I didn't think it was an accident.

"Why is that?" Gil asked.

"Because, for one, when she T-boned me all of the air bags went off, except hers. Her head was twisted around and looking through the side window. When I got up to her, it was like she was staring at me. It almost seemed set up."

"That could have been accidental, though." Wendy sucked a shot from the IV and let out an exaggerated, *Ah*.

"Maybe, but it didn't look right. Besides, she left the tea place before me. What was she doing there? There is no way it was coincidental. I think she talked to Karkaroff and Karkaroff sent Rochelle on a suicide mission."

"That makes sense," Gil said. "Everyone knows the Devil doesn't do her own dirty work."

"So I decided to take a look around at Karkaroff, Snell and Associates."

"What?" Wendy yelled. "Are you fuckin' crazy?"

In the bed next to us, smoky-eyed heads were turning, their mouths in dramatically shocked O's, like all the vacant blow-up dolls got the night off from the local sex shop.

"Shut up. I don't need any more attention drawn to me than already has been. Now listen. This morning, I got in to see Snell and he was none too happy to see me. He also didn't have a problem letting me know he has some serious power."

"What do you mean?" Wendy was distracted by the hot zombie ass passing the bed again. It did seem remarkably solid for dead flesh. She cranked her neck around to get a full view.

I waved off the question and continued, "He was called out of the room, during our meeting, and I snuck in to Karkaroff's office . . ."

"Jesus."

". . . so, there's like nothing in the room. Nothing but mirrors and weird carpet. It's massive. Oh, and a desk, chair, and get this . . . a telescope."

"Telescope?"

"That's right and the lens is trained on a man in an office. And you'll never believe who it was." I stalled for effect.

"Who? Who?" Wendy perked up, right on cue[83].

"Shane King." The vampire was the man about town and every female within lubricating range was wet or frustrated. I'd remembered seeing him on a separate occasion with

---

[83] I love an unexpected rhyme.

Liesl. *Just talking*, she'd said. Although Shane was clearly smitten, hanging on the succubus's every word. Dangerous for him. We'd only met once, Shane and I, at some club. Ricardo introduced us I think. Shane wasn't particularly interested at the time, but he was pleasant, polite. Probably gay, I'd thought. Gil had insisted, no.

"Yum." Wendy brightened.

"That's not possible," Gil spat. "He's a vampire and you said it was this morning."

"I know. Freaky, right? Broad-fucking-daylight. So I sneak out of her office and Snell comes back and we talk and he says two really interesting things. One: Rochelle was not Oliver's girlfriend; and two: Oliver had joined a bowling league, and went to it the night before he went missing."

"Why would Rochelle lie about being his girlfriend?" Wendy asked.

"No clue. But the league is tonight. Assuming it runs every week. And I checked. Lutefisk Bowl is the only alley that was marked with the supernatural diversity symbol[84] in the phone book." I held up my index finger and smirked. "Mmm-hmm, 'cause who's the number one smarty?"

"Are you going over there?" Wendy asked.

"No. *We* are," I slipped in, and continued without a breath. "But let me just tell you this, after I left the meeting with Snell, something happened that made me certain that Rochelle running into me was no accident. I got into the elevator and the lights flickered off . . ."

Wendy and Gil had transformed into saucer-eyed story-time children. I find this amusing considering Gil's gaping mouth is full of razor-sharp teeth and Wendy's blue veins created a paper maché grid under her foundation. The story turns into campfire fodder.

---

[84] A circle with horns, the inside is a rainbow. Co-opted from the gays. Easy to overlook.

". . . the lights flicker on and off. And the floor jerks and trembles. I reach out for the sides to steady myself and then, and then—"

"What?" Gil shrieked, at exactly the correct moment when a flamboyantly gay man should, although Gil does not fit that stereotype.

"And then, I'm on the ceiling, cheeks shuddering with my screams. The elevator is plummeting thirty floors to my second death. Très dramatic."

Because of my articulate and lively storytelling style, Gil and Wendy are rapt and gasping. I left out the part about the eyes. I probably seemed paranoid enough.

"And then, just as quickly as it started, the elevator slowed, and, I shit you not, I drifted down to the floor like an autumn leaf."

"Whatever," Gil said, the spell broken. "You probably hit that floor like a raw ham. Hah! Autumn leaf." He was laughing and Wendy's shoulders were heaving in silent hilarity. Bitches!

"Let's go!"

Chapter 17

In League with the Devils

Tired of cocktails with the in-crowd, or just looking for something different? Why not head down to Lutefisk Bowl, the country's first supernatural-friendly bowling alley . . .

—Otherworld Weekly

Lutefisk Bowl hadn't been remodeled since it was built—in the '50s or '60s, straight out of *Laverne and Shirley*; *Happy Days* would have been too suburban. The lanes were shiny—all twelve of them—and the family man behind the counter carried a friendly grin like a first place trophy. When we arrived, he greeted us warmly and sent his son, a miniature version of himself, down to the lanes to deal with a stuck ball return. The owner's face was a full house of rosy cheeks, but the sunglasses he wore veiled demonic flashlight red eyes. His name tag read: Gordon.

"I'm sorry, folks," he said. "All our lanes are full. League night and all."

I stepped up. "We were hoping to talk to some people that might know an Oliver Calver."

"Oliver Calver, d'ya say? That name does sound famil-iar." He walked away to a clipboard at the far end of the counter. "Here he is, Emerald City Devils, lane 9. Ought to be interesting down there even if no one remembers your fella."

"Why's that?"

"The Devils are up against the Hounds of Hell, they're tournament champs. Gonna be tough to beat. But, I think the Devils have a shot. See here." Gordon slid the clipboard in our direction. A list—and, I do love a list, OCD me—counted off the teams by lane (see inset). Two were of interest. The Emerald City Devils, and The Horny Incubi—someone there might know Liesl.

> ### *League of Supernatural Bowlers*
> (Men's Division)
> Lane Assignments
>
> | Lane | Team |
> |------|------|
> | 1 | Bigfoot Balla's |
> | 2 | Strikes and Sprites |
> | 3 | The Horny Incubi |
> | 4 | No Pussy Cats |
> | 5 | Shiftin' 4 300 |
> | 6 | Vampirella's Fellas |
> | 7 | Supa Chupas |
> | 8 | Wendigo Tossers |
> | 9 | Emerald City Devils |
> | 10 | Hounds of Hell |
> | 11 | Strikers of the Dead |
> | 12 | Paddy's Strikers |

"Thanks Gordon," I said. "Do you mind if we head down there and chat up some of your patrons? We promise not to make a fuss."

"Have at it." He picked up a pair of shoes from the counter and sprayed them with disinfectant. I feared there wouldn't be enough sanitizer in the world to clean the germs from this pit. I wondered how much fecal matter I'd picked up since our arrival. I found myself scratching my palms, arms, and oddly, my ass.

We stepped around the service area, which completely blocked the view of the lanes, and for good reason. Daddy could boot the humans before they got too nosey. A retro bowling alley spread out in front of us, decorated in pastel diamond shapes and linoleum. The lanes were sunken and split by conversation pits, each corralling a subset of supernatural beings. It could have been the Illwill games[85]. Vampires vs. werewolves, zombies vs. leprechauns, chupacabra vs. wendigo; they all mingled and guzzled various drinks from frosty mugs like longshoremen.

"So what do you hope to get out of this?" Gil ground his pointy teeth; his eyes twittered over the space like butterflies. He pulled out a cigarette with a shaky hand and stuck it unlit into his mouth.

"I hope to either, get another lead on Oliver, or . . ." I looked over to the far lanes. The low numbers, 3 in particular. I pointed it out. "Look down there." They followed my finger. "Incubi."

We trooped across the room on pastel flecked linoleum until we came up on a short stack of stairs that led down to the pit for lanes 3 and 4. A muscular blond man of about twenty-eight, stood there leaning against the bowling ball cabinet. His jaw was chiseled from Carrerra marble and his eyes were deep pools of spa mud. Gil and Wendy stopped a few yards behind me, both were busy ogling the specimen.

"Excuse me, are you on the team?" I asked pointing to lane 3.

"I am," he said, lip curling into a smile and then fading, as if a realization swept over him. I didn't need to rack my brain over what the epiphany had been. It went something like this:

> *Hot girl, could she be a vessel for the seed? Her skin's a little pale, but she has good bones. There's no warmth coming off her. This bitch is dead. Why am I wasting my time?*

[85] I would have to check if that had been done. I do love to facilitate.

Time frame from smile to frown: less than a second, the cute blond was an efficient demon. Why is it I didn't feel any better for that knowledge?

"I'm looking for a friend of mine. You may know her. Liesl Lescalla?"

The incubus stared at me, and checked his watch, the progress on the lanes, anything to avoid the boredom of his present situation.

"Does the name ring any bells?" I asked, my lips pursed, my eyes mid-roll[86].

"Nope." He didn't make eye contact. Like I was beneath him—that might have been a possibility before he got all high and mighty, but now, no way. The fucker. I was riled.

"Bitch, you better ask your friends, then. I don't know why you think it's okay to be rude. I'm just asking for a little help here. My friend happens to be a succubus, if that changes anything." I planted my hand against my hip.

That got his attention. He called out to his buddies, "Hey guys!" They turned. Each one precision carved from a delectable food item (cream cheese, chocolate, etc.). Hot as Hell, their hometown. "Do any of youse know a Liesl? She's our kind."

There was a welter of voices in the pit, but I couldn't hear. Not that I was wrapped in gagaland over the incubus. Even if he weren't a total asshole, the use of the word "youse" would have been a deal-breaker.

A brunette and tan god of a specimen in tight blue jeans broke from the crowd by the ball return and jogged up the stairs. "I'm Nick, you asking about Liesl?"

"Yeah, I'm Amanda." I offered my hand. He took it. "She's been gone almost a week. I'm really worried."

"I haven't seen her in a while, either. Have you talked to her mate?"

"Her 'mate'?"

---

[86] Standard Operating Procedure for show of irritability.

"Yes her 'other,' her incubus, whatever."

"I don't know who that is."

He looked at the floor and the ceiling, his brow furrowed in puzzlement. "Shit, come to think of it, neither do I. I think he's from out of town, though. Los Angeles, I think."

"Is there somewhere she might frequent? Somewhere, or someone else I could talk to?"

"You could try the tracker, but he's very confidential. I doubt he'd give you an appointment without doing him a favor."

"Anything would help."

"Let me see if I have his card."

Nick dug in his jeans, causing the fabric to tighten across his crotch. I couldn't help it; I stared. His thick penis was outlined in denim. It trailed down his leg, in a most inhuman and frightening way. *Were there two heads?* He pulled his hand from his pocket, withdrawing a business card. I glanced upward to find that he'd been watching me the entire time. He was beaming with pride or evil, but certainly not charity.

"Here you go, Amanda. Talk to Clevis, he might just help you."

"Uh . . . thank you, um, sorry for . . . well, you know, whatever." I spun and took disingenuous steps across the linoleum. I refused to add to my embarrassment by slipping on cheap flooring. I didn't deserve an afterlife. I'd be better off dissolving into bile in a cheap pine box. Let the maggots have a home and puff me up with a *snap*, *crackle* and *pop*. So embarrassing.

Gil and Wendy were bounding up the stairs that led from lanes 9 and 10.

"They didn't know shit," Gil said, letting his fingers slide through his hair. "Cute though. Is the one in the jeans looking?"

Wendy shook her head.

"Or anything about Oliver, either." Wendy smooshed her

face and shook her head[87]. "Oh . . . except that he went to a twelve-step group over on Grant."

"A twelve-step group?" I asked. "For what?"

"They wouldn't say." Her mouth hung open, eyes searched the ceiling for anything remotely interesting.

"Okay, let's get out of here. I for one am exhausted. I don't even think I could manage a kill, tonight."

"Oh, come on, not even just a little one?" Wendy chided, in a French waiter accent.

"Nope." I had no intention of giving in, just because Wendy chose to invoke Monty Python movie lines.

"Not even a wafer-thin kill?" Gil mocked in a bored, this-has-*so*-been-done tone. He searched his manicure for leftover ridges.

"Knock it off!"

We bickered back and forth, all the way to a freeway underpass, parked, and devoured a particularly beleaguered homeless man—that's right, Wendy and I know how to share. Gil drained his wife from a tear below her breast. It seemed so wrong for a gay vamp to feed this way.

---

[87] Her trademarked look. It indicates the presence of either unacceptable males, or dirty diapers in a grocery store parking lot.

Chapter 18

Severine and the King

*The humans are definitely on to something here;
Seattle is absolutely buzzing with inattention. We think
it's the caffeine. Give Starbucks a shot (pardon the
pun) for a latte and a fresh victim. They are a yummy
combination . . .*

—Undead Times

I remember once wondering how I would die. These thoughts
weren't old, either. I think they occurred a mere week before
the embarrassment of the actual event. I was just lying
around on my patio, drinking iced tea, thinking about
death—nothing wrong with that. This is how it played out:

*A great plague is sweeping Earth, as a result of hu-
manity's mindless consumerism—as if, obviously, in
there for dramatic effect, mindless consumers are the
bread and butter of advertising—every day the news
reports are increasingly bleak; people are dying and
the medical establishment is impotent to cope with the
strengthening viral power. Then, hope arrives on American shores. A tribe, hidden deep within the jungles of
the Amazon, sends an emissary to the United Nations.*

He explains, through hand signals and primitive drawings, that a powerful woman must be sacrificed to appease the Gods and end the contagion. A televised search for the perfect martyr, hosted by Ryan Seacrest, ends at my doorstep. I agree, of course—who could resist the global attention—and proceed on a trek to join the tribal leaders in the Amazon, a camera crew follows my every move—it's no wonder, my skin looks flawless, simply perfect, clear, even toned and it ought to—remember my skin-care regimen? After a fantastic cocktail party with surviving celebrities, dignitaries and a few of my closest friends—two hundred and thirteen on the guest list—I am led, in Versace, through the lush vegetation to a fantastic hut that opens in the rear to a cliff and an amazing panoramic view of the rainforest. Martin, my boyfriend/psychotherapist, is waiting. We become lost in a swirl of lust and passion, and as we both explode, the tribal chief and a gaggle of what must have been warriors burst in (gaggle?), and drag me away. They toss me over the precipice. In super slo-mo, my naked body twirls and writhes (and looks fabulous) as I meet my demise in a shallow pool at the foot of a tragically beautiful waterfall. My blood flows into the water and from the pool into the river, and from the river into the seas, it evaporates and takes to the clouds where it showers upon the earth, dissipating into the air, entering the deteriorating lungs of the afflicted, healing and destroying the virus. In the end, I live on forever in the bodies of the living.

If only my reality were a Technicolor dream. As it is, my own skin is taking on hues of black and white, and not the shiny cleaned-up Turner Classics, but dull and dingy greys, like the Sunday afternoon movie on a local channel. Still, there was something about this fantasy that stuck in my head like a popcorn husk digs into your gum line.

Was it Martin? No. And best not to think about him too much, that's a story for another time. My mind cleared of its haze, revealing the tasteful décor of Wendy's apartment. A haze is what I have, now, instead of sleep. The apartment is the obvious result of a totally consuming catalog addiction, Pottery Barn couch ($2499, in plush loden), Crate and Barrel coffee table ($2100, mahogany stain); you get the picture. Wendy was gone, but left a note, next to the Museum Company euro vase ($229+SH). It read:

> *Good Morning Bitch*
> *I'll be home at 4:30. Feel free to wash your snatch and*
> *watch my satellite (channel 766, particularly).*
> *Let's do the fun run[88]!*
> *Wendy*

Even after a brisk morning shower, I wasn't ready to face a hellish day at the office. The mundane tasks of advertising and creativity were weighing on my nerves—I wasn't even sure those worked—like a too-tight seaweed wrap, dipped in the pissy stink of Puget Sound water. My business was, simply, interfering with my fabulous supernatural life. And that's really something you have to make time for, cultivate, you know? I think if you spend too much time focusing on deadlines and copy and office politics, there's no time left for the really important things like flesh eating, cocktails, undead body preservation and supernatural investigations. What's death without them?

I needed to get my priorities straight. I called in sick; I'd been doing that a lot.

I was putting the phone back in the charger, when I noticed a note slid under the door. Apparently, this was a morn-

---

[88] Every now and then—and I've never done it—a bunch of zombies heads down to the welfare office and picks up some deadbeats for a feast. They set them loose in a fenced-off field and have at it. Hilarity ensues.

ing for notes. I wondered if it had just happened. I opened the door into the hall. A grey haired woman with a walker trudged down the corridor, with a zip, shuffle, shuffle, shuffle. The elevator *ding*ed and a sweat-suited man emerged carrying a paper, heading back in for his morning crap.

Zip, shuffle, shuffle, shuffle. I closed the door.

The top of the note was blank. It was folded in quadrants. It read, in all blocky capitals like screams:

AMANDA

MEET ME AT THE STARBUCKS IN THE OLD WASHINGTON MUTUAL TOWER. THE ONE ON THE WEST SIDE, NOT EAST.
NOON.
MAKE SURE YOU'RE NOT FOLLOWED.

S

P.S. (AND NOT THE ONE ON THE 15TH FLOOR EITHER)

I checked my watch. 7:30. Who was this? A secret admirer? I followed the curls of the S with a fingertip. Shane King? Mmm, yummy, if only. With the crowd I'd been bumping into lately, it was more likely from a horned devil with a razor spiked double-cock, than a tasty morsel like Shane King.

I wasn't getting my hopes up. I flipped the paper around. Nothing.

Another option floated from the back of my head to just behind my eyes, blossoming like a migraine worm.

The blue van.

I hadn't given it much consideration; I'd completely forgotten to tell Wendy and Gil about the damn thing. They were clearly filming me, and "they" were at least two people, one driver, and one cameraperson. I'd simply played it off as paparazzi, downplayed it. But what if it were something truly sinister, even more so than myself, I mean? What if the camera lens was Karkaroff's eye on the scene? I shivered at the thought and crumpled the note and crushed it beneath my foot.

Fear or no. I'd be there, fashionable as ever. The reapers inspired me. I wore my Chanel schoolgirl dress, black with pointy cream collar and cuffs, and an ethereal overlay in a gauzy jet.

The Westside Washington Mutual Starbucks sat between two towering escalators, in a glass hothouse. The skyscraper stood above at such a stance, the coffeehouse seemed to be a premature birth, too small in contrast. But the coffee would be the same, it always was, plus, I'd worn my mutsuki[89].

I was inside, and then in line, before my mouth dropped open.

The coffee slaves weren't their jittery selves. There was no chatting or BlackBerry pecking, no fumbling through domino tiles or clicking on laptops. The people were doing the unthinkable in the kingdom of caffeine. They were dozing. Heads lolled and snapped as they tried to stay awake.

None of the line standers seemed affected. They were doing the ever-popular busy dance—the living are so self-important—feet tapped, arms crossed, body language with a capital B. There were three of them, a woman in a brown corduroy mini and kicky boots, and two short-cropped paper pusher boys in low-grade wool three-button suits. Totally inedible; not a hottie in the bunch. The puffy blond guy closest to me wore the pimply face of a steroid junkie—can I just say, fat-covered muscle is not sexy. The other man was a towhead with a big girly bubble butt, not cute.

[89] With a capital "M".

I didn't see Shane.

The counter staff and barista weren't doing much better than the seated customers; they seemed to be in a sleepy funk. The girl manning the metal behemoth coffeemaker seemed stalled behind the steaming milk; it bubbled over the stainless steel pitcher in clots. Her name tag read: Severine.

Her eyes were closed.

She sniffed the air.

Recognition flooded in. I knew that look. I'd seen that same face, in the mirror. And what comes next isn't pretty. I think you know what I'm talking about.

Severine's mouth opened and a pale puffy tongue thrust out like a schizophrenic on bad meds. She wheezed a whimpering cry, and her last two tears drained, and fell from drying eyes. She began to smell of hot urine and the thick musky rank odor of runny stool.

Crack!

Her jaw broke free from human; it began to ratchet down like a big plumber's wrench.

Behind me similar sounds and smells echoed from the tables. This Starbucks had gone zombie in stereo, the volume surpassed the cool jazz pumping from the speakers. The people in line were fucked. Deeply.

They began to look around them, leaving behind their meaningless dwellings for a real visceral experience that meant something—death, sure, but certainly that's more valuable than a triple shot Americano or an afternoon affair. Looking down death's throat changes your perspective.

The situation was going to get messy and there was not a damn thing I could do about it. I'd be damned if I got another injury protecting my own food from distant relatives. I backed past the shelves of bagged coffee and cute mugs, and slipped discreetly into the restroom alcove.

The living customers came unglued, screaming and stumbling over each other like the Three Stooges at a foam party. Drawing way too much attention to themselves.

Gravelly screams sounded from unhinged and gaping mouths, frothy drool bubbled up and spilled past teeth and gums. Severine's death progressed to a rapid seizure of her head, spittle flung from her mouth like dog slobber. She jumped onto the counter with feline grace and dove for steroid boy[90]. She tore off his pimply forehead in a puss-filled scrape of her lower teeth. His eyes blinked in shock, before closing as the zombie barista slammed her upper teeth into his skull, as teeth and bone fragments went flying. Severine dined on the man's brain like a back-alley Filipino delicacy, but unlike her human counterparts, she'd leave no waste.

The smell wafted into the little hall where I sheltered, like a Hostess snack cake bakery; I was nearly drawn in, my head gone fuzzy. The blood aroma was intoxicating, stronger even than the first time, with Ricardo. The only difference was maturity. Apparently, the longer I was a zombie, the more self-control I gained, much like a man's ability to maintain an erection. An adolescent can shoot his spuzz from a simple brush across the jeans, while a man has learned to think about dead kittens, or whatever, if his momma taught him right. I backed off the cravings and focused on the possibility of being damaged in a struggle. Beauty marks were my dead kittens.

While I settled into food deprivation, a battle for survival had begun in the back of the room. The other man was long dead; by the time I regained my senses, his body was roughly bisected in a snarling tug of war between staff and customers. Two on the bottom half and two on top, all of them wildly gorging on sweetbreads[91]. Behind that lovely image, the woman was fending off three growling ghouls with a busted bottle of sugar-free hazelnut syrup. Returning each reaching limb with a thin ribbon of flesh or sinew dan-

---

[90] Mistakes are not discerning eaters. Like how hillbillies eat possum.
[91] There. I said it. Sweetbreads. As it turns out, they are not so bad. Saying BRAINS would just be tacky.

gling off. Her face was stretched in an insane smile that said, I'm an animal; I'm going to kill you. I wondered if she'd make it, but then a zombie to her left leapt between her flailing arms and clamped onto her face like the mouth of an accordion boarding corridor at an airport. The bite radius was deep on the woman's face, stretching to just below her ears. When the creature retracted, he took with him both sides of her mouth, her cheeks, and vast chunks of muscle and sinew, the leavings curled back like New Year's Eve noisemakers. Her jaw thunked against her chest, exposing a writhing half tongue. She went limp. Must have fainted; I guess died is more likely.

The room quieted to gnashing and wet snarls. Billie Holiday whined a baritone scat in the background. Fine dining compared to a snatch and grab at DSHS or a midnight binge at tent city.

My head count came up zombies–8, humans–0. There was going to be a problem here, the food supply had dried up and the undead would soon be shuffling for the door. Outside, throngs of weekday shoppers, couriers and mid-day smokers littered the courtyard. There must have been forty people milling about.

The door to the coffee shop opened and a distracted woman toting files on a quick cart ran shoulder first into Severine's waiting mouth. The ghoul tore into the joint with butcher's precision. But, to her credit, the attorney[92] grabbed her dislocated arm before it hit the floor and wielded it like a weapon, leveling Severine, temporarily. The woman then turned to look at me.

"Help . . . me," she gargled, blood sputtering from her lips.

I shrugged a quick sorry and retreated farther into the

[92] The files strapped to a rolling cart, a striped suit and crème colored blouse, the look of angry frustration. What's your best guess? Mine was attorney.

space. The woman's eyes went white within the few seconds of our contact. Her jaw was crunching. This was going to be bad. In case you're counting, that's nine zombies. Ten, actually, but I don't count, I'm civilized. I dove inside the men's room and locked the door.

It occurred to me that this was the beginning of a major zombie outbreak. Outbreak. I was reminded of the plague in my death fantasy, and the gory scenes from that movie in the mall. I had suppressed what was actually happening. This was harkening back to that night outside the Starbucks near the Well of Souls. It didn't take a brain surgeon to figure out the two events were connected. If they were the same, I thought it would be over by now, that the reapers would come—at least one. Outside the door, I heard the scratching of fingernails, like a rat trying to get through drywall, but barely; Bebel Gilberto's snappy Brazilian tunes were competing for volume.

And then I heard a new sound.

Sharp *pangs*.

Two came from the distance, and then, louder ones, closer. *Pow, pow. Powpowpow*.

I kept track on my fingers. If the shooter was good all he'd need was nine.

Pow.

Close enough, you have to admit, ten shots for nine targets is pretty good. I unlocked the dead bolt and opened the door a crack.

"Safe to come out?" I yelled in my best damsel in distress.

"Someone's alive in here, Scotty." I heard a voice shout.

"Where at?" Another guy.

"In the bathroom," I answered.

I opened the door wide and hopped over the attorney's severed arm, like a lucky Southern bride over the groom. Then wished I hadn't, I slid across the floor on a thin puddle of blood and insides. Officer Scotty caught me in his burly thickly muscled arms. But all I could think was, *sloppy eaters*.

Scotty was a 6'2" hottie, with sandy curls, blue eyes and light afternoon shadow on a manly square of a chin. He held me in his arms. Stroking my hair and cooing consolations, "Sh. It's all going to be alright. Sh. It's over."

I was game for his macho routine—though, you could smell the irony of the situation, it reeked of butt—I played along. A dry shoulder-heaving sob, and the murmurs of "it was horrible," and "I just want to go home," were all it took, that and pressing my face tight into his puffy coat. He bought it, and hugged me tight as a baby. I won't lie; it felt great. Even if we were surrounded by blood, urine and bowels leaking loose stool. After all, I'd seen worse and it'd been a while since I'd been next to a man I didn't plan on eating.

When I pulled back to look up at my savior, he grimaced. I immediately looked from his sour face to his jacket. Sure enough, there it was. Mama left her face on the nice police officer. I tore myself from his grasp and ran out of the store.

The courtyard was cleared of bystanders and crowds gathered at the entry. To my surprise, Shane King was standing front and center of the morbid gawking hoard. When he saw me he blended back and disappeared. I tore past the grabby cop standing guard at the entry and straight through the yellow barrier tape, like a hundred yard dash winner. Behind me I heard shouts of protest.

"Wait!"

"She's a witness!"

"Stop her!"

But it was too late. I slipped around the corner, and through an alley. At the half block, I re-entered the parking lot to retrieve my car.

Chapter 19

All Looks and No Moves Make Shane a Dull Boy

There has been talk of demons re-creating the or-gies of Hell at secret warehouse parties. Attendance is strictly invitation only. But we know a guy . . .
—Otherworld Weekly

I drove back to Wendy's with one eye trained on the road and the majority of my face obscured by a spread hand. The rear-view mirror displayed a horrific mimicry of Baby Jane, streaks of mascara and eye shadow slid down scaly cheeks and lipstick smeared around my mouth like a hooker's after a back alley blow job. I was so obsessed by my make-up mal-function, that when a husky voice rose from the backseat, I swerved. The rental jumped onto the sidewalk, barely miss-ing a rusty truck and a howling woman shuffling out of an Asian grocer.

"Amanda?"

I knew the voice. I'd been damning the owner of it to Hell since seeing him with the not-so-innocent bystanders. I slammed on the brakes and felt his body pound against the front seats, and tumble into the foot well.

"Jesus!"

I leaned over the seat, and started in, "Shane, you piece of shit! You've got some serious explaining . . ."

"I know, I know. Just let me . . ."

I just couldn't take his voice. I reached back and pummeled him with my fist with the force of a little brother.

"Ow! Ow! Ow! Knock it off, Amanda!"

"What the hell was *that*, back there?" I asked as I slowed from punches to backhanded slaps, one for each word I spoke.

"Stop and we can talk." His arms flailed, trying to deflect.

Settling back in the seat, I pulled the Volvo back onto the road and headed for my condo. "Well?"

"It was exactly what you think it was."

"A bunch of mistakes at a buffet, then?"

"A zombie outbreak." He'd slumped back into the seat. Shane wasn't looking his best. His eyes were carrying dark bags, crow's-feet spread from the corners. His jaw was covered with a scruffy growth of sandy hair smattered with grey. If I didn't know he was a vampire, I'd say he was aging. "I'm sorry to involve you in all this." His head fell into his palms.

"All of what?" I slammed my fist against the steering wheel. "I don't understand what's going on at all!"

"I needed help. I needed for someone else to know." He paused, looked up into the rearview mirror. Our eyes met, but not in a romantic way. "I figured since you were . . . already in deep shit."

"Excuse me?"

"I saw you snooping around Karkaroff's office. You know that; you heard my call, and you saw me."

He was right. I'd even told Wendy and Gil, just last night. From the moment Karkaroff became a part of my life, at least verbally, I'd been fucked. Car accidents, haunted elevators, and now, zombie outbreaks.

"You have a point. But, Shane, what is it you want to

share? If it's obvious, then I must be an idiot. Or my brain is starting to rot."

"I needed you to see what was going on . . . with the mistakes."

"This wasn't the first time I'd seen them."

"What?" he asked, brows furrowing like caterpillars in a scrap.

"I was down on Western Avenue, four or five months ago. The same thing happened. Well, I assume it was the same thing."

"Not quite. In the Western Sample, the reapers were alerted to end it before it spread. In today's, what they are calling the Downtown Sample, humanity got lucky."

Samples? Alerting reapers rather than them coming on their own? This was news to me. I swung the car into a parking garage and drove down the corkscrew until a vacant floor was exposed. It was time to park. Think. Probably yell.

Shane went on, "Today's test could have been the big one. The humans worry about earthquakes and tsunamis and volcanoes. They don't know to worry about the final plague, and it's coming sooner than they think. Unless we stop it."

"But both times they seemed to be stopped easily enough," I said. "The reaper responded in a timely fashion the first time, and Officer Scotty[93] didn't need a whole lot of help blowing zombie brains out."

"True, and these seem to be isolated incidents. But where were they located?"

"Starbucks, yeah that much I figured out. So what?" I asked.

"I just said, they *seem* to be—"

"Okay, shit. I got it." Not so long ago, Starbucks was a single store in the Pike Place Market. But now it was global. Thousands of stores circled the globe pushing caffeine like crack in kitschy mugs. And regardless of your taste prefer-

---

[93] The oh-so-dreamy Officer Scotty. The hotness.

ence—I think they burn their beans—they are definitely consistent.

"Imagine what happened today, occurring at nearly every store simultaneously. The human race would be done."

"And we'd be out of food," I finished. "So while the humans dwell on natural disasters, we can worry about a famine, is that it?"

"Exactly what Karkaroff wants to happen. If we're all starving, then she can swoop in with the second phase of her diabolical plan, I guess."

"And what is that?"

He bit into his lip on one side with a canine and winced. "I have no clue. I haven't gotten that far." The blood beaded into a knob that his tongue caught before it could dribble down his chin. In the time it took to lick, the hole had healed. And all I could think was, the lucky bastard. I took a quick look in my visor mirror. I was giving unacceptable face, and covered it with my hand.

"You'll have to excuse me, but I really need to powder my nose. Go on talking though. Particularly, that interesting bit about not having a clue."

"Well, I have a clue. I guess I'm just feeling a little overwhelmed."

"Oh, oh, hold up, Shane." I turned and lifted my hand, I shook my head like he'd made some small mistake and mouthed, "no." "This isn't a therapy session. Leave that to the humans, and spill your shit. Go on."

"Where else is there to go?"

"Let's start with how it is that a vampire is working the day shift over at Starbucks. Emphasis on the d-a-y."

"I don't really understand how it works. It was a gift, the ability to day walk, not the job. *That*, I had to apply for." Shane's gaze drifted away, toward the window. He patted his chest.

"A gift from Karkaroff?"

"Yeah, she needed someone inside Starbucks Corporate to monitor their knowledge of the project."

We pulled into the garage of my condo and continued the discussion in my bathroom, him on the toilet with his chin in the cup of his palm, me working at my face like a Rembrandt restoration. I began wiping down with moist cosmetic pads, removing the streaks. Then it was routine, mindless work; I could have done it blindfolded—concealer, foundation, eyeliner, shadow, blush, lipstick, powder.

"It was my impression that the reapers just knew, when something like these outbreaks happened. I didn't think they needed to be told."

"That's true," he said. "The reapers keep an ear to the ground at all times. But the difference here is there's nothing to listen for. No scrambling mistake, coming across and then biting a victim and spreading his viral shit. The reapers pick up on that immediately. No, in these samples there is no patient zero."

I turned on the hot water to steam my face a bit, before I did my foundation. I found that I was getting increasingly dehydrated, the more days I was into my afterlife. I wondered if brining would help, like a Thanksgiving turkey. I could fill up the tub, add some rock salt and soak overnight. Maybe, I'd find the added benefit of plump succulent breasts—and the smell of rosemary is always so festive.

"Then how does it start?"

"It's in the water."

"What, the water supply?" I turned on the sink for effect. But there weren't any cameras on me. I turned it off. There's simply no reason to be dramatic unless you're being filmed, or working out some family issue, like why doesn't Daddy love me? Or, I'll prove I have value, goddamn it! Something like that. I snickered at the thought, and then cringed at being caught while insane.

"The sample is a tablet the size of an ordinary gel-cap that's dropped into the filter reservoir of the espresso machine. It's time released, so Karkaroff can estimate the point at which it sets off, fairly close."

"So Starbucks Corporate is in on this?" The thought sent a chill through my already cold frame.

"Not at all." He sauntered over and leaned against the counter in a relaxed legs crossed at the ankle way. Far too comfortable, considering. "Much like I got a job through Karkaroff's connections, she's priming would-be baristas across the world to take on positions."

"Severine!" I knew the bitch looked too coherent, not even comparable to the uncontrolled animalism of the other zombies. She was made. Does that sound too mafia? How about a deathbreath? I just thought of that. Moving on . . .

"Yeah. She was one of us." He shivered. "God, I hate that I'm a part of this." Shane was a sunken, curled-up cornhusk of a vampire. He looked beaten, and although I never wanted children, his sullen demeanor made my breasts feel swollen like an expectant mother.

I'm lying.

I was just turned on. There's not a maternal bone in my dead body. My breasts were swollen, all right. I stole a quick glance to check for wet spots on my blouse. If there had been any, I would have freaked out, as there was no way I could lactate. The milk would more likely be pus.

"Me too." I stroked the back of his chilly neck. "But you don't have to be part of it anymore, you've already taken the first step." I thought of Oliver's twelve-step group, and derailed my train of thought. I continued, "Well, at least you've told me."

"Karkaroff is going to kill me."

"A bit too late for that, isn't it?" I joked, straining for eye contact.

"Not funny. It's not like I'm immortal." He gave in a bit and tilted his face toward mine. Twitched. The expression was disgust, and he wasn't looking behind me, either.

"Oh, fuck you!" I turned back to the mirror to check out the scene. He'd been startled by my death mask. An oval of make-up removed in totality, revealing perfectly clean but blue-grey skin underneath, dark blue veins and thin capillaries marred the surface like adolescent cutting scars. "Not everyone can be as pretty as you."

He grabbed for my shoulders roughly and spun me toward him, clutching at me, fitting me into the line of his body. "I'm sorry," he cooed. "It just startled me. Your skin is almost transparent."

I certainly had a knack for it; I could have been an esthetician. It's nice to be noticed for your achievements[94].

Our lips were inches apart and his were quivering, with fear, I wondered. I dove in for the kiss, pushing in and opening and struggling with his tongue for dominance. It would have been a romance cover shot, if it didn't have the look of a grave robbing, turned horny necrophilia.

We struggled with our clothes and feet to make it to the bed, nearly tripping over each other. We fell on the mattress, hard. He fumbled for my bra hooks—his ankles trapped in his wadded pants legs like shackles—while I stretched to reach the nightstand and retrieve the lube. He helped to apply it. I opened my thighs. He tumbled into me and started to thrust.

One thrust . . .

. . . two (deeper this time, nice, come on) . . .

. . . three (right up there, yeah! Mm-hmm!) . . .

. . . done (Huh?).

He hovered above me with a hopeful smile, dolly eyes rolling into the back of his head. His bottom lip sunk in and the top protruded in a half-dome over his teeth, like a monkey's, or that actor, whose name I can't remember, but without the ears like handles. He barked, "Uh . . . Uh . . . Uh." The sound was sharp and seal-like. He coughed the words out—and, this is the only redeeming element, in his favor— the most remarkable curlicues escaped his mouth, like deep Chinese red filigree, vermillion. He collapsed on top of me.

[94] See how I skew?

My mind went to work with all the rationalizing.

We were just *way* too into it, so, of course, it was as disappointing and premature as scrambled prom night sex. Though props to Shane, at least he made it inside before he hit his ceiling. Dante Morris had shot his load into the underside of a cummerbund pleat, and then didn't even bother to help a sister out. The corsage was pretty.

And, my senses were just *off* [95], so I couldn't drift in the moment, like I'd like. The scents were so odd. I, primarily, picked up my own, the sweet florals of Issey Miyake, but buried underneath, (the soil, if you will, and I think you will), rot and death. Shane smelled of very little. Soap. Car carpet dust. Armpit hair. Wood chips. He needed a shower.

But he was cute. Next time I would be in control. He could count on that.

He rolled on his back when it was over and stared at the ceiling.

"That was great," he said, winded.

"Mmm-hmm," I agreed, resisting a cough of accent. Shane was either unbelievably deluded or had lasted longer than usual.

I changed the subject, lest he feel the need to comment more. I knew myself well enough that it wouldn't take much digging for me to reveal the inadequacies of the quick romp. So I said, "So how does Liesl fit in to all this?"

"Who?"

"Liesl Lescalla?" I propped up on my elbows.

Like a little boy, he sucked at his lips and shook his head in ignorance.

"Succubus? Tall, sexy, black chick?"

"You've got to be kidding me."

"Nope."

He continued with the same response. Nada.

---

[95] You know I tend to lead with my nose. Nasal, but not in a Fran Drescher way. Let's get that straightened out right now.

Shit! Wrong lead.

You try to do something nice for someone—find their de-capitated body, rescue them from a crazed toe-sucking kid-napper—and this is what you get. I'm embroiled in an end of the world zombie conspiracy and no closer to finding Liesl. Typical.

"Did you know Oliver Calver?"

"No, doesn't ring a bell."

I'm not just dead. I'm cursed.

I reached for the phone next to my alarm clock. 4:25 P.M. I left a message for Wendy on her home phone.

"Wendy. I'm going to swing by there with a guest. Proba-bly around sixish. Need to regroup a bit, and have some really interesting news, but, of course, nothing on Liesl."

I left the same message for Gil, who'd be sleeping for an-other half hour at least.

Beside me, Shane drifted into sleep; his breathing be-came an adorable misty wheeze. I thought of the last time this bed had been defiled by zombie love, and Martin. Sweet and sexy Martin.

Hmm . . .

---

*A Confession**

🔲

**Don't Expect Another*

I've done something horrible.

If I tell you, you've got to promise to forgive me, okay?

Good. Here goes . . .

Remember when Martin and I . . . um . . . did it?

Well, after it was over, and he was dozing, and I was

really relaxed and basking in the afterglow, and all that, I ate him.

Please, don't judge.

I didn't mean to.

He smelled so good. It was intoxicating, so full of life.

I couldn't resist.

I guess I was too young of a zombie. I should have known I couldn't control myself. But let me make something perfectly clear: it was quick and painless.

I hope.

I feel horrible about it, to this day.

I apologize for holding my cards so close to my chest. I promised myself to keep you with me through my journey. Then I go and hold something like this back.

I'm ashamed. I really am.

I suppose I didn't want to be judged, so I just didn't open up about the conclusion of that night. Maybe, Shane and the undead sex shook something loose—and not in my bowels, this time—in my heart.

The few clean bones that are left of Martin, I keep in a black lacquer box under the bed, next to the cremated remains of my precious Chihuahua, Celie. Little known fact: I'm kind of sentimental.

Well . . .

I'm glad I told you.

I feel so much better, don't you?

Good.

"Sorry Martin," I whispered into the dusk filled room.

"What?" Shane rolled toward me, draping a leg over my own.

"Nothing." I'd nearly forgotten he was there. I swatted his leg away. "Take a nap."

Chapter 20

Shit Squall

Lakeview Cemetery is a popular spot for late-night ghost watching, not only for the celebrity plants, and mood swinging, but for the proximity to Volunteer Park. This park is an infamous hunting ground—if you like your victims closeted. . . .

—Way Off the Grid

It seemed in those days, I kept the water company in business with all my showers. The Starbucks gore spotted my skin with stains, something awful—thank God for powdered detergent with bleach. There is just something about having deeper layers of dead skin and not enough sloughing. Could anything be worse than rough patches? Oh wait . . . maybe this: at some point during "the sex act," as it is forever to be known, the gash in my arm tore open again.

I dug through the recent and sour memories to figure out the moment it had happened, and settled on the position. Shane opted for a modified missionary, which is by no means on my list of favorites, although many rapists hold it in high regard. Instead of holding his chest off of me by bracing his hands against the mattress, he held me down, balancing on my biceps. Not cool. I don't care how old the guy was—nor had I asked—this wasn't his first time, and there was no excuse for a macho power play.

I wondered what remedy would Wendy suggest next. An iron-on patch? Staples?

I ransacked the vanity cabinets for something to cover my wound. Tins and boxes skittered across the marble floor as I tossed. Finally, I found an unopened box of nicotine patches under the sink, a leftover from a failed attempt to quit. I pressed one over the tear and then another, giving them a pat—'cause, what the hell. But, I couldn't get a hit.

On the drive over to meet the crew, I told Shane about my search for Liesl, and my disappointment at having followed the wrong course of action. He thought that the other leads were quite encouraging. In the end, *he* apologized for *my* mistake. *Aw*, I thought. He's cute again.

I, also, made a call to the incubus/succubus tracker guy. The card said his name was Clevis. Yeah, I know, straight out of a '70s blaxploitation flick, right? You've gotta love that. He answered on the first ring.

"What d'ya want?" His voice was scratchy, dry and Scottish, breaking up my fantasy image of him. I imagined strands of mucus turned to crystal stalactites—or stalagmites, for that matter, albeit, less believable—bracing the back of his throat like a jail cell.

"I got your number from Nick."

"So . . . what?" Two words stretched thin by the thick brogue.

"He said you might be able to help me find a friend of mine, her name is . . ."

"Liesl Lescalla," he finished, having either read my mind or been forewarned. "I can get you the information you need . . ."

"Oh good." *Finally*, I thought. My luck must be changing. The bad sex I suffered must have filtered into my karma bank, like how Angelina Jolie's ghoulish red carpet behavior was wiped clean by helping bloated African children. A ray of light spilled into the dark pit of incompetence. "Thank you so much."

". . . but the price will be a hefty one, it will."

"Money is no object." I hoped he meant money. I could barely imagine having to pay with another inadequate performance. It was just too soon to risk.

"And who said anything about money? Grab a pen."

I jotted down instructions that proved to be more frustrating than an empty bank account. I thanked him and said goodbye.

In the hallway outside Wendy's, I laid it all out for Shane. I had to. I'd been dwelling. I don't do dwelling. My hand splayed on his chest, applying solid pressure, I said, "So, here's how it is Mr. King: I'm going to chalk today up to nerves and anxiety. But hear me, sex will never be like that again. We'll work on your longevity, but until it's up to par . . ."

He wore the correct expression: fear-tinged guilt. Lovely. His mouth dangled open. I put my thumb in it.

". . . you'll finish me off with this." I patted his tongue, he closed his mouth around my finger and sucked. "Or, this." I grabbed his hand and massaged. "I'm going to take control of your body and make your blood scream. The bedroom will look like a red tornado, when I'm through with you."

We were outside Wendy's door and Shane's eyes were so wide I feared they'd tear at the corners. The knob turned with a click and I pulled my thumb out with a *pop*.

It was Gil. I nudged past him, making my hips move the skirt like feathers, calling for Wendy. Behind me I heard Gil say to Shane, "Ooh, did you win the lottery, Kitten?"

Wendy called out from the back room, "I'll be ready in a minute, Amanda." I heard footstep patter, then the ashy blonde hair and pert oval of Wendy's face appeared in the doorway. "Watch that one channel. Oh, which is it, Gil?"

"Seven sixty-six," he said, plopping down next to me in the deep fluff of the green sofa. Remote in hand he flipped on the wall mounted LCD and triggered to 766. Shane chose the

Horchow Collection chocolate-leather club chair (it's *very* expensive); it squealed a bit as his hip slid down a shiny arm, and stared at the screen with the face of a medicated mental patient. He'd get over it.

The TV sprang to life in surreal mimicry of color and life, or death, as it were. The screen was full of the dead, zombies, vampires, ghosts. One zombie eating a human skull and biting into a hidden orange, its face changing from a scowl to a crazy cocked smile; later a toilet stall door is kicked in to find the same zombie grunting, flipping off the camera; a vampire is chased down by a little girl in a bright blue Sunday dress, behind her a large mouth, is clearly made of wax, a fake reaper doorway. The show name appears in flashes.

Undead . . .

On . . .

Tape

A male voice-over repeats the title and says, "And, now your host, everyone knows him, living and dead, it's Cameron Hansen!"

My mouth dropped open. The greasy fucker was double-dipping. Is it not enough to be adored by humans, he has to take over the undead consciousness?

"How long has this show been on?" I shouted back to Wendy.

"Oh my God!" Wendy yelled, bounding into the room. "Can you believe that piece of shit? I've been meaning to tell you about it but so much has been going on. I started seeing the previews last week."

Undead on Tape looked like a prank show. It was *Punk'd,* with gore standing in for the good-natured humor. I was only surprised that Cam Hansen couldn't be *less* original in his project choices.

"Next up. One of our favorite things here at *Undead*, a fatality accident caught on tape." His gelled and spiked head snapped to one side, and yelled, "Roll it!"

The screen changed to an image of an SUV driving down a slick decline, at its base was an intersection, from the cross street a small car approached from the distance, picking up speed.

The annoying voice-over remarked, "This accident features a darling of the supernatural club world, and a minor human celebrity, let's see if you can pick them out . . ."

The cars proceeded on their nightmare course and at the point of collision, the speed of delivery slowed to a crawl. It was repeated incessantly, from multiple angles, sometimes at once, stealing a DePalma split screen effect. I was horrified, but not just by the poor quality of the production, but because I recognized the participants immediately.

"Get a load of this," I broadcasted to the room. Wendy slumped behind Gil, stunned.

The cameras pulled back to reveal a tall gorgeous woman, staggering and staring at a gash in her arm. Quick zoom into dead flesh! Duh. It's me.

Fuck.

It wasn't long before the camera came in for a headshot of me, and poor Rochelle[96]. What I hadn't noticed at the scene was: if you looked close enough at the outside of the windshield you could see her exposed brain. The cameras don't miss a thing. They even stuck around to catch a seagull pulling at the grey matter with its beak like a half-eaten tuna salad. The real question is this: if I'd seen it, would that be me pecking away at the weathergirl's brain?

Cameron popped back on, "That's right folks. We caught Rochelle Ali in her last living performance and zombie debutante, Amanda Feral, a fresh face on the scene that many of you first took notice of in our special *Undead on Tape: Binge Party*.

There we were. No grains or tiling. The shot was crystal clear. Wendy and I chowed down on the teen runaway out-

---

[96] Is that a '60s doo-wop song?

side of Convent, our faces stretched into footwide bear traps and clamping down on the boy, bloodlessly chomping like a couple of Ms. Pacman. The boy was gone in less than a minute.

"Oh my God. So awful." Wendy's mouth hung open in shock. "Can they do that? I mean without a release or something?"

"Who are you gonna sue?" Gil asked. "It isn't like there's a supernatural court."

The screen switched back to Cameron. He was nodding creepily, grinning and giving a big thumbs-up. I had an idea of where he could shove that thumb, and it wasn't in Shane's mouth. I looked over at him and wiggled my own thumb. Shane licked his lower lip. He'd been staring at me.

"You like that, Cameron? Bitch, you should have been followin' me today," I said to the TV.[97] "A fuckin' laugh riot."

The show went to commercial and spooky horror movie music expelled from the theater speakers.

A shiny black hearse pulls up to a roll shutter door.
The sign reads Mortuary. The camera pans to look
into the cargo area of the car. A dead little boy stares
from between the black drapes.
"Three days," he moans.

Gil clicked off the TV.

"We are totally going," Wendy said. "I've been waiting for Mortuary to open, forever. Or at least since Ricardo told me about it."

"Ricardo? What does he have to do with Mortuary?"

"He owns it, silly."

I swear to God. I used to know things first. Did you see the fucking show? The man said debutante, you heard him—

[97] I know it's an inanimate object!

I was in-the-know, if-you-will, and I promise, I will be again. As God as my wit—

Forget it. I knew my place: I'm Reality Show fodder.

And to think, Cameron Hansen was my personal stalker, my Hinkley? Yuck. But still. I knew any publicity was good publicity. I should embrace it. I could probably turn undead notoriety into bank for my under the table work. I'd charge supernatural businesses a premium for way better campaigns than I'd seen on Undead Satellite. Of course, I'd have to get rid of Pendleton, Avery, Prissy and Lollipop, eventually. Marithé would have to be made. She was too valuable to lose.

I needed Gil along for the tracker's task, not because he would be any more help than the others, but because we hadn't had a chance to chat. He and I talked every morning on the phone, before he turned in, but not lately. I missed that. He'd mourn some lost love of his life—they were all great loves; Gil only had *great* loves—well, except for Chase Hollingsworth, and he was my great love, because I loved to tease Gil about his one night stand with Winston Churchill—and I'd share stories from the human trenches. Crazy things like Lollipop's fall, or someone smearing feces in the unisex bathroom. It wasn't me. I swear!

Plus, I was getting bored with Shane's pretty face—absence makes the heart grow fonder, and shit like that. We sent Wendy and Shane ahead to the Well of Souls to get a VIP table. I wasn't sure how long the task would take, but Wednesdays at the Well were crowded until the early hours of morning, so we'd catch up to them no matter what.

"So how was he?" Gil asked.

"What?" I brushed off the top of my jeans. Jeans. I wasn't about to go on a secret mission in a Vivienne Westwood Basque. What are you thinking?

"The prom king? How was he for a gasm?" Gil's face registered distaste; his lips were pursed under cloudy eyes. Subdued but distaste, nonetheless.

I shook my head sorrowfully. "Not."

"I'm sorry. That bad, huh? He looks it, though. So pent up."

I opened the folded piece of scrap, with the tracker's instructions, from my pocket.

The first cryptic instruction was a cinch, as it wasn't particularly cryptic—oh wait, I get it, crypt. *Go to the resting place of Kato*. Although it could be for a pop culture junkie.

"Is Kato dead?" I asked, scrunching my face up.

"You're thinking about Kato Kaelin. No. I think this is about another Kato. Bruce Lee."

Oh yeah! I thought. Everyone knows that Bruce Lee was buried here in Seattle; his son, too. Brandon Lee was sleeping off the world's worst headache at . . ."What's that cemetery?"

"He's over at Lakeview."

Gil was already driving the Jag in the direction of Capitol Hill, but on hump day, traffic could be a bitch.

"You know, you never talk about the vampire that made you. Not since that first time I asked, in fact."

"There's not much to say . . ."

Oh. Really.

Here We Go Again . . .

Inconsiderate Interlude of the Bitter & Pathetic
Part Three: Gil, again

"His name is Rolf DeBeers—and before you ask, yes, those DeBeers, I think . . . I never actually asked. He'd slipped away from his home and family in Amsterdam, to take up surfing in Southern California. How he came to be in Tacoma, of all places, is another story, I don't know that story personally, but . . . anyway, we dated for a while, and I fell in love. I think I was in love from the moment I saw him in the Rusty Bucket. That coffee sniffin' bastard.

"It started out great. Long walks on the Sound, I told him everything about me, and he'd listen. He had great hearing; sometimes he'd just walk off and let me keep talking. I knew he was listening though.

"Rolf was distant, aloof—he called it—I like to think he was mysterious. I tried everything I could to keep him interested. I brought willing victims to him, wrote him cute love letters, sent him flowers. I even introduced him to my mother, God rest her soul.

"Then, one night, I got up for the evening and found a note pinned to his pillowcase—I say 'his' because I had his name, then mine embroidered through a little heart, it even had a cute little cupid's arrow going through it—the note said: Enough.

"We were together for a magical three weeks, a real whirlwind romance, and then he was gone. I just don't understand what happened."

"Um . . . maybe it was your love of life? Your free spirit and passion. Some men have difficulty expressing emotion," I suggested. Gil was clearly insane, and had no clue about relationships. Not that I was a fount of knowledge, but to tell him the truth might be dangerous. He might go crazy and suicidal and drive us into a telephone pole, or something. I couldn't risk it. Despite the temptation to say: Listen, you were too clingy, and you're not alone, it's a problem that many women have. I had to keep lying.

"What?" Gil started to sniffle. A bizarre action, since his tear ducts dried up years ago.

I reached across the expanse between us and patted his thigh. "Gil. You are a wonderful man. There's a guy out there for you somewhere. I'll help you find him."

"Thanks," he mewled. "You're a real friend."

"That's me."

The conversation filled the time from Wendy's place to the cemetery. Hump day traffic is atrocious. It was late summer, 7:30, and the gates closed at dusk. By the time we made the grounds it would be black as pitch. Gil parked in a residential area and we hoofed it to a service gate.

"What's next?" he asked.

I held the darkened paper out to the streetlight. No. 2 read: *Walk straight from the main gate through the beds until you reach the other side.*

No problem—in theory. We tried to follow the fence around but tripped as often as we took steps.

"Goddamn it." Gil toppled over a low inset of headstone.

"Shit." I stumbled on some unseen obstacle.

If there wasn't a headstone to stumble over, there were roots from a high grove of poplars, or mounds of dirt covered in tarp, or protrusions of board hovering over empty graves. A tall hedge provided far too much shadow. The path was treacherous, but before long we reached the main gate, and stepped out of the shadows, me with stubbed toes, and Gil with scratches up both forearms and a shining welt above his brow.

We headed west through the markers, headstones and crypts. A haze crept across the black swath of lawn, illuminated by thin tendrils of moonlight cutting through clouds that carried only misty patches of rain. Lucky day. Occasionally, we passed specters sitting atop their tombstones. Their ethereal frames blurred at the edges like charcoal rubbings. The phantoms glowed in a mood ring of colors; those that stomped and kicked atop their final resting spots were surrounded with a deep peacock azure; others lazed in sunken rectangles of lawn, like comfortable divans, shimmered emerald.

One ghost wore a vibrant red aura. A woman. She brushed her hair, with the aide of a hand mirror, her familiar face lit by reflected moonglow. She took particular interest of our movement, and our task. She uncrossed her legs and hopped from her headstone with the ease of a girl. Soon, she had caught up and tagged along.

"Where ya goin'?"

"We're on a bit of a mission, Ms.?"

"Ms. Mercer, thank you. If you're looking for Jimi he's over at Greenwood, now. They dug him up a while back. Family."

"We're not, ma'am," Gil said, politely. "But thank you. Good to know."

"What are you looking for then?" She skipped by and was walking backwards in front of us, passing through headstones, bushes and lawn ornamentation. She left trails of red glow on the stones, like phosphorous. "Brandon Lee's over there. Everyone thinks that his father's not, that he faked his death, but he's here, too. Right there next to him. Body's not, but he's there. Would you like to meet them? It would be no trouble at all. Lovely people."

"Some other time, Ms. Mercer."

She stopped dead in her tracks, her glow darkened into a regal purple shade. She planted her hands on her hips and roared, "Fine." My hair flipped back from the force of her . . . expectoration. She stomped off, mumbling something about *rude young people* and *heathens*.

"I somehow didn't expect ghosts."

Gil stopped ahead of me and turned, smiling. "Yeah, they kinda show up in the oddest places. Are you crazy? It's a cemetery. What'd you expect to see?"

"Nothing. I thought I'd seen everybody at the clubs."

"Ghosts are linked to things. Sometimes coffins, sometimes an object at the place they died. There's one over at Les Toilettes."

"Oh." I laughed. "Now it comes out."

"I've heard. I've heard there's one there."

"You are such a chubby chaser. I swear to God."

"Shut up."

We finished the trek to the far fence and Gil lit the note with his watch. Instruction No. 3: *Find the oval marker at the base of the oak and get to diggin' for the wee coffin.* This was the easiest, so far, as the oak was only a few steps away. We spread out on our hands and knees feeling for the marker.

"Do you think Liesl will appreciate our effort?" Gil asked.

"I've been thinking the same thing. It's my impression that most people don't appreciate a goddamn thing." The grass was damp and I felt moisture seeping between the fibers of my pants, staining them. I was unperturbed. I brought a change of clothes, anyway. Helmut Lang. I hoped Gil had remembered to do the same. I would have suggested Jil Sander. I've been meaning to talk to him about expanding his wardrobe.

"I don't know if I'd go that far, Amanda. I appreciate—"

"I was making a sweeping generalization, Gil. It's rhetorical, please don't respond. I feel ugly enough that I've even said it. I'm so negative." Had I said that? Negative? The living me would have never copped to that. Sleuthing must have suited me, or, perhaps my brain was rotting into a jaundiced slush. I hoped that wasn't the case; one needs a brain.

"Over here!" Gil was on the opposite side of the tree, knees between thick exposed roots.

Gil dug for the small coffin like a bowel impaction, his fingers crooked, widening the hole, and then picking at the dirt pocked with small stones, loosening it. Although, I would have never thought of it in quite that way if Gil hadn't remarked, the hole was tighter than a virgin's ass. Oh, why do I lie? I was already going to compare it to digging a corn kernel from a butt-hole, before he said a single word. I'm a sick fucker like that.

"This hole is so tight," he said, in all seriousness, like that, like that's not a funny statement, and hunched over it on his knees, pressing his probing fingers deeper and deeper. Honestly, that's a little gay.

"Oh, yes!" I screamed, then laughed, then screamed again. "Get in that hole, Gil. Yeah! Deeper! Deeper!"

"Shut up, Amanda!"

No bigger than a shoe box, the coffin was probably the top of the line of pet burial implements; mahogany, gold fixtures, doggy swank.

"Open it," I said. "Open it, open it, open it." Like the coffin was a morbid little Tiffany box, and this was *Black Christmas*.[98]

A small button on the side unlatched the lid and despite its diminutive size the coffin creaked with an echo across the graves.

"Can you keep it down?" Ms. Mercer shrieked in the distance. "I'm reading, for Christ's sake."

Inside the box was an amulet. Round and heavily carved, it hung from a thick gold-corded chain. But was it *the* amulet? Would it fit in that dusty shadow box, in Liesl's bloodbath of a room?

"The size of a monocle," I said. "Weren't those Wendy's words?"

"Yep." Gil picked at the dirt crammed underneath his fingernails. A look of annoyance spread across his handsome face. He dragged his hands across the damp grass then rubbed them together, repeating the action until his hands were skin-colored.

We carried the casket to a more lit area. The moon wasn't

---

[98] It's never inappropriate to reference bad Canadian horror movies, or their remakes, as it turns out.

illuminating for shit. The bronze pendant was the size and shape of a small compact. Its face and back were engraved and embossed in an intricate orgy scene, like a miniature Kama Sutra. A hedonistic variety of creatures in various ridiculous positions, flitting across its surface—you could almost hear the moans.

"It's a sex scene. That just screams incubus/succubus, no?" I asked.

"Oui, Mademoiselle. Très érotique."

"Lovely. But, I took Spanish."

"Let's go back to the car," he said, in a dull, disgusted monotone. "My eloquence is lost on the likes of you."

We crossed the street and the instructions must have fallen from my pocket, because they crunched under Gil's foot. He picked them up, and read them under the dome light, for a next step, presumably.

"Oh shit. You're such an asshole, Amanda."

"So much for eloquence. What is it?" I snatched the note from his hand.

There, following the directive to dig up the coffin, in my own handwriting, if you'll recall, was an important note.

It read: *Do not open the box.*

Chapter 21

God Grant Me the Serenity to Disembowel and Devour

Wherever you go, there's always the chance that you'll run into them. Seattle is certainly no different. Just remember the majority of us say that supernatural is supernormal. We have a right to exist . . .

—Uncanny & Out

After all the hassle of recovering the doggy casket, Clevis didn't answer his door. We knocked, just short of hammering blisters into our knuckles. A second-story window was lit behind a closed curtain, the light bleeding through the break. Someone was shut up in there.

My first thought? He knew we'd opened it. Clevis had somehow gained the knowledge that we'd debauched the coffin and fondled its contents. Probably in the same way Nick had detected my unwholesome interest.

I ended up leaving a curt message on his voice mail.

Gil floored the British racer, weaving in and out of traffic and, at times, bottoming out, after tight leaps from unexpected hills.

"That was a complete waste of time, Amanda," he railed. "What did we accomplish tonight, besides missing half-price happy hour?" Gil loved Ricardo's specialty vamp snacks; he called them blood crisps. Apparently when not managing the hottest club in town, or promoting his newest, Ricardo was an amateur chef and fan of late night infomercials. The crisps were pungent and snappy, but reminiscent of hard fruit roll-ups. Ricardo made them in a food dehydrator, a regular undead Ron Popeil.

"Don't forget ruining three hundred dollar jeans. I'm sorry. But, honestly, is there anything more important than jewelry?"

I reached into the floorboard and after some finagling with the latch, retrieved the amulet and donned it. I slumped in the seat like a pachuco, and gave him a nodding pout. Doing my best hand signal gang signs: the Chanel double C logo.

Gil looked over and his demeanor brightened. "No she didn't! Mary J. in the house!"

"Hey-Ho!" I waved my hand in the air and used all four of the required syllables.

The vampire slowed down a bit then, typical male, needed Mommy to soothe his precious little head. *Baby got a temper, he do.* He parked the car under the viaduct, and arms linked, we traversed the living obstacles in the gutter, on our way to the Well.

The club was packed as tight as Nick's jeans. Clumps of supernatural subgroups were plopped here and there in a vibrating throng of inhumanity. Heavy-handed description, to be sure, but, nonetheless true.

Wendy and Shane hung off the bar like utility disconnect notices, rejecting would-be suitors with flippant waves or disturbed shakes of the head, all the while, in rapt conversation. Gil bounded off ahead of me to join up, but I had slid into stilettos and had to maneuver dark stairs.

A blatant hand shot out from between a pair of translucent water sprites in Valentino. It latched onto my forearm, like a cuff. Before I could think to snatch it back, I was face to smiling face with the hand's owner, Elizabeth Karkaroff.

Let me give you the rundown: The Devil does not as has previously been reported favor the designs of Miuccia, Donatella, or even the man, himself, Giorgio. She wears Carolina Herrera, and wears it well, like the Brazilian seamstress pulled her as a muse. The dress was a tweed boatneck and ended below the knee where jet stockings took over. Her heels were high and rounded at the tip—now, those were Italian. Impeccable. Her long flaxen hair was streaked with platinum, and waved like Veronica Lake. Her eyes were as dark and stormy as a Victorian gothic novel. Her handbag was an Hermès Birkin, in orange ostrich. *Holy shit!* The woman was intimidating.

I turned back to scream for Shane. The hand pulled me close. I shut my mouth.

"Ms. Amanda Feral," she cooed. Up close, her tongue could have circled the fleshy knob, dead center of my ear, if she'd wanted. "I've been meaning to have a word with you." The accent was studied and aristocratic, as if harked up from a wet lung. South African, perhaps, smooth as dark roast coffee.

She dragged me through the crowd, her arm enveloping my waist, feeling far larger than its appearance. We stopped at the farthest table, with the highest vantage. She guided me deep within. I tried to spot my friends, but would have had better luck plucking grey hairs from a child. My memory started to speak, shout. *Don't look her in the eye.* Who'd said that? *If you appear rude, you're dead.* Now, I know I've never heard that before. *She'll put thoughts into your head.* That was me. *Make you kill yourself.*

"I certainly would not," she responded, her hand to her chest.

"Did I say that aloud?" I asked, apologetically, staring thoughtlessly into her cat shaped eye, the left one. I began to feel faint.

"Well . . . no." She pushed her hair back over her shoulder—it fell with the luminous weight of a shampoo commercial[99]—and spun a single pearl on a pink lobe. "I hear you took a meeting with my man Snell, yesterday."

"Yes." I fumbled through my purse looking for something important, or just something to avert my eyes. She needn't know there was a difference.

"I was expecting a bit more of an answer, dear."

"Yes, I met with Snell. I had questions about Oliver Calver."

"Lovely boy." Her brows shifted suggestively. "I hope Snell answered your questions adequately."

I wondered if it were possible that Elizabeth Karkaroff was, actually, a polite, genuine woman?

"It's entirely possible," Ms. Karkaroff replied, looking off into the cavernous club. "And before you launch into an internal dialogue, yes, I am reading your thoughts." She reached over and patted my thigh. "Darling, you've nothing to fear from me."

I caught up with my train, surprisingly able to continue talking despite the shock of the brain rape that was going on. "Mr. Snell was cordial and helpful. Although, I haven't found Oliver, as of yet. I'm not sure if you're aware but his girlfriend, Rochelle, was killed in an accident."

"Oh, but of course." She muffled a snicker behind a long-fingered, porcelain-white hand. "Everyone knows. Cameron Hansen. *Undead on Tape*. I suppose there are many here who find that sort of thing entertaining." As if on cue a

---

[99] "It's not just soft," the model said. "It's devilish! New Beelzebub Shampoo, with Satan proteins." I can see it now, simply evilicious.

clown-grinned photographer blew in and offered to take a picture, snapping it with a big Hasselblad before a comment could be returned. I imagined that Karkaroff had set it up, that the camera *had* stolen my soul, like primitive tribes once believed.

Elizabeth continued, as if uninterrupted, "But, regardless, your statement is flawed. That weathergirl may have been killed in the accident. But she was not Oliver's girlfriend. I'd question where you got that bit of information."

I thought of my conversation with Claire Bandon. She had told me, and Rochelle hadn't denied it. But had the weathergirl actually said that she and Oliver were together?

Karkaroff winked at me. "Now you are thinking. I wouldn't be surprised if you've been getting quite a few things jumbled."

She means Sha—I immediately tried to layer over the thoughts. *Dead kitties, dead kitties. No! Lalalalalalalalalala.*

Elizabeth was locked on to my eyes; her wan smile faded to a flat line. "What are you on about, girl?"

Lalalalalalalala. A pressure seemed to envelop me like saran wrap and tighten. Elizabeth was exerting the same force Snell had back in the conference room. Only with more power behind it.

"Fear is such a sad emotion, so common. And, how do I get this through to you, child? So futile. I've told you you've nothing to fear from me, but you choose disbelief. I fear our chat is over." Karkaroff motioned for me to depart. I'd been excused.

I did it, I thought. I had successfully kept Shane's name from my head.

Oops.

"Ah. Shane King, such a beautiful boy. How is he?" Elizabeth called from the banquette. When I looked back, she toasted me with a crystal flute (see inset).

**The Well of Souls'
Champagne Cocktail**

*1 cube sugar
2 dashes bitters
Chilled Bollinger*

*Add sugar and bitters to chilled
flute. Muddle. Add champagne.
Garnish with lemon curl.*

I ran down the risers to the bar. If I'd had functional lungs I would have been breathless. Shane and Wendy were talking about live skin transfer, a new procedure they'd seen on a supernatural cosmetics show, and Gil was making out with a werewolf, who'd begun to change with arousal, his fingers elongated with sharp knuckle pops. Ricardo intervened.

"Chuck! Gil! If you guys like it rough, you're going to have to take it somewhere else."

Gil looked over and mouthed an exaggerated *nosy*. They detangled like a Johnson and Johnson's sex show. Chuck's claws retracted like ten hairy lipsticks.

"What'll you have, Amanda?" Ricardo was in front of me, so smooth you barely see him move that lanky undead frame.

"Something strong, I just had a run-in with Elizabeth Karkaroff."

He reached for an unlabeled bottle and poured it into a thin frost-glazed glass. It tasted of jet fuel. My skin turned pink before the liquid made it to my stomach.

"Holy shit!" I gritted my teeth.

"That'll take your mind off anything, right?" he asked, beaming. "Just got it in. It's called Life Fuel."

"Well, cheers. Have you tasted this shit?"

"It's great, right? What did you mean run-in?"

"She took me aside and assaulted my thoughts. Up in the rafters over there." I tried my best to look wounded and aloof, but damsel-in-distress doesn't really work for me. Ricardo caught on immediately.

"You mean you couldn't contain yourself and she read your mind? What? Were you afraid, or something?"

"Of course! Jesus! How many supernaturals in this town can read minds, Ricardo? It seems like everyone I run into lately is in my head. It's like a rape. Especially her." I looked into the upper banquettes. Snell had joined Karkaroff and the two were rapt in a serious conversation. Brows were furrowed and eyes locked on each other.

"Someone's been filling your head with a line of bullshit, then."

"What are you talking about? I've heard she's the Devil." I felt the urge to cross myself, but onlookers might have been offended, so . . . I crossed myself—and I'm not even Catholic.

"The Devil? Well if I'd known she was *The Devil*, I might have sent up some Cristal. Someone's pulling your chain, Amanda. I know a lot of people say that about Elizabeth, but it's simply not true."

"Could we not talk about that now? Something big is going on. She mustn't hear." I pushed in close and mouthed *shut up.*

Ricardo rolled his eyes. "Fine."

"Whatever. Listen, do you know of a recovery group for werewolves?"

"Not for werewolves, specifically, no."

"What about for supernaturals in general, then?"

His eyes scoured the floor and his forehead cringed into a W. It loosened. "There is a twelve-step over on Magnolia, but you couldn't mean that."

"Why?"

He shrugged. "Oh, no reason. Check it out. It's the only thing I can think of. Plus they'd be more likely to know of other groups."

"True."

He leaned in and put his hand over mine. "And princess, be careful; you seem to be caught up in something."

Yeah, I thought. Caught up in the drama of it all. And going nowhere. I brushed him off and marched up to Shane and Wendy. "What's the topic?"

"Lost love," Gil said. I thought of Martin.

"Bad sex," Wendy said. I thought of Shane. I decided to just listen. The conversation ultimately turned to the rollicking topic of favorite foods, it continued deep into the night.

The group met on Thursdays, the female voice on the machine said, "Supernatural to Supernormal and Beyond, meets on Thursdays at 11:00 P.M., at McAlinden's Tavern on Magnolia, newcomers welcome." No beep.

I took another sick day from work, locked up in my apartment[100]. I drove out at 10:45. I wanted to watch as people arrived. McAlinden's was an ivy-covered brick building with a black lion statue out front and a smoking tent in the rear. The parking lot was nearly full, so I parked on the street with a full view of both the main entrance and the back door, which was covered by a slapping screen. It got a ton of use, as the humans had passed a no-smoking-within-twenty-five-feet-of-a-building law. Bullshit, posturing. There were certainly more deadly things than cigarettes, and they were convening at McAlinden's.

A stumpy army jeep whipped past, nearly clipping the bumper and parked with a skid in the damp lot. A tall man, about twenty-five, got out and headed for the back door, his hands buried deep in his ass pockets. A woman parked on the opposite side of the street. She took some time getting out of her aging Crown Vic, and seemed to be talking to her reflection in the rearview. She gave her ratty hair a sloppy

---

[100] Surprise. Surprise.

brush-out and shuffled to the building in bright orange garden clogs.

It was 10:55.

I grabbed my purse and reached in, circling the amulet and then digging for some gloss, checked my face, applied and stepped out onto the curb.

McAlinden's reeked of sauerkraut and dirty butt. Small tables were scattered about like driftwood, and surrounded by small segregations, secretaries at this one, college students at that, etcetera. The bar was oak and mirror; its top probably carved by a drunken stupor of regulars.

"What can I do you for?" asked the keep. An older man with Brillo-pad hair and sparse muttonchops, his nose carried the telltale signs of alcoholism, a multitude of broken capillaries. I could sympathize.

"I'm looking for the meeting."

His brows raised and he nodded to the back of the building. "Back behind the restrooms, right past the smoker's door. You can't miss it."

I couldn't help think, he'd rather not have the group there at all. Couldn't blame him. Who'd want a bunch of zombies, vamps and other threats to the national welfare so close to the vulnerability of an exposed ass? I wondered how many of the customers knew that they were opening themselves up to possible attack, every time they pulled down their pants in the john. So close to the evil, but with vulnerable assholes exposed, it would be so difficult to run.

Three hanging globes lit the room, each in milky glass.

I stood at the door surveying the occupants. The young man I'd seen enter was there. He sat in the corner with his arms crossed and eyes burning. *Or were they glowing?* The clog woman either didn't belong to the group or was smoking. A Korean man in a dark suit stood thumbing through brochures at a nearby table. I had my contact. He seemed professional and approachable.

"Excuse me, sir?" I pressed in and touched his forearm.

"Yes?" He responded in a quick burst. He glanced at me once and then looked away. He had a nice face, roundish with glasses that did nothing for him, and bangs that intruded only slightly on his brow.

"Is this the twelve-step group?"

"Yes." He nodded, turned and sat on one of the wooden folding chairs, already gathered in a circle.

A woman with wild red hair, like a lucky bingo troll doll, but with a halo of gray at the forehead, stood from another seat and crossed the hall, offering her hand. "I'm Samantha Baumgartner, I facilitate *Supernatural to Supernormal, and Beyond.* We're glad to have you. Sit anywhere you like." She gestured toward the circle.

She thought I was here to join the group. It didn't feel right to lie about my real purpose; wouldn't it compromise the integrity? That was always a concern in advertising focus groups, sample size and predictability—too little is bad, too many and the results have been manipulated. Wouldn't an outsider jeopardize safety, or comfort, or some shit like that? Shouldn't a group be safe? Or had I been watching too much *Oprah?*

"Oh. Uh . . . no. I came to ask some questions about a member."

"I'm sorry, that's not possible," she said. A sour look spread across her face like someone had polluted her chocolate with raspberry. "You see, our group—like all twelve-step groups—is anonymous. We only use our first names, and even those are confidential to outsiders."

She started to walk away, when I stepped forward. "Then I'll stay, I'll talk, whatever."

The clog lady entered and shut the door behind her. From close up, she had the wide-eyed gawkiness of a muppet— Beaker. Her face was long and her hair too high.

"Hello Lenore. Welcome," Samantha said.

"Thanks." Her eyes darted in my direction. I thought they

might roll out and over to my shoe. She sat and fingered an ironic lifeline on an open palm.

So there we sat: Samantha and Clog Lady, Blue Jeans and the Korean Businessman, oh . . . and don't forget, the Undead Socialite. I began to sense an itch in the center of my back. It would certainly drive me crazy for the extent of the meeting.

Samantha began: "Let's start with the Serenity Prayer, shall we?"

The group spoke, in unison, minus me, "God grant me the serenity to accept the things I cannot change; the courage to change the things I can; and the wisdom to know the difference." *Can you say: Crap?*

"Now. Who'd like to start? Lenore? Richard?" Samantha's gaze lit on one after the other.

Blue Jeans spoke up. Why wasn't I surprised that a Southern drawl marred his speech. Was it the shit kickin' boots he wore? "My name's Richard . . ."

"Welcome Richard," they all said, interrupting the man, and so did I. But the Korean businessman said "Witch-it" so I wanted to pee myself laughing, then flagellate with guilt.

". . . and I'm a recoverin' vampire. This week, I sucked the blood from a hamburger pack, instead of a human."

They clapped and my mouth dropped open in horror and judgment. "Hamburger pack? What the hell for?"

Samantha's head snapped in my direction. "Richard is working *very* hard on reducing his intake of human blood. He's working on becoming super*normal*. Good job Richard." She gave him the big thumbs-up, and me a suffocating grimace.

"But aren't you a vampire?" I leaned forward onto my knees, for what I hoped was an empathetic stance.

"I certainly am, ma'am, I don't need you to point that out. Samantha? This doesn't feel very supportive."

Samantha sat next to the vampire and gave him a hug while sneering in my direction. "Richard, we are all very proud of you." And then to me, "Maybe our guest could introduce herself and explain why she's here."

They turned sour faces with blank eyes in my direction. Waiting.

"My name is Amanda, and I'm really happy to be with you here this evening." I know that was probably laying it on a little thick, but hey, I was just trying to spread the love.

"Welcome Amanda," said the group.

"I'm here because I'm looking for my friend." There seemed to be some interest, so I continued. "I don't have many friends because I'm new to this zombie flesh-eating thing, and she's missing. She's a succubus. Her name's Liesl, and I miss her." They seemed to be genuinely sympathetic. "While looking for her someone told me about another guy who went missing and thought it might be connected so I followed some leads on him and I met his girlfriend but she ran her car into me and she died. I went to his work, which was really scary, and then I nearly got killed in an elevator and then, a bunch of mistakes jumped me but that's okay 'cause I got laid that night." They hadn't started clapping so I went on.

"I went to his bowling league and there was an incubus there with the scariest dick but I got some info from him so I guess he's cool and now I'm here at his "supernormal" group[101] even though I'm pretty sure everyone knows he's a wereleopard and in that prayer thingy you said that you should accept the things you can't change and for sure he can't change being a wereleopard any more than Richard can change being a vampire or Lenore can change her fashion sense." I wrapped up my speech, with a quick point at Lenore's clogs.

Blue Jeans guy was right; this group wasn't very supportive. They looked shocked and judgmental.

But, I felt better. I really did; more relaxed, too. Maybe

---

[101] Don't worry. I used the air quotes.

there was something to this group therapy bullshit, and sharing. A smile began to spread across my face. I just knew it would look welcoming and open the group up to a discussion. They'd be willing to help me now. I scanned their faces.

The group expression: Anger.

Samantha lit in, "We are horribly sorry about your friend but we can't help you either. Oliver hasn't been here in weeks."

Then, a subtle change.

A hesitant voice crept from the corner. "I can not change been unday'd. Group stupid. I reaving."

"Oh, no, Mr. Kim," Samantha said, mothering. She shot a quick glance my way. Hatred. "You are doing so well here. You know what they say, fake it until you make it!"

"Then I be fake uh-til etern-tea. Fuck you. I outta here." Mr. Kim pulled a cigarette from out of his suit jacket, lit it and crumbled the empty pack, tossing it into a mesh wastebasket by the door. As he strode out of the exit, a thin trail of smoke in his wake, he uttered a second, "Fuck you."

Samantha, Richard and Lenore were tight lipped and their body language was closed off. Arms and legs crossed, looking at the floor.

"Oops." I shrugged. "I guess Mr. Kim *outta* here."

"Get out!" screamed Samantha. Her face was pomegranate red and seemed to be shifting beneath the skin.

"But, I—" I reached for my purse.

"Out!"

I stood up and straightened my skirt. I wouldn't be treated like this. I was a celebrity for Christ's sake. Lenore and Richard were smug and accusatory; both had crossed their arms, and shifted away from me.

"Do you even know who I am?"

"Get the fuck out!" she squealed and charged me with fists in the air. She seemed to get bigger as she approached, almost bear-like. Her eyebrows grew together, forming a single caterpillar across her broadening forehead. Her tits sunk to her waist and her chest puffed up like a pony keg. Her head engorged to the size of a Pilates ball.

Shit! I thought. A werebear.

I rushed the door as fast as my stilettos would carry me. Speeding past McAlinden, or whoever the guy behind the bar was, and out onto the sidewalk. I expected to hear four fat paws pounding the linoleum, but there was nothing but the soft sprinkle of rain.

Peering back into the bar, I was happy to see that Samantha's freak-out had ended at the group room door. She had returned to her human state and stood there flipping me off.

Chapter 22

A New Friend, a Revelation

If someone approaches you selling maps to super-natural celebrity homes, beware: this is likely a scam . . .
—The Bacchus Guide

Unscathed by the nasty potential of a botched werebear at-tack—what was Samantha going to do, after all, lose her group space?—I settled in to drive back downtown. But my brain snagged thinking about Claire Bandon. Was she, in fact, completely unreliable? I sat in the car outside McAlin-den's and warmed. It did seem I'd been led down a path never traveled, and guess what, there's no one here waiting at the end, no one to ask. No leads.

Crick, crack. A ringed knuckle rap sounded on the car window. Passenger side.

It had started raining again; and the individual was ob-scured by rivulets of water on his side and the dewy musk of condensation on mine. The interior of the Volvo was sub-tropical by this point, Antiguan only without the mosqui-toes—wet clothes can, certainly, create atmosphere. I pressed down on the window button. It slid into the sleeve of the door. A breezy hush entered the car.

The round face and angled eyes of Mr. Kim appeared. I hadn't looked at him with any real curiosity before, and he wasn't old, probably thirty five. His poor make-up job bled in the streams of rain, revealing a cage of blue veins.

"Get in," I told the zombie.

He did as he was told. Wouldn't you? Or maybe it was simply the rain.

"Thank you. It Miss Amanda, yes?" he asked. His clothes and mouth smelled of smoke. The heat of the car warmed that scent and carried it to me, served up like tiny nibbles in a dirty ashtray.

"Amanda Feral." I extended my hand. I remembered making fun of his accent, and started to feel marginally guilty[102]. He reached out and shook. His hand was all thumbs. I mean literally, he had five fingers the size of thumbs, like the regular set had been ground down to stubs.

"Please to meet you. I sorry for disturb, I saw you sit in car. Thought I say thank you."

"Thank you? For what, ruining your group?" I asked; then thought, *Did I just come across another clue, does everyone live like this*?

"For showing me right." A thin trickle of water left his hairline and traveled to his jaw, before dripping onto what could easily have been a Members Only jacket, minus the epaulets.

"Showing you *right*?" I repeated.

"No. Not right." His small mouth was twitching, and his tone was elevating. "Right, rike rightswitch."

"Light," I said, nodding. I'd shown him the *light*; that was so sweet. Now, if only I could do the same for Karkaroff or

---

[102] Marginal Guilt: From where you're sitting—the soft cushion of disinterest—look out across the border. You should just be able to see guilt crossing the river on a makeshift tire raft, three deep.

Lollipop, even. Lollipop certainly needed to see the light of subtle fashion. Even a dim beam would help. Mr. Kim spoke in that all to easy to make fun of accent, free of articles and verb conjugation; R's shoved in where the L's should be.

"Great, glad to help." I waited for explanation.

He smiled and blinked.

And, I continued to wait for explanation.

"Anything else, Mr. Kim?"

"Uh, uh. I could. Uh, uh," he scrambled, either searching for words or stalling to spend more time with me. "Uh . . . I know." He raised his brows and pointed a finger into the air. "I tell about Mr. Oliver? Yes?"

"Uh . . . yes. You could, absolutely, do that. That would be *so* super great of you, Mr. Kim." I put my hand on his knee to prompt him to begin. He looked at my hand and smiled. Then at me. Another smile. "Go ahead and tell me about Oliver," I stopped patting and withdrew my hand. I slid it under my leg.

"It a sad, sad story. Mr. Oliver very dead, right now."

"Dead! Shut . . . up!" I cried and twisted my body to promote full attention. "What happened? How do you know?"

"Oliver stay with me, for a while. Tell me he afraid of ex-girl-a-friend, Rochelle."

Mmm-hmm. I thought. *Ex*-girlfriend.

"She follow him to work and to bowling alley. She cragee stalkuh gull[103]. One night. After come home from Supernatural to Supernormal and Beyond—bullshit, as you say—front door broke, scream inside. I look through crack. Rochelle pound Oliver body. He dead."

He gesticulated wildly in the seat as he recounted the tale. Mimicking Rochelle's facial expressions (insane, then evil) and the spryness of her maneuvers, and the strength of her blows. Which didn't sound like Rochelle, at all. I would

---

[103] Interpreted: Rochelle was a crazy stalker girl.

never describe her as spry or strong—whore, bimbo, idiot—those worked. Sorry, if that offends[104].

"Then, I run for stairs and go out front of building. Hide in bushes. She come out and get in car, drive away."

"Where's the body now?"

Mr. Kim looked like a sheep guarded by wolves. "I eat."

I stared at him for a moment and then acquiesced. It was as good a source of protein as human[105]. A world of food opportunity opened. I asked, "Is that it?" It would have been enough if it were. It was the most information I'd retrieved since the zombie outbreak and finding Shane in my car. So, I was pleased.

But, Mr. Kim shook his head. "There something wrong with weather woman."

"Wrong? Well yeah, she's a psycho bitch. What do you mean wrong?"

"After get in car . . . change." Mr. Kim's face lost its helpful glee. A frown and slow darting eyes took its place.

"Change?"

"Yah, change." He measured his words out slowly, stressing each. "Face, head, body. Change. Make different."

"You mean like a werewolf, leopard or bear? That kind?"

"No, change to different *person*. Rochelle like *Playboy* centerfold . . ." He acted out breasts with shy hands at his chest.

"Yeah, yeah," I said. "Fake tits."

". . . and, long yellow hair. New woman, short." He brought tensed hands to his head to indicate a mannish cut, his facial features sharpened in expression.

"Was her face severe?"

"What means severe?"

"Sharp. Angry." I was more hopeful with that description.

---

[104] No, I'm not.

[105] Werewolf, it's what's for dinner—the other, other white meat.

I furrowed my brow and pursed my lips. That fit the image I already had in my head.

"Severe. Yes."

Hmmm. Short-cropped hair on a mannish face—a T.L.D.[106], if you will—and a professional shapeshifter? Are you thinking what I'm thinking?

Claire-fucking-Bandon.

There's that name again. The route she'd sent me on led straight back to her. That bitch.

I kidnapped Mr. Kim and brought him along on my way in to downtown. I couldn't help but think that I was in danger, not that he'd be much protection. But, two zombies were better than one in a scuffle—at least, it spreads the skin damage around. The fear crept in through my cracks, like a rat flattening itself. Maybe it wasn't just the proximity to the story of Oliver's bludgeoning death. But, the degree of manipulation, the lengths Claire had gone to pull off this ruse. And for what? I was freaked out. The woman had really run a number on me, not to mention Oliver.

The tracker's house was lit up like a holiday sale, every window shone bright through wide gaps of curtain, even the second-story advertised party. The street was crowded on one side, with a long line of parked cars, Mercedes, Bentleys, and a few Italian sports cars, as slim as anorexia. I pulled into Clevis's circle drive. The house was an unfashionable Tudor, with rough, crème-colored walls blocked in by broad stripes of walnut boards. Beside the entrance a tall window climbed to the second story. Celebrants could be seen dotting the stairs in party dresses and funerary suits, cocktails held high and clanking.

I changed my mind. Mr. Kim stayed in the car, for this was no concern of his, and I'd no intention of causing him

---

[106] T.L.D.: Traditional lesbian 'do.

harm, after the favor he'd paid me. I carried the coffin from the back seat, and knocked on the heavy wood door; my knock barely made a sound.

A woman answered, Asian, with a black shiny oil slick of hair that reflected light like onyx; her plump mouth was a pincushion of collagen. "Are you here for the shower, darling?"

"Um . . ." I looked around at the party guests, and saw no ribbon bouquet–carrying bride or expectant mother, and there was no rain, just then. Confused, I responded, "No. I'm here to see Clevis." I lifted the box; she looked down at it, nodded.

"Follow me. I think he's in the lounge."

She slinked off like Ms. Scarlet and I followed, hoping to get a clue[107]. The house was splendidly appointed, compared to most houses—antiques mostly—though the main hall was home to an enormously lavish chandelier that hung like a pierced clitoris, among more sedate furnishings. In competition with mine, it would rank a close 100th, but I'm being generous.

At the top of the stairs, Nick, the incubus from Lutefisk Bowl, chatted up a similarly blonde model-type. She giggled behind an oversized cocktail. I didn't think she'd be giggling with that big pitchfork of a dick in her.

Just past the stairs, a passage led off to the right, its walls lined with small Picasso figure prints lit from above. It ended in a cracked door, light filtering from its edges, spilling into the thin space to create a checkmark across the floor and up one wall.

Inside, a small bald man—I hesitated to think the word midget, considering my track record of misjudging mind readers—sat behind a broad banker's desk. He did not look

---

[107] When I say things that are ridiculously obvious, *please*, just ignore it. It's a pathetic attempt at humor, really. It should come naturally, like it usually does.

up from his work. Behind him, the wall was plastered with street maps pinned liberally. Small colored flags dangled from the thin tacks.

This was him: the tracker. He looked up at me.

The Asian woman crossed the gap between the door and the immense piece of furniture and sat on top, leaning backward and accepting a kiss from the little man. Her dress, a cascade of chestnut satin, dripped down her legs. She'd be considered gorgeous if it weren't for the overly enhanced facial features. *Cosmetic surgery doesn't have to be ugly, people! Go for the natural look. Bold strokes are for Pollack paintings. Slight accentuations are much more attractive.*

I stepped forward and placed the casket on the desk. The man was brown on brown on brown, eyes, skin, suit, with only minor fluctuations in hue.

"What's this?" he asked in the deep Scottish voice of a more robust presence. His eyes scanned from coffin to me.

"I'm Amanda. I called you about my friend a couple of days ago?"

His eyes were unblinking, unimpressed. Had he known I'd looked inside, even so far as to have fondled the amulet, worn it like a video star, he might be more animated, to my detriment. I decided he had no clue. So much for Milton Bradley.

"Liesl Lescalla? You sent me on a task?"

Still no response. The Asian woman smiled and looked me up and down. I decided she was Chinese; she had the posture of an actress. Hong Kong, maybe. She said, "Nice shoes."

". . . up at Lakeview Cemetery?" I stuck my tongue out of a menacing face and clawed my hands in the air. "Ghosts and shit all around?"

"Ah, yes," he replied finally. He scrawled his signature at the bottom of a letter and folded it in thirds, slid it gingerly into an envelope. He sealed it with a wet sponge from a china bowl, and gestured to the casket. "Well, there it is."

"There what is?" I refrained from asking what I really wanted to ask, which was, *Did everyone have to be so fucking vague?*

"Open the box."

"But you said, 'Don't open the box'."

"Dramatic effect! Just open it."

Asshole, I thought. It is really too bad that I pay attention to people at all. They are so disappointing. I pulled off the lid and lifted the pendant from the black satin cushion, handling it as delicately as an egg. I made sure to widen my eyes, as though I'd never seen it. "Now what?"

"It's a necklace, is it not? So. Put it on. Go ahead."

The Chinese woman nodded, a coy smile curled from her lips. I did as instructed, expecting something mystical to happen, a glow perhaps, or the sudden movement in the amulet itself, the emblazoned bodies writhing, something. In the end, not so much. It just hung there. I lifted it and let it thud against my ribs. Nothing.

"What is it supposed to do?"

"It's just good luck. Like a rabbit's foot." He giggled and the woman laughed silently, covering her mouth. "Just kidding. It's your ticket."

I lifted the amulet and looked at it again. Ticket? Things were looking up. "For what, where?"

"To the nursery." Clevis narrowed his eyes.

"Nursery? You mean like a garden center?"

"No, no. The nursery where you'll find Liesl." He scribbled a few lines of letters and slid the piece of paper across the desk. "Here's the address. Do be quiet when you knock."

Chapter 23

A House on Bleak Street

A note on the weather: It does not always rain in Seattle. During certain supernatural spawning there may be some instability in pressure. Do not be alarmed, why not instead watch the human news stations make it into a catastrophe, that's always fun . . .
—Paranormal News @ One

The directions led us to a slick walled modern house on the appropriately named Bleak Street. It hung over the freeway on stilts like a creepy French clown. Its windows leaked faint illumination, seemingly from candles. I left Mr. Kim in the car again, though this time he seemed sheepish and disappointed. He was growing on me, like a stray cat.

I lightly rapped on the metal door. Trying to be quiet. So much so, I thought I wasn't heard, until the *clip clop* of high heels came, and the door opened. It was wider than a regular door and spun on a central hinge like a revolving hotel entry. A woman answered it.

When I saw the tall black woman before me, the first thing I noticed was her amulet, the same as mine. Then I saw her face, those regal cheekbones and light brown eyes—she was smiling through plump *Shiseido* Red.

It was Liesl.

"Oh . . . my . . . God. Where the hell have you been?" I asked. It's amazing how quickly one can move from happy to see, to . . . want to see dead. I was furious.

"Right here. What's the problem?" she said, turning and clip-clopping back into the house. I noticed her attire. A fluffy white bathrobe stained a bright crimson in more places than not. Through a doorway to our left three similarly stained women lounged at a dinette set, smoking, drinking coffee, and flipping through magazines.

"Smoke 'em on the deck, ladies!" Liesl called.

"Well, seeing as how you've been missing for a week, now?"

"What are you talking about? I haven't been missing. I'm not sure you're aware—and how could you be, really—but this is the time of year when we multiply."

"No," I said, refusing to believe that this whole escapade was an elaborate mistake. One that could still prove deadly, considering. I started to whisper, "I don't believe it. Where are the kidnappers, Liesl?"

A nerve throbbed on Liesl's head, pulsing. Across her forehead a slash of red substance bled from her hairline. "You're such a tweaker, Amanda. Did they come up with cloud for zombies, while I've been working?"

"Working?" I crossed my arms. Because really? What the fuck?

"This is the nursery for the little baby inkys and suckys," she said in a horrendously mouthed baby talk, accentuated by a rapid clapping of her hands. "They are *so* cute, I just want to eat 'em. Want to see?"

She trod off down a hallway. I followed. Windows lined one wall, they looked out over Interstate 5. I flinched at the sight of the speeding cars, blurring past mere feet below.

The hall opened into a large vault of a room, its far end furnished with a row of seven bassinets, in its center, a mattress soaked in blood. There were leather binding cuffs and chains strewn about. In the corner to my right, two green garbage bags bulged. Even my barbaric nose could detect the subtle hints of iron and slick sweetness. I wondered what had gone on here. A feast? I noted the amount of waste and thought about the poor children in Ethiopia, although, on second thought they probably wouldn't be interested in my idea of food. But, if you are hungry enough, who knows? I'm just being insensitive; of course, they'd eat it.

Liesl was standing by a bassinet, rocking it gently. When she looked at me, I gestured to the mattress and the bags in the corner. "Rough birth?"

She smiled. "Not particularly." Her expression was flippant, eyes blinking rapidly, playing dumb. "Come look. They're so lovely."

And, they were rather cute little critters, which is a much more accurate word than babies, as these were more, well, crittery[108]. They were round, and long, like those kid toys, *Glo-worms*, I think they're called. But their eyes brandished spiraled pupils and were dark red. They were wrapped in plush blankets, like breakfast burritos. The one I was looking at made kissy mewls at me, from a tiny mouth. It must have been a baby incubus, or—what had Liesl called them, inkys?

"This one's already a flirt," I remarked. "You're right Liesl, they are precious."

She gleamed with pride. ". . . and deadly dangerous, too. But mostly just cute." She patted the closest infant's belly, if that's what it was.

I had learned so much, over the past few hours, but in many ways, more questions loomed. "Liesl?"

"Yep." It was in her arms, now. She rocked gently.

"You've got to bring me up to date, girl. This is a lot to take in." And, frankly the whole coming from Hell thing is sort of intriguing, don't you think?

---

[108] Crittery: Coined phrase number 27.

Unlike those other hambones, Liesl actually had a fascinating story, and a knack for the telling. It is quite rare to hear first hand accounts of Hell, particularly straight from a genuine devil's mouth. They're usually so secretive. So I wasn't completely bored with her yammering.

Liesl elucidated the story with the poise and regal elocution of a debutante, pure finishing school, a real classy bitch.

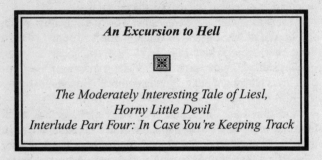

An Excursion to Hell

The Moderately Interesting Tale of Liesl,
Horny Little Devil
Interlude Part Four: In Case You're Keeping Track

"You've probably noticed an absence of red skin, horns and tail, and I can assure you, I have no pitchfork—because really, do I look like a farmer? The vermillion paste you saw is only for our rituals, to mimic the look of our former selves. You see, we slough that look in the transport process." Liesl's eyes wandered off, as though remembering. "I kind of miss the wings though; walking everywhere is so tedious, and these human shoes are pure torture.

"It comes down to this: I got lucky. I received a job offer that beat anything I could be doing in Hell. I have no regrets.

"I was born in a rural community far from the bustling Beelzehub of Hell. Which, if you haven't guessed, is not the fire and brimstone pit the Bible beaters would have you believe. Oh, to be sure, it's hot, sweltering even, but no more so than a rainy Vegas summer, or August in Orlando. What makes Hell Hell isn't burning in a lake of fire, it's constant work and no vacations. And, I was sick of it.

"Sick . . . of . . . it!

"It's laid out like any other country, only on a much larger scale—imagine the population! The Beelzehub is at its center—a bustling metropolis that in its cynosure breaches the clouds and spreads out to its lowest storied buildings in a circumference the size of Texas. Two hundred highways stretch off across the desert dunes—where the heat can reach glassblowing highs—like spokes on a wheel to populous regions where villages are as big as Tokyo.

"Each village is assigned a duty, which is managed by the Undermastor, who reports to the Mastor of the specific Highway, who reports to the Liaison to the Synod Speaker, who reports to the Synod itself. From there it gets confusing. All you need to know is that they're all in bed together, sometimes literally, and you can't trust any of them.

"Despair, where I'm from, is more of a hamlet than a village, about the size of Los Angeles. It lies far enough from a main highway, that it gets few visits from the Undermastor himself. Our work was simple enough, though, requiring little effort and repetitive. Lower-level soul sorting has never been a priority to the Synod. They just let us do our thing, which was essentially job placement for petty criminals, political figures, and children who stepped on cracks despite clear evidence of its outcome. We spent what little free time there was fucking—that's the number one leisure activity in Hell; second is masturbation; there isn't a third.

"So it was a surprise to be called into my manager's office one day, and come face to face with the Undermastor, who looks a bit like Kevin Spacey, I must say. Except for the crimson complexion and the skinned horns protruding from his forehead like a calf. He wore his wings down, and cloaked under a light black trench, which is the style in the Beelzehub, but in Despair it came off as elitist. My manager was shooed away and the honcho asked me to sit. The window behind me whispered with the etching of a sandstorm. He said he had a proposition.

" 'We've had our eye on you for some time,' he said.

'You're a lovely girl, dedicated to your work, scored high on grey matter, omni-orgasmic, and seemingly impervious to distraction of any sort. These are amazing character traits for Earth, but here, quite an accomplishment. Satan himself couldn't have conjured a more appropriate set of attributes.' The Undermastor's black eyes stared over the temple of his clasped hands, index fingers tapping his nose.

"I shifted in my seat. There seemed to be a question hanging out there. I thought I might be in recruitment for Satan's League of Whores, which despite the title was not just a concept, but an actual pack of female demons sitting around in mud baths waiting for the Big Guy's forked dick to twitch. Revulsion coursed through my flesh. I preferred to choose sexual partners, you see, and while that belief is not the norm in Hell, I planned on maintaining control of my own body.

" 'Liesl, how would you like to spend some time in a cooler climate?'

"I cocked my head. Cooler, I thought. Did he mean the hub? The League of Whores is said to have air conditioning. I cringed, my left stomach roiled.

" 'I'm of course referring to a tour of duty on Earth. Now, don't answer yet. I know that life in the Corps sounds glamorous, but it can be very nasty work. Very nasty. You'd have to leave Despair and travel to the Beelzehub, immediately. I'll give you a few minutes to consider your options.'

"The Undermastor strode to the nearby window overlooking the steaming factory floor. Thousands of thick pipes rose and curved like shower nozzles on either side of a wide conveyor belt. Steam rose from the open ends creating a shimmering haze. Souls ejected from each of them with a plop, turning from milky misshapen masses to corporeal form as they connected with the moving surface. Red arms snatched at the new arrivals with the efficiency of machines, tossing them through the air into various bins, marked deprogramming and trade school and upper management. From the sorters, workers sucked the dead up into huge vacuum hoses, delivering them to their assorted destinations. The workers were drenched with a feverish sweat that beaded on their red skin like white candy dots; nearly all flapped their fleshy wings to create a bearable breeze. This was a 'sweat shop' in the truest sense of the word, but the swing shift crew only had another ninety-seven hours until half-shift fuck-break. The home stretch.

"He started to move for the door. This was not a choice. It was like winning the lottery. 'That's not necessary. I'm ready now.'

"The Succubus Corps Basic Training Camp is a twenty-story building connected to the Great Mall of Indecency in Southwestern Dreary, a major suburb of the Beelzehub. The Undermastor was right; in addition to being more spacious than the factory in Despair, it was significantly cooler.

"In my first days at camp, I was assigned a partner and a tracker, Clevis, who you've obviously met. The job was laid out simply: Fuck humans, strip and deliver souls, increase our number through hybridization. That last bit I can't go into specifics on. You've seen too much as it is and must promise to keep your mouth shut. I know you will.

"The trainings at SCBTC were minimally pleasurable exercises in human mating rituals. The complex utilized a recreation of an Applebee's Restaurant, where we ran pick-up drills and familiarized ourselves with your wonderful cocktails. I became enamored of strawberry margaritas from the first day. The sex act took a little getting used to, logistically speaking. Humans are so fragile and soft. I hate to tell you how many I broke just getting on top of them—the size differential had a bit to do with that, I think. Really tedious machinations, as you can imagine, but the unit orgies were amazing. They had to be, to make up for all the boring human sex.

"The orgy stadium was intentionally the most comfortable of spaces. The coaches made sure of that, and only the top one hundred grunts of the day got tickets. Needless to say, I was there every day. The floor of the place was a massive tufted cushion made from a slick vinyl-like material that was hosed and mopped off regularly to avoid the accumulation of noxious fumes that our fluids can sometimes generate—a little known fact, don't spread it around. The ceiling expands to allow for various aerial positioning and for flying mounts. Just thinking about the room gets me going, a little bit.

"I remember this one orgy. It lasted nearly two hundred and twelve hours. I ran through every possible maneuver and left there sore from my asshole to my nasal passages. My red skin was raw to the point of purple. I needed a real hosing down after that one, and more than a few gauze pads.

"After training, our group was assigned to Seattle. We had a glorious graduation parade through the streets of Dreary. The citizens threw streamers of ash and blew stolen horns from the Lights, the angelic sound blistered in the heat, warbling. The wonderful smoky odor of a forest ablaze filled the air. The Liason to the Synod, herself, presided.

"We left for Earth the very next day.

"That experience wasn't so wonderful, and I'll leave it at that. I did mention the sloughing of our natural bodies rite? Dreadful."

Despite Liesl sharing so very much of her personal life, she left some questions unanswered. I reached into my purse, digging for that hunk of plastic that had got me into all this in the first place, her cell phone.

"Liesl, if you weren't in any kind of trouble, why did you text me the message?"

"What message?"

I pulled the phone from my purse and clicked on the saved message. "Help me" glowed. I handed it to her. "This one."

"I didn't send you that message. In fact, I lost that phone, before I was called away for the harvest."

"The what?"

"Oh, no, this." Liesl swept her arms about indicating the birthing. "When my other called to me, I had to drop everything. I guess that included my phone. I can't be sure where I lost it."

"Then I wonder who sent the message?"

"No clue, Amanda."

Liesl busied herself tightening blankets. I sensed it was time to excuse myself, as I had a guest in the car. I looked at my watch. 2:30 A.M.

"I'm going to leave you to your mothering." I turned to walk back down the hall. Then, turned back. "We could use some time to catch up. Is there a chance you can come to the opening of Mortuary on Saturday? I have a feeling it's going to be eventful."

"I'll see if my other will escort me. I'd love for you all to meet him."

Liesl was so polite. I loved her for that.

"Okay, then. Call me tomorrow night and we'll set it up. But plan on dressing to impress." I thought of the tracker's moll and her chocolaty satin. "I'm thinking satin slip dresses, what do you think?"

"Pretty."

Hey. I'm not above idea thievery. I let myself out.

Chapter 24

Duck and Cover

Supernatural crime statistics show that Seattle has the lowest number of violent crimes committed against other undead by vampires, zombies, demons, and the assorted faerie breeds. Unfortunately, the data confirms a tendency toward impulse control problems amongst the shifting population . . .

—A Taxonomy of the Dead

Mr. Kim was so happy to see me, and he followed directions so well. He hadn't even removed his seat belt. He just sat there with a huge grin on his face that didn't move. His eyes held my gaze. They were unblinking, dry dusty marbles—so very dry. From a small hole in the center of his forehead, a slow ooze of aging yellowed pus glugged, like a leftover squeeze of Mrs. Butterworth's gone stiff on the side of the bottle. Behind him, on the headrest, was a reef of grey coral, spattered with brown beads of blood and lumps of hairy scalp.

My eyes skipped to the windshield. I'd seen enough CSI to know that the bullet had come from the opposite direction of the big splatter on the headrest. There on the center of the passenger side, the glass was pocked and thin cracks radiated from the hole like roots.

Poor Mr. Kim. He was so nice and helpful.

Oh, wait . . . hello.

Danger.

I stumbled from the Volvo and backed away in a feral crouch, hands gone instinctively to claws. What if the shooter were nearby? *Was it stop drop and roll?* From off to my right I heard the shirring slide of metal on a track, the slamming of a door. I craned my neck to see the blue van, any other time a sight to elicit fury—now quite welcome. Behind its window, the red light signaled record. Maybe they'd caught it, *Undead on Tape*, and all. At the very least they might provide some protection. A bullet hole didn't really go with my outfit.

I charged the vehicle, weaving in a crooked line, to avoid being "scoped" or "sighted" or whatever the fuck a sniper might do through his viewmaster. The only thing I was sure of was that he was not flipping through Disney cartoons.

I scrambled low across the blacktop, reaching the van in a matter of seconds. I slid twice on the slick toes of tan Coach pumps, nearly cracking my ankle. But they were too cute. I pressed my face to the window and clawed at the door handle. Locked.

"Open up Hansen! Jesus! I could use some help here!"

I heard a quiet *pfft* as a bullet whizzed past followed by a hollow *thunk* when another punctured the van's side. I flattened myself on the concrete, ruining a Calvin Klein skirt in the process, and not just muddied, a full-on tear spread east of the seam[109]. The door slid on the opposite side and that familiar voice called out.

"Get in here, we're gonna get killed," Hansen cried, and then to someone else inside, "Yes, goddamn it. Did I say to stop filming?"

"But? But?" the other voice stuttered.

I crawled around the van, hugged close to the ground, my

---

[109] Damn all this intrigue!

left shoulder skimming the fender and bumper, cleaning road grime and tar from it, another ruined item—reminder to self, time for a shopping excursion. I certainly would have been up for some browsing then, or anything, even a ride on the senior citizens bus to the dollar store—desperation is horribly unfashionable. As I rounded the driver's side fender, I felt hands reach for my waist out of the darkness, pulling me forward and up into the open gap of the van door.

We were face-to-face then, probably mirroring open-mouthed horror. Cameron was attractive despite the height difference, which wasn't revealed from a sitting position, indicating a longer torso—totally proportionless—but, his skin was tan and flawless—damn him—like mine used to be[110]. The cameraman was obscured behind the big lens and a spotlight. It was pointing at us.

I turned back to Cameron, panting, and out of breath. Odd considering I didn't actually breathe, but that's nothing you don't already know. I was reminded of the buffet in the south-side motel room, and the breath that had squeaked out into the computer geek's face sparking something within him. I realize that the spark I saw was undeath. Now I was exhaling, and the breath had emerged, again in thick white tendrils, uncoiled and undulating like the stingers of a Portuguese man-o-war. Cameron shifted his body away to avoid connecting with the solid air, his neck stayed stiff, like the animations of a puppet. An "*ew*" came from behind the camera. I tried to inhale the breath back, but found myself merely biting at it, taking it in chunks, and swallowing. Finally, when the breath hung in loose zeppelin shapes, I sucked in the last of it with a gagging painful intake of air. My pipes were getting rusty.

"Wow, Amanda," Cameron said, nodding smugly. "A socialite and a breather, I'm impressed. But you're going to have to keep that in check."

---

[110] Please join me in a moment of silence.

"Whatever, little man. Who's shooting and, why? I thought as supernaturals, we'd be past guns?"

He looked up toward the window. "You're right, we are. They . . ." He pointed a shaky finger out the window. "Are not."

"Not past guns or not supernatural?"

Before he could respond, the back window blew out and we were sprayed with glass, gore and chunks of cameraman, suitable only for stew meat, and, then, only if you picked out the glass. Who am I kidding? He was totally inedible. A shame to waste so much food, though; did I mention he was overweight? Cameron was scrambling over a padded center console into the driver's seat and fumbling for drive on the tree.

Approaching from behind were three shadowy figures, two in pants, the other in a skirt. The bitch carried a thin rifle, while the other two were armed with heavy looking shotguns. As the van shifted forward, Mr. Kim's assassins broke into a run, raised their guns, and began to fire. I saw a green apron with a Starbucks logo on the front as they passed under a streetlight. I ducked out of the way of a spray of fire. They were silent between shots.

Cameron picked up the pace and took the corner with such ferocity that I was left tumbling in the van's seatless cabin. I slammed into the door with my arm bent back far enough to jar the nicotine patches loose. The cameraman's body slid toward me, releasing a putrid wave of liquefied innards. He had been a zombie. I, apparently, would have been right to leave him unbitten—quite a good makeup job, though.

The ride smoothed out. We left our assailants and my rental behind.

"Those were Karkaroff's people," I said, blinking away a slick gob of fat from my splattered face.

"Karkaroff?" he sneered. "What the hell are you talking about?"

I began to explain the zombie plague scheme, but the actor was wild-eyed and fumbling for something in a cargo pant pocket. He withdrew a phone and held down a key with a decidedly pointed thumb, speed dialing.

"Are *you* all right, sweetheart?" he asked, breathless. "I know. I know . . . They were shooting at us . . . Mmm-hmm . . . Bill's dead . . . Yes . . . I know, it's horrible . . . Are you safe?"

Who was he talking to, I wondered. Someone else knew we were being targeted? And before I realized it, I uttered the famous line of every bad horror movie, "What's going on here?" Usually, it would signal my death, but in this case, that would be the least of my problems.

Cameron either hadn't heard, or didn't give two shits; he continued his call. "They haven't tried to get in the house . . . how are the babies?"

Click!

The lights are now on. He was the other.

I only had to wait a few seconds for confirmation.

"Okay, Liesl, call Clevis and let him know to get a guard over to the house . . . I know they'd need an amulet to enter, but the bullets wouldn't . . . Just humor me . . . Tell the guard to get that Volvo in the garage before the cops see it . . . I love you, sweetie . . . I will. Bye." He pressed *end* and the phone darkened.

Do I need to state the obvious? Cameron was Liesl's other. Gross, she must tower over him. I'd need to talk to her about self-esteem.

"Now, what's all this about Karkaroff?"

"I'll tell you later. Let's take this party to the Well and re-group."

In the shock of the realization, I'd nearly forgotten about Karkaroff's barista death squad. My head needed to settle. Cocktails were in order, many of them. Looking down at myself, and the state of my designer fashions, caused a pit to open in my abdomen. My stomach sunk inside it. I decided on a detour.

"On second thought, Cam, let's head to my apartment, I

need to get presentable." The truth was, he didn't look much better.

Behind its ice waterfall, the Well of Souls hid a secret room. In the future, the space would become our lair, the VIP party spot. We were all there, except Liesl, who had more important duties, namely, the care of newborn hairy maggots with glowing eyes[111]. A series of bistro tables was lined up, draped with white linen, and surrounded by chairs. A variety of crystal chandeliers hung at random heights, shaded in delicate fringed paper. The walls were striped in multiple colors. Someone had been to Le Cirque. Lowballs and glass pitchers of various cocktails sat in metal bowls of crushed ice, on antique French sideboards.

Roll call: Wendy, Gil, Ricardo, myself, Shane and our odd new compatriot, Cameron Hansen, film star and sleazy reality show whore.

The conversation flowed along with the liquor, while the group was let in on the events of the night, everything from my first meeting with Claire, to the crash with the stalker bitch, to supernatural bowling leagues and werebear attacks, to our miraculous escape from the Starbucks Gestapo.

I finished with, "Since we know that Liesl is safe and was never in any danger, I say we just drop everything else and pretend we don't know anything about a plague of zombies.

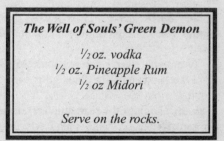

The Well of Souls' Green Demon

½ oz. vodka
½ oz. Pineapple Rum
½ oz Midori

Serve on the rocks.

How about it?" I drained my green demon (see inset) and reached for the half-full pitcher of glowing lime liquid.

[111] It's a living.

Shane interjected, "Well, we can't really do—"

"I was being ironic, Shane. Obviously, we can't. It's too late for that and people are dead . . . or, *deader*." I thought of poor Mr. Kim and his permanent smile, a line of yellow goo bisecting his face like a court jester's mask.

"I prefer deadish," Wendy said with a wink, and held her glass in a toast.

"I say we just call the bitches together and lay it out," I said. "Like an Agatha Christie drawing room scene."

"I'm afraid that might end in a bloodbath, and of that Ms. Christie would not approve." Ricardo had entered the mix. During my monologue he stood against the wall, holding his bottom lip between his thumb and index finger. He'd opted for the natural look, no make-up, and I could easily picture him standing off to the side in a Spanish firing squad painting, by Goya. "I know you two . . ." he motioned to Shane and me. ". . . are certain that Elizabeth Karkaroff is behind this Starbucks doomsday plot. But I'm unconvinced. If Claire Bandon's ability to shape shift, as you say, has progressed to the imitation of human likeness, then I propose that *she* has been imitating Karkaroff."

"What?" I was shocked. It hadn't occurred to me at all. Though, I'm sure it would have come to me, eventually. "If that were the case then, perhaps she's someone in this very room," I proffered, pointing a stiff finger at each person in turn.

"Whatever spaz, drama much?" Wendy tossed back her drink and reached for a pitcher.

"It is possible," Shane said. "I, for one, had never met Elizabeth Karkaroff before the day she approached me with the job offer."

"Describe it." Ricardo slid a cigarette from a metal case and tapped the loose tobacco.

"Wait, wait," I said. "What makes everyone think that Claire couldn't be among us?"

"Well," Gil said. "It could be that she was out in the club dancing with some human woman—who had victim written all over her—when we walked in here."

"What? Here? What if she tries something? Tries to kill us?"

"I thought it was Karkaroff that was trying to kill us," Cameron said, keeping copious notes on a small PDA.

"She is!" I leaned across the table to snatch at his chin. ". . . and this is not TV show material; if you're going to be in on this, then at least pretend to be helpful."

"Then why would she want to kill Mr. Kim? He seemed to be the only witness against Claire Bandon." Ricardo swallowed a Hypnotiq® blue slurry of fluid, from a frosted glass.

"I don't know, okay! Why do you think I've got all of you around? It wasn't either Claire or Elizabeth shooting anyway. It was her barista goons."

"Just calm down." Ricardo's voice vibrated like calming cello strings. "We can't have you exerting your lungs. There are people in this room who would be adversely effected by your breath." He gestured to the vampires—I wasn't aware of that fact, although Cameron had reacted like it was the plague, so maybe he could be harmed in some way, too? Wishful thinking.

Ricardo continued, "Now, Shane, detail your contact with Elizabeth Karkaroff."

"I was working on my doctoral dissertation at the university library—night classes, obviously—when this woman approached, quite striking and regal, but she wore the jeans and cable knit sweater of an undergrad. She asked me flattering questions about my work."

"And what was the subject of your dissertation?"

"The efficiency of drug delivery systems. Capsules versus gels, injections, blast delivery, patches. She seemed genuinely interested. She seemed to be flirting and I asked her out on a date, for the following evening."

"When we met, again, she rushed the conversation past

the romantic, and continued to press for information on time-release paradigms, and the dissipation of certain chemical compounds. We talked briefly about my financial struggles and she revealed herself to be a competent businesswoman and attorney who could help me a great deal. She arranged for an interview at Starbucks and I went. Despite my complete lack of experience, and to my complete surprise, I was given an executive position, with few responsibilities and a great salary. It was later that she gave me the gift of day walking, which obliged me to her."

I noted that Gil had crossed his arms tight across his chest and clenched his jaw at the comment. Jealousy is so ugly, particularly in vampires. For some reason, they don't see the need to hide it.

"While this is completely interesting, it is not exploring new territory. This isn't what I need from you," Ricardo said. "What I'm asking is that you tell us about the experience of being around Elizabeth. How it felt within you." Ricardo met my eyes. I recalled our run-in. The same force that Snell expressed came from Elizabeth. They were like moons altering the tides. That couldn't be said, as I recall, about Claire Bandon.

"I felt . . . uh . . . flattered by her attention. She is a beautiful woman—"

"Exactly!" I shouted. "Claire Bandon *is* behind this."

"Why do you say that?" Shane asked, confusion spreading.

"Because Elizabeth, and Snell, too, send out a vibration that presses into you like a bear hug. It's a threatening feeling. Although, now, I'm not sure if it's meant to be."

Ricardo nodded, with a small smile. "Elizabeth would be furious if she knew she was being impersonated. Or that we were having this conversation, at all, without her presence."

"Is she coming to the opening?" Wendy asked.

"She's been sent a personal invitation, of course. But it would be rude not to alert her as to what is happening."

I wasn't following the train of thought. "Why don't we just march outside and drag little miss copycat in here and interrogate her?"

"I'd think that would be fairly obvious."

"Well, as it turns out . . . Not so much."

"Claire has gathered an immense amount of strength around her, the ability to change at will into another person, as you say, and some kind of mind control or manipulation of these coffee girls, not to mention, Ms. Ali. At least in regards to the car accident."

"Rochelle? I hadn't thought she'd been under anyone's control. I was just thinking crazy stalker. I thought she was gunning for me because I'd expressed interest in Oliver."

"I can't imagine that's true, but we'll agree to disagree, and maybe we'll never know," Ricardo said, with his palms up. "I believe it is in our best interest to meet with Elizabeth and discuss a plan to stop Claire. As it stands, we could nab the changeling and still be unsuccessful in stopping the plague."

"I'm not sure about that," Shane said. "There seemed to be a missing piece. An ingredient that was sparse in the capsule. Karkaroff . . . uh . . . Claire had mentioned it once, in a conversation with one of her associates. An elderly man, zombie, I think."

My memory twitched like fresh road kill. Elderly zombie? "Black man?" I asked.

"Yes," he responded. "Come to think of it."

Wendy and Gil looked at each other, then me. "Let's take a meeting with Ms. Karkaroff."

"I think I'd better do that," Ricardo said. "Elizabeth and I have an ongoing relationship, of sorts."

Again, with the vague. Do you see what I mean? It's no wonder I'm not figuring stuff out. There must be a global brain rot going on, for people to be so forgetful and chintzy with their info.

Chapter 25

No Rest for the Wicked

Seattle is home to the exclusive Riyadh Morte, a four-star supernatural spa, catering to the elite of the otherworld. The spa provides low-impact treatments, safe enough for the deadest skin . . .

—Undead Times

I always liked to think of my Riedel glass of Pinot Noir as half full, while yours, on the other hand, is and will always be half empty. To my dismay, I found the opposite might just be the case. Not only was I seemingly unprepared for the cerebral task of solving mysteries, but I was starving and hadn't even thought to eat. I told Wendy I'd meet her at her car, but she was busy chatting up Gil, about the plot, and how horrifying to think that there'd be no more life to feed off if the zombie plague was successful. I'd already thought of other options. I'd start with the werebears—in human form obviously—they seemed particularly meaty.

On the way to the car, I snatched the closest hobo—yes, they still exist, although they've ditched the stick and hanky bag for stolen Chanel and Louis Vuitton knock-off duffels. Before he had a chance to scream, I'd unhinged my jaw, alligator-like, and swallowed him in five bites.

"Impressive efficiency," Wendy said, coming up from behind me. "Weird about Cameron and Liesl, right?"

"God, gag." I mimed an anorexia finger.

Cameron had gone back to the birthing center to be with his other, while Gil and Shane went on a blood hunt, although it was highly unlikely they'd gone together. Wendy suggested that we needed bonding time, and pampering. The slew of revelations and near deader experiences had me exhausted. I needed a massage and more cocktails.

Wendy knew of an all-night supernatural spa on First Avenue, just past the rescue mission[112]. To human eyes, the retreat was a boarded-up brick apartment building, to ours it was an oasis of shimmer and relaxation.

"Welcome to Riyadh Morte." The female greeter wore white silk pajamas, a white fez and sparkly bright vampire teeth that looked like she'd undergone Zoom!® Her hair was pinned into a loose up-do; copper curls trailed down the side of fake tan cheeks.

The front doors swung open to reveal a dark pool shimmering under a heated moon. Lofty potted palms anchored the four corners of the courtyard and shiny teak daybeds lounged under tents of striped cottons in blues and golds. Males and females of various breeds reclined, warmed by a gentle equatorial breeze, pumping its way through the room; it seemed to come from thin air, though the atmosphere was dense, scented by dates, frangipani, and flavored tobaccos.

Our vampire hostess led us to a private lounge to change into silk robes for our treatments, which apparently didn't require discussion.

"Your assessor will be by shortly to detail your luxuries," she said in a French accent and an obligatory smile, that somehow came off as genuine—and, I didn't even see any cloud Band-Aids—so, go figure.

Luxuries. That single word nearly erased the toxic events

---

[112] So it's perfect for those late night cravings.

of the last week. I wondered what kind of pleasures were in store. We disrobed and waited on the thick fluff of silk floor pillows for the mysterious "assessor."

"God, I really need to just chill out." I rolled my head in a circuit from right shoulder to left, and back again. "All the shit seems to be dropping down the chute."

"You've been through a lot. A massage will do the trick."

The private lounge was sectioned off from the courtyard by a thick curtain, and the interior had the appearance of the inside of a round pouf ottoman. Shantung, in cocoa and raspberry, was drawn up the walls in pleats and across the ceiling in a swirl, tightened by a single fabric-covered button, the size of a dinner plate, and resembling a dimpled nonpareil.

A shirtless young man entered; his hair was wavy black and hit just above muscular shoulders attached like epulets. He'd walked off a cheesy romance cover, to sit between us on the pillowed floor. His dark nipples, erect despite the humid warmth, stood out on olive pecs glistening with oil that smelled of cinnamon. Or, maybe, this was just a perception. The assessor was clearly Middle-Eastern, with large brown sinister eyes ringed dark to the point of shadow[113]; I wondered if he tasted like baklava, or even Turkish delight. Did I just drool, I wondered and pressed my fingers to the corners of my mouth. He smiled graciously, and looked not only at our bodies but around them, as well.

"Ladies, you seem to be tense. Your auras are dark and swirling with black notes. I interpret these to be confusion and fear, on the one . . ." he remarked in a thick Arabic accent that hummed as though escaping the dense sweetness of a bowl of medjools, ". . . and ooh," he said, as though finding a rare album of Islamic prayers, and rubbing his palms together. "Anger, on the other. Both are treated the

---

[113] In this new world, sinister was the new soothing.

same. We'll start with the aural massage and proceed to the venal shower and wraps."

"Oral massage?" I asked, gulping. I envisioned his mouth moving over every inch of my body. "And, venal shower?"

"Yes, our own patented technique of reenergizing the flesh of the dead, by infusing it with the platelets of the living. It's so relaxing. It's my favorite treatment." He licked his lips and winked from a naughty place. "You're going to love it. Follow me."

He led us through the courtyard. This time, a trio of Italianate beauties in the short white robes of Cinemax softcore porn, lounged at the edge of the pond. They hummed and chirped back and forth, in such a way that even the assessor strayed from his course to be near them. Their cadence churned around us. We were standing before them without any real desire to do so.

"Good evening ladies," the assessor said, "How were your treatments?"

They hummed in response, and a vibrating flutter of pleasure rippled inside my chest.

"Excellent, glad to hear it." The assessor led us from the courtyard through a hall lined with fluted columns interspersed with statuary. He explained, "The sirens take so little time for self-care. So dedicated to ship disasters, mainly ferries, you really have to respect them for centuries of hard work."

I imagined ships broken and impaled on rocky crags, dead and dying sailors and passengers strewn about or floating lifeless. Nearby the sirens filed each other's nails and spray tanned. Wendy and I nodded and continued to follow.

The passage funneled into a sunken chamber, at the base of a shallow stair. The floor was covered in a voluminous layer of pink sand. It shifted under us, enveloping our weary feet in subtle warmth. Two pillars of stone provided the base for massage tables, topped with sumptuous mattresses, one for each of us. The brown-skinned boy gestured for us to lie on the beds, and then exited with a tight bow.

The ceiling above us appeared to be the natural stone dome of a cave, slick, and flecked with gold sparkles and veins of ore, but free of artificial accessories—one of the few times it's excusable. There were no obvious lights in the room, yet it was illuminated.

"Neat trick with the lighting." I lay on my back and turned my head to the side to connect with Wendy.

"Mmm-hmm." Wendy's eyes were glued to the ceiling. She was not at all talkative. So unusual for her. I decided maybe we should discuss her favorite topic.

"Didn't you say you were going to bag Julian?" I asked, making up the name. They changed every day anyway.

"Yep, nailed him. I'm going to see him tonight, as well."

"Oh," I said in reply, but thought, what had she just said? She "nailed him and was going to see him tonight, too"? Odd, that never happened. Wendy's style was unwavering: pick up, fuck, eat. I decided to dig.

"You're going to see a human man, on two separate occasions. Since when?"

"What are you talking about?" Wendy said; her voice had taken on a tone of defense. And, as you know, I don't *do* tones.

"Nothing, nothing. How did the first date go, then?"

"You know, getting to know him. We talked a while. I think he likes me."

I sat up on the bed with a start, and jumped at the other woman, "Bitch, you better tell me what you did with Wendy."

"What?" Wendy's face registered wide-eyed shock, as she struggled under my grasp of her upper arms.

"I know it's you in there Claire. Don't make me beat it out of you."

But, even as I said the words, I knew they were empty. My mistake was a lack of subtlety in a situation that demanded it. The muscles in Wendy's arms began to thicken. Her pale smooth skin was replaced with a rapid growth of coarse black hair. In her last human words, before they were replaced by rumbling growls and that morose wilderness inspired howling, Claire said, "I thought you were too self-centered to notice."

Claire was shifting out of her Wendy costume into an animal. Something I'd only witnessed from a full-on run, in brief over-the-shoulder glances—Samantha had every right to be pissed, I imagined, but she did go overboard with it and stopped herself before she'd done something she'd regret. I feared Claire wouldn't have any regrets for tearing me into little chunks. Before I could withdraw my hands, her ironically feral arms slid through them. Her lengthening claws clamped on my wrists.

The skin of Wendy's face hovered over an active construction site of bone and muscle. Her brow and cheekbones extended to either side of her large pointing ears and her muzzle stretched out to resemble the snout of a giant German police dog; a dense covering of hair followed and grew long. The monster's chest heaved as though she'd drawn in all the air in the room and stayed puffed out while her waist thinned to an enviable degree. I followed the line of her body to her legs, which stretched out a few feet past the edge of the mattress. They were copiously corded with muscle and crunched loudly to bend in an odd angle above the foot.

But why go on? You know the drill. The bitch had turned werewolf on me.

I felt the proximity of her hot breath, before I noticed the transformation in her mouth. It washed over me in a heavy perfume of rot. Her canines expanded into blades, punctuating the horrors chattering around them. Her gums had sprouted seemingly endless rows of short, spiky, snapping teeth.

She sat up and stood, heaving me from my position of misguided attack and throwing me across the domed room with a roar.

I heard the crack of my head before I realized I'd even hit anything . . .

I became aware of motion, first by a jarring back and forth from head to feet and then by several jittery hops. I was laying on my side in a small space. My wrists were bound behind me and seemed to be connected to my equally pinioned ankles. The space smelled of oils and musty towels. I opened my eyes, initially to darkness and then, a thin line of muffled light became visible. But, I was drifting, again. My brain felt the soreness of a blow, like the fall in the garage that had essentially killed me. The last I knew of the space was a low pace of guitar strums accompanied by bass rhythm . . .

I awoke, for the second time, inside a rusty barrel at least twenty feet in diameter and towering into unknowable dark heights. I was confined to a dental chair by heavy bands of fabric tightened through metal buckles that reminded me of airline seat belts. Across from me was the huddled heap of a vacant body. His skin was dark and separated, to reveal dried muscle and tissue, the consistency of beef jerky. The remainder of his face was a lacework doily that exposed the inner workings of jaw and sinus. But, despite the state of decay, his identity was obvious.

Rude Wingtip Guy.

In an effort to determine the cause of his death, which immediately brought to mind torture, considering the state of his body, I scanned the perimeter of the room. My chair was surrounded by a roller coaster of hanging glass containers and rubber tubes. These were lit by several lamps standing on tripods of the sort mechanics use to do work on cars in driveways. Space heaters glowed red, and humidifiers hummed and sputtered puffs of moisture into the tropical climate of the room. Above my chair and slightly to the side was a stainless steel tray table crowded with nefarious metal tools, none of which looked particularly dull.

Just outside the ring of suspended glass jars and tubing, a TV flickered an image of a damp room with a single-paned window covered in condensation, its edges spotted black with mold. The walls appeared to be vinyl panels of a color not seen in this century. The carpet was shag and specked with browns and greens, but had probably been gold before the housekeeper quit. A woman was tied to an oak armchair and dressed, not in a silk bathrobe, or a terry sheet, but in obvious synthetic fibers, poly-somethings, that itched against skin like methamphetamines. What's worse, her feet were bare, and touching the filthy floor. I realized she must be in that most horrifying of residences—if you could call it that—a trailer[114]. I'd normally be only superficially disgusted, but as the woman raised her head of blonde hair, her pale skin revealed the image of my friend. Last seen exploding into a hairy monstrosity.

It was Wendy.

A jarring of turning metal sounded from within the room, followed by the squeak of decrepit hinges. Fresh air followed it into the room.

A voice projected from behind me, the direction of the damp breeze. "How are you dear?" Footsteps followed, closing in. I was in that instant enraged; I struggled against my bonds with every bit of energy I could muster. A *wondertwin* couldn't have tried harder.

---

[114] Unatrailaphobia: the fear of a single-wide.

Chapter 26

A Barrel of Laughs

Dentistry after death? What once was a ridiculous question has become the plastic surgery of the dead set. Supernaturals are crowding Mystical Dental for procedures like tooth sharpening to mechanical implants—saw blades, micro-drills, etc. . . .
— The Undead Science Monitor

The voice belonged to Shane.

I'm fucked, I thought, and not in a good satisfying way, either, but in an abrupt Shane way: unremarkable, disappointing, brief. My taste in men apparently hadn't improved; if only my taste for Martin hadn't been so literal. I regretted not turning him zombie—or allowing him time to transition, a more appropriate description—and keeping him by my side, a partner, a lover. He certainly had a knack for it. But here, with Shane up in my face, my anger slipped right past self-loathing as easily as if I'd been buttered. I lashed out, slapping Shane where it would hurt, right across his big fat ego.

"You were a fucking lousy lay, Shane!"

Even Claire, who'd entered the echoing room behind him, giggled, back in her Wendy mask. She stationed herself

somewhere off to my left obscured by the glow from the
television. On the screen, the real Wendy struggled against
the ropes that restricted her to the chair.

Shane's smug grin dropped into grimace with the velocity
of an amusement park thrill ride. And, I most certainly was
both amused and thrilled by the reaction. Until the bastard
slapped me back . . . hard. His wide palm barreled into my
right cheek, snapping my head to the left, with a painful jarring of my neck. The skin there seemed to drag my lid down.
The bastard had done facial damage. He had to die!

"You seemed to enjoy it at the time, bitch."

"Absolutely, Shane. You're *so* right. All ten seconds of it."
And that was being generous. "And, before you even bring
up that shit I said in the hall as a defense, that had everything
to do with your incompetence in the bedroom, and my personal generosity to tutor. I pitied you, thought maybe I could
put you through some training, so you wouldn't embarrass
yourself in the future. How old are you, anyway?"

Shane's mouth resembled a shrew's. The response came
from Wendy-Claire, "He's two hundred and ten."

"Two hundred and ten years old!" I barked, with much
mocking. "In that time, you'd think you could learn how to
please a woman." I turned my head to address Claire. "Three
jabs with that sorry wiener and he was done. I'd do better
with you." Then back at Shane. "At least she could figure out
how to get me off!" The words spit from my tongue like
venom.

Claire's Wendy-body shook with uncontrolled laughter;
she was bent in two, supporting her torso with her hands on
her knees. Shane powered a ferocious slap to the opposite
cheek—the force of it brought my face to within an inch of
his. His gorgeous face, made so ugly by the personality behind it, had the look of a gargoyle perched for centuries[115].

"Listen. I don't want to hurt you." His face was chang-

---

[115] At least two.

ing, now, all charming smile and white teeth. "But I am going to . . . gonna hurt you bad."

"Now don't fuck her up too bad," Claire said. "She's still your date for the Mortuary opening."

"The fuck I am!"

"Shh." Wendy's voice attempted to soothe, but had the opposite effect, considering the source. "You won't even remember this when we're done."

"Done with what?" I asked, voice shaking into a vibrato, glancing again at the tray of sharp dental tools. My sight bounced between Claire and Shane; both wore disturbing grins I'd rather not try to imagine again.

"The remaining ingredient to turn this planet into my kingdom."

"A kingdom of zombies, Claire? That's just crazy talk. Who will they eat?"

"They'll eat everyone, then when there's no human left, or they've all turned, they'll starve! Oh do go ahead and beg. 'Please don't go through with it, Persephone, please!' " She clutched the sides of her face mimicking the horror of that far-off situation, and faking a reaction that would *never* come out of my mouth. It was clear she didn't know me at all.

"Persephone? Persephone? Is that who you think you are Claire?" I vaguely remembered the goddess of the damned from a high school English assignment. Daughter of Zeus married to Hades, blah, blah . . . and blah. "And, who's this hambone?" I twisted my wrist under my restraints and jabbed my thumb toward Shane. "Is he your husband Hades? Sorry excuse if he is. You're both fuckin' nuts.[116]"

"Enough!" Claire ordered. She motioned to Shane. "Start the process, we need every puff of breath you can squeeze

---

[116] Now, before you get all high and mighty, thinkin' that this is no way for someone in jeopardy to act toward their captors, remember, this one's *already* dead.

from that bag of rot." She came up to the chair and bent down into my face; her expression was hatred, skin stretched over nothing at all, but hate. "I *will* bring the dark, girl. That is a certainty." She stomped off for the door, yelling back to Shane, "Every ounce of fucking breath!"

"Absolutely, my goddess." He seemed to do a nervous jig.

In the distance, footfalls on what sounded like hollow metal stairs. They trailed off into silence.

Shane inventoried the variety of tortures on the tray. I watched as his hand passed over a pair of nasty looking shears, slowed to a hover at a glimmering scalpel, and, finally, lighted on a curved pick, with a point so miniscule it could pry open pores. He stroked the tool as though it were a lover, tenderly, lightly pressured.

"Absolutely, my goddess." I turned Claire's order into baby talk for Shane. "Jesus Christ! You even sound like an impotent little turd. I guess she's lucky to have someone as servile and vacant as you, Mr. King. Oh wait . . . I just got it, Mr. King. King of the Damned."

Shane backed into a court bow. "At your service." he said, in a ruinous British accent, which had absolutely nothing to do with what we were talking about, and everything to do with him being an idiot. Jeez, what did I see in this guy? He spoke again in a more menacing monotone.

"I'm going to start you out like this . . ."

His voice trailed off and he leaned into me. Grabbing the sides of my jaw and popping my mouth open he inserted a square of metal, a spacer, which forced my mouth and jaw agape, wide enough to accept a small fist. From somewhere above my head, he closed a mechanism that framed my face; it held me so securely, I felt paralyzed from the neck up.

"And, this is the next part . . ."

The tray was beyond my vision, in that state, but I could hear the piercing clank of steel against steel. The bastard made sure to draw the tool across my line of sight, and my eyes followed it wide and with the first real horror since my change.

I mewled and pulled up off the chair with my hips.

The curved pick dipped down into my mouth, found an anchor and then blind pain ignited; my body screamed for my mind to go blank.

He withdrew the instrument and brought his face in line with my own. His mouth churned and he puckered. A thin rivulet of spittle dripped from his mouth into mine.

"That'll cool it off."

I heard him fumbling on the side of the chair. It shook and then began to move with the sound of electronic gears. My head was lifted to give a direct line of sight to the TV. Off to my right, Shane was typing a message into a Black-Berry.

"Watch this," he said.

On the screen, Wendy had stopped struggling with her ropes. Her head hung down, the back of her skull even with her arched shoulders. She heaved occasionally, sobbing, I suspected. It was torturous to watch. I shut my eyes.

"No, no, no, lover. This next part is very important."

I gargled dissent.

A clanking on the tray, and he drew a mechanism that looked like an eyelash curler. The tool had two flexible metal strips, attached to a pair of tong-like handles. Shane demonstrated that with a squeeze, the bands sprang into an oval shape. The sight of them blurred as he brought them closer to my left eye.

"Don't move now. I'd hate to slice it open, eyes are quite messy and pop like grapes with even a minor pressure from something this sharp." He squeezed the tongs lightly and they made an ominous, *click-click,* to accentuate his point. Shane was the worst kind of sadist, the cliché. He just *had* to describe the events, self-gratification barely hidden behind the wavy lip of a Peanuts character. I hope you never meet up with his type. The spank and nibble sadists are fun, occasionally, just to change things up. But this guy was totally out of control.

I howled with frustration and pain as he pressed the slivers between my clenched lids and pried my eye open. I felt a horrible scraping inside the socket. I forced myself to look straight ahead, lest he get sloppy and blind me. The corners stretched to the point of tearing. I relaxed a bit for a second one, for fear of cutting my eye in the struggle.

With both hostile appendages adhered, I had no choice but to watch the screen. A person entered the dingy room. A woman, in a white shirt, black pants, draped in a green logo apron, one of Persephone's Starbucks death goons, strode up to the chair, circled, and positioned herself behind Wendy.

She must be mortified, I thought. Wendy prefers the upper hand, in every situation. She's in control, even when she follows my ass around. Her suggestions are always welcome, and appropriate for the situation. She's my Betty Crocker Ho, and she was in trouble. I fought with the belts again. Every part of my body tensed, probably compressing the empty honeycomb of blood vessels, collapsing them.

The barista wrapped her right arm around the top of Wendy's head, pulling it backwards and lengthening the bound woman's throat, exposing it to vulnerability. My mind dragged a memory from its fat trap. Hostage footage from Al Jazeera. Serrated knives and beheadings. I tried to shake my head as though cold, frozen, to vibrate my eyes and blur the image, disrupt my suspicion of where this was all leading.

The woman drew up her left hand and pointed a scraggy unmanicured nail toward Wendy's cheek. She continued until the nail was touching the hollow of a dimple. Then, she started scratching, slowly at first, lightly, a caress. The victim's pale skin issued a deep purple hue and Wendy began to mouth the word "no," barely audible, over and over, like a chant.

The scratching became more direct, always at the same

spot, until the already loose covering gave way and a gash lit into the dead cheek. The woman began to pick at the tear exposing grayed mealy muscle. She looked up at the camera, and instructed Wendy to do the same, which she did. I hoped she was drugged; her eyes were sanded with defeat.

Then, the unthinkable.

The torturer pinched onto the tear and slowly pulled at it, until it gave, releasing a long ribbon of skin from Wendy's face. A scream echoed from the speaker as the ribbon, as if reaching the end of the Christmas roll, caught hold of some stronger attachment. The woman looked down at her work, wound the strip of skin around her finger and jerked it taut; it released with a further pull.

My eyes ventured to the body of my creator, lying on the floor. I could feel the thin pieces of metal cling to the balls. His face was stripped in a similar fashion. I feared this would be my fate. Even if I weren't killed, I'd not be suitable for viewing, not ready for prime time.

The woman loosed Wendy and stalked off camera. My dearest friend collapsed forward, spent from the pain, or the frustration, or more likely, the knowledge that her ability to draw male victims had been dismantled with no more effort than a child would exert.

"Startling footage, don't you think?" Shane asked.

He brought his index finger into my line of sight. There was dirt under the nail, or blood, the cuticle was shaggy and curled and the nail itself was jagged—he, obviously, chewed his nails. He wiggled it in the air, a prelude to a scratch, I supposed. But then withdrew it and continued to babble on, incessantly.

"I can't imagine how any of you'd think that I could jeopardize my new position as a day walker. I mean really, I'm just going to give it up and go back to being a slave to time?" He was moving around, now. Adjusting the heights of the glass bottles, which I saw were strung on some sort of pulley system. He removed the openers from my eyes.

I had wondered whether Gil had suspected such at our meeting in the Well VIP room. He appeared so disgusted with that particular topic and Shane, in particular.

"When Claire acquired the gift from Mr. Norris here . . ." He motioned toward the heap of rotting flesh in the suit. ". . . I would have done anything to get it. I was tired of living my afterlife in the dark. I'm bound for more important things. For greatness."

Does he hear himself? How does one become so grandiose? I feared it had to do with eternal life. They must be bored. But, to the point of insanity? Ricardo was perfectly sane, Gil . . . eh, probably not a good example, but I'd met some people who had it together.

"It's sad to think that the breather thought he could buy his life with such a gift. But I'm rambling . . ." He gazed down at the still corpse.

What was that; did he actually have some insight?

"I bet you'd like to know more about the gift itself; well let me tell you . . ."

Nope, not so much, not a lick. Shane went on to talk about an amulet of great power, stolen from the, and I quote, slut-u-bus's. I thought of the empty shadow box. As long as he wore it he would be safe from the sun and any other harm, almost. He brought it out of his pocket. A thin layer of dust highlighted the etchings.

I don't need to describe it again. You know it's just like mine. Except mine is where? Oh yeah . . . purse. Where else would you keep your super protection amulet? I wouldn't want to wear it, at all, or anything. I'm such an ass. I was sure they'd texted the help request, too. Probably left that phone lying there on purpose. Everything else seemed to be set up, including me spreading shit about Karkaroff. Shane had seen to that.

He rambled on, ". . . so it was kind of sad, then, that after we got your maker's breath, he didn't have any life left in him. So rare, you breathers—one in a thousand's my understanding. They say that you even have the ability to heal yourself over time; of course, it would take far longer than a human would. Heh. Beggars can't be choosers, right? Don't worry, I'll be more careful with you. After all, Persephone has plans for you. Of the servant variety."

Servant. You caught that, too, right? Now, I think we all know: that would be a tad inappropriate.

Nope, I thought. That is *not* going to happen.

Shane readied a plastic anesthesiology muzzle and covered my open mouth with it. It smelled of rubbing alcohol. Shane's wrist smelled of musky butt and nut sack[117].

"Give it to me, Amanda. Don't make me take it from you. That process will drain you. Just ask your daddy; he can vouch for that." He poked a thumb at the carcass.

I'm not proud of what came next.

Shane brought his fingernail up to my cheek and scratched lightly once. I glanced at the TV. Wendy sobbing.

Then, he scratched again, still lightly.

I panicked, heaving out every ounce of breath from my dead lungs. If I could, I would have vacuumed them clean and handed over the bag, too. The rubber hoses bulged with the white viscous breath and tendrils coiled into the glass receptacles like soft-serve vanilla. I half expected to see black specks of youthful nicotine addiction, pocking the coils of zombie breath, but it was clean. So *there*, take *that*, Surgeon General.

Actually, come to think of it, I'm not sure if it was a finger-*nail,* specifically. It might have just been his soft spongy . . . fingertip. But, in my defense, torture is like a Christmas present; it's the thought that counts, right?

"Wow. I knew you were vain. But, I don't even need to ask. That's all the breath you have. It's more than enough to supply our baristas with their little deadly gel-caps[118]." He

---

[117] That's a lie. It smelled like soap. I was just bitter and looking for derogatory comments.
[118] Little. Different. Deadly. New Maximum Strength Zombil. It's not just a sleeping pill. This one'll just kill ya.

busied himself with checking the bottles, spinning some in his palm to examine the process.

I wondered what my breath could do a supernatural; to Shane.

He wandered around the room, mumbling. "Have to be quick though, the breath is so fragile . . . dissipates in the water after a few minutes, only get a few doses out of a serving . . . something about the gel-cap turns the pure breath back into a mistake generator . . . haven't quite figured out why."

He removed the mask and the separator from my mouth and jaw. I clenched and unclenched my teeth. My jaw was numb from the abuse, like the ache of a prolonged blow job. Shane was watching the breath dissipate and bead up into moisture in the different jars. The final bottle accrued a fine powder that floated inside it like Sweet'n Low.

I had to *lay* into him.

"You bastard!" Spittle flew from my lips.

"Now, now. You're alive, aren't you? What's to complain about?"

"This isn't the playground, Shane. It's real life . . . er, death, I mean. If you think that dyke is going to take you as her *Hades*, you've got another thing coming."

"Shut up, you fat bitch!" he yelled and raised a whitening fist.

Oh . . . hell . . . no.

Mmm-mmm-mmm.

No . . . he couldn't possibly have spoken it. I hadn't heard it in years, but the feelings came springing back from the seventh grade. Janelle Cooper and Katie Swan holding me down, filling my mouth with the thick mud of a diet shake. I was literally seeing stars, but too angry to count the points. Whatever blood was left began to boil in my veins—you may want to cover your children's ears, although, frankly this will be nothing they haven't heard before in grade school.

"Fat?" I screamed and twisted in the chair, straining

against the bonds. "You motherfucker! At least I'm not some crazy lesbian werewolf's impotent little chew toy. You're a worthless piece of shit, you know that, Shane?"

"Shut up, shut up, shut up!" Shane's hands were clamped over his ears like Tupperware seals, he shook his head from side to side, eyes tight as screws.

"What do you think? Ms. Persephone is going to rule a world full of those mistakes that marched out of Starbucks the other day. There's no ruling them, you idiot. They're gaping, snapping mouths, on legs. When they run out of humans to eat, what then? I'll tell you what. They're coming after lycanthropes, and any other warm-blooded creature. That's right, *Hades*; even your carpet-munching wife will go straight down a gullet. Then what'll you do? Huh?"

That's all I had to say. But he didn't respond. Couldn't blame him really. But then, I thought of the anger, and *could* really blame him. I just had to add, "That's probably the most strenuous fucking you've had in a long time, huh, Shane?" I really couldn't help myself. What can I say? I just love to hear myself talk.

Shane was devastated; he'd collapsed on his knees trying to eke tears out of dry ducts. What a fool. P-thetic.

I let him cry for a bit and then let him off the hook, when I noticed a change of circumstance on the TV. Wendy was no longer alone in the room.

"Hey Shane, take a look." I jabbed my chin toward the TV.

Wendy was smiling directly into the camera. Around her were three little blonde girls in baby doll dresses, their hair hung in perfect ringlets. They took notice of the camera and wandered over until their bodies filled the frame. In unison, they wagged their little fingers in chastisement. They would have been RKO cute, had it not been for the pools of black tar they had for eyes; their obsidian depths brought to mind the hungry mouths of the reaper's transport. The girls disappeared.

"Oh no," Shane whispered.

Within the barreled chamber, three glowing black slits appeared, resembling snaggle-toothed vaginas. This was followed by a low hum that echoed into a growl in the circular room. The reapers stepped in unison from their doorways. The one on the far left held Wendy's hand, and motioned for her to stand back. They approached the weakened vampire and stood around him, as though they would clasp hands and play a game of *ring around the rosies*. Their tiny hands stretched out toward him, becoming claws, their blunt little Chicklet teeth gone needle pointy. Their eyes were deep black death holes, portals to somewhere else—where the screams live (or·go to die).

He was on his knees when one reaper grabbed his face and opened his jaws. Another squeezed and prodded his gums until his second canines slid from their garages of flesh. The third went in with a shiny pair of wire cutters.

It was Shane's turn to scream.

And, he didn't disappoint.

Chapter 27

Mortuary: All that Glitters

The opening of Mortuary—nightlife guru Ricardo Amandine's newest offering to the Seattle Otherworld—promises to be the social event of the summer, if not the year. If you haven't gotten an invitation you'll have to see if there's anyone left to blow . . .
                                                    —Otherworld Weekly

Wendy and I readied, primped and spackled. We opted for complementary colors and matching make-up. We curled and ratted our hair out, until it looked coiled to strike, Medusan; her hair was ash, mine a lush brown—it never hurts to remind you. Rather than downplay our dead skin, we highlighted it, showcased it in white powder, and shadowed our eyes and cheeks in kohl. For the lips, a dull blue shade was toned down to a dark as midnight hue. All in matte. Duh. We looked like a couple of MAC counter bitches, only more lifelike.

We donned satin slip dresses, braless. It was, after all, to be red carpet runway. Wendy's dress was black and low-cut to the navel, it trained behind her like cum-hungry groupies. Mine was gunmetal and backless; it clung to my form in smooth waves. I wore a long strand of pearls backwards, so they traced down to a diamond pendant that pointed to my ass. An advertisement, natch.

"Check it," Wendy said, spinning on the marble.

A quick side glance. I said, "Hotness."

I reached for a metal case embossed with the letters AF, and withdrew a cigarette; its paper dyed to match my dress, and twisted it into a long ivory holder. I held it out like a coy contract star.

"Oh my God!" Wendy shouted, not at all elegantly. "That is *so* the perfect accessory. I love it."

"I know."

We were ready.

The wait line rounded the corner, the usual sinister crowd, but the sirens from the spa were up front. A toilet clog of paparazzi were ten deep along the velvet rope. A trio of vampire criers in Victorian Morticiana shouted long streaming blood quotes into the night air; the words expanded and ribboned brightly like spotlights into the first clear night sky in weeks. The sign above the door glowed with fire, from cute little crematoriums; each of Mortuary's eight letters silhouetted by blazing gas.

The six of us fell out of the limo Gil rented, black and stretch, out into the throng of flashbulbs and video spots. Wendy and I shined like blind China dolls, skin as delicate as rice paper; both Gil and Shane wore Armani well, though the former was inordinately more robust and less boyish; he'd have me add that he stood at least four inches taller as well. Unfortunately, the black suit combined with Shane's white hair had the effect of a glowing voodoo candle—a dour one from the look of his face.

I jabbed him in the side. "You better make it chipper, Torquemada!"

The second crew from *Undead On Tape* yelled my name and got the finger. I grabbed Shane's arm—*why is he even alive*? Tortured, fangless, downtrodden, and along strictly for appearances, bait for the bitch—while Gil tucked his into the crook of Wendy's. Liesl and Cameron brought up the rear, as they'd been making out furiously like a couple of twelve-year-olds, despite repeated groans of protest, *so* gross[119]. I would have pummeled them with picket signs, if I'd had them.

A short dark hall led to a pair of swinging doors. They opened into a lobby of chintz wallpaper and travertine floors; the furnishings were funeral home chic, grandmotherly sofas, oriental carpets and a liberal dousing of artificial dust and webbing—way over the top. A grim top-hatted gentleman in a dusty topcoat attended to the coat check. He introduced himself as Lucien.

"Memorize these faces," I said. "We're going to be around, a lot."

Ahead of us, stairs led off to a passage labeled "The Drawers," while another sign pointed through a hole toward "The Embalming Room," and yet another to an area for "Viewing."

I glanced at a smirking Wendy.

"Please be appropriately somber," she said. The irony wasn't lost on her. We met in a funeral home, and now, were heading in to a showdown with Claire, in the aptly titled club. It was like a good luck charm.

The plan was in play. Karkaroff was furiously insulted at Claire's impersonation, vowing to help, to hear Ricardo tell it. She'd been the one to contact the reapers and arrange for our safe liberation—they were, likewise, on board for the plan. Shane talked to Claire, under heavy mental manipulation by Karkaroff, and insisted that everything was fine. As soon as she arrived, we would lure Claire into the ladies' room and confront her, keeping her there until the reapers arrived to do their jobs.

---

[119] Public displays of affection, while romantic to those involved, are, in fact, disturbing and icky. Leaving the witnesses as violated as molested children. Offenders: please make a note of it, and correct your behavior.

For it to work, everything must appear normal. So far, so good.

"We'll embalm her ass," Wendy said, stroking the thin, fading scar that ran from dimple to ear. The reapers had worked a bit of evil little girl magic on the cut, and it sealed up like a real live girl's would.

"No shit," I said.

Ricardo stood by the main entrance; he wore black Dior, but to be truthful, he also wore the building, like it was an extension of him. "Everything is prepared," he said as we approached. I winked at Wendy and Gil, Shane winced, Liesl and Cameron made out. He led us through the entrance into the main hall of the club.

Mortuary was a freak show. The design was fantastical and bizarre and I loved it. Upon entering, the patron experiences a sense of shrinking down to the size of a rat. Dead center of the space is the bar, set into the base of a massive steel embalming table. A giant body lay there, three stories above; its feet were visible, calloused, realistic. The body was draped by a gauzy shroud that cascaded down the table in pleats, drawn back to expose the bar beneath and secured to the table legs by surgical clamps the size of a fireman's jaws of life. Beside the bar, a massive machine pumped what appeared to be cognac up a thick rubber tube, which curved and undulated, ending in a metal spike that disappeared into the body. From the opposite side, viscous red ooze drizzled from a drain in the bottom of the table. It collected in a metal pan beneath it—the water feature preferred by nine out of ten serial killers.

The crowd was an eclectic mix of species. All types of were-animals and vampires mingled with shimmering apparitions and zombies. Clevis Walls and Mata Hari of the "nice shoes," stood nearby. The sirens made their way into the room. Ricardo greeted them, but ran his fingers across his lips like a zipper—I was to later find that they actually did not have names. So, Siren number one nodded agreement. A grumpy group of mylings sat in the booths that hugged the walls like platelets in a centrifuge. Near them, as though segregated by race, were the water sprites, wood nymphs and yetis. A large contingent of chimerae admired the blood pool, most notable among them a Jersey Devil and a densely haired chupacabra. A wendigo with tall antlers stood to their side, disgusted and ignoring them. The room was near capacity, but a scan of faces showed no sign of Wendy-by-Claire, at least not yet.

Ricardo clapped his hands twice, demanding immediate attention of his guests.

"Thank you so much for accepting my invitation. You are all most welcome here at . . ." He swept his arms out, theatrically. ". . . Mortuary!"

The wall of drawers began to click and shuffle open to various degrees, revealing the VIP seating— the destination for the stairway, designated to the Drawers—it makes perfect sense now, in an insane surreal way.

Ricardo was looking back into the lobby and gesturing to someone. "Enjoy!" He yelled to the crowd and the music began: Ladytron (see inset), thumped from the speakers and the overhead lights dimmed, leaving the club lit eerily by small lamps on the tables and uplights every

Mortuary Opening Night
DJ Malice
Set List

Ladytron • *Destroy Everything You Touch*
Oakenfold • *Faster Kill Pussycat*
Shiny Toy Guns • *Le Disko*
Scissor Sisters • *Filthy and Gorgeous*
Sasha • *Immortal*
The Prodigy • *Voodoo People*
Le Tigre • *Deceptacon*
Curve • *Hell Above Water*
Crystal Method • *I Know It's You*
Chemical Brothers • *Under the Influence*

few feet on the perimeter. The dance floor occupied the
space on the far side of the bar. It filled with a glowing fog,
dissected by a grid of laser light, and hosted a crowd of
dancers so mixed, it was like nothing seen before at any of
Seattle's clubs. People were going to remember this.

Ricardo waved us over and we followed back out into the
lobby and up the flight of stairs, down a hall to an elevator door
with a keyhole instead of a call button. He reached into the
interior pocket of his tux and withdrew a length of black ribbon, at the end of which was a key. With a twist of the key,
the elevator opened.

It took us to the uppermost loge, an aerie both lofty and
luxe, befitting our new status, I might add. Liesl and
Cameron took up a position[120] on a tufted couch, set farthest
into the balcony. Wendy, Gil, Ricardo and I crossed the
space and stood looking down over the club. To our right, at
slightly decreased elevation, natch, hung another balcony;
this one was occupied by a familiar, yet scary, face.

It was Wendy. Wendy-Claire.

Gil and I pushed the real one down to the floor, where she
sniveled something about dust on satin. I pivoted to see a
glum Shane, stalled near the elevator door. *Get your ass over
here*, I mouthed, pointing to the spot, where I expected his
feet planted. When he did so, I hissed into his ear, "If you expect to survive the night, you'd better follow directions."

Ricardo added, "Now, call down to her and tell her we'll
meet her downstairs."

He cantilevered forward, over the edge of the drawer and
yelled, "Wendy!"

Claire peeked up and simpered. She gave Shane a
quizzical look, to which he responded with a dorky team
sports thumbs-up. Claire nodded, a slow sneer spread
across her bland face.

---

[120] Not missionary, something more exotic.

"Meet us in the lobby!" Shane shouted. He twisted toward me, but averted his gaze.

"Yes!" Claire screamed and grabbed a wrap and her clutch, an apropos beaded albatross[121].

On our way out, I stopped to ask Liesl, "These are going to work, right?" I patted my chest.

"They should." She shrugged. Her face expressed little sympathy or concern as though we were simply going shopping.

"It should? That's not very comforting, Liesl. I would expect you to be more maternal just now—"

"It will, I mean. I'm nearly positive. Besides, Ricardo has a backup plan. Quit being such a puss."

I glared up at Ricardo. He shrugged and rocked his head, as if to say, "maybe no, maybe so."

"I want to thank both of you for *really* putting me at ease. It's so . . . soothing. It really is," I said, mouth split in a fake pageant smile one second, cat anus the next.

Wendy-Claire abandoned her corpse drawer before us, yet was nowhere to be seen.

"Maybe she's in the bathroom," offered Shane. He dusted imaginary lint from the lapels of his tux.

I glanced at Ricardo. He gave another unhelpful shrug.

What, exactly, do these people know? I wondered. *I'm pretty sure I'm more aware of; let's see . . . uh, everything. Jesus! No help, here.* I slunk off for the ladies'.

The Mortuary restroom was dark except for fabulous lighting over each sink, a muted pink, great for make-up application, not so good for watching your back. I propped my purse on the stainless vanity and touched up my lips, adding powder to take down the gloss. If I did say so, a look this

---

[121] It never ceases to amaze me. What *can't* Judith Lieber do with crystals and a hot glue gun?

flawless deserves to be on the nightly news, or front page of the supernatural gossip rags. I'd taken heroin chic to its next logical step: postmortem elegance[122].

Behind me, two vampires applied neon Band-Aids of cloud in an open stall, one, an atrophic redhead with a pinched overworked nose, wore a trail of ten hits running up her arm. She needed to check herself in to a clinic or, at least, trade in her addiction, for one more stylish[123]. The other one kept busy, squeezing the heady paste from a repurposed tube of Crest Whitening.

In the far stall, a pair of low-heeled training kicks gave away a certain hidden counterculture element.

"Is that you back there, Claire?" I called to her, emphasizing the name—I had no intention of referring to her as Persephone; I wasn't feeding into that delusion. I blotted the corners of my mouth, with a particularly soft facial towel, supplied from a shallow basket on the vanity. Next to it, various accoutrements, lotions, perfumes, even a small jar of vein concealer. Ricardo was so detail oriented. *Why weren't we together?* I wondered. *So similar.*

Claire left the stink of her stall and parked herself at the next sink. "Retardo thinks of everything," she said.

"Yes. Ricardo is quite fastidious." My eyes darted to the drugged out skanks in the john. "What's it going to be Claire? A meeting in the ladies' room?"

She shot a terse eye at me, as if not sure whether to laugh. Hmm? Oh . . . wait, that's a song from the '80s, right? *Klymaxx*, or Klymaxxx, or something. The tune began to weave its way into my brain like a parasite.

Before it could take hold, one of the wasteheads started singing it. "I got a meetin' in the ladies' room, I'll be back real soon . . ." They gyrated '80s style, authentic, except for the flat hair.

---

[122] Bitch! That's coined, right there. Postmortem Elegance.
[123] Shut up. Bulimia is making a comeback. I'm a trendsetter, remember?

"Shut up!" Claire barked.

"Yell much?" I turned to her and tilted my hip, resting against the vanity, exerting ownership. "I have to tell you Claire, I'm really surprised that you even wanted me alive."

She crooked back to the mirror and applied way too much blush, with a brush so overworked it was curled at the ends. "I was certain that Shane wouldn't be able to keep his mouth shut. I guess I was wrong. I need you around for *special* projects."

Special projects. Care to join me in a spine shiver? What the hell did that mean. *Special projects.* It brought to mind knee pads and dusty poon—*ew.* I don't think I need to tell you; that was not going to happen. Claire would have to shove handlebars through my head and work it herself.

"I have to tell you, Claire. The word 'special' creeps me out a bit. I'm not going down on you."

"Oh, do you have to be so dirty?" She scraped her nails around a shoddy lipstick job. The color bled up the fine lines that spread from her lips like drool.

"Well, *dirty* suits me like *fucktard* suits you, Persephoney," I said, but it even sounded lame coming out. *Stop it*, I thought. *Why must I be so self-critical? I sounded like my mother.*

"That's very amusing, Amanda."

"No, it wasn't." I pivoted to face her. "What is amusing is that your little world destruction plan has gone straight down the poop-hole."

The vampires giggled, one whispered, "Poop-hole." More giggles.

"See Claire, even the junkies think that's amusing." To the vampires, I remarked, "Stick with me while I wing it, girls."

"What the Hell are you talking about?" Claire clutched the marble counter hard enough to turn pink knuckles white. "Spit it out, girl."

"Sorry, but your supply of zombie pills . . ."

"What?" she bellowed.

". . . has been confiscated by the proper authorities."

"Excuse me?" Claire appeared to be ready for an aneurism, although I suspect that the bulging veins were the first sign that she'd be shifting.

"Oh, but surely you must know?"

Claire tensed and then curled her fingers into fists, cracking every knuckle in the process.

"No? Well, it seems the reapers—nice girls, really, sharp teeth, though, right?—were very upset about your last zombie experiment, and decided to pop in for an inspection. You can imagine their surprise when they found a full-blown extraction of zombie breath going on. Apparently they didn't get the memo."

Claire's ears sprung into points, and her fingers took on that scary claw look, that's *so* in right now, all that in perfect time to Shiny Toy Guns, booming through the speakers. It was impressive. Claire was a fully mature werewolf in a matter of seconds, and stalking toward me[124]. I stood my ground. Okay, so I was shaking a bit—but not a whole lot.

"They even raided your barista training ground," a new voice said, entering the mix. Wendy sauntered in like a rolling bead of mercury. "They said your goons couldn't pull a decent shot if their lives depended on it. Unfortunately, we'll never know for sure. All dead. Those reaper mouths can't seem to get enough food. I'm worried there may be an eating issue."

Claire's snout exhaled a plume of hot stinky breath. Her jaws snapped open, twisted to the side, and clamped down on my head; at the same time, she grasped at my body, trying to pull me toward her.

I grinned. She had hold of something but it wasn't me.

Claire was propelled backward and slammed into the wall leaving a distinctly werewolf shape in the bent stainless steel. The air came out of her lungs and she hunched over on the floor, like the dog she was.

---

[124] And by mature, I do mean geriatric, yes, to answer your question.

I picked between my breasts until I found a slick knot hidden there. I pulled the gold cord up, drawing the lucky charm from my cleavage. I slid the necklace over my head. Liesl was right, not just a ticket, the amulet was powerful magic. So, much love for the amulet.

Claire sprang up again, this time lurching toward Wendy. She spread her claws and tore at Wendy's face attempting to slice it into ribbons. But, her hand seemed to strike an invisible wall, hard as an anvil. Her claws snapped backwards, the sound of their breaking echoed against the metal walls.

"Ew," groaned a stall-stoner.

Wendy patted the front of her dress. "I'm afraid I've got your stupid henchman's amulet. Is that a problem?" She looked around as if actually concerned.

Our eyes met. We snickered.

The Clairewolf staggered, panting. She cradled her destroyed paw across her forearm.

"Well isn't this something," commented a familiar voice from behind me.

I swiveled in time to see Elizabeth Karkaroff make her entrance in what I believed was a lovely pre-Dior Galliano. What was certain? The frock was most definitely salary-consuming. It clung to her like a newborn, or as though she'd grown it herself, cultured off her own skin. It was a remarkable fashion achievement.

"Ms. Karkaroff, I really have to apologize," I said. "I was completely snowed by this bitch."

Wendy and I parted as the woman passed between us, and took a motherly stance over the werewolf. Karkaroff patted and stroked the fur of its head. Claire's eyes were damp with tears; her animal voice mewled with fear.

"Turn!" Elizabeth commanded. Her skin had a radiance not cosmetically possible[125]. Her energy squeezed around our bodies. The vampire stoners shut their stall door.

---

[125] But totally desirable. It would look hot on the dance floor, absolutely.

Claire's fur receded into her follicles in that instance; her skin sucking at the hair like straws. Her skeleton reconfigured, with several snaps, spasms, and loud cracking sounds. Claire's skin was bruised and her hand hung loosely as though the bones had liquefied.

"I think you are done, Claire. In fact, I'm sure of it. You've done quite enough damage in my town."

I envied the expression, *my* town. She asserted ownership and said it without a hint of irony or self-aggrandizement. She, simply, knew it was true.

"Please, Persephone! Have mercy!" Claire cried out. She shivered like a blizzard had swept into the room, and in a sense, it had.

"I'm all out of mercy, dear. What I have, for you, is peace."

Elizabeth made a slow circular gesticulation with her hand. She closed her eyes and the room seemed to void of air for a second. Her hair swirled around her, in an undercurrent of power. The lights over the vanity and in the stalls dimmed and went dark. Karkaroff's energy squeezed in on my body like a blood pressure cuff.

Below Claire's shaking body, the floor began to quiver like a vibration on the surface of water. Her face crimped into a cringe of fear. She sunk straight into it, like a stone.

The lights returned and the floor solidified. The air lost the density and pressure that held us all still.

"That was amazing," I said. Wendy shook her head next to me. I was worried she might ask for an autograph. I stepped forward and offered my hand. "Thank you. Persephone, is it?"

It made perfect sense. Claire was infatuated with Persephone, so why not disguise herself as the real thing, sans extravagant power, of course.

"We can stick with Elizabeth. Persephone was a long time ago." She smoothed the front of her fabulous dress.

"Absolutely. I've always believed in the importance of a

future orientation," I said, blowing off the supernatural events, as if they were commonplace.

"I'm glad you think that." She came up close and took me with an arm around my shoulder out into the lobby. Wendy trailed. "I have been thinking of some new business opportunities and I think you would be the perfect person to implement a marketing campaign."

"Mmm-hmm, go on," I replied, but inside I was doing cartwheels through a field of daisies—no, those smell like shit, don't they—through a field of jasmine. That's a pretty smell. Wait . . . is that a vine?

"The size of which would require the attentions of your entire firm. I'm afraid it may require some restructuring of your company." She was focused on me, intently, unblinking.

I thought of what would have to be done to those callous knuckleheads, Pendleton and Avery, and of the day of my death, their lack of interest. I certainly wouldn't miss them. It would beat selling out my shares and giving my baby away to incompetence.

"Sounds good. Dangerous."

"Yes!" She beamed. Her eyes seemed to flash red. "But lucrative." Maybe the flash was green.

The business chat was cut short by screams from the lobby.

Chapter 28

New and Improved
Zombie Chow

*I can't stress this enough: maintain a safe distance
from any zombies deemed mistakes. They are not at all
particular, and will claw you despite your inedibility.*
—A Taxonomy of the Dead

Outside the ladies' room, Mortuary erupted into a scene out
of bedlam. All the beautiful undead were running back and
forth, climbing over each other, turning the lobby from funeral home into a psychotics nightmare.

"Outbreak!" a voice yelled nearby, and then another, another. It was the supernatural consensus.

From the bottleneck of the front door sprayed an endless
flood of mistakes, each in a consecutively more advanced
state of decay. Some simply gnawed, others were missing
limbs, or torn open, bowels dragging the floor. Each mouth
was jacked open wide, and ready to eat.

Behind them, I could just make out the back of a tractor-
trailer. The zombies unloaded from there, some taking the
time to hunch down before jumping down, others marching
off and falling onto a heap of malfunctioning ghouls.

Once inside Mortuary, they tore into the nearest bodies, regardless of species. To our right, a group of wereleopards were mid-change, when a deluge of mistakes attacked them, clamping onto throats, lacerating arteries. The wallpaper was awash in blood spray and bile patterns[126]. It looked like a Jackson Pollack, if he were to work a new irritable bowel method.

The most statuesque of the sirens started to drone, from beside Lucien at coat check. Five zombies split off from the horde and attacked. Three crowded Lucien, drawing at his limbs until they loosed from the sockets and were flung into the lobby air; a leg came next. The siren's face turned piranha; she launched onto the other two pecking at their dead flesh with thin spiky claws like a pointed Thai dancer.

Cash Zinsser dashed away from a small huddled mass near the "viewing" room. He cradled his precious bichon frisé, Claudius, in one hand, a ubiquitous steno pad in the other. A pen bounced between his whiter than white fangs. He bounded across the lobby toward the bathroom. Halfway there, a huge mistake—probably a football player in life—snatched Claudius from Cash's hand, and bit its head clean off. The vampire screamed like a little girl, as he was hosed with the last of the dog's blood gush. The linebacker advanced, pounding the furry carcass against Cash's head, forcing him to take stumbling steps backwards. He fell over a pile of leftover bones and formal attire, landing square on his ass. The notepad hung in the air for a second, fanned out before smacking across his forehead. The zombie jumped on top, chewing into the vampire's cheeks.

I grabbed Wendy and Elizabeth and headed for the stairs. Gil was at the top, yelling something inaudible, above the roar. A zombie charged us, reaching for Wendy, but was unable to connect. I unhinged my jaw and snapped off the back of its neck as it passed. The mistake dropped in a heap; I spat

[126] Which are not fashionable, no matter what they tell you.

out a chunk of its spinal column. It chattered across the floor like fake teeth.

"Nice work," Elizabeth said, her face as placid as Sunday morning. She was on her cell phone, presumably contacting the reapers. It was about time for someone other than me to be useful. She shot me a quick sneer. A zombie broke for her from a nearby pack gnashing its exposed jaw. The demon glanced at him—a painfully bored expression—and produced a glowing whip of light in her free hand and slashed the zombie into flapjacks of meat. The pieces fell to the floor with the accuracy of a griddle cook, slapping wetly.

Sorry, I mouthed.

We continued bounding toward the stairs.

Gil was near their base calling to us. A flash of zombie appeared from the right. Before I could shout a warning, a brutish looking mistake grasped at him and latched onto Gil's shoulder with teeth the likes not seen since Ginsu ads[127]. Liesl and Cameron rushed from above, spewing a long strand of guttural howls, chants, perhaps in an unfamiliar language. An arc of electricity seemed to spring from the couple and charge directly into the ghoul mauling Gil. It dropped to the floor twitching as smoke rose from its charred eye sockets.

Wendy and I rounded the banister and headed up, just as a second wave of mistakes came from the entry. The floor below was slick with blood, gore, and bile. Body parts flew through the air like spears, some finding targets. Those they found, were knocked to the ground and quickly covered in zombie mouths, gnashing and grinding into their bones.

Above us, in the entry to the loge hall, Shane slouched, a blasphemy of a grin spread across his face. He was holding the BlackBerry I'd seem him with in the torture chamber. He looked far too smug not to have arranged this massacre.

A masticated hand reached between the balusters, dripping flesh from drying bones. It clutched my ankle, spilling

[127] God, I hate Grillz.

me onto my knees. Another hand reached for me, slinking through the cord of my charm. I reared up pulling away and the cord snapped. Before I could reach it, the amulet was snatched back through the rungs of the stairway and into the teeming bloodbath.

Another zombie slipped from behind Wendy, lunging for me. It wore a paper fast food hat and a striped polyester uniform. I was certain the fabric would do me just as much harm as the mistake. Already off balance, I fell back against the stair and raised my leg to try and push the creature away. It dove then. Its head quivered with excitement, its mouth wide and tongue flicking in grotesque vulgarity. I reared back and drove the heal of my stilettos sole deep between its eyes. It heaved twice and then fell to its knees. Its clawed hands hung flaccid against the sides of my hips, staining the satin with gore.

"Damn it!" I yelled and tried to kick him free. But, the heel was stuck in there good. The impromptu lobotomy tool had claimed two victims, the zombie and a beautiful pair of Guccis. I slid my foot from the shoe and the body dropped. I discarded the other.

I darted up the stairs, leaving Wendy below. Shane withdrew into the shadows of the drawers. I shouted to Wendy, "Hold on to that amulet, girl. Liesl would be pissed!"

I stopped at the top of the landing. Shane was not in the hall, likely hiding on one of the balconies. Below, Ricardo had joined the group and was battling the mistakes with a large mace[128]. From this vantage, the group looked horribly outnumbered, at least fifty ghouls were in active combat and that was just in the lobby—I hadn't seen the actual club yet, but the screams were thunderous.

I trudged off into the hall. The elevator door was closed so I tried each of the balconies in turn. The first two bal-

[128] It's a spice *and* a weapon.

conies found only frightened party guests, cowardly zombies in the first, unwilling to expose their flesh to the possibility of damage. I couldn't really judge them. Without the amulet, I'd probably be hiding, too. The second contained the worst kind of supernaturals, the disinterested. They sat chatting and turning their noses at the noise. Their flamboyant leader held court from a central pouf, his hairy legs splayed out like a murder victim. Bernard Krups didn't seem at all concerned.

"Darling, what are you on about? Come to take me up on my offer to paw around?" He slid his hand down the front of his flabby chest, into the waistband of a pair of bulging gold spandex hot pants.

"Gag," I said. "I'd sooner blow an actual goat, you perv."

He waved me off like an impetuous child.

I crossed the balcony and shooed two of his glommers. I looked over the edge at the main space to find that there were no more mistakes loose. The club guests barricaded the entrance with dismantled banquettes and the Yetis were using their backs to hold them against the entryway.

I moved back into the hall. It was empty.

At the next balcony, I located my quarry. Shane was waiting there, a gun in his hand. That's right, a gun. P-thetic.

I rushed him.

He fired.

The bullet blazed through my upper leg and I dropped to the ground, wincing with surprising pain. I actually had some functioning nerve endings. Score! Shane dropped down on his knees.

"You didn't think I'd shoot, did you, dead bitch?"

I pretended to faint from the pain, lolling onto my back, my leg splayed at an odd angle—more for the effect than out of any real damage. Shane's head hovered over mine.

"You couldn't possibly think we'd come unprepared. You see, the reapers only cleansed one of our training camps. The other was clean and ready to go. As you can see, if you'd just open your eyes." He reached for my face. I felt his thumb on my left lid.

I lunged at him. Clutched his head on either side. I brought his mouth down to mine. The fool opened it.

I exhaled.

The breath came from deep in my lungs. Its form was dense and scratched my throat on the way out, like the removal of a chest tube. It passed through my mouth like I'd conjured up a wet sausage and was forcing it into his throat. Shane's eyes bugged out. He made a muffled moaning sound and then was quiet. He seemed to relax.

I pushed him away. He fell against the wall, defeated. He wore a sullen face.

Was that it, I wondered? Had my breath simply calmed him, sedated?

No, was the answer.

Wrinkles formed rapidly in Shane's skin. Deep creases caved in around his lips and eyes, unraveled across his forehead. I flashed back to Bowie in *The Hunger*. The rapid aging was even more disturbing in person. I looked around for my purse. Gone. I was going to have a make-up breakdown.

The skin on his neck began to sag and hang like fabric rouging. The age spots were next. They appeared as though flecked from a paintbrush nearby and bled out from their initial spots, growing, unevenly. His skin darkened with multiple cancers. Lesions appeared and opened. Thin rivers of blood drained from soft flaccid puckers, like swollen entry wounds.

The curtain from the hall opened and Wendy peeked in. She looked at the pile of clothes and decomposing flesh that was Shane and said, "*Ew* . . . Pretty. Nice boyfriend you got there." She kicked a loose tuxedo pump off his shriveling foot.

"Thanks, figured it out a little late. But, you can't say I don't know how to take care of my man."

She crouched down, poking at the grey flesh around the gunshot wound. "Hmm. I'm not sure if Liquid Leather's going to patch that up."

"Whatever."

"You'll have to tell me one day how you killed that piece of shit."

"Maybe. Right now, though, help me up, bitch. This leg is killin' me."

Chapter 29

Afterparty of the Living Dead

Even if you encounter some unforeseen bit of nastiness on your visit, such as a gash or errant spell, the supernatural community has you covered. For a small fee, any one of a large group of reapers that call Seattle home, can be called upon for a touch-up . . .
— Supernatural in Seattle

In the corner closest to the dance floor, the three reapers were enjoying some downtime. Which would be fine if they didn't appear to be celebrating a victory of the Little Miss Emerald City Pageant, all made up like hookers and slurping body shots off a near-naked male sprite.

"Excuse me." I bounded away from Wendy. I needed to thank the "girls" for the healing.

Their mouths dropped as I approached, as if shocked by my intrusion. The dark-haired one stood on the seat and held out her hand. "Hold up, bitch. Don't try to horn in on our action."

The sprite was about their height and pale as paper. He climbed on the table, gyrating for them, thrusting, wearing nothing but a japonica leaf and an unwholesome grin. I pushed down a gag.

"Nonono. I just wanted to thank you."

"Oh there's no need. You'll get the invoice in the mail, sweetie," the blonde said.

"With interest." The redhead threw back her head, snorting laughter into the air like a choking victim. The others joined in.

"Okay. That's fine," I said. "Thanks again." I backed away. The girls appeared to have completely dismissed the interruption and were salting the sprite's pectoral cleavage. I noticed the redhead clung to a bottle of tequila the size of a ham. She held it like a baby doll.

I couldn't get away from the snotty bitches fast enough. But they did fix the bullet hole in my leg, the tear in my arm, and a nasty scratch on my ankle, so I was thankful. At least, I wouldn't be subjected to any more of Wendy's craft projects. Let's face it, she's no Martha. They should have stuffed Wendy in Camp Powderpuff for that *As Seen on TV* shit.

Wendy was waiting with Gil by the bar.

Gil's shoulder, of course, healed on its own. He'd been the one to carry me down the stairs—my hero[129]. To say I was jealous of his healing ability was an understatement. But don't think for a minute that I didn't take note of Shane's insane ramblings in the torture chamber. I fully expect to be able to heal, myself, one day.

Just like a big girl.

As for Ricardo, he survived unscathed, of course. Not a single scratch, like someone rubbed him down with four-leaf clovers. The weeks ahead would prove that the opening of Mortuary was a success, despite the melee. As far as opening night P.R. goes, infamous is the new fabulous. The club would be a hit, once it was remodeled. Ricardo figured it would be two months before he could reopen. The candy

[129] Or was it My Pretty Pony?

asses in the actual club had done the most damage with their damn barricade.

I sat with Elizabeth for a while. We worked out some strategy to clean house at Pendleton, Avery and Feral. I was all for it, but the devil is in the details, and not as Elizabeth has pointed out sitting in the booth with me. She pulled out all the stops on the zombie horde after I left for the balconies, tore through them with something she called a lightning whip. I was totally jealous. And she had nothing but great things to say about Liesl and Cameron; apparently, they fought like savages, ripping the zombies apart with the zest of healthy German women carving into a plate of overboiled brats.

Speaking of the two sex killers, they sidled up to the bar next to Wendy, Gil and me. "Hey y'all," Cameron said. "We've got a little announcement to make."

He pulled Liesl to him and anchored her around the shoulders. She produced a gigantic ruby engagement ring, shook her fingers with pride, and shouted, "We're getting married!"

"Jesus!" I turned my face and gagged.

"Tell me you're joking?" Gil asked, barely raising his mouth from his glass of blood. A William Shatner donation, if I'm not mistaken.

Wendy had no response, except for a cold stare.

"What?" Liesl glared at us.

I only hope Cameron wears lifts to the ceremony. I'm not sure how he'll explain it to the Hollywood crowd, either.

Liesl got her amulet back, by the way. She'd had to pull it from the pulsing stomach of a mistake, but she got it. It belonged to her grandmother, so it was special enough to claw through rotting intestine and undigested human meat to get back. Don't make that face; that's what they make soap for.

As for its thief, Mr. Norris, I settled on a conclusion about the man who made me. I like to think it went down like this: Mr. Norris got hooked up with Claire's batty ass and couldn't disengage without getting killed. But, he was always looking for a way out. When he stole the amulet from Liesl's, he found her phone and looked me up. He'd known me all along, of course, and since he made me figured I'd help.

The sad part is . . . I'm not sure I would have.

Now . . . yes.

But back then, unlikely. He'd never come to me and been civil, after all. It would have been nice to have a choice in the matter of one's death.

Anyway, that's how I'll remember the man.

The other amulet never turned up. Scary, huh? A mistake shuffling around invincible—I'm sure it'll turn up.

It has to eventually.

One last thing . . .

I was telling Wendy recently, "Now I realize that therapists are meant to send out a welcoming empathic vibe, but Martin really got me. He could finish my sentences."

"They can all do that," Wendy said, hiking her shorts up another inch and stretching back to expose her long legs to the sun and to the men waiting at the Starbucks drive-thru. We liked this spot for the effortlessness of the hunt. It was a sunny patch of concrete, a home for umbrellas and black iron bistro sets, between the coffeehouse and the drive-up lane. Despite its reputation as the hub of the high maintenance woman, you'd be surprised how many men go to Starbucks for the grande decaf misto with heavy whipping cream and sugar free vanilla. Most times we would bring books to alert drivers of specific traits we were after; sci-fi or computer how-to would often lure a needy, eager-to-please programmer[130], some literary fiction, Roth or Updike, may snare some pseudo-intellectual panty-sniffer. Sometimes, and

---

[130] I don't really need to say "geek" here, do I?

believe me, Wendy frowns on it, I'll pull out my copy of *The Heroine's Journey* to rope a lonely lesbian or an experimental feminist coed from the liberal arts college.

"No, no, I mean he was like a psychic. We didn't even talk that much and he knew. He knew. He knew how lonely I was, how eating is so tricky for me. How dirty doorknobs and faucet handles can be, even after a good cleaning."

"You have to stop mooning over him. He's gone," Wendy said. "Maybe you should find another therapist that can help you work all this crap out. I've been through five in the last ten years and I still wake up screaming from my mother's backhanded compliments."

I decided to skim over the mother comment. Ethel Ellen Frazier could stay exactly where she was—Chicago I think, at least that's where the bitch was the last time I checked—thoroughly out of my mind.

"Yeah . . . no. I'm swearing off men."

Wendy tsked.

"Well, except to eat, obviously."

She rolled her eyes and lit on an Asian man eyeballing her from a gunmetal Hummer. Her tongue traced the outline of her lips. "What do you think about Chinese?" she asked, making her way to the tank's high window.

"Yeah, that's fine, I had Mexican last night." I packed my book and pulled the sunglasses from my hair.

"Maybe we could do the chocolate cake trick, later."

"What?"

"Oh come on, Amanda, you remember . . . on the buckets?"

I honestly don't know what she was talking about. You should know me by now. I don't do *that*.

I don't.

Anymore.

Amanda's
Très Importante
Authorial
Acknowledgments

Despite the opinion that writing about oneself is just mental fingerbanging, the process of a memoir is a major undertaking[131]. I couldn't have done it without my new friends.

Thank you Wendy, for the late-night snacks:—she knows what I mean, oh . . . wait; you do, too.

To Gil, my main vamp, for endless readings of first draft drivel. The price? A paltry 2007 Lance Bass brut—Thank you Mr. Bass[132].

And, of course, I offer a huge debt of thanks to my mentor Ricardo. Equal parts teacher, savior, and smarty-pants.

My editor tells me the book can't help but be a hit. It'd better be, because I tend to eat when I'm disappointed, and I know where he lives. Food is love, after all.

As always, to Martin Allende. You will always be in my heart, and, well—heh, heh—my stomach.

---

[131] No pun intended.
[132] He was soooo accommodating.

**Please turn the page for an exciting sneak peek of
ROAD TRIP OF THE LIVING DEAD,
now on sale!**

Chapter 1

Raising the Dead
for Fun and Profit

Nowadays, anyone with a wallet full of cash and a little insider knowledge is getting into the Supernatural life. And, I do mean anyone. Criminals, politicians, even—brace yourself—entertainers are plopping down tons of cash for immortality.
—Supernatural Seattle (June 2008)

Gil brought lawn chairs to the cemetery—not stylish Adirondacks, not even semi-comfortable camp chairs (the ones with those handy little cup holders). No. He dug up some cheap plastic folding chairs, the kind that burrow into your leg flesh like leeches.[1] He arranged them in a perfect semicircle around a freshly sodded grave, planted an iBoom stereo in the soft earth, pulled out a bottle of '07 Rose McGowan,[2] and drained half of it before his ass hit plastic. Granted, he managed these mundane tasks in a pricey Gucci tuxedo, the tie loose and dangling. On any other day, this would have

[1] It's like he had a time machine and a white trash childhood.
[2] Celebrity blood donation is quite lucrative. You'd be surprised who's giving it up for the vamps.

been his sexy vamp look, but tonight . . . not so much. His eyelids sagged. His shoulders drooped. He looked exhausted.

I, on the other hand, looked stunning.

One of those movie moons, fat and bloated as a late-night salt binge, striped the graveyard with tree branch shadows, and spotlit your favorite zombie heroine reclining starlet-like on the polished marble of the new tombstone—there was no way I was subjecting vintage Galliano to the inquisition of plastic lawn chairs; the creases would be unmanageable.

Wendy didn't take issue with the cheap and potentially damaging seating. She wore a tight pink cashmere cardigan over a high-waisted chestnut skirt that hit her well above the knee. She crossed her legs and popped her ankle like a 1950s housewife, each swivel bringing attention to her gorgeous peek-toe stilettos—certainly not the most practical shoe for late-night graveyard roaming, but who am I to judge?[3]

The dearly departed were our only other company; about twenty or so ghosts circled the grave—in a rainbow of moody colors and sizes. A little boy spirit, dressed in his Sunday best and an aqua-green aura, raced by, leaving a trail of crackling green sparks; the other, older specters muttered to each other, snickered and pointed. Popular opinion aside, zombies do not typically hang out in graveyards—ask the ghosts. We don't crawl out of the ground all rotty and tongue-tied, either. We're created through bite or breath, Wendy and I from the latter. So you won't see us shambling around like a couple of morons, unless there's a shoe sale at Barney's.

"You're killin' me with The Carpenters, can't you skip this one?" I stretched for the iPod with my heel trying to manipulate its doughnut dial. Karen was bleating on about lost love from beyond the grave—and just a little to the left.

---

[3] I'm a total shoe slut. Jimmy Choo, Manolo Blahnik, Christian Louboutin: this is an open invitation. Feel free to run a train on me. The cost? Stilettos, duh.

"She's forcing me to search my bag for a suicide implement. I swear I'll do it."

"No shit. Her warble is drawing the less-than-present out of the woodwork." Wendy looked over the top of huge Chanel sunglasses—she seemed to wear them as a joke, so I refused to comment. She'd be more irritated with every second that passed. Such a simple pleasure, but those are often the best, don't you find?

"Bitches." Gil opened an eye. "This is a classic. Besides, Markham put this playlist together."

"Who's that?" I'd decided against self-harm and opted for a smart cocktail. I pulled a mini shaker from my bag and followed that up with miniature bottles of vodka, gin, and rum. Who says Suicides are just for kids? I mixed while Gil chattered.

"Him." He jabbed a thumb toward the grave. "That's Richard Markham; they call him the Beaver King. He's a millionaire, entrepreneur, and genuinely bad guy. He owns a chain of strip clubs, you might have heard of them. Bottoms."

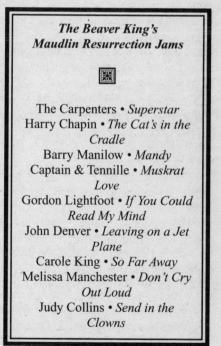

The Beaver King's Maudlin Resurrection Jams

The Carpenters • *Superstar*
Harry Chapin • *The Cat's in the Cradle*
Barry Manilow • *Mandy*
Captain & Tennille • *Muskrat Love*
Gordon Lightfoot • *If You Could Read My Mind*
John Denver • *Leaving on a Jet Plane*
Carole King • *So Far Away*
Melissa Manchester • *Don't Cry Out Loud*
Judy Collins • *Send in the Clowns*

When neither of us registered a hint of recollection, he became animated.

"You know. He's been in the news recently because of some shady business deals. He also coined the phrase 'All Bottomless Entertainment'."

"Don't you mean 'all nude'?" Wendy asked.

"No. 'All *Bottomless.*' He's decidedly anti-boobs. His clubs feature blouses *and* beaver. It's a very specialized niche."

"Well then, this should be fun." I stuck a straw into the shaker and sucked.

It was nice to see Gil's enthusiasm; he had been a complete ass-pipe since he'd opened Luxury Resurrections Ltd., stressing about every little detail. I had to hand it to the guy. After the money dried up—his sire left him a hefty sum in their bank account and then left (said Gil was too needy)—he launched his plan to charge humans for vamping. He was one of the first in Seattle, but the copycats were close on his heels. A few months later he bought into my condominium—not a penthouse like mine, but a pretty swank pad, nonetheless.

"Explain to me again why we're out here?" Wendy struggled to separate her legs from the sweaty straps—I cringed, afraid that she'd leave some meat on the plastic; we were fresh out of skin patch—they finally released with a slow sucking sound. She massaged the pattern of dents on the backs of her legs. "It's not like vampires need to rise from the *actual* grave. It's a little melodramatic. Don't ya think?"

"Yeah." I drained the final droplets from the shaker with loud staccato slurps. The alcohol seeped into my veins, flooding them with welcome warmth.

"I told you, I have to provide an experience with the Platinum package," Gil huffed, then snatched up his man bag and dug through it. He pulled out some Chapstick, spread it on in a wide "O," retrieved a crumpled brochure, and tossed it at me. "Here. Service is the only thing that's going to set my business apart from the chain vampire manufacturers. I provide individualized boutique-like vamping, at reasonable prices."

"Mmm hmm." I slid from the headstone, carefully hop-scotched across the grave—I'd hate to misstep and harpoon Gil's client, or worse, break off a heel in the dirt—and stood next to Wendy. I smoothed the crinkled paper and turned to catch the moonlight.

"The Platinum Package," I read aloud. "Includes pre-death luxury accommodations at the Hyatt Regency, voted by readers of *Supernatural Seattle* as the best undead-friendly hotel in the city, a thorough consultation with a vamping specialist, a fully realized death scenario, including funeral and interment, bereavement counseling for immediate family, and an exclusive orientation to the afterlife from the moment of rising. Hmm."

"I spent a lot of time on that." Gil beamed.

"Yeah, at least fifteen minutes." My eyes found a series of numbers after the description, that if it weren't for the dollar sign, I'd have mistaken for binary code. "Can I ask you a question?"

"Sure."

"Is this the price down here?" I pointed out the figure.

"Yep."

Wendy took a slug from a crystal-studded flask—she couldn't find her usual Hello Kitty one.[4] Immediately, her skin took on the rosy glow of most living alcoholics. I love the look: almost human.

"One million dollars, Gil? You call that reasonable pricing?"

Wendy did a spit take that flecked the brochure and my hands. "Jesus! So, if that's the platinum, what's the bronze package, then?" Wendy asked, wiping at the Grey Goose trickling from her nose. "A drive-by vamping?"

---

[4] The folks at Sanrio are really kicking their adult line up a notch.

"Cute." Gil tongued and sucked at his fangs in irritation.

He shrugged off our outrage and plopped down in his own lawn chair. "Five hundred grand is the going rate nowadays, the markup is for my fabulous luxury features. It's not cheap, but look what you get . . ." He swept his hands from his head to toes like a game show hostess. ". . . a super hot greeting party. And . . . a couple of hot go-go dancers."

"Where?" I looked around. "Are they late?"

"Why, you two pork chops, of course. You remembered to leave the panties at home, right?"

"Oh yeah. Of course." I plucked a miniature Goldschläger from my purse and drained it. "When am I not airing out the chamber of horrors?"

"Me, too," Wendy said. "Totally commando."

"Gross." Gil covered his mouth, heaving. "Let's not talk about the vage, anymore. I think I'm traumatized."

"You started it." I tossed the empty bottle aside and dug for another.

From there, the conversation dwindled to nothing, an uncharacteristic silence settling over us like a late summer fog. The ghosts had even settled down. Except for a particularly downtrodden specter pacing under a nearby tree, the rest seemed content settling into their various routines (friendly visits to neighboring graves, a spirited game of cards over by the mausoleum, a display of ghost lights in the woods). Relaxing, even.

And that's when I opened my big fat mouth.

"I got a weird call today."

"Oh yeah?" Wendy asked. She must have been bored because this normally mundane news had her wide-eyed.

"My mother's hospice worker."

"What?" Gil twisted in his chair to face me. "Hospice? She's dying? You never even talk about her. I thought she'd already kicked it."

"Yeah, right?" Wendy muttered.

The dead are so sympathetic. If you're looking for an

honest opinion, and don't want any handholding or softeners, this is the crowd for you. Not that we're auditioning for friends, just now.

"Nope. She's still alive. The doctors say she's in the end stages of stomach cancer; it's pretty much spread everywhere. Been at the hospice for a few weeks now. Apparently, it's not pretty, nor is she." Inside *or* out, I thought.

"Wow."

"That's bad."

"Yeah." The truth was, I wasn't feeling any pain about it. Ethel Ellen Frazier had been a rotten mother, wife, and human being. You name it. Now, she was rotting inside. Ironic? Harsh? Sure, but she'd earned it. Every wince of pain, bout of vomiting, and bloody toilet bowl—the caller had gone into some unnecessary specifics.

Let me give you a little "for instance."

When I was young, Ethel convinced me—through months of badgering and ridicule—that I could benefit from a gym membership. Dad tried to talk her out of it, but like always, he had no say. So, off we went to Happy's Gym and Pool. Happy was just that; he had the kind of smile I could never seem to muster, broad and beaming. I think it was even real. The gym and pool were in the same room, a massive barn-like structure with the pool in the center, the equipment to the right, and the men's and women's locker rooms on the left, separated by a dry sauna. With about ten minutes left on the treadmill, I noticed a growing number of horrified expressions. I took off my headphones. Screams were coming from the sauna. Long screams. Then, choppy short bursts. And in between low gurgling moans reminiscent of the ape house at the zoo.

I scanned the room for my mother; I didn't expect to see her. She was behind closed doors. And I was out in the open, fifteen years old and humiliated. Happy's smiling face was nowhere to be found, either. I suspected it was crammed firmly between my mother's thighs. But I was wrong. The security guard cleared up the mystery by opening the sauna door. There was Mom. On all fours and facing a captive audience, Happy behind her caught up inside like a shamed dog; his perpetual smile replaced by an embarrassed "o". I could see the words play across Ethel's lips, as I ran for the exit. "Shut the door, dimwit!"

Now, tell me she didn't buy herself some cancer on that day.

Did I mention how lucky I am to have friends like Wendy and Gil? I can always count on them to turn the conversation back around to . . . them, and I was glad to have the heat off this time.

"Oh my God!" Wendy grabbed my arm and shook it like an impatient kid in the candy aisle. "I totally knew about this. I was talking to Madame Gloria just the other day and—"

"Here we go." Gil snatched up the bottle of McGowan and finished it off.

Madame Gloria was Wendy's telephone psychic. According to our girl, she was "moderately accurate," whatever that meant.

"Shut up, Gil. Madame Gloria said that someone was going to die and that we . . ." she pointed at Gil, herself, and me, "we would be going on a trip. A road trip."

"Jesus." I swatted her hand away. "You think she's talking about Ethel? I'll be damned if I haul my dead ass across three states for that bag of bones."

"It might be good to get some closure." Gil's face was attempting sincerity. It missed. He did succeed in pulling off a smoosh-faced version of constipated.

"Alright. So, before the two of you go all psychotherapist on me, let me tell you a few things. The reason I never talk about my mother is that she's a bitch. In fact, the last time I saw her was my high school graduation, where she blew me off to go to my ex-best friend's party. I can't say as I miss her."

Wendy waved me off. "None of that matters, anyway. Madame Gloria says we're going. It's fate."

"Yeah. It's fate." A sly smile played on Gil's lips.

"Like Hell it is." I punched his arm. "What was all that shit about breaking free from your family?"

He sneered, rubbing the spot. "What are you talking about?"

"When I first met you and you took me to see Ricardo?"

"Not ringing any bells."

"Ricardo told me that I needed to make a clean break from any living family and friends."

Ricardo Amandine had filled me in on a lot more than mere survival tactics. The club owner had become a mentor of sorts, doling out words of wisdom over drinks, shopping, and the odd kill. He was hot as hell, but as is the rule with male zombies, totally asexual.[5] Shame.

"True," Gil said. "But this is different. Your mother's gonna die, anyway. And look at poor Wendy. Don't her feelings count?" He gestured to the other chair.

Wendy's lips pursed into a pathetic pout. She was even batting her eyes.

Christ.

He continued. "She's totally bored. Would a road trip be so bad?"

I imagined dirty rest-stop bathrooms, rows of trailers substituting for motels, a general lack of shopping opportunities. A zombie has certain needs. The upside? Cute country folk have cute country flavors.[6]

Wendy nodded. "What were *you* planning to do about the situation?"

"I thought I'd pretend I'd never gotten the call. Denial's my friend, and all."

"Yeah, okay. Just say you'll think about it. Please?"

---

[5] Something about the lack of blood flow.
[6] Without all the nasty additives you find in city meat.

"Fine. I'll think about it."

I lit up a cigarette; the smoke caught on the thinnest of breezes and spun off like cursive. The trail stretched off toward the single ghost who was still interested in our presence. He stomped through the haze, passed us and then stopped about ten feet away, leaning against a rather confusing headstone of a gargoyle eating a hoagie—or was that a salmon?

"I've been meaning to talk to Hans about making me some of those," Wendy said. She was pointing at the black-papered cigarette dangling from my lips.

"I'll ask him to make you some. Any particular colors, or outfits you're trying to match?"

The ghost started coughing. Expansive rattling coughs. He must have wanted attention, as he never looked away. So dramatic. "It's not gonna kill ya, buddy!" I yelled. He scowled.

Wendy disregarded the exchange and continued. "An assortment would be great. Only no orange. I look horrible in orange."

"Tell me about it. Remember that track jacket you kept trying to wear out in public. You looked like a road worker. I was fully prepared to club you."

"Oh yeah," she said, as though I'd brought up some long-lost treasure. "Where'd I put that?"

I shrugged. The truth was, Wendy hadn't put the track jacket anywhere. I'd snuck it out of her hall closet while mama was putting her face on and promptly dumped it in the trash chute. I was doing her a favor, really. She looked like a big pumpkin in that puffy satin piece of shit.

Gil adjusted his butt in the chair. He'd taken note of our visitor. "Is that ghost eavesdropping?"

"Probably."

"I can't have anyone, or thing, fucking up my shit. Not tonight. Markham's not a flexible guy."

"Maybe he thinks you need a third judge of your vampire making—"

"Vampires?" The ghost choked the words out from over my shoulder. I staggered to the side to avoid any spectral germs or whatever. "I can't stand me no friggin' vampires. Piss on 'em. They should all rot in iron boxes."

"That's a little harsh," Wendy commented.

"Harsh?" The ghost spit a glob of violet-hued mush at Wendy's feet. "I don't know 'bout that. Seein's they're the one's suckin' people dry. I'll say it again. Piss on 'em."

Up close, the ghost looked like a vagrant. His face was all scruff surrounding a nose the size of a kosher dill, his eyes obscured by thick tufts of brow hair. Dirt clung to his ethereal form in spots, as though even death couldn't hide the residue of boxcar or alley dumpster. There was even a scent in the air, pungent and sour like milk gone to clot.

"You one of them fuckin' vampires, boy?" He kicked at the back of Gil's chair, foot moving right through and ending up somewhere inside Gil's stomach.

"What if I am?" Gil stood and faced the bigot. I almost interceded but thought it might be important to witness some honest-to-God vamp bashing. If only just to say I had been there, and act disturbed and offended. I could give my report to the late evening edition of *Supernatural Seattle Tonight.* They love me.

"Then I got somethin' fur ya. You stinkin' mosquito." The ghost started to reach down inside his pants.

We all gasped in horror. Well not all, Wendy seemed genuinely interested—craning her neck to get a good look—but she doesn't count, being a slut and all.

A low scraping rose from beneath us, a lonely hollow scrabbling, as though rats were burrowing through wood or Gil's client had shredded the tufted silk of the coffin lid and was clawing through mahogany. Yeah. It was that last one for sure.

The noise drew the ghost's attention, as well. He hiked up his pants and re-secured them with what looked like an electrical cord.

The scrabbling gave way to several deep thuds.

"Couldn't we just dig him up and save his manicure?" I asked.

Gil shrugged. "It builds character. Besides do I look like I'm dressed for grave digging?"

Gil was up out of his chair, folding it and gesturing for me to do the same. I looked around for Wendy and to my immediate dismay caught sight of the homeless ghost. He stood atop the soon-to-be vampire's headstone, pants unzipped, and dick in hand.

"*Ew.* What do you think you're doing?" I asked.

"What does it look like, girly?" He bounced on the balls of his feet in preparation.

It hit me then. "Oh . . . shit. Gil, he's gonna piss on your guy's—"

"Piss on 'em. Piss on 'em," the ghost chanted.

Gil looked up from packing away the chairs just in time to catch Boxcar Willie pissing a steaming stream of ectoplasm onto the grave. It glugged from the guy like Mrs. Butterworth's, glowing an enthusiastic obscene purple.

"Gross!" Wendy yelled from behind me.

"Jesus!" Gil dropped the folded chairs and made for the ghost just as the Beaver King broke ground. Markham breached the surface and was birthing straight through the manhole-sized puddle of ghost piss. Globs of the stuff dribbled down his arms and mingled with the mud on his face. The ghost shook a few errant drops loose. They plopped on Markham's face like thick blobs of mayonnaise.[7]

"What the fuck!" The new vampire spat, scooping the ectoplasm off his face. It oozed from his hair and plopped onto

---

[7] I don't have to tell you, this kind of treatment would not be considered luxury service, by any means.

the shoulders of an expensive pinstriped suit that really seemed like overdressing for either digging oneself from a grave, or pee play, for that matter.

Gil started backing away, and gesturing for Wendy and me to do the same.

Markham had extricated himself from his burial place; he stood there like Carrie on prom night: humiliated, covered in that obscene fluid. He swung at the ghost, pummeling the air with impotent fists. The hobo's laughter echoed across the cemetery. The spirits playing poker by the mausoleum looked up.

One said, "Earl must have found him a vampire."

Their laughter joined a growing cacophony, as news spread amongst the dead.

"Where's that piece of vampire shit? I'll kill him!" Markham yelled.

Those were the secret words, apparently. We took off through the graveyard like someone had announced happy hour, bounding over headstones, and skirting spectral presences. Wendy broke off a heel in a concrete vase holder. I nearly tripped on a wreath Gil knocked over in his mad dash for the car.

In the distance, Markham was still screaming. "Luxury my ass! I want my money back, vampire! Every fucking cent!" Despite being the evil villain type, the Beaver King couldn't chase for shit.

I turned to Wendy. "Did Madame Gloria see that one coming?"

In Seattle's undead circles, Amanda Feral is one of the beautiful zombies. Of course, when you're socializing with werewolves, devils, and rampaging yetis, there's not that much competition. Still, Amanda has a stylish rep to maintain, which is getting tricky now that her tanking ad agency is obliterating her finances. The fastest way to make some cash: appear on a new reality show, *American Minions*, hosted by lecherous wood nymph Johnny Birch. Classy? Maybe not, but a girl's gotta eat.

With zombie gal pal Wendy posing as her bitchy agent, Amanda settles in to "Minions Mansion," crowded with 24-7 video cameras and undead fame whores. When Johnny is found incinerated in a locked room, Amanda decides to channel her inner Miss Marple (minus the fugly cardigans) and find who's responsible. Was it Hairy Sue, the white trash stripper yeti? Tanesha, the glamorous trannie werewolf? Angie, the Filipino vampire with a detachable head? Unveiling the culprit in a heart-stopping finale won't just save the show from cancellation, it might just keep Amanda alive—or as close as a ghoul can get . . .

Please turn the page for an exciting sneak peek of BATTLE OF THE NETWORK ZOMBIES, coming next month!

Chapter 1

Hillbillies, Whores, and Horrors

Saturday
2–2:30 A.M.
CH. SS12
Tapping Birch's Syrup

The remaining "ladies" share
a group date with Birch and
another challenge: create
evening gowns with the
local flora . . . poison ivy!
Plus, Ludivine reveals a
secret deformity.

Its official name was the H & C Gentleman's Club—that's
what it said on the tax statement, at least, and in the phone
book—but everyone in Seattle knew it as the Hooch and
Cooch, the Northwest's first hillbilly-themed titty bar, and it
certainly lived up to its backwoods inspirations. The exterior
was dilapidated, a hodgepodge of boards nailed up at weird

angles and intervals as siding, while rust from the corrugated-metal roof striped the building a gritty orange. It clung to the hillside above Fremont on pilings so rickety, the slightest bump threatened to dump the shack's smutty guts onto the quiet neighborhood underneath.

I'd applaud the audacity, if the owner weren't Ethel Ellen Frazier, vampire, mega-bitch, and, worst of all, my mother.

I considered leaving the car idling in the space—a sound getaway plan was looking like my best option—then fished out my cell and hammered in Marithé's number.

"Seriously?" I asked the second she picked up, fondling the address she'd written on the back of my business card.

"What?" My assistant's voice always sounds annoyed, so it's difficult to assess her tone. A good rule of thumb is just to assume I've interrupted something very important like saving time in a bottle, writing the great American novel, or ending the plague that is zombie crotch rot—more likely, at that hour, she'd be using the Wite-Out to create a budget French manicure.

"The Hooch and Cooch? Since when is one of my mother's strip clubs an appropriate meeting place?" My eyes took in the stories-tall cowgirl on the roof, lit up old school—in lightbulbs rather than neon. Several were burnt out, but most notable were the cowgirl's front teeth; on closer inspection, those seemed to be blacked out on purpose—it's nice to see an attention to authentic detail. The ten-foot-tall flashing pink beaver between her legs was a subtle choice, if I do say so.

"He insisted," she said, her voice echoing on the speakerphone.

"Fucking pig."

The pig's name was Johnny Birch, and he was famous for three things: crooning jazz standards like that Bublé or Bubble guy or whoever, screwing anything with a hole (including donuts), and doing it all publicly on his own reality show, *Tapping Birch's Syrup* (shown exclusively on Channel SS12). He was also a wood nymph, but even though that's all ethereal and earthy, it's really secondary to the pervert stuff. Apparently he had a proposition and from the look of the Hooch and Cooch, I had a pretty good idea it wasn't business related.

"Seriously, this better be a for-real deal or I'm gonna be one pissed-off zombie."

"Karkaroff was very specific that this was a *priority* meeting." I could imagine her making air quotes in the cushy office chair, leaning back with her ankles crossed on the desk, admiring her trophy shoes.

My business partner was already fuming from our recent clusterfuck with Necrophilique. How was I supposed to know the fecal content of the cosmetics? Do I look like a chemist? Still, we needed the money after word spread and the launch tanked. What was the saying, beggars can't be choosers? Not that I was a beggar by any count, but . . . shit, mama's got bills to pay.

"Fine." I gripped the phone to my ear as she yammered on about her day and I started loading my purse with all the important undead accoutrements. Flesh-tone bandages (you never know when you'll get a scratch, and humans are normally surprised when they don't see blood seeping), cigarettes (why the hell not) and lastly, Altoids, of course, because dragon breath doesn't even begin to describe the smell that escapes up this rotten esophagus.

I did take a moment to wonder if I was dressed appropriately for the venue. The Gucci skirt was definitely fitted and might draw some roving hands, but I could certainly handle those. My big concern was the white silk blouse.

It was Miu Miu, for Christ's sake.

The Hooch and Cooch didn't look like the kind of place that any white fabric could escape without a stain, let alone designer silk.

As if on cue, two drunken slobs slammed out of the swinging doors and scattered out onto the red carpetless cement.[1] One landed on his ass with his legs spread, an expanding dark wetness spreading from his crotch outward. His buddy clutched at his stomach in a silent fit of laughter, but then fell against a truck and puked into the open bed. The rest dribbled off his chin and down his loosened tie as he slid to the concrete. I guess that answered my question about fashion choices. Pretty much anything will do if your competition is piss and puke stains, though clearly the blouse was in danger and the stains were much more dubious than I'd imagined.

"Ugh. Christ. Call me in ten minutes. I know I'm going to need an excuse to get out of here."

I stuffed the phone in my Alexander McQueen red patent Novak bag—yes, you need to know that, if for no other reason than to understand that I've moved on from the Balenciaga; it's a metaphor for my personal growth—and headed in, stepping over the passed-out figure on the threshold. The urine smell was unbearable. Someone had enjoyed a nutritious meal of asparagus.[2] I shoved the splintery doors into the strip club's lobby and was greeted by a wall of palsied antlers, Molly Hatchet blaring some '70s bullshit, and my mother's pasty dead face beaming from behind the hostess stand.

"Darling." She crossed the room in three strides, cowboy boots crunching on the peanut shells coating the floor and arms reaching—the effect was more praying mantis than loving mother, I assure you. "You should have called."

I submitted to a hug and, over her shoulder, caught a glimpse of Gil, arms crossed and leaning on the open bed of a Ford F-150 that seemed to have been repurposed as the gift shop—how they got it in there, I have no clue. A pair of those ridiculous metal balls dangled between his legs from

---

[1] No. No paparazzi, either. Yeah. I was glad about that.
[2] Don't pretend you don't know what I'm talking about. That piss is rank. Good for getting rid of some quick water weight, though. Just a tip.

the trailer hitch behind him. I couldn't help but giggle. He tipped his Stetson in my direction and winked.

"You're right, Mother. I'll definitely call next time."[3]

She pulled away, concern spreading across her face. The vamping achieved the kind of freshening a top-dollar Beverly Hills facelift aimed for, but no amount of magic could revive Ethel's sincerity.

"It's just, we haven't had a whole lot of time to sort out this . . . tension between us, and I'd like us to be a family, again."

Again. Just like that. Like there'd ever been anything remotely resembling a "family." Unless her definition of family was the people one ridiculed, judged, and rejected, then yeah, I guess we had a "family."

I clenched my fists. If blood flowed through my veins rather than thick yellow goo, I might have turned beet red. But instead of appearing angry, I took on a sickly jaundice, which is never cute.

I decided to stuff it and pushed past her to find Johnny Birch. "Sure, Ethel, let's work on that."

"I don't appreciate your sarcasm." She sang the final word, as she did when pretending something didn't actually bother her. I grinned, triumphant.

I bounded up to Gil. "How do you put up with that bitch?" I stabbed a thumb in Ethel's direction.

"Who, your mother? Oh please, she's wonderful to work for and so funny . . ."

His voice trailed off, replaced by the twangin' guitar of Southern rock. Mother had obviously brainwashed Gil to spout this pro-Ethel propaganda, and I wasn't about to listen to it. "Yeah. Yeah. Awesome. A real peach."

"A better question is, how do I put up with this seventies-ass rock."

---

[3] The authorities, that is; nothing disrupts business like a vice raid.

The music changed. "Slow Ride," by Foghat. "Seriously. What's the deal?" I asked.

"Part of your mom's plan; it's all she'll play here. She says seventies rock forces guys to buy beer. Something in their genes. Oh . . . and look at this." Gil reached into the truck bed, which was lined with various Hooch and Cooch promo items, T-shirts, CDs, pocket pussies— that sort of thing—and retrieved a DVD. A sleazy, greasy-haired dancer grinned from the cover, one of her front teeth was missing, and she wore a wife-beater that didn't do a good job hiding the fact that his boob job looked like two doorknobs. It read: Learn to Strip with the Girls of the Hooch and Cooch (see inset).

Music from the DVD . . .

Learn to Strip with the Girls of the Hooch and Cooch*

Thin Lizzy • *Jailbreak*
Foghat • *Slow Ride*
Heart • *Barracuda*
Ted Nugent • *Cat Scratch Fever*
War • *Low Rider*
Nazareth • *Hair of the Dog*
The Runaways • *Cherry Bomb*
Blue Oyster Cult • *Burnin' for You*
Kansas • *Carry on Wayward Son*
Boston • *More Than a Feeling*

*for instructional purposes only!

"Jesus. Like one of those Carmen Electra striptease workouts?"

"Yep." He tossed it back in the truck. "Sells like hotcakes."

"I bet."

I looked past Gil into the club for the first time and witnessed the horrors of uncontrolled testosterone production. A drunken mass of homely men and a few semi-doable ones, surprisingly, crowded around two spotlit islands, shouting obscenities and waving dollar bills. It was nearly impossible to distinguish them as individuals; they'd reverted to some sort of quivering gelatinous state. A few appeared near death, eyes rolling in the back of their heads as though they'd never seen a used-up hooker—I mean, nude woman—writhing in a metal washtub, scrubbing herself with a moldy bath brush and kicking suds off dirty feet at her sweaty admirers. Maybe it's because we were indoors.

Between the two performance spaces—though really I'm being overly generous with that description—was a large shack built into the back of the club complete with everything you'd expect to find in the backwoods of the Ozarks, or in a typical Northwest suburb, for that matter—a covered porch, rocking chairs, even a butter churn.[4] Everything, that is, but a little inbred blind kid playing the banjo and showing off the graveyard of teeth in his mouth.

He must have been on a smoke break.

Booths lined the edges of the room, where hillbilly chicks chatted up customers under the watchful glass eyes of various stuffed animal heads. Fog lights on truck grills jutted from the walls lighting up the tables and the assorted (or sordid) activities taking place there.

"This place is a regular Rainforest Café. Only instead of cute plastic animals, you've got dirty whores."

"Absolutely." Gil crossed his arms and beamed, as proud as a new father—sure, he had a stake in the place, but he was overdoing the satisfaction considering the place reeked of bleach and I'm pretty sure it wasn't emanating from a big load of laundry.[5]

"Pays the bills," he said.

---

[4] I didn't want to even think what these girls would use *that* for.
[5] It's a curse that my sense of smell is so acute. A curse!

"Listen. I'm supposed to be meeting a guy. Johnny Birch, that fame whore from TV. Have you seen him?"

"Um." He scanned the room. "Totally. What a freak. I think he's just finished up with Kelsey." Gil pointed to a hallway flanked by two columns of chicken coops. A lanky, dark-haired man emerged with a jug of moonshine in one hand and a skanky redhead in the other.

"Christ."

The guy was tonguing the girl's ear as I approached.

"Excuse me," I said. "Are you Mr. Birch?"

He spun the girl away like a Frisbee, absolutely no regard for where she might land. She twirled a few times, collapsed in some other perv's lap, and started gyrating. Birch measured me in long, sweeping stares. Head to toe, lingering on the tits and back to the head. "Sure am." He extended his hand. "And you're Amanda. Lovely to meet you."

He pulled at my hand as though planning to pull off a gentlemanly knuckle kiss, but I snatched it back, wishing for a Clorox wipe. "Yeah. Um, you have some sort of business proposition, I've been told. Do you want to talk about that here, or do you have a table somewhere? Maybe a private booth they reserve for regulars."

"You mean V.I.P." He winked.

"No." I shook my head. "Just regular."

Birch nodded and chuckled off the jab under his breath.

The next moment, the blaring '70s rock was silenced, an apparent signal for the strippers to make way for the principal dancer in this redneck ballet. They scrabbled off on bruised knees, wet hair dangling in clumps, and bulldozing collapsing pyramids of dollar bills in front of them.

Birch pointed toward the shack.

The lights dimmed, and a jaundiced glow rose behind the dirty shower curtain covering the front door of the facade. At the edges of the porch, slobbery men set down their jugs and hushed each other as though in reverence to approaching royalty. It became so quiet, I could hear the chickens scratching in their cages and crickets chirping or rubbing their legs together or whatever the fuck they do. Though that last bit was probably being pumped in through the speakers to set the mood. The stage light brightened until columns of dust motes stabbed into the audience from between the rusty metal curtain rings, stretching across the waves of corrugated roofing above and the five o'clock shadows of drooling businessmen below.

And then *she* stalked into silhouette—no . . . shuffled is a better word—to the opening cowbells of Nazareth's "Hair of the Dog"—'cuz really, what else would you expect?

"Harry Sue!" I could have sworn someone yelled.

"Harry Sue!" the crowd shouted back in liturgical response.

"*Harry* Sue?" I asked Birch.

"Short for Harriet, maybe?" He shrugged without taking his eyes off the dirty play unfolding.

When the guitar roared in, Harry Sue snatched back the curtain and stomped out onto the porch in Daisy Duke overalls and the most hideous high heels—since when did Jellies make a heel? Her blond hair was teased and tortured into massive pigtails, hay jutting from the strips of gingham holding them in place. Her face was pretty enough, if you could get past her wild eyes, bee-stung lips, and the mass of fake freckles that sadly recalled the broken blood vessels of an alcoholic more than the fresh sun-kissed face of a farmgirl.

She didn't tease the crowd of howling men much, making quick work of the denim overalls with two rehearsed snaps at each shoulder; they slid off her bone-thin frame and pooled around her ankles. The ensuing slapstick of Harry wrestling her feet out of the denim mess would have been charming had my eyes not been stuck to her undergarments. Not satisfied with a dirty wife-beater and some holey panties, the stripper wore cut-off Dr. Dentons complete with the trapdoor. Of course, in true trashy stripper fashion, Harry Sue wore hers backwards.

The room was filled with redneck boner and there I stood in the middle of it, without a vomit bag, a designer cocktail, or a canister of mustard gas. You couldn't move through the room without rotating aroused men like turnstiles and I had no intention of doing that. I did notice that Johnny Birch was standing awful close to me.

Glad to see you, close.

Too close.

"That's my asshole, asshole." I jerked away from his probing fingers.

Johnny grinned in response, totally deserving the punch I threw into his kidneys.

"Ow!" He ran his fingers through his hair, eyes darting nervously at the men around us, as if any of them were looking for anything other than a beaver shot. "Jesus. It's all in good fun."

"Touch me again and we'll see who's having fun."

"Aw." He scowled.

Harry Sue slunk down in one of the rockers, and the men whimpered in unison—apparently prepared for what Harry Sue had in store for us. She rocked slowly, pivoting her ass forward on the edge of the chair until the flap was front and center. She toyed with the buttons, tweaking them like nipples.

I glowered. Shot a glance at Birch. Wished I were drinking.

The stripper got my attention when she unbuttoned one side of the flap, then the other, finally, exposing the biggest 70s bush I'd ever seen.[6] It was massive. Afro-like. Harry Sue needed to be introduced to the wonders of Brazilian waxing, though she'd likely be charged extra. And then it clicked. The men weren't yelling Harry Sue.

They were shouting *Hairy* Sue.

Still. It didn't make sense.

I've read *Cosmo*. I know men prefer shaved to bouffant.

---

[6] Hey. I've always kept mine neat and trim. Don't go making assumptions.

Yet they were clearly enthralled by this stripper. I watched more closely.

Hairy (let's just drop the Sue part; it never had any real value, anyway) reached for the butter churn and pulled out the plunger dripping melted butter down the front of her jammies.

She peeked at the mess, frowned, then licked the end of the plunger before returning it to the churn. In one motion, she slipped out of the Dr. Dentons and reached into an aluminum pail next to the rocker and retrieved an ear of corn, which she preceded to shuck using her teeth. She sprinkled her breasts with corn silk. With the ear she traced circles across her belly, her thighs, and then, as though by accident, she dropped the cob on the porch, gasped, and then slipped from the chair into a full split, hovering briefly above the ear before nestling it against her buttery crotch.

I shifted from one foot to the other.

There was absolutely nothing sexy about this. These guys were all perverts.

Hairy Sue rose then and bowed to the wild applause and showers of dollar bills. She posed there like she owned that porch, corncob dripping and a fat smile spread across her face.

The lights dimmed.

"I'd sure like to see *your* bush." Birch again. His lips curled into a lewd smile.

I nearly vomited up my dinner (let's not go into what that might have been, just yet). "Is that some kind of wood nymph joke? 'Cause I'm done with your poor impulse control."

"Hey." He stepped back, spread his arms, and wiggled his fingers. "I can control the trees and stuff."

I let my eyes wander down to the tent in his pants. "But not the wood?"

He sagged.

"Maybe we should just talk." He covered his crotch with cupped hands, a flush rising in his cheeks.

I followed him back to a booth underneath a monstrous

moose head, where he laid out the scenario. It was the first time I'd seen his face in full light. He wasn't hideous, though his features were sharp and his nose a bit too thin. The brown of his eyes shimmered with veins of gold, and his lips, though pale, were full and unexpectedly alluring. He looked much better on TV, but that was probably the makeup.

Mmm. Makeup.

"The calls started coming about three months ago," he said. "At first the caller wouldn't say anything. Just hang up after I'd answered. The phone company said they were always from phone booths. I didn't even know those still existed, but they do."

I nodded, though I couldn't remember the last time I'd seen one, either. Still, why do people feel the need to tell me the most random crap? Like I care. I'm dead.

"About a month ago, they started getting threatening. Not overtly so, just freaky. Like letting me know that I was being monitored. 'You're at the Texaco on First.' Like that. And then they'd just hang up and I'd be standing there at the pump, not just worried that my cell was going to spark and blow me up, but now that someone was nearby watching. Then a couple of weeks ago I get the first one."

"First what?"

Johnny reached into a briefcase he must've stored under the table before his lap dance and pulled out a plastic shipping envelope, the kind lined with Bubble Wrap. He placed it on the table between us and leaned forward, searching the room for observers. Half the crowd had been culled into the back rooms, and the other half were busy drinking themselves into stupors.

I made eye contact with Gil across the room. He looked concerned. It must have been my expression of pure boredom. My eyes dropped back to the envelope.

"I'm not a private detective, Birch. I'm in advertising. Can we get on with this?"

"I know. I know. But, I don't need you for that. I need you for your celebrity."

Celebrity?

Oh, yes. He'd snared my attention with that. "Go on."

He opened the end of the envelope and pulled out a thin shingle of wood. Stretched across it and attached with thick pins was a creature like none I'd seen, almost insect-like, with wings that clung to its sides like a termite. Its flesh was as black as obsidian and shiny from toe to its segmented abdomen to its horribly humanoid head. The creature's waxy face was frozen in a torturous silent scream.

"Gross. What the hell is it?" I was unable to look away from the little body, pinned as it was like a lab experiment. Better there than flying around, though, or I'd be snatching a flyswatter.

"I don't really know. But it looks like a fucking threat to me." He slid it back into the envelope and tossed it into his bag. "Anyways! I'm going on tour this spring and clearly, with this shit going on . . ." He kicked at the briefcase. "I'm going to need some protection."

"All right. How is my 'celebrity' going to do that?"

"It's not. I'm putting together a team of bodyguards, and what better way to do it nowadays than with my own fabulous reality contest show? Can you see it? Celebrity judges and weekly death matches. It's exactly what Supernatural TV is aching for. Cameron Hansen would host, of course, and all we'd need is our Paula. You'd be our Simon."

"Simon? I'm too cute and, anyway, you'd be our fucking Paula. What we'd need is a Randy." I reached for my purse and began to scoot out of the booth. The idea was ludicrous.

"Maybe." His voice thundered. "But I'm a nut with financial resources and I'd be willing to pay."

"So you're looking for more than just a guest judge here, then? We're talking about exclusive advertising contract with product placement?"

"That could be arranged."

"Let me think about it." I looked around the Hooch and Cooch and couldn't quite believe that such a gross experience might lead to a potential financial windfall. "All right, let's plan to meet somewhere less . . . disgusting, and then we'll talk about it. Sound good?"

"Up to you."

"Well, let's figure it out in the parking lot. I don't think I can stomach this place much longer."

As we stood to leave, a commotion began in the hallway to the private rooms. A steady stream of men were rushing from the exit, most of them screaming and none of them attempting to shield the bulge in their trousers. Following them was a roar that vibrated through the room and a crash as the chicken coops shattered sending several birds flapping and skittering off toward the door in the shack. Gil and Ethel ran into the room, my mother brandishing a machete, Gil some sort of short club.

"We better get out of here." I turned to Birch, but he'd already darted for the front door. Behind him a massive hairy beast emerged from the tangle of metal cages. Its bulbous head sheared the ceiling as it lurched, creating a groove across the ripples of metal. Its thick, muscled arms ended in raking claws that shredded the floorboards into mulch with each powerful swipe. It stopped in the center of the room, head twisting wildly from one patron to the next until it found its quarry.

The creature howled with such force, the floor shook under me. Slobber clung to foot-long fangs like sloppy pennants flapping in the direction of Johnny Birch, who let out a quivering whimper.

It rushed forward.

Dammit, I thought. There goes the TV show.